ALL OR NOTHING

Also by Lynda Page

Evie
Annie
Josie
Peggie
And One For Luck
Just By Chance
At The Toss Of A Sixpence
Any Old Iron
Now Or Never
In For A Penny

ALL OR NOTHING

Lynda Page

First Published in 2001
by HEADLINE BOOK PUBLISHING

10 9 8 7 6 5 4 3 2 1

British Library Cataloguing in Publication Data

Page, Lynda
All or nothing
I.Title
823.9'14[F]

ISBN 0 7472 7051 1

Typeset by
Letterpart Limited, Reigate, Surrey

Printed and bound in Great Britain by
Mackays of Chatham PLC, Chatham, Kent

HEADLINE BOOK PUBLISHING
A division of Hodder Headline PLC
338 Euston Road
LONDON NW1 3BH

www.headline.co.uk
www.hodderheadline.com

For Rene Saunt

With very precious memories of a wonderful lady who, through no fault of her own, become my second mum. On more occasions than I can remember, during my deeply troubled teenage years, Rene took me into her home and, through pure kindness of heart, treated me as one of her own. Her compassion, unique observations and sense of humour will stay with me for the rest of my life.

This book is for you, Rene, with my love

Thanks to Richard Thomas, nephew Richard and all the lads at Mototechnics, Leicester. My succession of jalopies and I have much to thank you for, not least because the origins of this book began life one bitterly cold morning as I stood in your garage waiting for something or other to be fitted or fixed.

And thanks to my beloved grandmother, Annie Pearson, who, at the age of 92, soon to be 93, never ceases to amaze me. I hope I'm as lively, sharp, and as good a cook as you are when I reach your age. And please hurry up and win the big one at the bingo because you've promised to go halves with me!

Chapter One

1960

'I DON'T WANT TO SEE HER. TELL HER TO GO. OI, YES, YOU! Go and stop that woman from coming in here.'

Elsie Shawditch, a middle-aged, homely type of woman, was passing the bed, pushing a metal cart holding a frayed mop and dented galvanised bucket of steaming water and detergent. She stopped abruptly to stare, bemused, at a pair of terrified eyes peering over the top of a sheet. The patient was obviously shouting at her. Elsie turned and looked down the ward. Coming towards her was a very smartly dressed young woman in her late-twenties, she guessed, wearing a dark grey woollen fitted coat with imitation leopard-skin collar, matching cuffs and pill box hat perched on top of a mop of Titian curls. She wore a pair of smart black court shoes which clicked purposefully over the hospital tiles as she advanced.

She was neither slim nor plump but attractive enough to catch the eye of the male visitors. They all turned to look admiringly at her as she passed, much to the annoyance of the other women patients. Elsie thoughtfully pursed her lips. Though the new arrival looked like a woman with much on her mind she did not appear in the least threatening and Elsie wondered why the patient seemed so frightened of her.

Not relishing the task, she took a deep breath and placed a sympathetic smile on her face as the unwelcome visitor arrived by the patient's bed.

'I'm sorry, me duck, Mrs . . . er . . . Miss . . . er . . .' Her eyes flashed to the medical chart hanging from a bull-dog clip at the end of the bed. 'Miss Simpson dun't want any visitors ternight. She's . . . er . . . not feeling 'erself. Maybe termorrer, eh?' she suggested.

Francine Taylor smiled kindly at Elsie as she pulled off her gloves and unbuttoned her coat. 'She'll see me, I'm sure. I'm . . .' She hesitated for a moment before adding . . . 'an old friend.'

'No, you ain't,' a voice declared from under the covers which were then pulled down to reveal Stella Simpson's face, now contorted angrily. 'I don't want to see you. I might be hospitalised but I still have rights,' she spat harshly.

Feeling that trouble was brewing and not wanting to be caught in the middle of it, Elsie decided to make a hurried exit. The water in the bucket slopped dangerously as she scooted off, quick as her legs would allow her.

Frankie stared at Stella for several moments before pulling out the visitor's chair at the side of the bed. She sat down, then hesitated momentarily before laying her hand gently on Stella's arm. 'Despite that bandage around your head you're looking good, Stella. Still as attractive as ever.'

Stella sniffed haughtily as she tucked a lank strand of her usually well-groomed natural blonde hair behind her ear. 'Pity I can't say the same for you. You look every bit your age and more. You look to me as if you haven't slept properly for a week.'

Frankie momentarily froze at her cutting retort. As unkind as it was, though, she had to agree with Stella. What she had faced and dealt with over the last five years was telling on her visibly, and added to it now was the trauma of two days ago. She shuddered at the memory of that terrible incident. She was still reeling from the shock of it.

Coming to the hospital tonight was the very last thing she had wanted, but something she'd felt compelled to do. It had taken all the courage and strength she could summon. At the entrance to the ward a tremendous surge of panic had engulfed her. How she hadn't spun around and raced off would always remain a mystery to her. But her conscience wouldn't allow her to leave until she had spoken to Stella and in doing so hopefully put matters right between them. Not just for her own sake but for the sake of the woman in the bed, the woman who used to be her friend.

She forced a smile to her face. 'I know I'm the last person you want to see right now but we do need to talk,' she said, putting her hand on the other woman's arm.

Stella's lips tightened grimly, her eyes narrowing to two thin strips. 'You're right, the very last person. I'd sooner the devil himself were here than you. I said all I was ever going to say to you five years ago, and I meant what I said then,' she hissed, wrenching away her arm as though she'd been burned. 'I haven't changed my mind. Now go, *Mrs*

Taylor, before I call the nurse and have you thrown out.'

Frankie's face filled with dismay. 'There's no need for this attitude, Stella. We used to be best friends.'

'*Used* to be,' she retorted then added icily, 'A good friend wouldn't have done what you did. Or a bad friend come to that. And don't think you can sweet talk me five years later, thinking my memory isn't what it used to be. I remember very clearly what I saw, like it was yesterday. And it wasn't just me, was it? I had company. Or had you forgotten?'

Frankie shuddered at the memory. 'You both drew your own conclusions about what you saw, Stella. But it wasn't what you thought, honestly. If only you'd given me the chance to explain at the time we could have avoided all these years of hostility.

'Explain?' cried Stella. 'There was nothing to explain. I saw you with my own eyes. Now I've asked you to go and if you don't, right this minute, I *will* call for help.'

Frankie ran her hand despairingly over her forehead. 'All right, Stella, I'll go, but I have to tell you something before I do.'

'Whatever it is I don't want to hear it. NURSE!' she yelled.

'Stella, please,' Frankie pleaded. 'It's to do with Eddie.'

On the verge of shouting for a nurse again, Stella's mouth snapped shut and she stared at Frankie, her mind whirling frantically, praying the feeling of foreboding deep within her wasn't showing. 'Eddie?' she finally faltered. 'What about him? He's your husband, not mine. Why should anything concerning him be of interest to me?'

Wringing her hands, Frankie looked at her meaningfully.

At the expression on her face Stella was shocked and quickly turned her head, making a great show of searching for her handkerchief in the bedside locker as she fought with all her might to compose herself. She knows, she thought. Frankie knows about me and Eddie. Oh, God, her mind screamed. How long has she known? But far more worrying: if Frankie knew, did anyone else? Her stomach heaved and she had a dreadful fear she was going to be sick. With all the strength she could muster she fought to control herself. 'I want you to go,' she repeated. 'And if you don't, right now, I'll scream blue murder and have you thrown out.'

Frankie stiffened. 'Stella,' she said resolutely, 'I came to tell you something, something you must know. Now you can cause a scene or you can act in a civilised fashion. Either way I'm not going until you've heard what I have to say.'

At this calm declaration Stella's fear escalated to near blind terror and her mind whirled frantically. For Frankie to walk brazenly into the hospital – a public place – and find her after all these years there could only be one reason, and that was to confront her. At this precise moment Stella wasn't prepared. She needed time to gather her thoughts, to concoct plausible excuses and denials of all Frankie's accusations. If only Eddie could somehow find a way to visit her discreetly, he would tell her what to do. But she hadn't seen or heard anything of him since she had been brought in here unconscious two days ago and this lack of any contact from him was causing her bewilderment and distress. But then, maybe Eddie didn't know she was here so how could he visit her?

'I don't care what it is you have to tell me, it'll have to wait,' she blurted. 'I'm . . . I'm not feeling well. The doctor's told me I need peace and quiet or I could have a relapse. I am very sick, you know. You are unfeeling, Francine Taylor, coming here like this after all these years and me on my death bed.'

Frankie sighed, shaking her head. 'You've suffered a mild concussion, Stella. You've many years of life ahead of you. I had a chat with the ward sister before I came in and she told me you'll be fit enough to go home tomorrow.' She paused and took a deep breath, her face wreathed in distress. 'You need to know the truth about Eddie, Stella.'

'Truth about Eddie!' she blurted before she could stop herself. 'I know all there is to know about Eddie. I know him better than . . . better than . . .'

'Me, Stella? Is that what you were going to say?' Frankie exhaled, shaking her head sadly. 'You don't know him at all, Stella. You only know the bit of him he chose to let you see. The nice, fun-loving Eddie. But that isn't the real man. Far from it.'

Stella's jaw dropped, eyes wide in horror as the full force of the truth hit her. Frankie knew about her and Eddie. She eyed her boldly. 'You know about us, don't you? Well, I'm glad it's all out in the open. Maybe now you'll do the decent thing and let him go. We'd have been together now, happily married with a couple of children, if you hadn't stolen him from me in the first place.'

'I never stole him from you, Stella.' Frankie eyed her beseechingly. 'Oh, if only all those years ago you'd let me explain . . . But you wouldn't talk to me, would you? I tried again on several occasions but you wouldn't have anything to do with me.'

'And can you blame me?' the other woman snarled, incensed. 'He was my man, Frankie. *Mine.* I was beside myself when I caught you and him together like that. Have you any idea what it did to me? Well, have you, eh? It was like I'd had my guts ripped out.'

Frankie gulped. 'Well, yes, I know how hurt you must have . . .'

'Hurt! I was devastated and that's putting it mildly. I thought at first you'd both double crossed me. Eddie had a hell of a job convincing me it was *you* who'd enticed him, of all people, and after all we'd meant to each other. I couldn't believe it of you, Frankie. But I couldn't blame him, could I? Well, no man refuses when it's handed to him on a plate, does he? It's a well-known fact. Eddie begged me to believe that it was just a one off with you, he got carried away but was sorry afterwards. I'll never forget the night he had to tell me you were pregnant. He cried, Frankie. I'd never seen a man cry before, not like that. It was the end of everything for him.'

She glared at her visitor with hatred. 'Oh, I could have killed you! I hated you then for the pain you put me through, the pain you were putting Eddie through. He had no choice but to marry you, did he?' She paused eyeing Frankie with disgust. 'You wanted him, Frankie, and you got him by using one of the oldest tricks in the books. And you ruined our lives. How did you ever expect me to forgive you for that?' She paused again and added gruffly, 'I was sorry that you lost the baby, believe me when I say that, even if you did use the baby to force him to marry you.'

Frankie let out a deep sad sigh. 'I wasn't pregnant then, Stella,' she whispered.

Stella eyed her, astounded. 'What? Not pregnant. Don't lie,' she spat. 'You were, I know you were, Eddie told me. Then you lost it. The night you did was horrendous for him. All that blood . . .' She gave a violent shudder.

'Eddie lied. I did lose a baby but that was much later, and now I can't have children.'

Stella frowned in confusion. 'Now! What do you mean, you can't have children *now*?'

Frankie lowered her head. 'Just believe me, I can't.'

Stella looked at her for several long moments then said, 'If you knew about me and Eddie, why didn't you say or do something? Why didn't you give Eddie a divorce when he begged you? Was that spite?' she harshly accused. 'To stop me and him from being happy together?'

Frankie's face crumpled with hurt. 'No, Stella, no. Eddie never asked me for a divorce.'

'Stop lying! He did, lots of times, but you always threatened him with what you'd do to yourself. He couldn't live with your suicide on his conscience, could he? No decent man could.'

'Oh, Stella,' Frankie sighed despairingly. 'Eddie has *never* asked me for his freedom. And if he had I wouldn't have agreed, but not for the reasons you think.'

'What reasons then? Come on, Frankie, tell me? What earthly reason could you have to stay married to a man you knew hated you and wanted to be with someone else?'

Frankie eyed her for several long seconds. She took a deep breath. 'I wouldn't have divorced him because I desperately wanted to protect you.'

'Me? Protect *me*?' Stella scoffed. 'What from?'

'From Eddie himself, Stella, from Eddie himself.'

She looked at Frankie as though she was crazy. 'You're mad. *You* protect me from *Eddie*?' she repeated mockingly. 'I admit he's a bit of a lad when it comes to business but in every other way he is the gentlest, kindest man who's ever walked the earth. Eddie was right. He said you should be locked up and the key thrown away.'

Frankie stared at her, aghast. 'Eddie said that about me?'

'And more. Want to hear what else he said about you, Frankie?'

Her face contorted in anguish. 'I don't need to, Stella, I know exactly what he would have told you. I'm not perfect by any means but whatever he said about me isn't true. None of it. I have to say again that you didn't know him, Stella. Not the real Eddie.'

'Oh, spare me,' Stella cried. 'You can't stand the fact that he never stopped loving me despite being shackled to you.' She pulled herself upright in her bed and thrust out an arm in Frankie's direction. 'I'm not quite sure what you came here for, Frankie, but I've had enough. I want you to go,' she demanded, eyes blazing.

Frankie took a deep breath. 'I'll go, Stella, but I have things to say first. I'm not leaving until you've heard me out,' she said resolutely.

Stella's face paled. Frankie was determined to have her say, and she couldn't face it. She opened her mouth to protest but just as she did so the curtains parted and a young nurse popped her head through. 'Everythin' all right, Miss Simpson? Staff Nurse told me she okayed your visitor a longer time if yer don't disturb the other patients.' She smiled. 'It isn't like Staff to turn such a blind eye. Must be true what's being said about 'er and the Chief Surgeon.' She suddenly realised she had spoken out of turn and bristled. 'Not that I listen ter gossip myself.' She suddenly noticed Stella's pale face and frowned worriedly. 'You okay?'

'I'm fine,' she snapped.

'Oh! If I dind't know better I'd say you'd 'ad a terrible shock. Yer've gone all white. I'd better fetch Sister.'

'No, I don't want you to call her. If I did then I'd ask. Now, do you mind? Me and Mrs Taylor are having a private conversation.'

The young nurse sniffed disdainfully. 'Suit yourself.' She made a hurried departure.

'Does that mean you'll listen to me, Stella?'

She looked at Frankie for a moment then, sighing heavily, said stonily, 'It seems I've no choice as you seem determined not to leave until you've said your piece.'

Frankie's face was filled with relief. 'Before I begin, can I get you anything, Stella? A cup of tea?'

'No,' she snapped. 'Just get on with it. The sooner you do, the sooner I can be rid of you.'

Frankie flinched at her tone, then her mind drifted back to happier times, just before Edwin Taylor breezed into their lives and this whole shocking business all began.

Chapter Two

1955

'So how much d'yer reckon yer dad'll gimme then, Frankie?'

She looked doubtfully at the articles in question, then at the bedraggled boy holding them towards her, his grubby face wreathed in hopeful expectation. In truth, the articles were worthless. 'Well . . .'

'You'll be lucky to get a kick in the teeth for them, Jimmy.'

'Stella!' Frankie scolded.

'I'm only speaking the truth. Where did you get them from?' she asked the boy.

'The canal.'

'I thought as much, and by the state of you nearly drowned in your wasted effort. Them things look as though they've been in the canal donkey's years, you should have left them where you found them. You might get a ha'penny down the scrappy but I wouldn't bank on it. Come on, Frankie,' she urged, giving her friend's arm a tug. 'We'd better get a move on. You know what the lads are like if we keep them waiting.'

The young boy's face fell in dismay. 'An 'a'penny, is that all? I wa' hopin' for a tanner. Said I'd treat me brothers ter some chips,' he wistfully added.

Frankie's heart went out to him. She knew the O'Connell family well. Knew that the five boys, ranging in age from eighteen months to this one, Aidan, the eldest at seven, sometimes went for days without hot food in their stomachs. Their father had long ago vanished and their poor mother survived as best as she could on the money she earned from any menial job she could procure, what pennies could be made by what her sons managed to scavenge, but mostly on the charity of others. 'Well, maybe my dad might find a use for them,' she said kindly.

The boy's face lit up and he eyed Frankie eagerly. 'D'yer reckon?'

She smiled. 'I do. You know what my dad's like, Aidan, he finds a use for everything. Er . . . as a matter of interest, what happened to the spokes?'

The boy looked thoughtfully for a moment at the disintegrating metal bicycle rims he was clutching. 'I think they must still be in the canal.'

Along with the rest of the mangled bike, I expect, where the owner dumped it, she thought. 'Oh, never mind, I bet Dad has some somewhere in his shed that'll do the job. Tanner, was it?' she said, groping in her handbag for her purse.

'You must be mad,' Stella exclaimed, nudging her hard in the ribs. 'Even your dad won't be able to do anything with those. And that tanner'll buy us some chocs for the flicks.'

'Or three bags of chips for those famished lads,' Frankie whispered back. 'Stop being selfish, Stella.' She gave Aidan the sixpence and relieved him of his precious cargo. She watched as the happy boy galloped off down the street then turned to face her friend. 'Now wasn't the look on his face and the knowledge that the O'Connell boys'll have a meal tonight worth us going without those chocolates?'

Stella sniffed disdainfully. 'I suppose. You're too soft, you are, Frankie. You're a sucker for a sob story. You'll never have any money to speak of while you're handing it out to every Tom, Dick and Harry. And it ain't as though you earn much yourself. Oh, don't look at me like that. Yesterday you promised your old coat to Granny Wicks.'

'Stella, how can you begrudge that poor old duck a threadbare thing that was past its best when I bought it second-hand four or five years ago? You've seen the one she's wearing. It wouldn't keep a dog warm in the height of summer, let alone her old bones in these March winds. I'm only too glad to let her have it. It's no use to me anymore, is it? Anyway, what do I want with two coats? I've only got one back and two arms,' she said, laughing.

Stella shook her head. 'For one thing you could have put it in the rag bag along with the other stuff to take down the yard and got a couple of extra pennies for it. Oh, never mind, I know I'm wasting my breath with you. So what are you going to do with them?'

'With what?'

'Those pieces of rust you've just paid a fortune for.'

Frankie looked at them and laughed. 'Put them back where Aidan found them is the best bet, I think. Anyway, this'll bring the smile back to your face, I've still a few coppers spare for some sweets. Unlike you I don't spend what's left over from my wages on frivolities.'

'Frivolities?' Stella exclaimed. 'Make-up and stockings and a bit of costume jewellery from Woolie's sale is hardly frivolous – it's essential.'

'Yes, I suppose. But having five shades of lipstick when you only use one is a luxury, Stella. Even you've got to agree with that.'

'They were on sale,' she exclaimed sulkily. 'Saved half a crown, I did. I'd have to be mad to turn down a bargain like that. Look, hadn't you better run else you'll never be ready in time. It'll take a month of Sundays to get all that muck off you.' Stella cast a critical eye over her friend and shook her head. 'Why can't you get a proper job like any normal woman? At least with a proper job you wouldn't get in such a state.'

Frankie laughed. 'I *have* got a proper job and it's the only thing I've ever wanted to do, as you well know. My dad always says it's in my blood. Shall I call for you then?'

'Eh? Oh, no, I'll call for you. My mam's in a right mood at the minute. There's no living with her these days.'

'What's the matter with her?' asked Frankie in concern.

'Nothing that getting rid of my dad wouldn't cure. I don't know why those two ever got married, all they do is argue. Mind you, I suppose if they hadn't, me and our Simon wouldn't be here. Oh, did I tell you, our Simon's leaving home?'

'Leaving home? Really! Where's he going then?'

'Far enough away so me mam and dad can't visit,' her friend replied, laughing. 'Seriously, it's only for a while. He's got a job up north. It's navvying for some digging firm on the roads and he'll have to sleep in a bunk in a wooden hut with all the other men, but it's good pay and he's as pleased as punch. It's on that new M something or other.'

'Oh, I've heard about that,' Frankie said, impressed. 'It's a huge road that's going right from near Leeds, past Leicester and down to London. M . . . 1. Yes, that's what it's called. And your Simon is going to be helping on it? Well, I never. When does he start?'

'In a week or so. Look, we can talk about this later. Just get off home, will you? Roger's annoyed with me enough as it is for not handing over any money last week towards our wedding savings, and I don't want to give him another excuse to have a go at me.'

'You do exaggerate, Stella. Roger has never had a go at you for anything. Worships the ground you walk on and has done since he first clapped eyes on you in the school playground when we were eight.'

'Seven.'

'Well, seven then. And I'll see you about seven, okay?'

Five minutes later Frankie unlatched the back gate and walked down the cinder path towards the back door of the little terraced house she lived in with her mother and father in Wand Street, off the Belgrave Road on the north side of Leicester. Belgrave Road stretched from the edge of the town right down to where it joined the Loughborough and Melton Road about a mile on. Its whole length was made up of terraced properties of varying ages and conditions – some were kept in reasonable repair but most properties were damp and crumbling, the landlords who owned them indifferent to the plight of the poor tenants who had to reside within such inhospitable walls.

An assortment of shops and factories, trade yards, pubs, working men's clubs and places of worship served the large community that lived in the Belgrave area, mainly poor working-class families, not all of them lucky enough to have a breadwinner in regular work. Branching off the main thoroughfare were warrens of other terraced streets and cul-de-sacs. The busy Grand Union Canal and River Soar ran close by and harassed mothers searching for children well past their bedtime could often find their offspring playing on the tow paths or tormenting the barge folk whose brimming holds of coal, steel and other commodities were destined for the ports of Manchester and Liverpool for onward journeys far and wide.

The cobbled back yard Frankie picked her way across was littered with all manner of bicycle and motorbike parts and other odds and ends gathered over the years by her crippled forty-four-year-old father to enable him to carry out his work as a motor and push-bike mechanic. There was nothing Sam Champion did not know about two-wheeled machines of any description or make, and over the years his reputation for skill and fair rates had built up until his little back yard was the first place people from the surrounding area and beyond would bring their precious machines if a problem arose.

He lay sprawled on the wet cobbles now, a spanner in his hand, face tight with concentration as he laboured to loosen a stubborn bolt off the wheel of a machine that had been brought to him earlier in the day by its distraught owner.

'Need any help, Dad?' Frankie asked as she knelt down at the side of him. 'Good gracious, this is a Triumph model TT and it's still got its sidecar. I haven't seen one of these for years.'

He lifted his head, the dirt-filled lines on his weather-beaten but still handsome face creasing into a welcoming grin on spotting his beloved daughter. ''Ello, Frankie love,' he said, sweeping aside with an oil-stained hand strands of thick greying hair that had fallen across his kindly bright blue eyes. 'I got a shock when I first clapped me eyes on it meself. I need a bloody sledge hammer for this, I reckon. I don't think this bolt 'as bin budged since the day this bike left the factory thirty years ago. Ooof!' he grunted as he gave a tremendous heave at the offending bolt. 'No, it ain't gonna shift. Could you pass me the monkey, lovey?' he asked, pointing to a pile of well-worn tools scattered around a large battered box by the out-house door.

She scrambled across and grabbed the monkey wrench then passed it to him. 'What's wrong with the bike, Dad?' she asked keenly as she scanned her eyes across it.

'You name any ailment you can think of, Frankie, and this bike's got it. This wheel's buckled for a start. In truth the bike's only fit for the knacker's yard but the poor chap who owns it relies on it to get him back and forth ter work so I promised him I'd do the best I can to get it up and running again. I just hope I can and that he can pay the bill as he didn't look ter me as though he'd two 'a'pennies ter rub tergether.' Groans and grunts followed as Sam heaved on the bolt. Finally it gave way. 'Ah, that's got the beggar,' he said, relieved. He quickly undid the rest of the bolts and pulled the wheel off. Heads bent together, father and daughter scrutinised it.

'The buckle ain't that bad, Dad, we can straighten it out with a bit of luck, but the housing pin's bent, there's a few ball bearings missing and it needs a couple of spokes replacing.'

At the mention of spokes, Frankie quashed an eruption of mirth that threatened as she remembered the disintegrating rims, now back where Aidan had found them. She wished she had brought them home and with a serious face presented them to her father, just to see his reaction. He would have been astounded for a moment, mouth dropping wide, then the penny would have dropped and he would have laughed until his sides ached and probably not stopped all night. The only reason she had decided against it was because she knew he would have insisted on replacing the sixpence she had given Aidan. One day she would tell him, though.

'Oi, who's fixing this bloody bike, me or you?' Sam asked, a twinkle in his eyes. 'But you're spot on. Well done, Frankie. Right, while I mek a start on the wheel, you can give me your opinion as to what else yer thinks wrong. But first I need me bits box and bearings tin. Can yer find 'em for me, lovey? They're here somewhere,' he said glancing around.

'Oh, there yer are, might 'ave known. I thought you were going out ternight, Frankie?'

Her head tilted up and she smiled a warm greeting at the person addressing her. 'Oh, hello, Mam. I was just helping Dad.'

'Our daughter is just protecting 'er inheritance, Nancy. Weren't yer, ducky?' Sam chipped in, laughing.

'Yeah, that's right, Dad.' Beaming brightly, she held her arms out wide. 'Just making sure you leave me something worth having. But not for many years yet, eh, Dad? I kinda like having you about.'

'Inheritance, indeed,' Nancy Champion said, shaking her head. She folded her arms under her ample chest as her eyes flashed around the cluttered yard. With a mischievous twinkle in her eye she said, 'If this is all you've got ter look forward to, Frankie, I'd make a run for it now while yer can.'

Sam feigned a look of hurt. 'Nancy Champion, what a thing ter say. If I thought yer were serious, woman, I'd scalp yer backside.'

She grinned cheekily at him. 'That'll be the day, when you take yer 'and ter me. You know as well as I do, Samuel Champion, Frankie's inheritance, as you put it, keeps the wolf from our door and for that I'll be forever grateful. At least I can pay me bills most of the time. There's many round here who can't.' Her eyes fixed on their twenty-two-year-old daughter and she fought hard to suppress her laughter. What a sight Frankie looked.

Her vivid Titian curls, the very same colour Nancy's own hair had been before it had started to show the signs of ageing, was hidden underneath a blue workman's canvas cap, tendrils sticking out wildly at the side; her lovely face with its fine spattering of becoming freckles was streaked by dirt and oil, her nicely rounded body hidden underneath a most unflattering pair of bright blue overalls, which were filthy. 'You should have bin a lad, our Frankie. And if I were given a penny for every time I've said that, I'd be a very rich woman. Just look at the state of yer. Bathed in oil today, did yer?'

Frankie scrambled to her feet and cast her eyes down over herself. She had to admit, although clean on that morning the overalls didn't look as though they'd been washed for weeks. 'A leaking petrol tank emptied itself all over me when I was struggling to unbolt it,' she said sheepishly. 'Sorry, Mam.'

'Well, just lucky for you I got yer other pair dried today else it's you who'd have bin sorry, havin' ter put that disgusting pair back on again termorrow. I'll have ter get another packet of soda crystals in the morning, I used all I had left today. The both of you,' she said fondly, looking at each in turn, 'cost me a fortune in detergent. And Granddad too, come ter that. I'd be a rich woman if I didn't have ter spend nearly all me 'ouse keeping on washing powder. How's yer Uncle Wally, Frankie?'

'He's fine, Mam. Said to thank you for the pie you sent. He's going to have it for his dinner tonight. Although when he'll get home is anyone's guess. He was still at it when I left. We had three cars in today, all needed urgent.' Her eyes sparkled excitedly. 'One of them's an Alvis 3-litre with six cylinders. A right beauty it is. The owner's normal garage was snowed under and couldn't promise when they'd get around ter looking at it and someone the chap knew recommended Champion's. Uncle Wally said I can help him on it. I offered to work late but he wouldn't hear of it. Said him and Taffy would manage. He knew I was going to the pictures tonight, bless him.'

'Well, yer won't be going anywhere if yer don't get a move on. Yer bath's ready and yer dinner's on the table. Take yer pick which you choose to let go cold. Oh, and on yer way to the pictures, can you drop yer granddad's dinner in to him? It's all plated up and keeping hot on a pan on the stove. And tell him I'll pop in his clean washin' in the morning, and I'm off into town in the af'noon so if he wants any shopping doing, tell him to have his list ready.' She turned her attention to her husband. 'And you, Samuel, get yerself inside. I cooked a hot meal for you and you'll eat it hot.'

He shook his head. 'By, yer a hard woman, Nancy Champion, asking a man ter choose between one of your dinners and fixing a bike.'

'Yes, and I know you, Sam Champion. If push came ter shove you'd choose the bike. The way to most men's hearts is through their stomachs. Not you. I won yours by agreeing to ride pillion on that clapped-out contraption you had the nerve to call a motorbike. I was the only girl friend you ever had who would risk her life for you and *that's* why yer married me.'

Sam opened his mouth to offer a response, but instead issued a loud sneeze.

Nancy pulled a knowing face. 'I knew it were too soon for you to be back outdoors after yer bout of influenza the other week, despite you convincing me otherwise.'

'I'm fine, Nancy. Stop fussing.'

'No you ain't. You shouldn't be lying on those wet cobbles. Where's the old blanket I dug out for you?' She spotted it crumpled up at the back of him and grimaced in annoyance. 'What's the good of me trying me best to look after you, and you not caring a damn?'

He turned the top half of his crippled body around and made a grab for the blanket, trying to manoeuvre it under himself. 'I do, Nancy, you know I do,' he replied sheepishly. 'It's just that . . . that . . .'

'You lost yerself in that damned bike, that's what, and the fact the doctor warned you to keep yerself well wrapped up went flying out the window when you insisted on returning to work,' she finished for him. 'We nearly lost you, Sam, yer were that bad. And don't deny it because yer was. I should know, I nursed me mother through it and lost *her*. Now, either you lie on that blanket or I tell yer, Sam, I'll barricade you in the house and not let you out. I'm not risking losing you again, so be warned.'

'All right, I promise, gel. Oh, yer do go on,' he said, a twinkle in his eye.

'Yeah, well, it's a good job I do otherwise you'd never eat or sleep. You'd be out here twenty-four hours a day fixing those bloody machines.' She shook her head at Frankie. 'And yer daughter's heading that way too. In fact the pair of yer are as bad as each other, and Wally works all hours God sends in that garage of his. It's a wonder he hasn't wasted away. He'd never eat decent if I didn't send food down to him. In fact it's your dad I blame, Sam, he's the one responsible for encouraging you both to watch him fixings things when you were boys.

'Now come on, let's get you inside. Where's yer chair?' she asked, looking around. On spotting the wheelchair at the side of the outhouse, she tutted disdainfully. 'Samuel Champion, the seat of yer chair ain't a place to store mucky parts. If there's oil leaked on it I'll never get it off.'

He eyed her sheepishly.

'I'll clear the seat, Mam, and help Dad into it,' offered Frankie.

'I've told you to get inside, I can manage yer dad. I've bin doing it for twenty years now and the day I can't, I'll let you know.'

Frankie opened her mouth to protest then thought better of it. This was no rebuff from her mother nor was it anything to do with stubborn pride. Nancy Champion cherished every fibre of her husband's half-crippled body and showed her feelings in everything she did for him, from helping him up in the morning to easing his useless legs into bed of an evening. It was a pure labour of love to her.

Frankie watched her parents for a moment, giggling together like naughty schoolchildren as they struggled to manipulate Sam's hefty body into the cumbersome wheelchair. Her father, at over six foot, the top half of his body with well-developed muscles forged over the years as he heaved himself around in order to carry out his work, was no lightweight. How her mother managed at not much over five foot herself and apparently without the strength to lift a bag of potatoes, let alone grab her sixteen-stone husband around his chest and haul him into his chair without mishap, was something that always amazed Frankie.

She smiled, her heart swelling with love, and her thoughts drifted back over the events that had brought her family to this situation.

The accident that had caused this state of affairs had been Sam's fault alone. Since it had happened, and with such devastating results, not once had he wallowed in self-pity when he so easily could have done.

A couple of years married, with Frankie herself then only a toddler, an over-enthusiastic Samuel had insisted on road testing a motorcycle that he and his elder brother Walter had been labouring over for months. Sam could no longer contain his need to see if their painstaking labour had achieved the desired result.

The Champion brothers had always been passionate about anything with a motor attached to it, an interest nurtured from a very early age by their own father. Every spare minute of Edgar Champion's time had been spent mending or rebuilding anything he could lay his hands on, from clocks to lawn mowers, crystal wireless sets to bicycles, much to the dismay of his long-suffering wife Hilda, who had constantly complained about the mess in her parlour and back yard.

The brothers, both having finished much-coveted apprenticeships as machine mechanics – something they were extremely lucky to get at a time when apprenticeships were few and far between, and fought over – were employed by a local hosiery factory to keep their machines running, a fact which later kept Wally, much to his dismay, from being enlisted for the war effort. His skills were far too much in demand during this dreadful time helping to keep the armed forces clothed, though he desperately wanted to fight for his country.

Back in 1935, both men having saved for months every penny they could from their pittance of a wage, they bid successfully for a ramshackle 1928 BMW R63 motorcycle at a local auction, the idea being to restore it in their spare time then sell it, and with the profit hopefully buy two more to do the same with. Their ultimate aim was to have their own business with a natural progression into repairing motor cars. With hard work and patience, hopefully the venture would provide each of them with a decent living.

The weather that fateful April evening had been wet, the cobbled roads slippery. With his brother's warning to be careful fresh in his ears, Sam kicked the machine into life and, full of exhilaration, roared off. His journey was short-lived, coming to an abrupt halt as he misjudged a sharp corner at speed. Squeezing too hard on the brake, the front wheel had skidded on the cobbles, slammed against a kerb and Sam had been catapulted several yards into a brick wall. The motorcycle was barely scratched. Sam wasn't so lucky. His spinal cord was severed. A young, inexperienced doctor clumsily broke the news that Sam Champion would never walk again.

Despite his utter devastation Sam was very mindful he had only himself to blame and was just grateful he'd only lost the use of part of his body. His young wife, also, was thankful he was alive, only too aware what the alternative could have been.

As he recovered in hospital all Sam could think of was how he was going to provide some sort of living for his beloved family. The answer became obvious to him: to carry on with his dream of being his own boss, but in a slightly different form. He'd lost the use of his legs. Well, mechanics spent most of their lives lying or sitting on the floor as they carried out their work. He could still do that. And the rest he could manage sitting in a wheelchair. Instead of the garage premises the brothers had hoped one day to have, his own back yard with its leaky outhouse would have to suffice. His business would only ever be a small concern, one that he could manage on his own, but as long as he made enough to keep his family, he'd be satisfied with that.

Nancy's reaction to his decision had been to inform her husband she would support him fully in whatever he did, a promise she'd never once broken in twenty years and never intended to.

Wally's reaction was a different matter. Despite his brother's incapacities, as far as he was concerned nothing had changed, they could still carry on with their joint plan. But Wally had reckoned without the fierce determination and pride of Sam. He had no intention of hindering his brother's chance of becoming a success. The accident was the result of his own pig-headedness and it wasn't right that Wally's plans for his own future should suffer as a consequence. Sam's decision was final and despite strenuous efforts by Wally to dissuade him, there was no budging him.

With a heavy heart Wally continued on his own. All his spare time was spent rebuilding machines he bought cheaply and then selling them off reasonably, every penny of profit he made put safely away into his garage fund. The arrival of the war put a halt to his plans to a large extent as his working hours increased dramatically, but then so did his wages and what he managed to save. In 1946, as soon as peace returned, Wally gave in his resignation to concentrate fully on his plan for the future.

After extensive searching he found just what he was looking for, albeit dreadfully neglected, at a very reasonable rent. It consisted of one decent-sized building which had once been used as a blacksmith's and wheelwright's, with a much smaller building attached to the side of it which Wally intended to use as office-cum-reception facility. There was a smaller building at the back which presumably had originally been stabling but had later been converted to some sort of storage room. The moment Wally discovered it he thought of Sam and hoped he could persuade his brother to use it for motorcycle repairs instead of his yard. There was even room at the back for the good-sized scrap heap that Wally knew would gradually build up as business expanded. To the front of the premises was a plot for customers to drive on to and also a place to park cars awaiting work inside the garage.

With a few repairs and alterations the premises would admirably suit Wally's purposes, and more importantly leave him enough money to purchase from auctions or second-hand all the equipment he needed.

After weeks of hard labour, fraught nerves and many sleepless nights, finally an exhilarated Wally was ready to pull open the garage's double doors. Above them, in large black and yellow lettering, was spelt out: W. CHAMPION – MOTOR ENGINEERS. Using the last of his savings, he placed an advert in the *Leicester Mercury* informing the whole of the city that Champion's Garage was now in business to repair their cars. Then he prayed.

His prayers were answered and within months he was busy enough to employ his first mechanic, a giant of a Welshman named Morgan Thomas, Taffy to his friends, who had learned his invaluable skills servicing Army vehicles during the war on a base in Leicestershire, and stayed after it was over to marry a local woman.

Despite working at least fourteen hours a day, sometimes longer, and six days a week, nine years later Wally's dreams of owning several garages had still not materialised but the one he did have was ticking over nicely and earning himself and his now expanded workforce of two mechanics and a fitter a decent living. It had also afforded Wally the opportunity of buying his own home, something that otherwise would never have happened. It was a good-sized semi off the Loughborough Road, three-bedroomed and with a long garden out the back, and Wally was proud to say it was all his. Life was good and he was happy.

Sam, meanwhile, had had much to overcome before he was able to realise his own dream of supporting his wife and child. For many months after the accident life was very hard, and to Sam's chagrin they survived mainly thanks to the resourcefulness of Nancy. While her beloved husband healed the best he was ever going to, nothing was beneath her. Rising at five in the morning, she cleaned at the local school, minded children and packed socks for a penny a gross as an outworker for the factory Sam had worked for when his accident had happened. All this she did while still caring for her own family, and all uncomplaining.

Without Sam's knowledge, Wally would slip as much as he could spare to Nancy. Despite her reluctance to accept it, being very aware at the time that her brother-in-law was desperately trying to save as much as he could towards his future business, many times only Wally's generosity enabled the purchase of bare necessities which otherwise they would have had to have gone without. Nancy hadn't liked deceiving her husband but Wally had insisted Sam was kept in ignorance. He was facing enough, coming to terms with his disabilities, without risking any further hammering to his already battered pride.

Prejudice against Sam's disabilities, in so much as people doubted a cripple could do the job of an able-bodied man, was hard to overcome. Sam's strong will and perseverance, but most importantly his skill, gradually won the public over and work started to come his way. Finally, to his relief, the time came when if a motorcycle or push-bike needed expert attention, it was to Sam Champion people first turned.

He was fully aware that due to his disabilities any hope of ever expanding his small operation was out of the question, but despite the fact that when bills had been paid there was not much left over for luxuries, at least he was providing for his beloved family and Sam was content with that.

Like her father before her, Frankie's love of anything mechanical had been nurtured as soon as she could toddle down the yard where she would sit for hours, entranced, as she watched her father work. By the age of three she knew the names of every individual tool. From then on it was taken for granted by all the family where Francine Champion's future lay. The fact that she was a female was of no consequence.

When she was five years old, one bitter Christmas evening, her Uncle Wally, after indulging in a large quantity of festive cheer, promised her a job in the garage he one day planned to own, and he never forgot that promise. In September 1948, at the age of fourteen, the first Monday after she'd left school Frankie arrived, shaking with excitement and fired with enthusiasm, for her first day at work in Champion's Garage. Eight years later she was still loving every minute of it.

The first couple of years had been very frustrating, though, as despite constantly pestering her uncle, apart from fetching and carrying and failing miserably to keep the garage in some semblance of order, she was only allowed to watch and learn. She had almost given up on ever being allowed to put what she had observed into practice when, on arriving as punctually she always did at seven-thirty one bright June morning, her Uncle Wally steered her towards a large cardboard box at the back of the garage. Inside was a brand new pair of overalls and a metal tool box, her name boldly printed on it in black paint. Inside the box was her first set of spanners, a screwdriver, hammer and monkey wrench. Frankie was overcome with joy.

As time passed, paid for out of her own wages or received as gifts at Christmas or birthdays, the tools in her precious metal box were added to and a proud Frankie, having sailed through her five-year apprenticeship, now owned all she needed to carry out her trade.

Most customers were shocked at first to find a woman with her head under the bonnet of their car in what most people perceived as a male-dominated profession, but any doubt as to her capabilities was soon dispelled when, nine times out of ten, she immediately diagnosed the car's problem and informed them how it could be put right.

As she stood in the back yard now watching her parents' antics, Frankie heaved a contented sigh. What a lucky woman she was. Not many people could boast two loving parents who had always provided for her the best they could; or having the best job in the world with the best boss possible; or good friends and a beloved boyfriend who she hoped would one day ask her to marry him.

This is the best it gets, she thought. Some people have nothing; I have it all. I'm so lucky.

'FRANKIE?'

She jumped.

'You're miles away, grinning like a Cheshire Cat. What's up with yer, gel?' Nancy asked, as after heaving Sam into the wheelchair she arrived at her daughter's side.

'Oh, I'm just happy, Mam, that's all,' she replied, eyes shining.

'And I'm glad ter hear it. Now being's yer still loitering wi' n'ote better to do, you might as well push yer dad the rest of the way while I rush ahead and mash a fresh cuppa.'

Frankie leaned over and kissed her mother on the cheek. 'With pleasure, Mam.'

'Soppy 'a'porth,' chuckled Nancy, hurrying off.

Chapter Three

A while later, Nancy dropped her knitting in her lap and with a merry twinkle in her eye proclaimed, 'By 'ell, would yer look at that, Sam? It is a daughter we've got after all. You look a picture, gel. Don't she, Sam?'

'She always does ter me,' he said, peering over the top of his newspaper. His daughter did indeed look lovely. Out of her unbecoming work attire, she was a different person. She had pinned up the sides and back of her mop of red curls with kirby grips, letting the fringe fall naturally across her forehead. Her shapely curves were covered by a pair of yellow Capri pants and a bright blue cardigan. 'Yer do look smashing. New cardi?' he asked her.

Frankie tutted, shaking her head. 'What am I going to do with you, Dad? If I brought home anything with an engine attached to it, you'd instantly know the make, model, when it was manufactured and how much it cost me. This cardi's at least a year old. Mam knitted it for me last year.' Then, grinning, she added, 'My pants are new, though. I bought them off the market last weekend for two and eleven.'

He gulped sheepishly. 'Well, er . . . yer look lovely, me darlin'. What picture are you going to see?'

'She won't be seeing any if she doesn't get a move on,' chipped in Nancy. 'You ain't forgot about yer granddad's dinner, 'ave yer, lovey, or the message to give him?'

'No, Mam,' she replied as she went over and kissed each of them on the cheek. 'I'll give Granddad your love, shall I?'

'Yes, do that, please,' they both replied.

'Ta-ra then. I won't be late.'

'No, you see as yer not, you've work in the morning,' said her mother. 'I'll 'ave yer cocoa ready for eleven.'

Frankie smiled tenderly. It was no use telling Nancy not to wait up for her, knowing she would never go to sleep until she heard her daughter was safely home. And despite his never admitting it, she knew her father too would be lying listening for her key in the lock. With that in mind she always made sure she was home at a reasonable time. 'Thanks, Mam,' she said sincerely.

Moments later Frankie was tapping on the back door of an identical house several doors down the street.

'If that's you, Enid Smart, then yer can bugger off, I'm busy,' a gruff voice shouted.

'It's only me, Granddad,' Frankie called as she entered.

'Come away in, Frankie, me duck. I thought it wa' that busybody from two doors down. Getting on my nerves, she is. She'd be in and out all day long if I let her.'

'She fancies you, Granddad,' Frankie said jocularly as she walked into the dim interior of the tiny back room.

'Fancies me! I'm seventy, Frankie, far too old to be fancied.'

'Oh, I dunno,' she said, pretending to scrutinise him. 'You're not bad for your age. I'd fancy you myself if I was seventy. Might do you a bit of good to do a bit of courting. Better than sitting in here night after night straining your eyes fiddling with these odds and ends for the neighbours.'

'Odds and ends! I'll give you odds and ends. They're good stuff are some of the bits I get asked to fix. And courting! I'll give yer courting, and certainly not wi' Enid Smart. She's only after me money.'

'You haven't got any, Granddad. Well, not that I know of.'

'Ah, well, yer don't know everything, Frankie. I've a few bob put past. Enough to pay for me funeral. This fiddling, as you put it, brings in a few pennies and it all adds up. Oh, is that me dinner?' he said, eyes lighting up. 'I was beginning ter think I wasn't getting any tonight. Put it over there, lovey. Mind that . . . Oh, bloody 'ell, Frankie, I'd just fixed that!'

'I'm sorry, Granddad, I didn't see it,' she said remorsefully as the tin clock she'd accidentally knocked off the table crashed to the floor. She picked it up and shook it. It rattled loudly and she grimaced. 'I think it's broken,' she said, stating the obvious. 'It's so dark in here, I'll turn the mantles up.'

'You will not. There's still a bit of daylight left yet. Gas costs money. And it's gonna cost me more when the 'lectric goes in. Why people can't leave things alone is beyond me. Have ter stick their oar in, don't they, and most of the time it's only ter mek themselves look good when they mek these decisions. They never think of the consequences for us ordinary folks. I can manage the gas. I can have the mantles as dim or as bright as I like. Can't do that wi' 'lectric, can yer? And yer can't smell 'lectric if you've left it on by accident and the bulb's blown.' He screwed up his aged face in disdain. 'They'll be wanting to put baths in next. Yer can't 'ave a good soak in front of the fire in one of them new-fangled baths, now can yer? Them tap contraptions sticking in yer back . . .'

'I shouldn't worry about it, Granddad. You've got to have the electric put in because the government says so but I can't see the landlord insisting he puts a bathroom in, not when it takes him years to get around to carrying out simple repairs, can you? And especially considering how much it would all cost him.'

'No, I s'pose not. I'm still waiting fer that leaky gutterin' to be replaced that I asked to be done three years ago. Can you pass me that screwdriver, lovey?'

She did as he asked, then proceeded to give him her mother's messages, and finished off by saying. 'Are you going to eat this while it's hot or not?'

'What?'

'Your dinner.'

'Oh, yes, I forgot about that. Can yer get me a knife and fork? Oh, and the salt while yer at it. Mmm, this looks good,' he said, sniffing appreciatively as he lifted the enamel dish off his plate. 'Stew and dumplings, my favourite. Yer mam meks a mean dumpling. Ta, me duck,' he said, retrieving the cutlery from his granddaughter. 'So where you off then, all spruced up like a dog's dinner? Out with Ian? Nice lad, Ian. You could do a lot worse than 'im.'

She pulled a chair out opposite and sat down, resting her elbows on the table. 'I agree with you, Granddad.'

'You do? By, that meks a change, you agreeing wi' me. So when's the wedding then?'

'Granddad, he hasn't asked me,' she scolded.

'Well, 'bout time 'e did.' His bushy grey eyebrows rose as a thought struck him. 'Why don't you ask him? If I remember right it was your granny that asked me, God rest her soul. We'd never 'ave got married if it'd been left ter me. Right shy I wa', just couldn't seem ter pluck up the courage. How long yer bin courting? Must be knocking on a couple of years. I ain't got long left, yer know, and I intend seeing me favourite granddaughter settled, so you'd better do summat about it. No, don't bother, I'll 'ave a word wi' Ian meself when I next see 'im.'

'You'll do no such thing,' she warned severely. 'Now promise me,

Granddad, else I won't bring him around again. If Ian is ever going to ask me to be his wife, he'll do it when he's good and ready and not by being pushed into it by me or *any* member of my family. And as for being your favourite granddaughter. I'm the only grandchild you've got.'

His rheumy eyes twinkled. 'Oh, you're just like your mam you are, Frankie. Open yer trap before yer brain's in gear. I was just havin' a bit of fun.' He smiled warmly. 'But despite being a woman who speaks her mind, I ain't callin' yer mam, far from it. She's a wonderful woman. Best day's work my son ever did wa' to marry Nancy.'

'And that's another thing we agree on. See, Granddad, we get on better than you make out.'

'Cheeky bugger,' he said, shovelling a forkful of food into his mouth.

Frankie glanced at the clock on the mantle above the old-fashioned cast-iron range, a relic from bygone days he refused to have replaced with a modern fireplace for sentimental reasons. His beloved wife had spent many hours bustling around it cooking their meals, something he still liked to remember her doing in his mind's eye. 'Oh, goodness, is that the time?' Frankie exclaimed. 'I've got to fly,' she said, jumping up and rushing around the table to kiss him affectionately on his wizened cheek. 'Stella's calling for me at home, only I'm around here so I've got to try and catch her in the street before she thinks I've gone to meet the lads without her. I'll pop in tomorrow night, Granddad, okay?'

'All right, me ducky. Enjoy yourself, and don't forget what I said. I don't care how yer do it but get that lad to mek an honest woman of yer afore it's too late. I don't want the next time I wear me suit to be at me own funeral.'

'Granddad, you're as strong as a horse and never had a day's illness since I can remember, so stop it, will you?' she scolded him for the second time in minutes.

'I was only saying,' he commented innocently, and decided to change the subject. 'Can yer ask yer dad if I can borrow his soldering iron? And ask yer Uncle Wally fer a pint of oil and bring it all with yer termorrow night, will yer, lovey?'

She frowned quizzically. 'Engine oil? What do you want that for, Granddad? Are you fixing an engine of some kind?' Her eyes sparked keenly. 'Want a hand?'

'No, I don't. I'm not fixing an engine and I'm quite capable of tackling this job by meself without you taking charge. Oh, if yer must know, Nelly Dawson's mangle's seized up.' His face wrinkled thoughtfully. 'Now there's a woman I wouldn't mind fancying me, just a pity she's still her 'usband living. And he's a waste of space. All 'e does all day is sit on his fat backside issuing orders to poor old Nelly. The only time 'e leaves his chair is to visit the privy or go down the pub. Fancy treating that lovely woman like that! The number of times I've 'ad ter bite me tongue so as not to give 'im a piece of me mind.'

He suddenly realised he was voicing private thoughts out loud to his granddaughter and mentally shook himself. 'Her . . . er . . . cogs want a bit of lubricating. Engine oil is the best thing for the job and I've none left. I might as well 'ave a pint as a thimbleful. It's useful stuff to 'ave around is engine oil. And you, madam, are a nosey bugger. Now get off, if yer going. If not put the kettle on and mash us a cuppa.'

'I'm going, Granddad.'

'I thought you would be.'

'It's all your fault, Frankie,' Stella moaned as the four of them emerged from the Belgrave Road picture house later that night. 'If you hadn't spent so much time gossiping with your granddad we wouldn't have been late for the pictures and got the worst seats, and then I wouldn't have missed most of the film because I had to sit behind that stupid woman with the hat on! And she never stopped talking.'

'I did offer to change seats.'

'There was no point in doing that, Frankie. Your view wasn't any better. Neither was Ian's nor Roger's.'

'Oh, shut up moaning, Stella,' said Ian good-naturedly. 'I don't know why you're going on. You spent too much time whispering sweet nothings and necking with Roger to be bothered with the picture.'

Stella giggled. Roger blushed scarlet.

'So what if I did?' she said cockily. 'Oh, here's where we part company. I'll see you tomorrow, Frankie, when I call for you at the garage to walk home after work. Oh, and make sure you ain't in such a state as you were tonight. It's bad enough walking along the street with you in a boiler suit, let alone when you're covered in oil.'

Frankie smiled. 'I'm a grease monkey, Stella, and grease monkeys get covered in oil, it's a hazard of the job. And if you're that embarrassed to be seen walking with me, why do you insist on doing it every night? Anyway I shouldn't bank on me being able to leave on time tomorrow. We're really busy.'

'Oh,' her friend mouthed, disappointed. 'Well, I'll come past anyway, just do your best. It ain't the same walking home without you.'

'Yeah, I know, I look forward to it too. Gives us a chance to catch up.'

'Catch up on what?' both men asked.

'Just women's things,' the girls responded cagily.

'Ta-ra then, you two,' Frankie said.

'Yeah, ta-ra,' Stella and Roger called in unison. And Stella added, 'Don't do anything we wouldn't.'

'She's a case, ain't she?' Ian said good-humouredly to Frankie as, arm-in-arm, they sauntered slowly in the direction of her house. 'Roger certainly has his hands full with her.'

'Yes, she does try his patience at times but he puts up with her ways 'cos he loves her. And I do 'cos she a bloody good friend,' Frankie said, smiling broadly. 'The best. I couldn't imagine life without her around. Hit it off right from the start, we did, when we were put next to each other on our very first day at school and there haven't been many days since when we haven't seen each other. Even Christmas Day. Oh, the times we've had . . .'

Ian had heard the story of how Frankie and Stella had met many times before, and all of their subsequent escapades, the sort lasting friendships are built on, but he let Frankie carry on. He had more important matters on his mind.

'Ian, are you listening to me?' she asked a few minutes later. 'Ian?'

'Eh? Oh, yes, of course I am. You were going on about the time you and Stella got stuck in the lift in Lewis's and by the time they got you out you'd both eaten the pound bag of broken biscuits Stella had got for her mother and you'd no money to buy any more.'

'I knew you weren't really listening,' she good-humouredly chided. 'I was telling you about the cars that came in today and how much I was looking forward to helping Uncle Wally and Taffy to fix them.'

'Were you? Oh,' he replied distractedly.

She pulled him to a halt, frowning in concern. 'Ian, is anything the matter?'

Holding his breath, he stared at her. Something was very much the matter. But the problem was, he didn't know how to break it to her. He smiled tenderly, his dark blue eyes drinking her in. To others

Frankie might not have quite the slender figure other women starved themselves to achieve, or anywhere near Joan Collins's sultry film star looks, but to Ian the girl was beautiful. He loved her, loved everything about her. Her mop of Titian curls; the matching scattering of freckles across her nose and cheeks; her warmth; her understanding; her natural manner. He was very proud of her unusual occupation; enjoyed nothing more than to brag about it to his mates whilst they were discussing their girlfriends and to compare Frankie's occupation with their commonplace factory or office jobs.

Within a few short weeks of meeting Frankie, Ian knew without a doubt she was the woman he wanted to spend the rest of his life with. After nearly two years of courting her, he wanted to ask her to marry him, was desperate to do so in fact. The trouble was the wage he earned as a junior draughtsman at Jones and Shipman's, a large, long-established engineering company, was hardly enough to support himself living at home, let alone a wife and a home of their own. His future prospects were excellent but he had at least three more years of studying and exams to pass before he qualified and promotion changed his title of junior to senior.

Frankie, he knew without asking her, would not mind in the least if they lived in a shed at the bottom of the garden, but he did. He wanted the best for her. A nice little house with some decent furniture, albeit second-hand, and the choice of giving up her job if she wanted. That was out of the question as matters stood at the moment. A surge of excitement gripped him. But he had an idea, one he liked the thought of . . . A change of job. Something entirely different from what he was doing now but something he knew he'd be good at. His parents wouldn't be pleased at his sudden change of profession. They were good people but had set ideas about life and a change of career didn't figure in them, even for a very good reason. Frankie might be shocked at first by what he was contemplating but she would support him in whatever he did, he knew. Should he get this job it was better paid right from the start and, most importantly, if you were married a house came with it. To Ian that was lure enough.

Excitement warmed him. He had filled in the application form and was waiting for the postman to bring him a letter to see if he'd been granted an interview. The anticipation was almost killing him.

He was desperate to let Frankie in on his secret, but a wish to surprise her with a proposal if he got the job far outweighed this. Plus the fact that, should he fail in his quest, he would be spared her witnessing his bruised male pride.

As he stood staring at her, Frankie fought down a sudden urge to grab Ian by the shoulders and give him a shake. She knew instinctively he was desperate to ask her to marry him, she knew he had been on the verge of doing so before and that this time, just like all the rest, at the very last minute his nerve would fail him. And she knew why. Money. Or the lack of it. Did he not realise that she'd live in a hovel if it meant being with him?

She sighed, gazing tenderly at him. Frankie loved Ian, everything about him, couldn't visualise the rest of her life without him by her side. He was no James Dean or Marlon Brando, Frankie would liken him more to Danny Kaye in fact, but regardless to her Ian was the most handsome man in the world. He was four inches taller than she at five foot eleven and of medium build, neither thin nor fat nor muscly, just ordinary in fact. Thick light brown hair framed an unremarkable but pleasant face with kindly hazel eyes. He was the quiet type, a thinker, a very reliable man. Frankie felt safe with him, comfortable and secure. He was just the kind of man that suited her and she felt lucky and privileged to know that he loved her.

She pursed her lips. Was her grandfather right? Should she put Ian out of his misery and propose to him? She sighed. Despite what her grandfather had told her and her own desperation to become Mrs Ian Fields, to Frankie it wasn't the done thing for a woman to do the proposing. She had no choice but to wait patiently until the day Ian spoke. She only hoped that day came soon.

'N'ote's the matter with me, Frankie,' he said lightly, shrugging his shoulders. 'I was just thinking how nice you looked.' His eyes shone down at her, filled to brimming with unmistakable love. 'I'm a lucky man to have you,' he whispered huskily.

Quashing her disappointment, she forced a smile, wrapped her arms around him and gave him a hug. 'Then we're both lucky,' she said.

'Had a nice night, lovey?' Nancy asked Frankie as she walked into the backroom a few minutes later.

'Yes, thanks, Mam. The picture was good. Well, what I saw of it was. Stella and Roger were sitting behind a great big man and a woman wearing a hat, and me and Ian behind a couple who kept talking despite Ian asking them not to. Stella didn't stop grumbling all the way home.' She sat down at the table, picking up the cup of hot cocoa her mother had prepared for her. Frankie cradled it in her hands and gazed around the room, sighing distractedly. Of all the rooms in their house she loved this one the best. It wasn't lavishly furnished, just the opposite in fact, but she always felt comfortable here and safe. Her eyes fell affectionately on her mother sitting opposite at the well-used oak table which was covered by a red-checked cloth, set ready for breakfast the next morning, a task her mother always did before she went to bed.

'How did Dad ask you to marry him, Mam?' she asked.

Nancy looked at her daughter, taken aback by her unexpected question. 'You know the answer to that, Frankie, we've had many a laugh over it. We'd just been for a ride on a motorbike. I looked like hell on earth, me hair all blown everywhere, me face streaked with dirt, and he just turns and looks at me and laughs. Then he asks me: "Nancy Crabshaw, will yer do me the honour?" "What honour?" I ask, as if I didn't know. "Of being me wife. 'Cos yer must love me, after what I've just put you through!" '

Nancy gave an infectious giggle. 'And I must have loved him 'cos, believe me, yer dad had just terrified the life out of me, whizzing, along at forty miles an hour on that clapped-out machine, hardly slowing down to corner the bends. Yer granny, God rest 'er, would 'ave had a fit if she'd 'ad any idea what I was up to. "Well, being's I've n'ote better ter to, I might as well," I said. And we did, three months later, despite having hardly a penny between us. I wore yer gran's wedding dress, which was a bit too tight for me, and yer dad wore a second-hand suit which smelt of mothballs, and we lived with yer Granny and Granddad Champion 'til we could afford ter rent rooms of our own. And Frankie, lovey, I wouldn't change a thing.' Nancy folded her arms, leaned on the table and looked keenly at her daughter. 'But more to the point, why are yer askin' me this again?'

'I just wanted to know what prompted Dad to ask you, that was all.'

Nancy eyed her knowingly. 'Ian'll ask yer to marry 'im when he's good and ready, Frankie. It's plain to all that 'e worships the ground yer walk on but he's a man who needs ter set his stall out.'

The girl eyed Nancy quizzically. 'What do you mean by that, Mam?'

'I mean, he's a man who needs to do things right. You, Frankie, of all people should know that. God love me, it took the man six months to ask yer out, and me and yer dad had ter put up with you moping around in the meantime.'

'I didn't mope.'

'I can assure you, you did. You hardly went out in case 'e

happened to call. And you went off yer food. That's when I knew you'd fallen in love.'

'All right, it's true. I think I fell in love the first time I saw Ian. It was agony for me, hoping he'd ask me out. I did eventually ask him why he waited so long and he told me he hadn't a decent pair of trousers to take me out in and waited until he'd saved enough to buy a pair.'

'See what I mean about setting his stall out?'

'Yes, Mam, that's all well and good but I don't want to wait for years to marry him. We've both our savings. It's not much together, not enough for a deposit for a house, but enough to pay a month's rent up front and buy some bits of furniture. And we'd get wedding presents, wouldn't we? Mam, I want to be with Ian now, not in three years' time when he's finished his apprenticeship. That seems so far away.'

'Three years isn't that long. It'll soon pass. And I expect Ian knows how you feel, Frankie, but it won't change things. As I said before, he'll ask yer when he's good and ready and you, my darlin', will just 'ave ter 'ave patience. Anyway, what's all the rush? Anyone would think you were desperate to leave home.'

'Oh, Mam, I'm not, you know that. I'm very happy here with you and Dad. Compared to Stella and others I know, I'm very lucky to have you both as my parents. It's just . . . just . . .'

Nancy leaned over and patted her daughter's hand affectionately. 'I know, love. You've met the man yer want ter spend the rest of yer life with and yer can't wait ter start. But after a few years, lovey, yer will wonder why yer were in so much of a hurry. I love yer dad and bless each minute I'm with him. I nearly lost him once, well, twice if yer count that dreadful attack of the 'flu he caught a few weeks back, and those scares never leave me. But believe me, Frankie, men can test yer patience. They can be so inconsiderate. There's n'ote more offputting than a smelly pair of socks and dirty underpants that's been dumped on the floor for you to pick up and wash. They don't mean to be so untidy, it's just the way of men. Well, those I know at any rate. And it don't matter how many times you threaten 'em, they don't change.'

Frankie smiled wistfully. She'd do anything to be picking up Ian's dirty laundry to wash. To look after him in every way would give her so much pleasure. She heaved a thoughtful sigh. 'Why hasn't Uncle Wally ever married?'

'Oh, but he is, Frankie.'

Her jaw dropped in shock. 'Eh?'

Nancy chuckled. 'To his business, that's who yer Uncle Wally is married to. Believe me, 'e's had many a chance. I was always trying to pair him off. One in particular I wouldn't 'ave been sorry to 'ave seen him settle with. She was lovely was Maisie Turnbull. Still is, for all I know. Do you remember Maisie, Frankie?'

She shook her head. 'Can't say as I do.'

'Well, you'd only have been about twelve at the time. She's the sister of the woman who used to live next door. They moved to Northampton, but that's by the by. I really thought Maise was the one for Wally. Got on like a house on fire they did. She was besotted with him and I thought he was with her. But not even Maisie had quite what it took to come between yer Uncle Wally and the great love of his life. She was broken-hearted as much as the rest when he called it a day.

'But as yer uncle said at the time, what woman is going to put up wi' the hours he works? Maisie, like the rest, might say she will, but in the long run, he'd a feeling she'd start to resent the time 'e wasn't at home, even if he was earning them a living, and that wasn't fair to her. But in all honesty, Frankie, I think it was excuses, meself. Yer uncle ain't the marryin' kind and that's the bottom of it.'

'Shame,' said Frankie. 'He's a good-looking man.'

'Yer right, 'e is, nearly as 'andsome as yer dad. But just 'cos he's good-looking don't mean ter say he'd mek a good husband. Anyway, after Maisie I gave up trying to find a woman for him, I knew I was wasting me time. But getting back to you. Ian's a lovely man, Frankie, yer dad and me couldn't be more pleased about him. You think he's worth waiting for, don't you?'

'Yes. Oh, yes, 'course I do.'

'Well then, as I said, have patience. D'yer want some more cocoa?'

'I'd love some, Mam, but you sit where you are, I'll get it.'

Nancy watched as Frankie rose from the table and went off into the kitchen. She smiled to herself. She couldn't blame the girl for her impatience. Ian and her daughter made a lovely couple, just right for each other. Nancy was glad Ian wanted to do right by her, it showed his sincerity. She and Sam only wished they were in a position to help the young pair financially but as things stood they just got by themselves. Still, Frankie was twenty-two – by some people's standards well past marriageable age, 'on the shelf' as they would term her spinster status – but to her mother still her baby, still the little girl she did not want to let go of, and she knew her husband felt exactly the same so this state of affairs was not unwelcome to them. Although at the same time she did feel sympathy with Frankie and her need to be with the man she loved, remembering how she'd felt when she realised her deep feelings for Frankie's father.

'Tell yer what,' she said as Frankie came back into the room bearing two mugs of steaming cocoa, 'when I'm in town tomorrow I'll scour the market for some nice pretty patterned cotton and run you up a couple of pillow slips for yer bottom drawer. And when yer tell Ian at least he can see we're doing out bit towards helping yer both along, so ter speak?'

'Oh, Mam, that'd be great,' she said enthusiastically.

'Good, that's settled then. Now tell me about these great motor cars that came into the garage today? Yer dad ain't the only one interested, yer know. I was in on the planning of this garage right from when it was a twinkle in yer Uncle Wally's eye, and especially now you're working there it's of great importance to me how well it's faring.'

Chapter Four

'Now, Frankie, remember all I've taught yer. Listen. What can yer hear?'

Frankie listened, head bent over the engine, handle of the screwdriver against her ear, sharp end pressed hard against the rocker cover, her face screwed up in concentration. Seconds ticked past before, satisfied, she straightened up. 'They're knocking,' she said to Wally with conviction.

'Blooding banging if yer ask me, but knocking will do. Right, yer know what to do.'

She nodded. 'I need the feeler gauges to reset the tappets. If that doesn't work, we'll have to strip the engine down.'

'Yeah well, let's hope we can avoid that. This job is going to cost the owner enough without us adding to it unnecessarily. Bernard!' he shouted. 'Oi, Bernard. Where's that dratted lad got to now.'

'He's out the back, Uncle Wally, decoking that engine liked you asked him.'

'Is he? Oh,' Wally replied shamefaced. 'I wa' just going to ask him ter put the kettle on,' he muttered.

Frankie smiled, patting her uncle affectionately on his arm. 'I'll make a mash before I make a start on the tappets. I bet you could do with one, couldn't you, Taffy?'

Working on another car across from them, the giant of a Welshman, his broad face caked in grease, wiped equally dirty hands on his grubby overalls and looked across at her. 'Sounds good to me, Frankie, my lovely. Did your mother send any of her home-made cake today by chance?' he hopefully asked.

'I bet your wife didn't,' chipped in Wally.

'My wife hasn't worked out what the cooker is for yet, let alone baked in it,' laughed Taffy. 'We've only been married ten year, so I live more in hope than anger.'

'Your Mary doesn't cook because she's fed up with you never

being at home to eat it. And I can't say as I blame her,' said Frankie matter-of-factly as she made her way over to the table at the back of the garage where the tea-making was done. The whole area including the sink was in need of a clean and tidy up and Frankie made a mental note to try and tackle it before she went home that night before they all caught something nasty. There was no point in her hoping any of the men would do it. Their attitude was that anything remotely connected with domestic chores was women's work, regardless of the fact that what she did was considered men's.

'Ah, well, you could have a point,' sighed Taffy. 'But then she doesn't exactly moan when I hand over me pay packet and she's straight off up the town to buy herself something. She can't have it all ways. Anyway,' he shouted across to Frankie, 'have we cake or not?'

'We've cake,' she answered. 'Currant.'

Just then a bell jangled loudly.

'Go and see who that is,' Wally told Taffy.

Wiping his huge hands on an oily rag, he departed to return moments later.

'Was a suitcase chappy selling spares. I told him you were busy and to come back later.'

'Good man. With a bit of luck he won't,' Wally said, sliding down into the pit beneath the Alvis he and Frankie were working on. He began to examine it. 'I haven't time to listen to his prattle or promises he can't fulfil,' he shouted, assuming the others could hear him. 'Ah, there's a 'ole in this exhaust. Have yer gone to India for that bloody tea, Frankie?' he boomed good-humouredly.

Just before closing time that evening she was in the office seeing to Mr Willis, the owner of the Alvis. The office was a small area that had been partitioned off from the main garage and could be accessed by customers through a door at the side. A counter divided it in two. Whatever the weather the room was always freezing. The paraffin stove that was supposed to warm it had long ago broken and with everything else needing doing it was one of a number of things that never quite got attended to.

The space under the counter was used for extra storage and stacked there higgledy-piggledy were several cans of Duckham's engine oil, tins of fixative, a drum of Swarfega, a large sack of old cloths used for wiping rags, and five boxes of the Jeyes toilet paper Wally had bought as a job lot from a warehouse across town, temporarily replacing the newspaper squares they normally made do with. There was also an old safe Wally used to keep the takings in. Behind the counter was an old wooden filing cabinet stuffed to overflowing with all manner of paperwork covering the near ten years the garage had been in operation. Wally was a first-class mechanic but uninterested in administration and only did enough to keep the officials happy. Paperwork was not high on his list of priorities. Keeping his customers' vehicles on the road was.

Pushing shut an obstinate drawer of the filing cabinet with her bottom, Frankie addressed the customer. 'Your car is ready, Mr Willis,' she said, handing him the keys. 'Tappets needed resetting and you needed a new oil filter. Nothing serious this time, but my uncle says there was a small hole in your exhaust. He's repaired it temporarily but you'll need a new one in a few months. Oh, and you'll also need your brake pads replacing shortly.'

Mr Willis nodded, impressed, as he retrieved his wallet from his inside coat pocket and took out a pound note and several coins. 'I'm glad I decided to give Champion's a try,' he said, handing over the payment. 'My usual garage would have found a lot more than that wrong with the car and they wouldn't have repaired the exhaust, they'd have put on a new one. Nor would they have done the job so quick. I'd have had to have done without my car for at least a week, and I know for a fact the bill would have been much higher than this. Tell Mr Champion you'll be having my custom in future and I've a few acquaintances I'll definitely be telling.'

Frankie smiled happily at him. 'I will, Mr Willis, and thank you. Safe journey.'

'He looked a bit posh for this place. Lost his way, had he, and come in to ask directions?'

'Hello, Stella,' Frankie said, delighted to see her friend. 'Mr Willis is a customer actually. We just fixed his Alvis. He's ever so pleased with the job we've done – going to tell his mates, only he called them acquaintances.' She suddenly frowned, perplexed. 'Er . . . you're a bit early, aren't you?'

Stella shook her head. 'No, it's nearly six.'

'Is it? Well, I've a couple of things to do before I can possibly leave tonight. It might be best if you go ahead without me.'

Stella pouted in disappointment. 'Oh, Frankie, I've had a hell of a day,' she grumbled. 'The old battleaxe has been like a bear with a sore head and she took it out on me. Everything I did was wrong. Then to top it all the carriage on my typewriter came off. I only just managed to stop it shooting across the room like a catapult. It was really funny but Mrs Crompton blamed me. Said I'd done it on purpose. As if I would,' she said innocently, and gave a mournful sigh. 'Oh, Frankie, I hate my job. I hate everything about it but I daren't leave until I get something else. Are you sure your Uncle Wally couldn't do with me here?'

'I'm sure he could, Stella, but he couldn't afford your wage. Anyway, you'd be bored. Nothing exciting happens here, you know.'

Her friend tutted. 'And nothing exciting happens at Chawner's Accountants. In fact nothing happens, full stop. It's like working in a morgue. If you're caught talking during working hours and it's not to do with the business there's hell to pay. It's like being back at school only instead of the teachers bossing me about and treating me like an imbecile, Chawner's are paying me a pittance for the honour.

'Oh, surely your uncle could afford to pay me three pounds a week? I'd even settle for two pounds seventeen and six. I could tidy up this place and do all the paperwork. I'm really good at book-keeping now, I balanced the ledger last week,' she said proudly, then added as an afterthought, 'Well, nearly. All but two and eleven and that was because Mr Brown the chief accountant hadn't written some figures in clearly. They should have retired him long ago, if you ask me. He's eighty if he's a day and Mrs Crompton isn't that much younger. The pair of them together drive me daft. If it wasn't for Miss Biddles the senior typist, who's a sweetie, and young Kevin the junior accountant, I'd go daft, believe me. Look, Frankie, I could see to the customers.' Her eyes sparkled as another thought struck. 'Bring a touch of glamour to this place. That's just what this place needs: a glamorous receptionist to bring the customers in.'

Frankie hid a smile. Admittedly Stella was a very attractive girl but hardly glamorous, though given her figure, she could be in the right clothes. 'Stella, this is a little back-street garage,' Frankie said tactfully. 'We don't even sell petrol, although Uncle Wally said he's going to look into that in the future. Our customers' only interest is in getting their car fixed, not being pampered by a glamorous receptionist. We aren't one of those big car showrooms they have in London. I don't think even Sturgess's garage has a receptionist,' she mused, 'and they're just about the biggest in Leicester. They sell cars too. If you're that keen on working as a garage receptionist, why don't you go and offer your services to Sturgess's?'

'Because I want to work here, Frankie. Anyway that chap who just left looked like he'd expect to be seen by a receptionist.'

'Well, he might, but he wasn't here and let me assure you he's not our normal run of customer. If most of them came in and found you behind the desk done up like a dog's dinner, putting on airs and graces, they'd run a mile,' Frankie said, laughing.

Stella tutted disdainfully. 'You're behind the times, you are, Frankie. The war ended ten years ago. People expect better things now, and why not, eh? I went to the dentist the other day and even they've got a potted plant on the window sill and a few magazines to read while you're waiting, which is a damn' sight better than this place. It's depressing in here,' she said, gazing around. 'Look, all I'm asking is that you ask your uncle?'

Her manner was purposely childlike, a ploy Stella would always use to try and get her own way and which usually succeeded. But tonight it only resulted in irritating Frankie. 'You can stop that nonsense, Stella. I'm not in the mood. If you're serious ask my uncle yourself. He's through in the garage. But I'll tell you now what the answer'll be. We could do with taking on a youngster to learn the trade and when money allows that's what Uncle Wally will do before he considers someone for the office.' She looked at her friend for a moment and gave a kind smile. 'You're just fed up at the moment, Stella, and want something to cheer you up. Are you seeing Roger tonight?'

'No,' she said sulkily. 'He's going over to his sister's to put some shelves up in her kitchen. He asked if I wanted to go but Jackie's a miserable old cow and her kids drive me nuts. He might pop in on his way home if it's not too late, but if I know Jackie she'll find enough jobs for him to do to keep him going for weeks 'cos her lazy sod of a husband won't do anything around the house. Are you seeing Ian?'

'It's his college night. Look, I tell you what. Wait for me and I'll finish up as quick as I can, then you come back to mine. I'm sure Mam can rustle up some dinner for you, then after we can have a girlie night. How's that sound?'

Her friend's face brightened. 'Smashing. I'll pop home on our way and pick up my new Frankie Avalon record. Did you get a new needle for your Dansette?'

'I did yesterday lunchtime and . . .'

Frankie's voice trailed away as the outer door opened and a man sauntered in. Horrified to realise she was staring, Frankie closed her mouth sharply, suddenly extremely conscious of her working attire and of the mess she must look. Oh, but this man was handsome! A slightly shorter version of Rock Hudson, he even had thick black hair cut in the same style as the film star. Underneath his long fawn trench coat he was wearing a smart blue suit. Frankie guessed his age to be around twenty-five.

Stella too was gawping at him.

His eyes, a midnight blue colour, settled immediately on her. 'Well, hello,' he said seductively, stepping across to her. His back towards Frankie, he leaned casually against the counter and looked Stella straight in the eye. 'And what's a beautiful woman like you doing in a place like this?'

She gave a girlish giggle. 'My friend works here. I'm waiting for her.'

'I bet she's not as good-looking as you. She can't be.'

'Can I help you?' said Frankie tersely, offended that this man was blatantly ignoring her presence.

At the sound of her voice his head turned and he eyed her in surprise. 'Oh, I er . . . thought . . .'

'You thought right,' she cut in sharply. 'I am a mechanic.' She knew without doubt that on entering the office he had noticed her working overalls and assumed she was a man. He hadn't taken any notice of her because something far more important had attracted his attention. Frankie was not exactly an expert where men were concerned but she knew a womaniser when she met one. Her uncle would term this man a spiv. 'So what *can* I do for you?' she demanded sharply.

His attention was now back on Stella and without taking his eyes off her he said matter-of-factly, 'I've an appointment with Mr Champion. I called in earlier and was told to come back this evening. Tell him I'm here. The name's Edwin Taylor.' He winked suggestively at Stella. 'Eddie to my friends. I didn't catch your name?'

Frankie's eyebrows rose at his offensive manner but she kept quiet, with neither the time nor the inclination to waste any further time on him. As she made her way through the door at the back that led into the garage she heard Stella giggling and shook her head.

Her uncle was busy and it took her several moments to get his full attention.

'Oh, I can't be bothered seeing anyone this near knocking-off time, Frankie. Not that I'll be knocking off just yet. I've at least another couple of hours' work left to do on this car. Tell him . . . oh, I dunno,' he said, scratching his head. 'I did ask Taffy to tell him to call back so I suppose I ought to see him. No, no, I can't, I have ter get this car done. Can you deal with him, Frankie? I doubt this chappy's got anything we'd be interested in so just get rid of him as quick as yer can, then get yerself off home.'

She inwardly groaned, the thought of dealing with this man not appealing to her at all. 'Okay, Uncle Wally,' she reluctantly agreed. 'Look, I can stay tonight . . .'

'Oi, who's the boss around 'ere? Yeah, that's right, me. And when I say yer go home, yer go home.' He smiled affectionately at his niece. 'Yer offer's much appreciated, me darlin', but you've been working non-stop since seven-thirty this morning, so you've done enough fer one day. Me and Taffy will soon get this done between us. That right, Taffy?' he shouted across.

'If you say so, boss.'

'Besides,' continued Wally, 'I don't fancy yer mother charging down here threatening me with her rolling pin. She complains I work yer too hard as it is.'

Frankie laughed. 'All right, if you're sure, Uncle Wally. But I'll make you a mash before I do leave.'

He patted her arm. 'Yer a good gel, Frankie.'

She looked at her uncle for a moment. Like all his workforce, by the end of a working day Wally looked like he'd been soaking in a bath of oil. It was ingrained in his hands and streaked across his face, but that still did not disguise his handsome features, nor the warmth and sincerity that shone in his kindly hazel eyes. He was a lovely man and in his chosen profession something of a rarity. He was honest, sometimes too much so for his own good, but he was also one of the lucky ones. He was very happy in a job for which he was well suited and which he enjoyed. Like his father and brother, put anything mechanical within arm's reach of Wally and he was in his element. The only thing Frankie felt he lacked was a good woman by his side. Someone to look after him, care for him, have a hot meal ready when he arrived home of an evening, exhausted from the day's labours, his laundry all washed and ironed, his house warm and clean.

He seemed to sense what she was thinking and his eyes narrowed knowingly. 'Don't you start, Frankie. I've enough of that from yer mother.'

'I don't know what you mean,' she said innocently.

'Oh, yes, you do. I like my life as it is, Frankie. I don't want a woman fussing over me. If I'd wanted one, I've had plenty of chances. Some men, me darlin', ain't the marrying kind and I'm one of them. Besides, if I want a bit of fuss and looking after, I know where to come to get it, don't I?' he laughed. 'Yer mam and you never let me down. Now get and see that chappy before he thinks we've abandoned him.'

She eyed him tenderly. 'All right, Uncle Wally.'

Frankie was taken aback to find Stella on her own when she re-entered the office. 'Where's that bloke gone?' she asked.

'Oh, he . . . er . . . said he'd call back another time. Something about another appointment, I wasn't really listening.'

'Don't tell porkies, Stella. You *were* listening. You were hanging on that chap's every word.'

Her friend tightened her lips indignantly. 'I was not. Anyway, I've decided to have an early night, I've suddenly gone all tired. And I expect you'll be relieved 'cos you did say you had work to do before you left for the night and me hanging around will only make you feel guilty. So I'll get off and leave you in peace.'

Frankie stared at her, brow furrowing. Something wasn't right. Stella was definitely acting suspiciously. 'What's going on?' she demanded.

Stella eyed her innocently. 'What do you mean?'

'I mean, what's going on, that's what I mean. You were all for a girlie night in before that bloke came in. Now . . .' She stopped abruptly as a thought suddenly struck and her mouth dropped open. 'Oh, Stella, you're not?' she exclaimed, horrified. 'You are, aren't you?'

'What?'

'Going on a date with that chap that was in here?'

'So what if I am?' Stella said defensively. 'It's only for a drink. No harm done.'

Frankie was staring at her, stunned. 'But what about Roger?'

Stella shrugged her shoulders nonchalantly. 'What about him? Frankie, for God's sake, I'm just going for a drink, not planning to elope with the man. It's a bit of fun, and I can't remember the last time I had any of that. And Roger didn't think twice about leaving me on my own when he agreed to go and do that work for his sister.'

'When Roger said he'd help his sister out, I don't suppose for a minute he thought you'd be off gallivanting with another man. Anyway, you know what a nag Jackie is. He more than likely agreed just to shut her up. And you could have gone too.'

'Oh, and you call that fun, do you, Frankie? Sitting there all night listening to Roger banging and crashing around with three kids yelling in my ear and jumping all over me, not to mention Jackie moaning on about *her lot*.'

'But I thought you loved Roger?'

'I do. Look, I've had enough of this, anyone would think I'm about to commit a cardinal sin. What's the real difference between going for a drink with you and going with Eddie? It's just a friendly thing.' Her face suddenly filled with worry. 'Er . . . you won't mention this to Roger, though, will you? Or Ian, 'cos he might tell him?'

Sighing, Frankie shook her head. 'Of course I won't. I just hope you're careful, that's all. That man's a proper charmer if ever I've met one. He's probably got a wife waiting somewhere for him.'

'Well, more fool her for marrying him then. She must have known what he was like before she did. So I'll see you tomorrow night then after work, will I, Frankie?'

Lips clamped tight, she slowly nodded. 'I suppose.'

'And you promise you won't breathe a word to anyone? You won't, will you, Frankie?'

'I've said I won't, haven't I? What do you want me to do – write it in stone?'

Stella exhaled in relief. 'Thanks, Frankie. You're a proper mate, you are.'

'Mmm,' was her only response.

Later that evening Nancy eyed her daughter in concern. 'Not to your liking?'

Absently, Frankie lifted her head. 'Eh?'

'Your dinner. What on earth is up with you, Frankie? You're shoving my good food around yer plate like it's poisonous or summat.'

'Am I? Oh! Er . . . sorry, Mam.'

'Well, I thought that were grand meself, Nancy,' said Sam, pushing his empty plate away and patting his stomach. 'Nice bit of fish that.'

'Should be,' she said matter-of-factly. 'It cost me enough. So you gonna eat yours then, Frankie?'

She looked down at her place, then back at her mother. 'I'm sorry, Mam, I'm not hungry.'

'Not hungry? What d'yer mean, not hungry? Of course yer are, hard day that I know you've had.' She frowned disapprovingly. 'Not dieting, are yer?'

'No.'

'Thank God fer that. Now eat it up and let's have none of yer nonsense.'

'Now, Nancy,' Sam said firmly, 'if the gel says she ain't hungry then she's old enough ter know that.'

'She might be, but I'm the silly sod that's gotta look after her when she's ill through lack of sustenance.'

Sam laughed. 'One missed meal ain't gonna kill our gel, Nancy.'

'No, I grant yer. But it's a mother's job ter mek sure her children are fed properly and that's what I'm doing. Now are yer ailing for summat?' she asked Frankie.

'Not that I know of.'

'Got a headache then?'

'No.'

'Feel sick?'

'No?'

'Got toothache?'

'No.'

'Have yer had a row with Ian?'

'No, Mam,' Frankie said, beginning to feel agitated.

'Then yer've no excuse. Now eat that bloody dinner before I spoon feed yer. I'll not waste good food for no good reason. I remember when I was a kiddy we many a times never had a meal put in front of us because me mam had no money. Me and yer dad have been bloody hard up sometimes but we always managed somehow to put food in front of yer, and the least you can do is eat it.'

'All right, Mam,' sighed Frankie, resigned. 'Yer've made yer point,' she said, forking a piece of fish and putting it in her mouth. It tasted delicious which fuelled her appetite and before she knew it she had demolished the lot. 'That was lovely, Mam, thanks,' she said, placing down her knife and fork. 'Any pudding?'

Her mother smiled. 'Jam roly-poly do yer?'

'It will me,' said Sam.

'So come on, tell me?' Nancy pressed her daughter a while later after the table had been cleared, dishes washed and Sam was snoring softly in the armchair, the newspaper he'd been reading fallen in a heap on the floor to the side of him.

'Tell you what?' she asked.

Nancy pushed a mug of fresh tea towards her and picked up her own, sipping on it. 'What's troubling you? Summat is.'

Frankie sighed. 'Nothing escapes you, does it, Mam? It's to do with Stella. It's nothing really.'

'Nothing indeed. It's serious enough to have you worried. Oh, well, if yer don't want ter tell me that's fair enough. As long as you're all right, that's the main thing.'

Frankie's eyes fixed on the steam rising from her mug of tea. She longed to discuss her worries over Stella, but how could she without betraying her friend? She picked up the mug and took a sip of the strong sweet liquid. She had a terrible feeling in the pit of her stomach that Stella was heading for trouble. And what about Roger? Frankie liked the man, very much so. Like her Ian he was the genuine sort and loved every bone in his girlfriend's body, would do anything for her. Frankie knew that if Roger had any idea that Stella was at this minute out with another man, even for an innocent drink, it would devastate him. To Frankie what Stella was doing wasn't right, not when she had been courting Roger for over two years and been privileged to gain his love and trust. Although not officially engaged, they were busily putting away whatever spare money they could in the understanding they would one day get married. So far, though, Roger had done far more saving than Stella.

A vision of them rose before her. Their arms were linked, Roger staring adoringly at Stella who in turn was giggling over something shared between them. Frankie mentally shook herself. She was being stupid. She was getting this situation out of all proportion, letting her imagination run away with her. Despite Frankie's instant dislike of him there was no denying that Edwin Taylor was a good-looking man and she couldn't blame Stella for being flattered by his attentions. But he was definitely a Jack the Lad type who, if wasn't already attached, more than likely saw a different woman every night. No doubt after tonight Stella would be lucky if she ever saw him again. And hopefully Roger would be none the wiser.

Frankie lifted her head and smiled at her mother. 'I'm fine, Mam, honest. I'm getting all het up for nothing. Stella's . . . er . . . really fed up with her job and I'm worried she'll walk out without getting anything else first.' She felt terrible for not being completely honest with Nancy as to the real reason for her distraction this evening, but she wasn't exactly lying to her. Frankie really was concerned about Stella's employment situation.

'There's no point in you getting yerself in a tizzy over that,' said Nancy, topping up her mug from the old brown earthenware teapot and splashing in a drop of milk. 'You know as well as I do that Stella has a mind of her own, and should she decide to leave her job without 'ote else then n'ote you say will stop her, Frankie, love. I sometimes wonder how Roger keeps 'is patience with 'er. Runs him ragged she does, and 'im such a lovely young lad an' all. Don't get me wrong, I like the girl, Frankie, you two are good friends, but all the same – what Stella wants, Stella gets. She can be rather thoughtless at times.'

Frankie grimaced. 'Yes, I suppose so.'

'There's no suppose about it, and you're as guilty as anyone of giving her her own way.'

Frankie tightened her lips. 'The odd time, yes, I do, but it's only to keep the peace.'

'Huh, more than the odd time I'd say, Frankie. I've lost count of the times I've known you've wanted to go to the pictures instead of dancing but just 'cos Stella wanted to go dancing, that's where you ended up. And how many times has she come around here 'cos she's at a loose end regardless of you hinting you want an early night? She pouts and you give in. Anything for an easy life, that's you.'

Frankie was quite shocked to realise she was so accommodating towards her friend. 'Do I really give in to her so easily?'

'Yes, yer do. But that's not a crime, Frankie, it's just the way you are. You're considerate, and for the people you care for you're willing to put yerself out. Just like yer Uncle Wally, it's a Champion trait. But, as I see it, unfortunately Stella abuses that goodness in yer. That's the selfish streak in her. Still, that's what makes her Stella and you Frankie. I know which one I'd sooner 'ave as me daughter.' She leaned over and affectionately patted Frankie's hand. 'You, me darlin'.' Nancy turned her head and looked at her husband to satisfy herself he was still sleeping soundly then looked at her daughter. 'There's summat I want yer to help me with,' she whispered.

Frankie frowned questioningly. 'Oh? What's that?'

'Shush, keep yer voice down, I don't want yer dad ter hear.'

Glancing across at her father, Frankie grinned. 'He's out for the count. A bomb dropping wouldn't wake him.' She eyed her mother keenly. 'You're up to something, Mam, what is it?'

Nancy leaned further over the table, eyes sparkling excitedly. 'Well, I think I've found a lovely woman for yer Uncle Wally.'

Frankie's jaw dropped. 'Eh? But I thought you said you'd stopped trying to get him married off years ago?'

'Yes, I had, but I really think this might be the one. She's a widow. Her husband was killed in the war and she's bin on her own ever since. She's a lovely woman, Frankie. Hilary her name is. Hilary Thompson. She's ever so pretty. Just moved in at the bottom of the street – I met her in the corner shop. We got chatting and I invited her back for a cuppa. She's no children. Sad, really, I think she'd make a grand mother. Still there's time yet, I reckon, as she's not quite forty. She's a librarian. You have ter be clever to be one of those, yer know. Yer dad liked her. She had quite a chat with him, showed a real interest in the bike he was fixing. Anyway, will yer help me or not?'

Frankie slowly exhaled. 'Have you told Dad what you're planning?'

'Don't be silly, 'e's the last person I'd tell. Not that I make a habit of keeping things from yer dad, but things like this I do. If 'e got wind of this he'd put a stop to it straight away.'

'Yes, he would,' Frankie agreed. 'He'd say we were interfering and to leave well alone.'

'That's all well and good, but as yer Uncle Wally never has time to read a newspaper, let alone trot down the library to borrow a book, there's not much chance of those two ever coming face to face, so as I see it a little interference for want of a better expression is justified in this case. So are yer gonna help me or not?'

Frankie grinned, eyes shining. ''Course I am, Mam. I'd like nothing more than to see Uncle Wally settled with a nice woman. I was only thinking as much today. So what exactly have you in mind?'

'Well, that's where you come in 'cos I've no idea as yet. Whatever we come up with will 'ave ter be very discreet so neither of 'em realises . . . not your dad neither.'

'Mmm,' mused Frankie thoughtfully. 'I don't suppose we can invite them both to dinner?'

Pursing her lips, Nancy shook her head. 'Oh, no, that's far too obvious.'

'Yes, yer right. Then I don't suppose she's got a car that just happens to need fixing?'

'Don't be daft, Frankie. How many librarians do you know with a car?'

'I don't know any librarians.'

'Well, actually, Hilary is the first one I've ever come across, too. Not the sort of person you meet every day is a librarian.' Nancy looked thoughtful. 'Hilary never mentioned having a car . . . No, she can't have because she was saying how the eight-thirty-five bus never arrived the other morning and she was late for work.'

Frankie sighed. 'Getting those two face to face is going to take some doing then, isn't it?'

Nancy nodded. 'And cunning, but I'm confident we'll come up with summat 'cos if ever I've known a pair right for each other, it's them two. It'd be such a shame if they never got to meet.'

'Be a shame if *who* never got to meet?' a voice asked.

Both women looked guiltily across at Sam who was awake now, yawning and stretching his arms.

'Er . . . I don't know what yer blathering on about. Yer must 'a' bin dreaming,' said Nancy to him. She glanced hurriedly at Frankie. 'Mum's the word,' she whispered. 'Get yer thinking cap on and so will I, we'll see what we can come up with. Want a cuppa?' she asked Sam.

Chapter Five

'What's up with Stella?' Ian whispered to Frankie as he picked up his glass of foaming mild and took a gulp. 'She's been acting like a misery for a couple of weeks now. She's beginning to make *me* feel miserable. It's Friday night, Frankie. We usually enjoy ourselves on a Friday night. I've been at a funeral more lively than this.'

She stole a glance at her friend who was sitting across the table staring into her drink, seemingly miles away, while Roger at the side of her was trying his hardest to act as though everything was normal. So it wasn't just her own imagination, she thought. Stella's uncharacteristically sombre behaviour recently had to be glaringly obvious for Ian, who never said a bad word, to make comment. It was obvious to anyone that she was a woman with much on her mind and Frankie had the most terrible feeling she knew just who the cause of that distraction was, though vehemently hoping she was wrong.

She watched as Stella put down her barely touched half of bitter shandy, picked up her handbag and rose. 'I'm just popping to the Ladies,' she announced, and without waiting for Frankie left.

'T'in't like Stella to go to the toilet without you, Frankie. You two had words or something?' Roger asked.

Frankie shook her head. 'No,' she answered truthfully, shaking her head. How could the pair of them have had any kind of disagreement when for the past two weeks Frankie had hardly seen her friend? And when she had, all she had got in response to any question she asked was a mumbled 'yes . . . no . . . maybe . . . I don't know.' Added to that Stella had made trivial excuses for not walking home with her on an evening after work and that in itself was of great concern to Frankie. Whatever the weather, except during the odd illness, the girls always walked home together. As for their girlie nights – get togethers that took place at least three times a week when neither was seeing their respective boyfriend, when they would sit in Frankie's bedroom and play the latest hard-saved-for records by favourite artists on Frankie's Dansette record player; try out new hair styles and make-up on each other, flick through magazines discussing the new fashions or just sit and chat, mostly about their respective sweethearts – they had come to a sudden halt, Stella claiming to be tired or washing her hair.

Roger put down his glass and leaned across the table, his face the picture of misery. 'Frankie, d'yer know if there's 'ote wrong with Stella? Only she ain't been herself for days now and it's beginning to bother me. If I ask her she just tells me I'm being stupid. But you can see for yerselves there's summat not right, she's hardly said a word all night.'

His hurt and bewilderment were so apparent that Frankie's heart went out to him. But how could she tell him of her suspicions? After all, they *were* only suspicions and Stella's mood might not have anything to do with her date with Edwin Taylor. Grabbing her handbag, she rose. There was only one way to find out. If Stella wasn't going to talk, she would confront her and wouldn't give up until she had got to the bottom of it. 'I dunno, Roger, I'm as flummoxed as you,' said Frankie, hoping to appease him. 'I do know she's desperate to leave her job and it's probably to do with that. I won't be a minute,' she said to Ian before she made her way towards the Ladies' cloakroom.

Surprisingly the usually crowded place was empty and she immediately spotted Stella, with her back towards her, by the length of wall mirror, reapplying her lipstick. Frankie took a deep breath before she went across to join her. 'There you are,' she said lightly, placing her handbag next to Stella's on the narrow counter that ran under the mirror. She opened it up and began rummaging around for her own make-up bag. 'You've been in here that long I thought you'd gone home,' she said jocularly as she pulled her compact out, flipped it open, smoothed the pad around the remnants of ecru-coloured pressed power inside and, peering into the mirror, began to refresh her own make-up.

'Oh, I see, timing me now, are you?' Stella replied off-handedly.

Frankie stopped what she was doing and looked at her, frowning deeply. 'No, not at all.' She turned fully to face her friend, features softening. 'Stella, what's wrong with you?'

She glared back, annoyed. 'Oh, don't you start, Frankie,' she snapped. 'I've got enough with Roger asking that question every two minutes, and I'll tell you the same as I tell him. Nothing.' In obvious agitation she rammed the lid back on her lipstick and threw it into her make-up bag.

'Roger might believe you, but I don't. Come on, Stella, you've been acting funny for a couple of weeks now. Well, ever since you went out with that Eddie chap, really. Whenever I ask you anything about that night you say you just went for a drink, but something must have happened to make you like this, Stella.'

'Like what?' she asked innocently.

Frankie felt her temper rising. 'You know exactly what I mean,' she snapped sharply. 'It's not like you hardly to say two words all night. Even Ian's commented how strangely you're acting. Look how you've been avoiding me, and don't say you haven't 'cos you have. I can't remember the last night we walked home together, or when you last came around for one of our girlie nights. I know something happened when you went out with Eddie Taylor, 'cos you haven't been the same since. So what was it, Stella? What happened to make you go all peculiar?'

Tight-lipped, her friend stared at her then, unable to contain her burden any longer, blurted out: 'All right, if you must know something *did* happen. I fell in love with Eddie, that's what. Satisfied now, are you?'

Frankie was stunned, this declaration being the very last thing she had expected to hear. Suddenly her heart sank as her vision of her whole future, one she had cherished since she had realised she and Ian were serious about one another, and likewise Stella and Roger, seemed to crumble before her. The four of them got on so well together they had all automatically assumed that when they married the two couples would live close to each other and continue sharing their daily lives until the day they all died. Now Frankie felt that rosy future to be in jeopardy – and all because Edwin Taylor had seduced Stella with his good looks and charm over a couple of halves of bitter shandy. 'How on earth can you say you love this man, Stella, when you hardly know him?'

'You're old-fashioned, Frankie. You don't have to know everything about someone to fall in love.'

'All right, I agree, but surely you can't know someone well enough to have feelings like that for them after a couple of hours spent in the pub?' Her eyes narrowed and she looked at Stella hard. 'It is just the once you've been out with him, isn't it?'

She gave a nonchalant shrug of her shoulders.

Shocked, Frankie gasped, 'Oh, Stella, how many times *have* you been out with him?'

'Only a couple. Well, three to be precise.'

'Three! But what about Roger? You're engaged to him, or had you forgotten?'

'I'm not engaged.'

'Not officially, but you've an understanding.'

'And that's all. Nothing that would stand up in a court of law. I owe him nothing.'

'Oh, Stella, how could you be so cruel? Roger loves you and he thinks you two are going to be married in the not-too-distant future. Just because you've fallen out of love with him doesn't mean to say you can treat him badly.'

The other girl stared at Frankie then suddenly her whole body sagged. Lowering her head, she wrung her hands, distraught. 'Oh, Frankie, this is all so awful. I never meant this to happen, you've got to believe me. I was . . . I was just wanting some fun and couldn't see any harm in going for a drink.' Her voice lowered to a whisper. 'Eddie's so different from Roger, he's such a gentleman. Opens doors for me, pulls out chairs. And you should see the jealous looks I get from other women when we walk into a pub. I like it, Frankie. I feel so proud. I've never felt that way with Roger, and nor has he treated me the way Eddie does, Frankie, like I'm really special. He keeps telling me how beautiful I am and he's so attentive to me all night. And we talk about all sorts of things and not one mention of football. Have you ever known Roger or Ian go a whole night without talking about football?

'When he saw me to my bus that first time I was desperate for him to ask to see me again and I can't tell you how I felt when he did. I was so happy I wanted to . . . to . . . jump naked off the West Bridge, screaming with joy.'

Frankie was staring at her agog. 'And he's never once tried it on with you?'

Stella looked at her. Was Frankie mad? Of course he had, at every opportunity on the way home. He'd had hands like octopuses and she'd lost count of the number of times she'd had to fight him off. Trouble was, though, she hadn't really wanted to fight him off, but she wasn't about tell her friend this. 'Of course he didn't. I told you, Eddie's a gentleman.'

Frankie sighed long and loud. 'Why didn't you tell me about all this, Stella?' she asked, hurt. 'I thought we were friends? We've always told each other everything. How could you keep this from me?'

'I wanted to tell you, really I did, you've no idea how much, but I knew what you'd think.' She looked Frankie straight in the eye. 'And I'm not wrong, am I, Frankie? You think I'm a slut and being disloyal to Roger.'

'I would never think you a slut,' she said with conviction. 'And I'm sorry you should think I would. But you're right, I don't think you're being fair to Roger.'

'Well, I can't help that, Frankie. I don't seem to have any control over what I'm doing at the moment, and that's why I've been avoiding you. I knew it wouldn't be long before I had to tell you what was going on. I knew you'd take Roger's side, and I didn't want a fight with you or to lose you as my friend. Try and understand how it is for me. I thought I loved Roger until I met Eddie. Now I realise I don't. Eddie . . . Oh, Frankie, he's everything I've ever wanted in a man and I can't stop thinking about him. I even dream about him. We have this little house in the country with roses round the door. We're standing at the gate and he's kissing me goodbye before he goes off to work. Can you imagine what it's like, Frankie, to care so much for someone that it makes you feel sick?'

She sighed despairingly. 'You like him that much, eh?'

Stella nodded. 'I do.' Then she shook her head. 'I never realised before how boring Roger is.'

'Boring!' Frankie exclaimed. 'How on earth can you say Roger is boring? He's nothing of the sort.'

Stella pulled a wry face. 'Compared to Eddie he is.' Suddenly her eyes flashed and her face lit up in a way Frankie had never witnessed in her friend before. 'Eddie is so . . . Oh, Frankie, he's so *exciting*.'

'Exciting?' Frankie couldn't for the life of her see what Stella thought exciting about the likes of Edwin Taylor. 'I admit he's good-looking, but exciting, well . . .'

'He is,' she blurted defensively. 'He's going to be somebody one day, you mark my words. Eddie Taylor isn't going to be selling car spares for the rest of his life. He has plans, Frankie, big ones, he told me. And Roger,' she said, ruefully shaking her head, 'doesn't have plans for our future – apart from us getting married that is. He's an electrician for Goodwin and Barsby,' she spoke derogatively, 'and he'll be an electrician with Goodwin and Barsby 'til the day he retires. I know there's nothing wrong with that, but after meeting someone like Eddie and hearing what he plans for the future, it's not enough for me any more.'

Frankie frowned. 'I see,' she said tersely.

Stella scowled at her friend. 'What do you mean, *I see*?'

'Oh, Stella, for goodness' sake, open your eyes. Three dates with this man and you think you know him inside out. I know I only met him the once but I know a spiv when I see one. Stella, I beg you, please think about what you're doing. You've known this man five minutes. For all you know, everything he's told you could be nothing more than lies to impress you. And please think about Roger. He loves you and I know deep down you love him. It's just you're blinded at the moment by what you think you see in this other man. You've told me how much you think of him, Stella, but does he feel the same about you?'

She cast down her eyes. 'Not in so many words, but I know he does.'

'How?'

Stella haughtily threw back her head. 'By the way he kisses me.'

Frankie ran her hand despairingly over her forehead. 'Stella, men like Eddie Taylor kiss every woman like they love her. It's my guess he's had plenty of practice. Mark my words, when he's tired of you he'll disappear as quickly as he appeared and you'll be left with nothing if you're not very careful.'

'Oh, and you're the expert all of a sudden, are you, Frankie? You who's only ever had one serious boyfriend in your life.'

Mouth clamping shut, Frankie stared at her, stunned. Stella was right, she was no expert, it was only her gut feelings that were telling her this situation was all wrong. But what if *she* was wrong about this man? Her mind whirled frantically. She had based her assumptions about Edwin Taylor on her first impressions of him. But was it really so impossible that he was the great love of Stella's life and Roger wasn't? She gnawed her bottom lip anxiously, suddenly realising it was very wrong of her to try to persuade Stella to act against her own wishes. If she was hell-bent on pursuing this relationship then she had every right to do so without Frankie's interference. A friend's job was to be there to pick up the pieces, to be of support if things went wrong, and as Stella's friend that was Frankie's role. Not to dictate to her as she had been doing. 'I'm sorry, Stella,' she said remorsefully. 'You're my friend, I love you, and whatever you do, I'll be there for you.'

She eyed Frankie in surprise. 'You will?'

Frankie nodded.

Stella threw her arms around her and hugged her. 'Thank you,' she whispered.

Frankie pulled away from her. 'What are you going to do about Roger?'

She sighed. 'I have to tell him we're finished.'

'Oh, Stella, are you sure about this?'

'I've never been so sure about anything in all my life,' she said with conviction. 'I hate the thought of hurting him, but it's no good, it's over between us.'

With sadness filling her, Frankie said softly, 'Then you must tell him how things are, and the sooner the better, Stella. He knows something is wrong and delaying it will only make things worse. I'll get Ian to take me home, tell him I have a headache or something, and leave you two alone together.'

Stella eyed her, horrified. 'Now? You want me to do it now? But I can't. I need time to work out what I'm going to say. I need a few days at least, Frankie.'

'Stella, you can't expect me to go back and join the boys and act as though I know nothing about this. I couldn't look Roger in the face. I can't lie to him, Stella. Please don't ask me to do that. You've got to do it tonight.'

'And I've told you I can't, Frankie. Just do this for me,' she implored. 'It's not much to ask, is it? Please, please, say you will? Oh, and don't say anything to Ian, will you, because he's bound to tell Roger?'

'What?' she cried aghast. 'You expect me to lie to Ian too?'

'No, not lie, just don't say anything.'

Frankie placed her hands on her cheeks and rubbed them worriedly. This gets worse, she thought. It's like a nightmare. 'I'll do my best,' she said finally. 'That's all I can promise.' Frankie took a deep breath and forced a smile to her face. 'So . . . when am I going to be introduced to Mr Taylor properly?'

'Introduced? You want to meet him?'

'Well, of course I want to meet the man who's stolen my best friend's heart?'

'Oh, er . . . soon, Frankie. Yes, soon. I'm not quite sure when I'm seeing him myself.'

A feeling of foreboding settled in Frankie's stomach and she eyed Stella gravely. 'Oh?'

'Well,' she said matter-of-factly, 'we never made definite plans. I mean, I was busy tonight and he's busy tomorrow so we sort of left it open. He said he'd meet me out of work one night and take me for a drink. I expect it'll be Monday or Tuesday, could even be Wednesday, depends how busy he is.'

'Oh, I see.' A thought suddenly struck Frankie. Did Edwin Taylor in fact know Stella was seriously involved with another man and that she was about to give him up? And if he did, was the fact that she was obviously thinking along the lines of a lifelong commitment to him welcome or not? Despite having a gut feeling that Taylor would run a mile if he had any inkling of what was going through Stella's mind, Frankie sincerely hoped she was wrong. Regardless she felt she must at least voice her concerns to Stella, she wouldn't be doing her 'best friend' duty if she didn't. She opened her mouth but was stopped before she could utter a word by the door bursting open and three women, each in their mid-thirties and very much the worse for drink, stumbling into the cloakroom.

'Hiya, Fella, Stankie,' the one in the middle being held up by the other two drunkenly shouted. 'Out wi' the young chaps tonight, are yer? We've left our old sods at home and it's the best place for 'em. Outta sight, outta mind. Oh, God, am I drunk!' She gave a loud hiccup and belched loudly.

'You pig, Ivy Ramsden,' one of the others slurred. 'Can't tek 'er anywhere.'

The third woman giggled.

'Well, it's your bleddy fault fer buying me that last sherry. I feel bleddy sick now!' Ivy announced, clutching her stomach. 'Quick get me ter the lavy.'

Grabbing hold of each other, all the women disappeared into a cubicle where loud retching and giggling could be heard.

'Hark at that.' Stella grimaced. 'I hope I don't act like that when I'm their age, it's disgusting. Come on, Frankie, let's get out of here before I'm sick myself.'

Before she could respond her friend had made a rush for the door. Frankie stared as it swung shut behind Stella. So this was what her mother had meant when she had voiced her disapproval of the way Frankie gave in to her friend. But in this instance it wasn't just a case of giving in to one of Stella's whims, it was agreeing to cover up for her. If her actions were discovered it might seem as though she endorsed Stella's conduct when in truth it was the opposite. But Frankie had agreed to stand by her friend and that was what she must do.

Sighing deeply, and with grave reservations, she followed after Stella.

Chapter Six

The Grapes, a seedy public house off a narrow side street in a rundown area off the centre of Coventry, was renowned for the dubious occupations of all but possibly a handful of its clientele. The landlord – a huge, bushy-bearded man, as wide as he was tall – controlled troublemakers either with a hefty thump from his own monstrous fists or a sharp kick from one of his size-twelve boots.

Jack Grimes, or Grim Jack as he was known, could have made a fortune from blackmailing his customers if he had chosen, but didn't because he knew he was as vulnerable as the rest down a dark alley late at night and valued his life more than the lure of a retirement bungalow in Mablethorpe that he'd probably never live long enough to move into.

He didn't care one iota what his punters did to supplement their living, his only interest being that they could pay for their beer – which was far from being the best pint of bitter that could be bought in Coventry, and not helped by the fact that most pints poured were topped up with slops from the drip tray. But it was a penny or so a pint cheaper than other pubs nearby and neither did they boast a landlord as deaf as Grim Jack. The law enforcers of the city knew beyond a doubt that any crimes committed within a twenty-mile radius of the city centre had more than likely been planned in one of the Grapes' gloomy alcoves, but proving it was another matter.

At eight o'clock on a Friday night the air was thick with the stench of smoke, stale beer, and the obnoxious odours of many of the customers, cleanliness not being high on their list of priorities. All the alcoves were occupied with old lags playing dominoes or bar skittles. Several tarty women, all over forty and looking every bit of it, dressed gaudily, their faces caked in make-up, bright blue-shadowed eyes beadily fixed on the outer door, were ready to pounce if a likely customer came in. At several tables groups of two or three hard-faced men, their heads bent close, were talking in hushed tones.

It was obvious to any onlooker what they were discussing.

Two men were sitting in an alcove by the door to the toilets.

'Jesus Christ,' one complained bitterly, holding his nose. 'Doesn't that bleddy landlord ever clean them lavvies? God, what a stink. It's worse than the sewers on a hot day when the wind's blowing in the wrong direction. Ain't there anywhere else to sit?' he said, casting hopeful eyes around the gloomy interior.

Edwin Taylor eyed the man sitting opposite him disdainfully. Considering the smell emanating from him, which was bad enough to kill a fly, he thought the comment to be out of order. 'Shut yer mouth, will yer, Kelvin? You're attracting attention and that's the last thing I want considering I ain't exactly flavour of the month in Coventry.'

Kelvin Mason – a lanky, thin, sharp-featured character – ran long bony fingers through the fine blond hair that was beginning to recede at his temples and laughed. 'They're still talking about yer, Eddie. Everyone's wondering where you disappeared off to.'

His face filled with alarm. 'Eh, you ain't . . .'

'What, blab me mouth off and possibly alert the rozzers to the whereabouts of the man who's promised ter mek me rich? I'd be fucking stupid to do that, wouldn't I? Anyway let's get down ter business, I ain't got all night. I've kept my end of the bargain, you'd better 'ave kept yours.' There was a warning tone in his voice. He leaned towards Eddie, his voice lowering. 'It's parked up the road. Ninety-five quid you owe me.'

Eddie gawped. 'Ninety-five quid? You said seventy-five.'

'Yeah, well, things 'ave changed. They went better my end than I expected. Once the lads in the factory got wind I was interested in buying whatever they offered me, I was overwhelmed. It's in the van, all ready and waiting.'

Eddie's heart thumped worriedly. He was twenty pounds short.

'You said seventy five and that's what I've got.' He put his hand in his pocket and pulled out his wallet, extracting a wad of notes which he held towards Kelvin. 'This is what we agreed. I'll make up the twenty when I've sold the spares and take the next lot off you.'

Kelvin reached over and grabbed the wad from him, counted it and then shoved it in his pocket. 'The lot or yer don't get the van. I've forked out nearly all of this already. Apart from a fiver, that twenty's my profit.'

Eddie's face contorted angrily. 'Now hang on . . .'

'A deal's a deal, Eddie mate. I won't be stuck for getting another partner. Twenty quid I'm due or the deal's off. And I wannit now,' Kelvin demanded.

Eddie's mind raised wildly. Twenty pounds? Where on earth was he going to get that from? 'I just need a bit more time,' he pleaded. 'Listen, Kelvin, everything's going great my end. I'll have no trouble getting rid of all the spares you can get me. I've garages gagging to do business. It's just that I had to get a lock up,' he lied, not wanting Kelvin to know that seventy-five pounds was all he possessed in the world, 'and somewhere to live. It cost me more than I'd expected. You'll get your twenty but I can't get it without the van or the spares. You know that, Kelvin.'

'Look, Eddie, this ain't personal. I'm sorry, but it's the lot or n'ote.'

Eddie knew Kelvin meant business, and he was in far too deep now to give up for a miserly twenty pounds – which it was compared to what he knew he could make in the future. The answer to his dilemma was glaringly obvious though Eddie didn't like the thought of it. But then, he didn't have any choice. 'I'll get the twenty, don't worry,' he promised. 'An hour, Kelvin. I'll meet you back here at nine.'

He shook his head. 'Can't. Sorry, mate, I've other people to see.'

'Fuck them,' Eddie hissed. 'We're partners, remember?'

'Yeah, and you promised me we'd be rich.'

'And we will be. Enough for you . . .'

'To get miles away from me misery of a cowing wife and screaming brats and start a new life wi' Sandra,' Kelvin finished for him.

'Yeah, well, whatever makes you happy, Kelvin. But you want to watch out for that Sandra. Before you know it she'll have turned into another cowing wife with brats of her own. Women have a habit of doing that,' Eddie said scathingly. 'I expect this Sandra of yours is the same as all the rest. Bitches, the lot of them.'

'Eh, don't you talk about my Sandra like that,' Kelvin hissed savagely. 'Yer can call my Eileen what yer like and I'll agree with yer, but leave Sandra alone. Anyway, stop changing the subject.' He leaned across the table, eyeing his friend hard. 'I'm beginning to wonder if I was wrong to trust you, Eddie. But I'll give you the benefit of the doubt, being's we're partners. An hour, no longer. You might think you're a hard man but you won't like the other side of me if you welch on this deal.'

Chapter Seven

A while later, coat collar turned up, shoulders hunched, hands deep inside his trouser pockets, Eddie quickly slipped inside a dark entry and flattened himself against the wall. From his pocket he took out a packet of cigarettes, extracted one, lit it and blew a plume of smoke into the air. He then turned his attention to a house opposite. It was an ordinary bay-windowed terrace with a minute overgrown walled garden to the front, a disintegrating warped gate hanging from one rusting hinge before it. Like all the houses in this slum area of Coventry, known to the locals as the Dales, this one desperately cried out for a coat of paint, repairs to the guttering and repointing of the crumbling brick walls, but even that would not have gone far towards improving its dilapidated condition. The curtains at the grubby windows were moth-eaten in parts, the nets yellowing, and the broken step leading to the front door hadn't been scrubbed for many a long year.

He watched as the occupant of the house arrived at the gate and put down her shopping bags to look in her handbag for a key. All her movements were slow and laboured, giving the impression of a lady of great age. Eddie knew different. She would be fifty on her next birthday. Fearing she would sense his presence, he slunk further back into the shadows of the entry and watched as, key unearthed, the woman heaved up her bags. She kicked the gate open with a shabby-shoed foot and trudged the short distance to the peeling front door, unlocked it and disappeared inside.

Face grim, he threw his cigarette on to the cobbles below and stamped it out. He tightened his lips and once again fixed his eyes on the house – a place he'd thought he'd never enter again; had in fact been warned never to do. But he had no choice. He badly needed money, and despite the occupant's looking as if she hadn't a penny to her name, it was the only place he knew where he was likely to get what he wanted without having to steal from others. Not that the pastime was unfamiliar to him, far from it, but recent events had proved to him that taking what didn't belong to you had its drawbacks. At this moment in time Eddie had a plan that was going to secure his future. All it would cost was another twenty pounds. He couldn't allow this chance to slip through his fingers.

The minutes ticked past while he waited. When he felt sure the woman had settled herself inside he stole across the road, walked down the entry at the side of the house, crossed the small square of cobbled yard and let himself in through the back door.

The room he entered, like the outside of the house, hadn't seen a paintbrush in years, and hadn't been thoroughly cleaned that often either. It reeked of stale cooking odours mingled with decades of must and damp. A rickety pine table still littered with the remains of past meals, three equally worn chairs, an ancient dresser and threadbare armchairs to either side of the old-fashioned black iron range, were its poor furnishings. The room was gloomy, the only light coming from the flames of a meagre fire which had just been lit.

The grey-haired woman who had entered minutes previously was now slumped in one of the armchairs, her shabby dress pulled up over her knees exposing hideous varicosed legs. Despite the deep criss-cross of lines on her face there was still a trace of the great beauty she'd been in her youth before the harshness of life had wreaked its havoc. She jumped as Eddie entered. 'What the . . .' Recognising her visitor, her voice trailed off and she glowered in displeasure. 'Oh, it's you,' she spat.

He took several steps forward. 'Nice welcome, I must say.'

'Waddid you expect?' she hissed, throwing down her dress to cover her legs. 'I thought I told you never to darken my door again, and I meant what I said.' Struggling up from the chair, her skinny arm shot out. 'Now gerrout,' she ordered.

Eddie sighed. 'Oh, come on, Mam, there's no need for that attitude. I *am* your son.'

'Son!' Evelyn Taylor's nostrils flared and she looked at him with loathing. 'Son you are not. I told yer that two weeks ago and I ain't changed me mind. Is your memory that short that yer've forgotten your own brother is rotting in jail? And I don't care what you say, I know somehow you're behind it.'

'Oh, Mam, for God's sake, how many times do I have to tell you? Neil getting nabbed is nothing to do with me. I'm speaking the truth.'

'*You* speak the truth?' she said sarcastically. 'You've never spoken one word of truth in the whole of yer life. You wouldn't know what truth was if it hit yer in the face. And yer brother's as bad as you in every way. I'm glad ter be rid of the pair of yer.'

'And whose fault is that, eh, Mam? Who taught her sons to lie, cheat and steal since before they could walk? We're a family of thieves, Mam. I was hardly off your tit when you had me crawling around next door to pinch lumps of coal out of Bella Hackett's bunker and hide whatever I could get down my nappy.' He glanced across at the pile of brown paper carrier bags stacked by the door where Evelyn had put them when she had come in. 'Still up to your tricks, I see.'

He stepped over and picked a bag up, moved across to the table and tipped out its contents. They tumbled across the table and he smirked as he surveyed them. 'Had a good day, I see. A cardigan and a skirt, neither your size. A baby's brush and comb set. A present for someone you know is pregnant, eh?' He laughed. 'I doubt it! You never give anything away, let alone a present.' He picked up another bag and spilled its contents out. 'Oh, that's nice,' he said in pretend admiration. 'Pity the colour's not me or I wouldn't have minded this shirt, but then it's too big anyway. Who do you know with a size 18 collar? Oh, cakes, biscuits, two tins of red salmon . . . a right feast yer've got here, Mam.' He looked at her. 'Must have cost you a fortune this lot. But then we both know that not one of these things has been paid for.'

'You bastard,' she hissed. 'How else d'yer expect me to live?'

He laughed. 'Other people get jobs, Mam. Me and Neil got up to things, I don't deny it, but we still brought a wage in each week legit. But then, you consider shop lifting your full-time job, don't you? Most of the tricks me and Neil learned, we picked up from you and the rest from Dad. Neil was unlucky that night and he's paying the price. You're just mad because with him away I couldn't stand the thought of staying in the house with you. But I know what *really* upset you most, Mam, and that's the fact you haven't Neil's and my money coming in any more.'

'How dare you?' she screeched, incensed. 'How dare yer speak ter yer own mother like that?'

'Oh, a minute ago you weren't my mother. Make up your mind.'

She folded her arms under her sagging bust, her prematurely aged face tight with fury. 'And you call yerself a son? Some son you are! You deserted me,' she accused. 'Left a poor defenceless woman to fend for 'erself. Didn't give a monkey's uncle whether I starved or not.'

'Defenceless woman?' he repeated sardonically. 'You're about as defenceless as a fully armed Panzer tank. Don't forget I've seen you in action, Mother. I've seen you physically attack an eighteen-stone man when he accidentally knocked your glass of beer flying, *and* you stole his wallet in the process, so don't tell me you're defenceless. Are you still selling fags to little kids for a penny a pop? And what about the time you brewed that spud wine from potatoes and turnips you bribed the kids around here to pinch off their dads' allotments, and then charged those same dads a shilling a jug for it?'

Evelyn's face turned purple as her anger mounted. 'And who was the little fucker who was charging one and six for me wine and only giving me a shillin'?'

He grinned. 'It's called enterprise, Mam. Anyway that was years ago.'

'Enterprise! I calls it robbing of yer own mother. And it might 'ave happened years ago, but I ain't forgotten and you ain't changed, yer still a thieving toe rag. If your dad were still alive . . .'

'Yeah, well, he's not, is he, Mam?' Eddie cut in savagely. 'But if he was he'd more than likely be sharing a cell with our Neil, and for a much longer sentence. Dad was a bigger tea leaf than all of us put together. The first thing he ever taught me was how to steal a purse from a woman's shopping bag. It was on my fourth birthday. He said teaching me that was my birthday present. Some father he was.'

Face thunderous, she drew back her arm and brought her hand up to slap him full force on his face. 'How dare you speak about yer father like that? God rest his soul, he did 'is best for us.'

'Oh, yeah, right,' snarled Eddie, rubbing his smarting cheek, fighting hard to control his rising anger. 'Doing his best by drinking himself to death by the time I was five and Neil four. And I expect you were glad to see the back of him considering how often he gave you a thumping just because he felt like it. No, don't deny it. Me and Neil used to listen to you screaming night after night. Yeah, some father he was.'

There was nothing Evelyn could say to that. Her son was right and she knew it. There had been no one more relieved than herself when Frederick Taylor had killed himself – falling off a ladder while trying to rob a house. He'd been drunk at the time. She glared at her son for several long moments then her eyes narrowed suspiciously. 'Just waddid you come back for?' she demanded.

Eddie shrugged his shoulders. 'Nothing in particular. Just to see how you were getting on.'

'Bleddy liar. The day you do 'ote for n'ote is the day the sun stops shining. Now I asked what yer came for and I want the truth this time.' Then a thought struck her. Mouth curving into a malicious smirk, she eyed him knowingly. 'Ah, yer don't need ter tell me, I know. Things didn't work out for the big I am in the wide world outside and so yer wanna come back. I knew it'd only be a matter of time before yer came crawling back, yer tail between yer legs. Spent all yer money on yer fancy clothes, I see,' she said scathingly, casting her eyes across him. 'That coat must 'ave cost yer a pretty penny and that suit didn't come cheap. I know a good bit o'cloth when I see it. The money you had in yer pocket when yer left 'ere would never 'ave paid for them, nowhere near it. So how did yer, eh?'

She smirked. 'Yer don't need ter tell me, son, I know exactly how you got 'em. Same as you just accused me of doin'.' She turned from him, lowered herself back down into the armchair, picked up the poker and gave the fire a prod. 'Yer room's as yer left it,' she said matter-of-factly. 'There's n'ote in the pantry so if yer want summat to eat yer'll 'ave to go down the chippy. Oi, and yer'd better get work quick 'cos I ain't keepin' yer. I ain't fergotten you left 'ere owing me ten shilling board.'

He shuddered. The very thought of moving back disgusted him. He'd have to be very desperate indeed ever to reduce himself to living under this roof again. No matter what happened to him in the future, what depths of despair he found himself in, this would be the very last place he would come. He'd sooner die. But then, he was never going to allow himself to get in such a position. By the time he was thirty Eddie Taylor had promised himself he'd have enough money in the bank to afford all life's luxuries. And he was already on his way to doing it. He lacked only one thing he needed to achieve his ultimate aim and that was the only reason he was standing in this room now.

He gave a distant smile and his thoughts drifted back. Everything he would ever achieve in the future was down to the actions of a woman: Amanda Sutton. He wondered if she had any idea that her such callous behaviour towards him had completely changed his life for the better. Her selfish attitude was responsible for opening his eyes, making him take stock and spurring him into action. Despite at the time being utterly demoralised and devastated by her treatment of him, and taking a solemn vow of vengeance against her, he now felt he owed her a great debt of gratitude.

Before meeting Mandy, Eddie had been moderately content with his life. He knew no better. His childhood had been rough, a hand-to-mouth existence, but no different from any of the other kids roundabouts. Threadbare clothing, bread and lard as a main meal, and a regular thumping for nothing in particular was a way of life accepted without question. Every other house in the street had a parent who supplemented their living by some dubious means or other and many like his own had both parents ducking and diving. But no matter what money they brought in, living conditions were poor to the point of deprived. Due to poor diet and dire living conditions many children died in infancy and the average life expectancy around here was the early-sixties.

Not themselves well educated, most if not all of the parents locally turned a blind eye to what their offspring got up to and praise was given not for any academic excellence but for the stolen booty they managed to bring home. All the kids regularly played truant from school and left at fifteen, some hardly able to read and write or add two and two together, to work in the local motor factories on the assembly lines for a paltry wage. Like their parents they would then supplement their living by pilfering whatever they could to sell on to whoever would buy it for a fraction of its worth, lucky not to be caught and sent to jail.

Edwin and Neil Taylor, born only ten months apart, had been blessed with lithe physiques and good looks. They were equally as arresting, never any need for rivalry between them. Both from the minute they were born had had an aura about them which drew people to them, and as they grew older they were both acutely conscious of their ability to charm and would never hesitate to use this gift in whichever way necessary to enable them to get what they wanted. Much to the disgruntlement of the gang of boys they mixed with they had their pick of the local girls. As they got older the girls matured to women and neither brother gave a thought to the number of broken hearts to their credit, never losing one minute of sleep over the sufferings they had caused those poor unfortunates whose only crime was to fall in love with either of the Taylor brothers.

Evelyn Taylor had told the truth; her son was a liar and a thief and lived his life not caring one iota who suffered as a consequence. The actions of Amanda Sutton, instead of making him realise what sort of person he was and forcing him to change for the better, had succeeded in making him worse.

A vision of Mandy rose vividly before him. Small and petite, long jet black hair flowing well past her shoulders, she was dressed in a pair of Capri trousers and a tight-fitting top, showing to perfection her pert shapely breasts. From across a crowded dance hall his eyes had settled on her stunning face and for the first time in twenty-four years his breath had left his body. She was the most beautiful creature he had ever clapped eyes on. His pulse had raced faster than he'd thought possible and instantly Eddie Taylor had fallen in love. She was standing in a group of other girls, obviously the centre of attention, as everyone giggled over something she was saying. It was a Saturday night and as usual he had gone with Neil and several of their cronies to the local dance hall. It was heaving when they arrived, the local group in the middle of playing their version of Frankie Lymon's 'Why Do Fools Fall in Love?' Couples were jiving like mad to it and Eddie and his mates had to elbow their way through them to get to the bar.

He had an arrangement to meet Gladys Putt, a pretty girl he knew was crazy about him and would not spurn any of his advances – providing, of course, he didn't meet anyone better than her before the close of the evening. His plan was to have fun with his mates first and leave Gladys until an hour or so before the finish. A quick dance then see her home via the tow path by the canal where he knew of some secluded areas where they wouldn't be disturbed. But these schemes flew from his mind the minute he spotted Mandy, and Gladys Putt wasn't given another thought.

'Who's that?' he whispered to his mates who were grouped around him supping on their pints.

They all stared across at the group of girls.

'I dunno,' Nobby Green piped up. 'But I wouldn't chuck her outta bed.'

Eddie turned on him. 'Watch your mouth, Nobby. Don't you know a lady when you see one?'

Nobby spluttered on his beer in surprise. He had never heard Eddie Taylor speak so defensively about someone of the opposite sex. 'Okay-dokey, Eddie, I wa' only joking. I didn't know you knew her.'

'I don't, but I intend to. I tell you now, lads, that's the woman I'm gonna marry.'

'I wouldn't take a bet on it. I tell yer now for nothing, Eddie, you'll get nowhere wi' 'er,' Steve Miller piped up. 'That's Amanda Sutton. She's old Surly Sod Sutton's daughter.'

'Surly Sod Sutton? Who's he?' Eddie asked.

Steve laughed. 'Who's he?' he scoffed. 'Where yer bin hidin' yerself, Eddie? You must 'ave 'eard of him. He's the manager of the paint shop. Right bastard to work for by all accounts. Get caught more than once having a crafty fag by him or sloping off for a pee when it ain't yer official break-time and you're given yer cards with no by-your-leave. The lads in his department 'ate the sight of him.'

'How do you know she's his daughter?'

'She came into the factory one day a while ago and it's obvious why. I asked about her just the same as you just did, and for the same reason. Only I ain't daft, Eddie. I know the likes of 'er ain't never gonna look at me, so asking about her is as far as I ever got.'

'And apart from who her father is, what else did you find out?'

Steve pulled a face. 'Not much. Only that the mam died when Mandy was a baby and that Sutton worships the ground his little girl walks on. She's spoilt rotten apparently. Get's 'ote she wants. What she's doing slumming it down here is anyone's guess. I bet Sutton doesn't know she's mixing with us common factory floor lot. Anyway, more ter the point, if he got an inkling yer were eyeing up his daughter he'd 'ave yer gizzards for breakfast and I bet before long he'd get yer kicked out of work. So, Eddie Taylor, yer might be an 'andsome devil but I'll tell yer for nothing, the likes of Amanda Sutton ain't gonna look at you as a possible 'usband.'

At that moment Eddie wouldn't have given a damn if Mandy's father had been the owner of Rootes and a millionaire into the bargain. He was well and truly smitten. As far as he was concerned Eddie Taylor was good enough for anyone's daughter and the reputed bullishness of Sutton was not going to put him off making a move towards her. Besides, Eddie was used to getting what he wanted. 'How much do you want to bet?' he asked. 'But before you tell me,' he warned, a satisfied smirk on his face, 'don't bet what you can't afford to lose.'

He gulped down the rest of his pint. Then, giving his friends a winning grin, conscious they were watching his every move, he swaggered across, wading through her friends boldly to ask Mandy for a dance. As he bragged to his mates afterwards, 'All it took was one look at me and she was putty in my hands.'

If Eddie's brother was envious of him he did not show it, just slapped him good-naturedly on the back and congratulated him on his good fortune in landing himself such a looker, and not only that but a woman with baggage that could serve Eddie very well if he played his cards right.

Their relationship, though, wasn't conducted in quite the fashion that Eddie was used to. It was Mandy not he who dictated where and when they met. He was so besotted, Mandy being the kind of woman he'd never dared dream of meeting, that he readily agreed to whatever she suggested, so eager even to spend an hour in her company it did not register that the places she chose were well away from where they both lived and at odd times too, not the usual dates courting couples would arrange at all.

Soon he was planning marriage, a commitment he'd vehemently shied away from before, in fact had never even contemplated. But everything about Mandy was different from the usual type of woman he escorted, and those not for long once he had got what he wanted. Not only was she extremely pretty, she was refined as well. Eddie couldn't believe his luck in actually landing her. He knew he was the envy of his mates just by courting her. Married to her, his prestige in this community would be assured for all time.

Eddie was confident that once Mandy was his wife, Sutton would insist on using his own position to better Eddie's job as a lathe operator in the machine shop. The stores was a cushy number and a position that would suit Eddie admirably, putting him in a premium location for pilfering whatever he chose to sell on the side. And with Sutton as his father-in-law, people would treat him with the kind of respect that Eddie had always felt he deserved.

Married to Mandy he was going to lead the life of Riley, and the sooner they cemented their relationship the better it would be all round.

As conceited as he was, it didn't enter Eddie's head for one moment that Mandy was not of the same mind.

Matters between them came to an abrupt head one warm July evening. They had met at eight-thirty in a quiet place on the canal tow path and had spent an hour kissing and cuddling, hidden from view behind a clump of dense shrubbery. Eddie had pulled away to gaze at her adoringly, his deep feelings for this woman readily apparent.

'Don't look at me like that,' she giggled.

'Like what?'

'Like you want to . . . you know what,' she said coyly.

He looked at her earnestly. 'I can't help it, Mandy. And anyway, I do want to *you know what*, very much so. God, Mandy, you must know you make my blood boil.' He took her dainty hands in his, squeezing them tightly, and eyed her tenderly. 'Look, we can't go on like this, we both know how we feel about each other.'

She frowned quizzically. 'Oh, and how's that, Eddie?'

He grinned knowingly. 'Stop playing games, Mandy, we love each other. We want to be together. Then we can do *you know what* every night if we want to. I wasn't going to say anything just now – I wanted to get it first, then surprise you.'

She screwed up her face, perplexed. 'Get what?'

He grinned. 'I suppose I might as well tell you. A house I've heard of.'

'House?'

'Yes, for us to live in. It's around the corner from where I live now, coming up for rent. An old lady's there at the moment but she's going to live with her daughter soon. It'll need scrubbing from top to bottom and sprucing up a bit.' He gave a laugh. 'Don't look like that! We'll get help from our mates. It's a house and it'll do us until we can get something better.' He stopped himself from saying that her father, once he saw where his daughter was going to live, would more than likely throw up his hands in horror and insist on getting them something better. That was Eddie's hope. 'Well, we can't get married without somewhere to live, can we? I don't know about you but I don't fancy living with my mother and I certainly don't like the idea of living with your dad. It could be ages before another house comes up with a rent we can afford. But it's only a start. We won't be in it forever. It just means we can be together now, doesn't it? Anyway you'll be glad to know my name's top of the list. I saw the landlord on my way home from work tonight.'

She eyed him in disbelief. 'Married? You're asking me to marry you?'

He beamed broadly, his whole face lighting up. 'Yes, that's what you want, isn't it?'

She sat upright, straightening her clothes. 'No, it isn't. I want to get married some day, but not to you, Eddie.' At the crestfallen look on his face she burst into a fit of giggles. 'You don't seriously think I would ever marry someone like *you*, do you? You're more arrogant than I thought if you did.'

His jaw dropped in shock but he told himself he had not heard her right. 'This is no time for joking, Mandy. I'm serious . . .'

Her face grew hard and she eyed him coldly. 'So am I,' she cut in. 'Oh, come on, Eddie. What we've had has been fun, but that's all. When I marry it'll be to someone with a lot more going for them than you have. I can't deny you're a good-looking man but you've nothing else that's of interest to me. When I marry it'll be to someone with prospects, someone who can buy me a house, not rent one, and especially not in the area where *you* live.'

He was gawping at her, utterly astonished. 'But I don't understand . . .'

'What don't you understand, Eddie? For God's sake, you work on the factory floor as a semi-skilled machine operator which is hardly more than a glorified labourer.'

He was stunned by this. Then enlightenment dawned and he nodded in understanding. 'You're talking like this because of your dad. Don't worry, I'll sort him out. He'll come round to the idea of us being together when he sees we're serious, you'll see.'

'My dad has nothing to do with it. I do what I like. And I'll marry who I choose. Anyway, I've already got a proper boyfriend, and when I decide it's time for me to settle down in a few years, he's probably the one I'll settle with. He's got a decent job and can afford to take me out to nice places and buy me gold jewellery, not the cheap costume earrings I suspect you bought me from Woolworth's. Or probably nearer the truth did a deal for with one of your mates. For your information they went straight in the dustbin. I wouldn't be seen dead wearing them.' Mandy smiled mockingly. 'I have to say that my boyfriend can't quite compare to you in the looks department, but then neither is he a petty thief like you are. I'm not daft, you see, I know all about that side line of yours. It was exciting for me going out with a man like you. It gave me and my friends something to laugh over.

'But that's all you've been to me, Eddie, a bit of a giggle. After I met you at the dance that night I asked around and heard of your reputation. You're not really a very nice man, are you? I was quite appalled when I found out how you've treated other women. It was obvious to me you thought your ship had come in when you met me, and as I was a bit fed up at the time I thought it'd be fun to give you a taste of your own medicine.' She eyed him in a superior fashion. 'My Peter is an accountant. His father owns the firm and will make him a partner in a few years' time so our future is secure. You've no hope of ever matching that, Eddie Taylor. And Peter has a car,' she added smugly. 'I doubt that if you live to be ninety you'll ever be able to afford a car, even an old banger. To be honest, I doubt you'll ever be any more than you are now, and that's a nobody, Eddie.' She looked at him nonchalantly and laughed. 'You seem so surprised. Come on, you're not that stupid. You never seriously thought we had a future together.'

He was staring at her dumbfounded, unable to take in just what she was saying.

Standing up, she brushed herself down, straightened her clothes, then looked at him hard. 'Now you know what it's like, don't you, Eddie? You think you're God's gift, Eddie Taylor, lady-killer,' she scoffed. 'Well, let me tell you, you're not. I know of men you couldn't hold a candle to and that includes my Peter. They know how to treat a woman properly, and more to the point have decent money to spend on them. Anyway, now you know how all those other poor women felt when you just threw them aside when you got fed up with them.'

She looked at her watch. 'Oh, is that the time? How it flies when you're enjoying yourself. I'd better go. I have to meet Peter. He's a late meeting with a client but said he'd be finished by ten. While he was busy I used the opportunity to have a bit of fun with you. Shame this all has come to an end, I shall miss the danger of it, and if I'm honest I shall miss you, Eddie. I am fond of you. Just a pity you couldn't give me what Peter can or I might have considered your proposal more seriously.' She made to turn from him then stopped. 'Oh, by the way, the kind of ladies *you* usually take up with scrub floors. *I* don't and nor do my friends. We have dailies to do that kind of thing.'

As she turned and walked away she gave him a dismissive wave. 'Cheerio,' she called, completely unconcerned that she had just broken his heart.

Chapter Eight

Shocked rigid Eddie stared after Amanda as she flounced down the path to disappear through a gap in the railings further down. He couldn't believe what had just happened. Of course she hadn't meant what she said, she couldn't have, it was all a joke, it had to be. In a second or so she would reappear, a broad grin on her face, run up to him, laughing, and tell him how stupid he was for believing her.

Eyes on the gap in the railings she had disappeared through, he waited. Seconds then minutes ticked past. A full ten minutes had crawled by before he allowed the truth to sink in. Mandy was not coming back. She had meant every callous word she had said. It was then that grief flooded him, pain so great he could feel it tearing him apart. Tears stung his eyes and for the first time since a very small child, having been thrashed by his mother for some innocent misdemeanour, Edwin Taylor cried.

Finally his choking sobs subsided and his pain was overridden by a surge of humiliation. He couldn't believe what a fool he had been actually to believe a woman like Mandy would ever settle for him. He had let himself become so beguiled by her that he did not realise she was using him as her toy, her bit of rough, a joke to laugh over with her friends.

Then anger exploded in him, building to a rage so great he thought his head would burst with the intensity of it. Wiping away the rivers of snot that were running under his nose with a swift swipe from the back of his hand, he clenched his fists so tight the knuckles shone white. How dare she? His mind screamed. How dare that bitch do this to me? A need for revenge against her filled his being. One day he would make that witch pay for what she had done to him. And as far as he was concerned *all* women could rot in hell from now on. One thing was for certain, he vowed, never under any circumstances would he allow this state of affairs to happen again.

Something Amanda had said flooded back to him and grim-faced he nodded. It all came down to money. He had the looks but not the money. If he had done, he knew for certain Amanda Sutton would have grabbed him with both hands, grateful that he was even looking at her. To avenge himself would take money so he would get himself some. But one thing for sure, he wasn't going to achieve the kind of revenge he wanted on the paltry amounts he made from his job and his bits on the side. He needed serious money to make her suffer as much as she had him.

But how would he get it?

As matters stood he hadn't much chance of succeeding round here, not without doing something stupid like robbing a bank. No one he knew of who came from around these parts had ever made good. People were generally happy that the few extra pennies their illicit dealings brought could buy them an extra few pints, a second-hand dress for the wife, a pair of shoes for the kids. They were born, lived their frugal existences and then died in these desperate streets, and that was all they expected. Until now that existence had been good enough for Eddie, but no longer. He was going to get himself out of these streets and make himself a fortune, enough so that people like Amanda Sutton and her ilk would hold him in respect.

But he didn't know how he was going to do it.

Then, like a miracle, the answer arrived with Kelvin Mason.

''Ello, Eddie, old mate, long time no see. What you doing sittin' 'ere looking like yer've paid ten shillin' for a shag and only got a flash of 'er drawers? I hope yer got yer money back,' said Kelvin laughing.

The unexpected voice shocked Eddie out of his stupor, and his head jerked up. 'Eh! Oh, it's you, Kelvin.' He sniffed hard, praying the upset of earlier was not showing on his face. 'What . . . er . . . brings you down here?' he asked.

'I'm just teking a short cut on me way to see a man about some business. Anyway, why are you here? You're usually out wi' yer mates, ain't yer? Or that fancy bird yer've landed yerself wi'. She's a looker, I'll say that, but what the likes on 'er sees in you is what I can't understand. 'Er dad's got a high position in Rootes so I've heard. It's my bet 'e ain't gonna tek kindly to you seeing his daughter when he finds out. Oh, I'd love ter be there when he does, though. 'E won't tek that lying down.'

Eddie's back stiffened. 'Yeah, well, he won't ever find out 'cos I've dumped her.' He lied to save face and also hopefully quash the rumours which he knew were bound to start once word of the break up got around. To be humiliated in front of his mates was something he wanted to avoid at all costs. The humiliation and hurt he was suffering now were bad enough without anything else.

'You've dumped her?' Kelvin said in surprise.

'That's right, I did. She was just a spoilt little tart. She had no idea how to treat a real man. I'm well shot of her if you ask me,' Eddie replied.

Kelvin smirked knowingly. 'Ah, what yer mean is that you couldn't get 'er to drop 'er drawers. Or, more to the point, you knew you weren't really anywhere near good enough for 'er and dropped 'er before she dropped you. Did yer know the lads 'ave bin teking bets on how long it'd last before Mandy came to her senses?'

Eddie glared at him icily, angry that his mates had dared act like this behind his back. He'd certainly be dealing with the culprits later and they'd be sorry for what they'd done. 'If yer know what's good for you, take note of what I say and tell the others. *I* finished with her, got that? Now drop it,' he warned.

'Okay, mate, if that's what yer say. No need to get shirty.'

Eddie was desperate to change the subject. 'As a matter of interest, what kind of business are you seeing this man about?'

Kelvin looked at Eddie as though he was stupid. 'Fuck off,' he said, jumping up. 'I ain't daft, I ain't telling you. I know you of old, Eddie Taylor. You'd think n'ote of going behind me back and doing the deal yerself.' He grinned in satisfaction. 'Only yer can't anyway, I set this dealing ring up and I'm the only one who knows all the contacts and that's the way it's staying,' he bragged before he could stop himself.

Eddie's curiosity rose and he hauled himself up to stand before Kelvin. 'Dealing ring? And what's one of them?' he asked curiously, eyes narrowing in interest.

Kelvin wished he had kept his mouth shut. Now he wouldn't get away from Eddie until he'd explained. 'Just buying and selling on a regular basis. I got contacts for getting all sorts of stuff from different places across town. Warehouses and factories, that sort of thing. There's always people bringing stuff out. Makes me laugh how some of 'em do it. A chap I know brought out a rug stuffed down the sleeve of his coat. Just like you lot at Rootes but this is on a much wider scale. I've got the monopoly on all the stuff that comes out of each place. I get it cheap 'cos they're glad to get it quickly off their hands, then I sell what I get on to people for a bit of a profit and they sell it on for a lot more. Clever, eh?'

Very, Eddie thought, his mind whirling.

'Right, can't stand around here all day. I've gotta go, Eddie, I daren't be late. Gotta pile of dresses to offload and the chap I'm seeing ain't the kinda man to be kept hanging about. I'll see yer around, Eddie,' Kelvin said as he hurried purposefully away.

'Yeah, see you,' he replied distractedly.

Chapter Nine

It took Eddie precisely forty minutes to plan what he was going to do. Tired with an excitement which blanked out his misery over Amanda, he raced off to find his brother.

Neil listened intently to what Eddie had in mind, then grinned enthusiastically, rubbing his hands. 'Sounds good to me, Ed. More than good, I'd say. It's the best bloody idea you've ever come up with.' He assumed, as he had been led to believe by Eddie, that the idea was all his. 'We buy everything the men in the factory manage to nick and sell it on to garages for a damn' sight cheaper than they'd pay legit *and* we make a huge profit. It's really that simple, eh?'

'Really that simple. Same as we do now, Neil, but on a far bigger scale. Of course, we'll have to make sure first that the garages we do business with are the type that don't care a monkey's where the spares come from as long as the price is right, but I reckon there's got to be loads who'll jump at what we have to offer. They're in business to make as much money as they can, just like we are.'

Neil looked at Eddie awe-struck. 'Genius, brother, pure genius.'

He grinned. 'I am, ain't I?' he said proudly. 'All we need to do is get a van which won't be a problem to us, will it?' he said, winking knowingly at Neil. 'And someone to do the work on it so it won't be recognised when we drive around. I can find someone from the Grapes. That's going to cost but we'll take that out of our first profits. We'll get the first lot of spares ourselves, too. Unless you've got any money so we can pay others and get this off the ground, quicker?' He knew it was a futile question but asked anyway.

'Don't be daft, Eddie. I'm as desperate for pay day as I bet you are.'

'Well, not for much longer,' he said with conviction.

'I know a chap who knows someone who's got several lock-ups where we can keep the van out of sight when we're not using it,' said Neil. 'He's a bit pricey but he don't ask no questions, apparently.'

'Good, that's that problem solved then.'

Neil frowned, bothered. 'But what if we get done for handling stolen goods, Eddie?'

His eyes flashed angrily. 'We won't because we'll make sure we don't by covering our tracks and being very careful who we deal with. And I don't ever want to hear you talking like that again. I've really thought this through. You see, brother, that's where some stupid idiots go wrong. They don't stop long enough to think of the pitfalls. All they see is the money in their grubby little hands.'

Neil nodded in agreement.

'Eh, and the men we buy off, we make sure they fully understand that if anything goes wrong they're on their own. If I hear one word that they've told anyone they're selling to us then I'll break their fucking necks.'

Neil laughed. 'I'm sure they'd be fully aware of that, Eddie, without us having to tell them.'

He laughed too. 'Oh, and another thing,' he said as a new thought struck him. 'Don't tell Mam anything, not a word, else she'll be wanting her cut. Least she knows the better. She's stashed away enough from us over the years. This is just you and me, brother. Just you and me.' He took a deep breath and then his face was split by a wide grin of satisfaction. 'This is all so brilliant, I can't believe I haven't thought of it before.' He rubbed his hands gleefully. 'This is going to be the making of us, you'll see. The bloody paltry wages Rootes pay for us to slave for them, it serves them bloody right.' He gave a laugh and shook his head. 'Makes me wonder if them lot upstairs have any sense. There's a few been caught but don't they realise how easy it is to get stuff out? And it's happening every day. Even the security guards take backhanders to turn a blind eye.'

A thought suddenly struck Neil. 'Ah, well, funny you should mention that. I've heard a rumour there's a random stop and search going to happen at any time. I'll try and find out more details. Wouldn't do for one of us to get caught, would it? I don't know about you, Ed, but I couldn't stand the thought of going to jail.'

He flapped his hand dismissively. 'Stop worrying, brother, we're too clever for them lot. We've had a couple of sticky moments in the past, like that time the starting handle fell from under my coat. The noise it made as it hit the ground nearly gave me a seizure, especially being's that new security guard wasn't far away from me at the time. He must have been deaf or something not to have heard it. Anyway, we ain't got caught before, so why should we be now?'

Neil looked worried for a moment, then his face brightened. 'If you say so, Eddie.'

'I do. Now just grab as much as you can lay your hands on, starting tomorrow, and I'll do the same. We haven't got time for dilly-dallying about. I want to get this all set up and the cash rolling in as soon as possible. Until we organise the van and lock-up we'll keep whatever we get in the dug-out under the outhouse. Even Mam doesn't know about that place. And the police, if they ever came snooping, would never find it even if they were right on top of it.' Eddie gave a sudden grin. 'It's the only thing of any value our dad passed on to us, Neil. A place to hide our booty. So I suppose we do have summat to thank him for,' he added scathingly. He rubbed his hands gleefully. 'Just think, Neil, us working for ourselves. Who'd have thought it, eh? In a few weeks we'll be able to tell those bastards at Rootes just where to stick their fucking jobs.'

Neil laughed. 'Too right, brother, too damned right.' He beamed with excitement as a thought struck him. 'D'yer reckon I'll be able to afford a car of my own one day then, Ed?'

'Several,' he said with conviction. 'You can count on that. We play this right and we could be rich, Neil, bloody rich, believe me.'

The brothers smiled at each other.

The next few weeks were productive ones for Eddie and Neil, far better than they'd envisaged, and the stock of spares in the outhouse was building nicely. They had enough to fill a large suitcase which they could sell for at least sixty pounds or more if they were lucky. More than enough to pay for the van but not quite enough to finance filling it again. At the rate they were going, though, another couple of weeks should do it and they'd be in business properly.

They still had to acquire a van. They had spotted a couple of potential ones while roaming the streets late at night but both times, just as they were about to take it, they'd been disturbed and had to abandon their plan. The brothers were hopeful they'd have more luck when they went out tonight, but if not there was always tomorrow. Then all they had to do was find a man who'd do the respray. Passing word around the Grapes and waiting for a response should do it. Getting rich was proving very easy to accomplish.

Eddie was humming happily to himself as he strategically positioned himself right in the middle of a swarm of at least two hundred men charging towards the main gate at knocking-off time. As he walked along he flashed a glance around, guessing that at the very least thirty of those men had something on their person they shouldn't have. Some of them, he knew, would have thrown what they'd pinched over the high perimeter fence for retrieval later, to save being caught by security guards who weren't open to bribery. Eddie inwardly smiled to himself. The bits the others had stolen would bring in a paltry amount compared to what he was carrying. Fired with enthusiasm over the way things were progressing, he had risked taking out far more than he normally would at one go and knew his brother would have too.

Concealed underneath his own over-large top coat, hanging from strings over his shoulders, were several bulky strips of brake pads and lengths of material to cut oil filters from. Filling his especially sewn deep inside pockets were all manner of bits and pieces he knew mechanics used regularly and were always having to replace, while secured around his waist were lengths of rubber door linings.

Concentrating so hard on acting unsuspiciously he was almost adjacent to the gate house when it registered that something was amiss. 'Something's up,' he heard someone close by say and the crowd he was amongst started to slow their pace. Eddie's pulse raced, his heart started to thump wildly and he stopped so abruptly several men knocked into him, expressing their displeasure in a string of expletives. Then through a gap in the crowd he saw what was capturing everyone's interest. Two gate men had Neil by the shoulders and along with two men in suits whom Eddie did not recognise they were manhandling him roughly inside the gate house.

'Oh, shit,' he uttered.

Sheer panic erupted in him then and without another thought Eddie spun on his heels, heedless of the interest he was creating in those nearby, and swiftly retraced his steps. After a desperate search he found a deserted spot behind one of the numerous buildings making up the huge car plant and hurriedly disposed of all he had on him, furious that his hard work had been wasted. Then, taking several deep breaths to compose himself, he made his way back towards the main entrance.

Most of the workforce on Eddie's shift had gone and the area around the gate house was practically deserted. With no fear now he waved a greeting to one of the guards as he sauntered past.

'Just a minute, Eddie,' the man called as he hurried out of the gate house. 'Orders.'

'Orders?'

'I gotta search yer.'

Eddie glared at him warningly. 'What's got into you, Sid? You never search me, you know that,' he hissed, pushing his face close.

The guard gulped. 'Gotta, mate, sorry. It's orders, I told yer. And me gaffer's watching me.'

Eddie's eyes narrowed. 'Whose orders?'

He gulped again. 'I can't tell yer, Eddie. It's more than me job's worth.'

'You listen here, *mate*, I've seen you more than right over the years to turn a blind eye. Now you fucking tell me whose orders or you'll be sorry, believe me.'

Sid Armstrong knew that these threats weren't idle. People with any sense did not make an enemy of Edwin Taylor. 'Okay, okay, but hold yer arms out. I have ter make it look like I'm searching yer. I told yer, me gaffer's watching.'

Eddie compiled. 'He can watch all he likes but you won't find anything on me,' he said, his voice rising loudly. Then it lowered menacingly as he hissed. 'Now, whose orders?'

Sid knew he had no choice but to divulge what he knew or he'd suffer the consequences one dark night on his way home from the pub. 'It's rumoured Sutton, the manager of the paint shop, is behind it. It's a strange one, if yer ask me. You don't work anywhere near the paint shop, do yer, nor yer brother? We got orders to stop you and Neil and were threatened with our own jobs if 'ote about it leaked out. I can tell yer though, Eddie, but yer didn't hear it from me, the order came from the very top. I'm sorry ter be the one ter tell yer but your Neil's bin nabbed. The daft sod was carrying that much on him it was weighing him down and a blind man would have spotted it. He's down the station now. The cops are gonna throw the book at him, the company want an example made. Poor sod. A decent stretch, I reckon he'll get, and it ain't fair, Eddie, not when yer think that every other sod that works in the factory is doing exactly the same thing.'

Eddie's brow furrowed deeply. Why had Sutton instigated this? As Sid had said, work-wise neither Eddie nor Neil had anything to do with him. So why . . . Then the truth dawned. Somehow Sutton had found out about Eddie and his daughter. Maybe Amanda for whatever reason had told him herself. This was Sutton's means of retaliation. The stupid bitch! He thought, and his need to get his revenge on Amanda mounted to fever pitch. He'd make her suffer if it was the last thing he ever did. And her father along with her. 'Searched enough?' he asked Sid icily.

'Yeah, Eddie, you can go.' His voice lowered to a whisper. 'Tek a warning, though, you're a marked man. I wouldn't try 'ote stupid, for the time being at least. Someone's got it in for you,' were his parting words as he turned and walked back to the gate house. Once there Eddie watched him talking to his boss and shaking his head.

Face thunderous, he made his own way home. He thought of Neil, probably locked in a cell by now, frightened and alone. But there was nothing he could do about that. He'd been caught and had no choice but to suffer the consequences. They were both well aware of the risk they'd taken. According to Sid it seemed very likely Neil was going to jail. What sentence would he get? A year? Eddie shuddered. It didn't bear thinking about.

Neil's misfortune, though, wasn't going to stop Eddie's plans. It was just going to take more work on his part to achieve it all without his brother's help. Besides he couldn't stop now. Apart from all the spares accumulated under the outhouse, there was the lure of decent money to be gained from selling them, the prestige it brought with it, and just as importantly his need for revenge against Amanda and her father.

He decided it would be best to appear normal when he arrived home. As he walked into the backroom, slipping off his coat and slinging it on a worn oak dining chair, his eyes settled on several bags on the table. 'Been busy, Mam, I see. What did you get today then? Anything worth having?'

Sprawled in her chair, her misshapen feet resting on the dirty cracked hearth, Evelyn flashed a disinterested glance at him. 'Keep yer thieving mitts off, you. Where's our Neil?' There was no warmth in her voice, no genuine concern for her younger son's non-appearance, the question had been asked purely to steer Eddie's interest away from what was in the bags. Not that there was anything of any great value but as far as Evelyn was concerned she had shoplifted it so any profit she made from it was hers alone.

Eddie shrugged his shoulders. 'Haven't seen him.'

She narrowed her eyes. 'You two always come 'ome together. You ain't 'ad a row, 'ave yer?'

'I'm not my brother's keeper, Mother. I told you, I ain't seen him. What's for dinner?'

She shrugged her shoulders. 'Whatever you get yourself, I expect.' She sniffed disdainfully. 'There's a tin of pilchards in one of them bags. Help yerself,' she said grudgingly.

He stared at her blankly. Other men came home from work to be greeted by a hot meal. He couldn't remember the last time his mother had cooked for him or Neil. As soon as they were old enough they had had to fend for themselves in more ways than one. Having made himself some toast with the remains of a stale loaf and put the pilchards on top, he poured himself a mug of tea and made his way up to the bedroom he shared with Neil, to collapse on the bed. The ancient monstrosity, bartered for many years ago by Evelyn, clanked loudly and the worn mattress sagged under his weight.

As he ate his solitary meal Eddie's mind ticked over. Sid's warning was still ringing in his ears. Bearing that very much in mind he dare not risk a repeat performance of today until the heat had died down at least. But he couldn't wait for that. Eddie knew that if he was to proceed with this scheme he would have to start selling the spares they already had and use the profits he made to finance buying further stock off the other men in the factory as well as paying for the work on the van, which he would now have to steal by himself. Then a thought struck him. Maybe he wouldn't have to wait to get the van while he earned the money needed to disguise it. Twenty quid should do it and there was one person he knew who should have that, despite her appearance and surroundings all declaring that she hadn't a halfpenny to her name. Whether she'd part with it without a fight was another matter, though.

He made his way back down the stairs and stood before his mother who was still slouched in the armchair. 'I want some money, Mam,' he demanded.

She raised her eyes to him and laughed, a sarcastic cackle. 'You can want all yer like, son, I ain't got none.' Her brow furrowed questioningly. 'Anyway, what do you want money for?'

'None of your business. And don't tell me you're skint 'cos I know you ain't.'

'Our Neil's still not home,' she said, rising, pushing him out of her way and making a grab for her coat off the back of a chair. 'I'm off down the boozer,' she announced, pulling it on. 'When he gets in tell him to finish the rest of the pilchards. If they ain't to his liking then it's the chippy.'

He stepped before her, blocking her way. 'Stop changing the subject, Mam. I asked for some money. I want fifty quid. I know you've got it.'

Evelyn eyed him suspiciously. 'Fifty quid!' she exclaimed, shocked. 'What the 'ell do you want that kinda money for?'

'That's my business.'

'It's mine when yer asking me for it. Whatever it's for you can sling yer hook. You're after me nest egg and you ain't 'aving none of it. That's mine, for me old age. Anyway I ain't got fifty quid in it, n'ote like it.'

'Pull the other one, Mam, you've been stashing it away fer years, probably got ten times that amount. And don't forget, most of that nest egg is what you've took off me and Neil over the years. Now it's payback time.'

'You're me sons so why shouldn't you stump up? If I managed to save some of it, then that's my good luck not yours. Now listen good, son.' Her voice was harsh, leaving Eddie in no doubt she meant business. 'However much I've got it's mine and it's staying mine. And don't bother ransacking the 'ouse 'cos yer won't find it anyway.' She eyed him knowingly. 'I know what a thieving rat you are. I taught yer, remember. If yer want money, you know damned well 'ow yer can get it. Now I'm off.'

Eddie stared after her, her actions confirming forcefully to him that all women, no matter whether mother, lover or some nameless creature passed by in the street, were the same: selfish bitches who were beneath his contempt. He would treat them accordingly. A vision of Amanda rose before him. She was laughing at him and his need for revenge boiled over.

He grimaced angrily. He knew his mother always was as good as her word. She had hidden that money – however much it was – somewhere clever and he could wreck the place and not find it. But her refusal wasn't going to disrupt his plans. Burglary was nothing new to Eddie. Another house in the area he had in mind wouldn't miss a few choice items and the money he got for them would be the making of him.

Having no spare cash to go to the pub with he settled himself in an armchair and thought briefly about Neil then focused his mind fully on his new venture. A while later Evelyn burst through the door. ''Ave you bleddy heard?' she screamed, waving her arms wildly.

He slowly turned his head and eyed her blankly. 'Heard what?' he asked as if he hadn't a clue what was upsetting her.

'About our Neil. I was 'alfway down the street when I met Constable Anderson coming the other way to see me. I've bin down the station all this time. The stupid idiot 'as only gone and got 'imself nicked, that's what.'

''As he? Oh! More fool him then.'

She froze, eyeing him suspiciously. 'You don't seem surprised?' she said accusingly.

He eased himself upright. 'I am. I'm as shocked as you are, Mam. It's just that I don't make such an exhibition of myself as you do. I expect all the neighbours know by now, with you screaming like that.' He stood up. 'I'd better go and see him. Which nick is he in?'

'Don't bother, he's locked up for the night and we're about to get a visit from the rozzers, so I've gotta get my stuff bundled up and out of here quick sharp. I hope Ida next door's in a good enough mood to hide it fer me. Meantime,' she scowled fiercely, 'I'll have to pay her a couple of bob for the privilege and to keep her mouth shut.' Evelyn wagged a menacing finger at him. 'They'd better not find 'ote of yours,' she warned.

Eddie smirked. 'They won't,' he said nonchalantly.

'You'd better be right. If yer interested, yer brother's in court first thing termorrow. The CID chap told me they're gonna throw the book at him. The firm wants an example made. It's not bloody right. Why should they make our Neil pay for all what the other blokes are up to? I've a good mind . . .'

'To what, Mam? Grass all the others up? I don't think they'd take kindly to that, do you, eh? Most of them involved are our neighbours.'

'Huh,' she grunted. 'I suppose not. But waddam I gonna do now?'

'Eh? Oh, you mean now you won't have Neil's ten bob board money coming in each week and the rest he tipped up when he'd done a good deal.'

'Exactly. We ain't exactly rolling in it, are we? And don't you dare bring my nest egg into this. That's not being touched.'

Eyes hard, Eddie shook his head. 'You make me sick, Mother. You don't give a damn about me or Neil, just how much money we bring in.'

'And that ain't much, is it, for all yer big ideas? At least when yer father did a job he made decent money from it. You two . . . waste of time, the pair on yer. Good job I've never relied on you two to look after me in me old age, innit?' she hissed.

Next morning he went into court and watched in horror as Neil was found guilty and sent to prison for two years. As they were leading him away the brothers looked at each other. 'I'll look after things while you're inside,' Eddie mouthed. A stricken-faced Neil nodded in understanding. Leaving the courthouse Eddie made his way to work. As soon as he clocked in he was summoned to the manager's office which he didn't think unusual as he was expecting a severe reprimand for his late arrival.

Norman Macclesfield, a tall thin man with a completely bald head and protruding teeth, eyed him coldly. 'I know why you're late this morning so you needn't bother explaining. But what do you know about these, Taylor?' he asked, pointing down to scattered items cluttering his desk.

Eddie frowned, then cast his eyes over the items in question. He shook his head. 'Nothing,' he answered truthfully. 'Should I?'

'We did a search last night and they were found in your locker.'

'You searched my locker?'

'We're entitled.'

'I didn't put them there.'

'I expected you to say that, Taylor. But all the same that's where they were found.'

Eddie's eyes narrowed. 'You set me up?'

Norman smiled. 'Prove it. We've known what you Taylor brothers have been up to for a long time but we could never quite catch you. It was lucky for us last night that your brother got sloppy and now he's getting just what he deserves. A couple of years in prison should make him think twice next time. As for you, you should count yourself lucky we've decided not to take this matter any further.'

'Yeah, only because you know you can't prove anything.'

Norman narrowed his eyes warningly. 'I'd advise you not to push your luck, Taylor. My gut instinct tells me you've still got a stash of Rootes' spares hidden somewhere. I know the police searched your house, but you are just too clever for them. Well, you've having no more company property, not while I'm working here at any rate. Collect your cards and what pay is due you from Personnel on your way out. They're expecting you.'

Eddie's heart was racing; he was greatly relieved he wasn't going to land in the same place as Neil. He sneered at Norman, 'You can stick your fucking job up your arse! I'm well rid of this damned place.'

Norman Macclesfield shook his head. 'No, Taylor. Rootes are well rid of you.' He paused and eyed Eddie for a moment. 'Just as a matter of interest, the police are going to be watching you closely in future and if they get even a hint you've got any idea about anything to do with Rootes, or you're seen with any of the people who work here, they'll pull you in and dig up something to put you away for a good few years. Mark my words. Now get out.'

A while later, sitting in exactly the place where Amanda Sutton had dismissed him only weeks before, a fuming Eddie counted the money in his hand. Fourteen shillings and eightpence three-farthings plus a pile of stolen spares he daren't now tout around this town for fear the police were watching him. A fat lot of good they were to him. After his mother had demanded her ten shillings board money – and there was no point in hoping she'd take less in consideration of his predicament – the amount left wouldn't go anywhere.

A shabbily dressed mother trailing two scruffy kids approached him. 'Eh, mister, can yer spare a copper for summat fer the kids?' she begged, holding out a filthy hand.

'Piss off,' was his blunt response.

'Curse you to hell!' she spat.

He grinned. 'That's a foregone conclusion, missus,' he replied as he returned to his thoughts.

A while later a very dispirited, miserable Eddie was beginning to wonder if his big idea would have to be abandoned. The only way forward that he could see was to involve his mother, hope that when she realised what was at stake she'd hand over her nest egg. But that was the last thing Eddie wanted to do. He'd sooner strike a deal with the devil than his own mother.

Devil, he thought. Dealing with the devil. Suddenly he wanted to yell in delight as the answer to his problem occurred to him.

It took him several hours to unearth the whereabouts of Kelvin Mason who then reluctantly listened to his proposition. When Eddie had finished he sniffed dismissively. 'You seriously expect me to be your middle man? Sod off. I gave you this idea in the first place, and anyway I don't trust you.'

'Very wise too, Kelvin, old mate. I wouldn't trust me either. But I don't personally give a shit. You're doing this. I'm not giving you a choice.'

Kelvin looked at him and laughed. 'What yer gonna do, Eddie, break me legs? Do that and you've no deal at all. And there's no deal anyway, not for twenty percent there ain't. Anyway, as a matter of interest, where a' you gonna get the money from to buy the spares off me? The only way I deal is cash on delivery. And you'll need transport. I take it you'll be lifting a van? You'll need to get it resprayed, false docs for it and a new set of number plates. That don't come cheap, though actually I know someone who'll do the lot fer about twenty quid, just say the word when yer get the van and I'll point you in his direction. For a fee, of course. So have yer come into an inheritance or summat?'

'Where I get the cash from is my business,' snarled Eddie.

'As long as you can,' his friend replied doubtfully.

'I'll up it to thirty percent,' Eddie offered, not liking the thought of seeing his profits dwindling. 'And that's final.'

'Fifty-fifty.'

Eddie's temper flared. 'For Christ's sake, man, are you thick or what? At thirty percent this deal could earn you a fortune. And your side of it is a piece of piss, it's only doing what you're doing now.'

'Yeah, but even so you're still forgetting it wa' me that gave you this idea in the first place. And I've heard about your Neil and that you've bin sacked. Your back's against the wall and you're up the Swannee wi'out a paddle,' said Kelvin, grinning snidely. 'No one in Coventry is goin' to go near you at the moment for fear the rozzers are watching yer. You can't do this wi'out me, Eddie. If a spare I sell you is worth ten bob, I want five shillin' from you for it. Don't forget I've to pay the men in the factory their share and then transport the stuff to you out of my percentage. Fifty-fifty or no deal.' It had crossed his mind to demand sixty but he'd thought better of it.

Eddie glared at him for several long moments. Kelvin had him over a barrel and he knew it. Still, once he was up and running and had good money coming in, which he'd no doubts about making, he could find someone else to be his middle man at a much reduced percentage.

'How much could you get me a van for and get the work done on it?' he asked matter-of-factly. 'Nothing special but it's got to be roadworthy. I don't want anything that'll break down,' he added, 'considering what's in the back. I'm going to start out in Leicester.'

Kelvin stared at him. 'Is this a serious enquiry?'

'Yes?'

He thought for a minute. 'Forty quid all in.'

Eddie already felt he had more than the means to get that via his stash in the outhouse. Getting the van through Kelvin would save him time and a hell of a lot of trouble as Kelvin had contacts he didn't. Eddie doubted he could do it himself any cheaper and there was always the risk of getting caught while he was stealing the van now he'd hadn't Neil to act as a look out. 'Thirty-five and you've got a deal,' he said.

Kelvin thought for a minute then nodded. 'And what about the money fer the spares yer want?'

'You'll get it. How much?'

'How the 'ell should I know 'til I see what the lads offer me? Yer want me to tek everything I can get, I take it?'

Eddie nodded.

'Then I reckon you should be looking at about seventy-five for the stock and van.'

'What?' Eddie cried, astounded. 'How the devil do you come by that amount.'

Kelvin gave a sarcastic laugh. 'You call yerself a businessman! My kid brother could work that out.' His eyes narrowed darkly. 'Don't underestimate me, Eddie. I know how much spares are worth, I've handled a few in me time. To fill the back of a van is gonna tek at least forty quid which can offload for at least eighty. That's fifty quid profit. Twenty for you and twenty for me. That leaves you forty quid to refill the van with. It's up to you how quick yer offload your end of it but if I'm getting' the lads in the factory geared up to sell only to me you'll need to tek at least one load a week. Can you handle that, Eddie, or d'yer wanna back out now?'

His brain was working overtime. How the hell did he know at this stage whether he could handle that amount or not, until he got out and assessed things? He just had to hope that he could. 'Yeah, yeah, I can handle that.'

Kelvin grinned. 'Right, we've a deal then.'

They shook hands. Kelvin's felt sticky and greasy. Repelled, Eddie wiped his own down the side of his trousers.

'So, when you off to Leicester?' Kelvin asked. 'Though why you've chose there I don't know. I heard it's a bigger dump than Coventry.'

Because it was the first city that Eddie had thought of and the nearest to Coventry for transporting the goods to. Besides, no one there would be watching him and it was as good a place as any in which to operate a business like this. It was a larger city than Coventry and more prosperous by all accounts, which meant more people had cars and as a result more garages fixed them. 'Tonight.' The sooner the better, he thought. 'How soon can you arrange the rest?' he asked.

Kelvin thought for a moment. 'A couple of weeks should do it.'

Two weeks was enough time to get things rolling his end. Eddie nodded.

Evelyn threw a tantrum when she found out he was leaving. In truth she didn't care a damn but the loss of his board money she wasn't happy about, especially so soon after losing Neil's. She would have been even less happy had she realised that before he left Eddie had emptied her purse of its three pounds in notes and loose change, then thrown it away so she'd think she had lost it herself. Her parting words to him were short and to the point. 'Leave and yer needn't ever bother coming back, I mean it.'

'There's no danger of that, Mother.'

Chapter Ten

The burly man before him, boiler suit he was wearing ripped and so heavily caked in grease hardly any material was visible, eyed Eddie warily. 'You can get 'ote I want in the spares line, yer say?'

Eddie nodded. 'Anything. Next week when I call I'll have a van stocked with everything you can use on a regular basis and more besides,' he said confidently.

Rubbing his hand backwards and forwards over his stubbly chin, the man weighed Eddie up. 'Warrabout an engine?'

Getting an engine out of the factory was risky and took a lot of organisation, but Eddie knew it was done. 'Might take two or three weeks for one of those, but I can get it.'

The other gave a mocking laugh. 'I can get it from the bleddy spares warehouse in a few weeks!'

'I said, two or three weeks,' said Eddie, hoping that's all it would take. 'And you definitely couldn't get one at the price I'd be wanting. Look, I ain't being funny but how much of your business actually goes on the books? I'd like to bet half doesn't. Think of the extra profit that can go straight into your pocket by dealing with me. I don't want to push you into anything, if you don't want to buy my spares that's fine, but there's plenty that do. I only decided to branch out my operation to Leicester this week and already I've half a dozen on my books in this part of town alone. As I said before, the spares in my suitcase are just to whet your appetite. But I warn you, if you don't take my offer up you could be the loser in the long run. When word gets around the chap a couple of streets away can do a repair cheaper than you because he's buying his spares through me.'

The man stared at him for a moment then a slow smile spread across his face. 'You're a cocky bugger, I'll say that for yer. I've had plenty of suitcase chappies in here before and never gave 'em the time of day, but there's summat different about you.' He stared at Eddie for a moment. 'Go on then, I'll give yer a try, but let me down once and yer needn't bother calling again. For now I'll tek a couple of fuel pipes and two sets of tappets. I've a car booked in next week that needs a gasket so how yer fixed for getting me one of them?'

As with all the other garage owners he'd coaxed to buy his spares, Eddie walked away from this one smugly confident this venture was going to prove every bit and more lucrative that he'd ever dared hope.

That hadn't been the case a week previously, though, when he'd first dragged the heavy cumbersome suitcase out of the Leicester train and taken stock of the city where he hoped to make his fortune. His heart sank at the sight of the grimy Victorian red-brick buildings that greeted him, reminding him strongly of the city he'd just left behind. A fight was taking place outside the rough-looking pub across the street and the men taking part looked no better than those who frequented the Grapes. Further up the street several prostitutes were plying their trade.

Two attractive, smartly dressed women had then passed by, taking a keen look at him as they did so, one smiling invitingly before they had stepped into a car waiting at the kerbside. Eddie watched intently but his interest lay in the car, not the women. They were two a penny as far as he was concerned but the car was a Humber and if he wasn't mistaken needed looking at, judging by the noise it made as it pulled away. Well, that was what he was here for. To supply the garage the car owner would use with the spares to fix it. And judging by the number of cars on the busy road in front of him there was not going to be a shortage of garages. All he had to do was smoke out the right type of businesses and the rest was easy.

But first things first, he ought to find somewhere to live. Depositing the suitcase in the railway's Left Luggage office, armed with a canvas bag holding his entire belongings, he went off in search of lodgings. After two days of solid searching, staying in cheap bed and breakfasts in the meantime, he finally managed to secure a dismal room in a dilapidated, ancient terrace in a miserable street off the Braunstone Gate, charming the arthritic, half-blind and filthy landlady into letting him off without paying a week up front, despite the fact he had the money courtesy of his mother.

The wallpaper in his room was no better than in the rest of the house, it was worn and peeling, and the paint on the doors was chipped and dirty. Cobwebs hung everywhere. The bed sagged worse than the one he'd left back in Coventry, and the bedding covering it had definitely seen better days and smelt as if it had never been washed since the day it had left the factory; he felt sure he could hear rats scuttling above in the attic when he took a look around. But this place was the cheapest he could find and would do him until he could afford something better. Which wouldn't be long if Eddie got his way.

His interim sleeping arrangements settled he then went on a shoplifting spree. Eddie was astute enough to realise that for people to take him seriously he had at least to look the part of a prosperous businessman and he knew he didn't in the clothes he possessed. Burton's the Tailors were very obliging and while the harassed assistant was in the back looking for a particular style of trousers Eddie had insisted upon, he walked out of the shop armed with a trench coat and an off the peg dark blue suit. He had taken a fancy to a three-quarter-length jacket with matching trims on collar and cuffs and piped trousers like the Teddy Boys wore, but had thought better of it and settled for a more sombre style instead to enhance the impression he wanted to give. He also took two white shirts and a tie. A stall on the market provided him, again free of charge, with a change of underwear and socks. He actually bought a smarter case from which to ply his goods from a pawnbroker, for a very good price considering the quality of it. With just a select amount of spares inside it would be much easier to carry around.

Dressed in his smart new clothes, carrying the suitcase of stolen spares and armed with a street map, he set off to search systematically for backstreet car repairers willing to do business with him.

His first outing was very encouraging despite a bad start when he was thrown out bodily from the first place he tried. But from then things picked up and apart from a couple of places that were too busy to see him, and several that looked too seedy for even Eddie to want to risk doing business with, he managed to sell six pounds' worth of spares and drum up interest in his future van sales.

As he traipsed the streets in search of his quarry it didn't take Eddie long to realise that despite the city having more than its fair share of poverty it also had its share of wealth. The grimy factories were owned by a prosperous middle class, their abodes sprawling gabled properties with staff to run them. They all had cars, two in many cases. And now the professional classes, like head teachers and bank managers, were earning enough in these post-war years to run a small car. This knowledge encouraged him.

At five-thirty on his fourth day in Leicester, tired and ready to call it a day but not at all looking forward to spending the evening alone in his room with only the landlady and rats for company, he was debating whether to spend a couple of shillings out of his fighting fund when he remembered the request to call back to a garage he'd visited earlier in the day. Despite the fact that it was near closing time and a decent traipse away, Eddie knew he could not afford to lose a possible sale or the future business it might bring.

As he entered the tiny office of Champion's Garage his eyes settled straight away on the woman standing at the end of the counter. Due to his inability to ignore a pretty face all thoughts of business immediately flew from him and he couldn't stop himself from turning on the charm, the possibility of spending a night with this girl of far more interest than a sale at that moment.

He arranged to meet her later that evening and hurriedly left to get rid of his sample case back at his lodgings. It wasn't until he was climbing the bare-boarded stairs to his room that he remembered why he'd gone back to Champion's in the first place. But he didn't let that bother him. The day had been a good one and as far as Eddie was concerned he could always call on Champion's another time.

The night passed pleasantly enough. Eddie found Stella very much the same as the girls back home: with limited conversation, convinced men found her irresistible, but obviously naïve and inexperienced. Toying with her affections was fun to him. It made him laugh inwardly how quickly his charm worked on her. Before the night was out he knew she was besotted with him. She hung on his every word, giggled girlishly at his quips, even paid for their drinks, believing without question his feeble excuses for his own lack of money. Well, he wasn't going to waste good cash on her. And because he had no better prospect in the offing he arranged to see her again two nights later.

Alone in his bed that night, staring up at the stained, cracked ceiling, Eddie made a bet with himself that if he allowed this particular relationship to continue, providing of course nothing better came along in the meantime, he would get his way with her before the month was out.

By the time he returned to Coventry for his prearranged meeting with Kelvin he had seventy-five pounds in his pocket and enough change for his rail ticket. It was upwards from here.

He was totally shocked when Kelvin demanded another twenty pounds, and his only means of getting it at such short notice was from his mother. This time he wasn't leaving until he had her nest egg or at least twenty pounds of it on his person.

He raised his head and looked at her, still sitting slumped in the chair trying to coax some life into an almost dead fire. Only moments ago she had mockingly informed him he could have his room back. He suspected she would announce later she was raising his board money.

'I don't want my room back, Mother. I told you, I just popped in to see how you are.' He took a deep breath and steeled himself. 'And . . .'

Poker in hand, she swivelled around to face him fully. 'And what?' she demanded.

'And I want my dues.'

'Dues? What dues?' Then realisation dawned and a malicious smirk crossed her face. 'If yer don't want yer room back, yer know where the door is. And, Eddie, take notice this time. *Don't* bother comin' again.'

'You have my word I won't, Mother, but I'm not going anywhere 'til you hand my dues over.'

Anger erupting, she waved the poker menacingly towards him. 'How many times do I have to tell yer? You 'ave no dues. That nest egg is mine and you ain't seein' a penny of it. Now get out or I'll use this.'

His face contorted. His mother was not using idle threats, she would do as she said. He hurriedly decided another tack was called for and forced his face to soften. 'Oh, Mam, come on. There's no need for this. Look, I've a deal going down. I didn't want to tell you before because I didn't want to build your hopes up but this one's the big one. Mam. We're going to be loaded. Rich. I just need some capital to get it off the ground and I'll guarantee you a big return. I'm giving you first choice, Mam, to be my . . .' he gulped before he said the word '. . . partner.'

'Partner, eh? Mmm.' Her eyes crinkled wickedly. 'As I said before, if yer not wanting yer room back, yer know where the door is.'

'But, Mam . . .'

'Oh, cut the crap, Eddie. Great ideas? Big deals? Riches beyond belief? I hear those kinda words day in, day out, out of the mouths of those prats down the boozer and I heard it all before from yer dad. Now it's spewing from you and our Neil. And it's all clap-trap! Neither you nor anyone else around 'ere will ever mek good, not with all the capital in the world behind 'em. And I wouldn't mind bettin' it won't be long before you join your brother.' She paused, her face contorting in disgust. 'I ain't wasting no more breath on you. Now gerrout and leave me in peace.'

Frozen, Eddie stared at her as all his plans for a bright future crumbled to dust before him. She had been his last hope. And she should be the one to help him, for Christ's sake, she was his mother. But then, he should have known from experience what to expect. She had never been a proper mother to him or his brother. Never shown any warmth towards them, never cuddled them, never kissed them goodnight, in fact exhibited no motherly acts towards them that he could remember. Her only interest was in what they'd brought home that she could sell. He and Neil would have been shown more signs of affection by an orphanage matron.

He tried one last time. 'You're not going to help me, Mother? Just a few pounds, that's all I want. You'll get it back, I promise, a hundred times over. Just show some faith in me for once, that's all I ask.'

'Faith in you?' she scoffed. 'Don't make me laugh.'

At her words anger filled him, a rage so intense he had to fight with all his might to stop himself from leaping over and putting his hands around her scrawny neck to throttle the life out of her. But he was having that money, he needed it, without it he was done for. Without a word he spun on his heel, ran up the stairs and into her bedroom, Evelyn's threats to batter him senseless and the thump of her footsteps as she ascended the stairs after him, no doubt still armed with the poker, rending the air.

By the time she reached the doorway, inside her bedroom Eddie's frenzied search was evident. Drawers in her woodwormed dressing table had been pulled out and the contents scattered after they had been hastily rifled through; wardrobe doors had been flung wide, her sparse collection of clothes wrenched off the hangers and thrown in a heap on the floor. Unsaleable items from her shoplifting sprees were strewn everywhere as were the contents of old shoe boxes holding all sorts of bits and pieces: her bed, an iron-framed monstrosity, had been shoved aside and Eddie, on his knees, was prising up a loose floorboard that had been concealed underneath.

Brandishing the poker, she shuffled into the room and as she did so he gave a triumphant yell and jumped up, brandishing a yellowing envelope.

'Not clever enough, Mother,' he smirked, ripping it open. 'You of all people should know that under the floorboards is the first place a burglar will look.'

'Pity you didn't then,' she said flatly, casting her eyes around at the havoc he had caused.

'Oh, put the poker down, Mother,' he ordered mockingly as he pulled out the contents. 'Both of us know you've no intention of going to prison for murder. What!' he cried as he studied the contents in his hand. 'Ten pounds! Ten measly fucking pounds.' He raised his eyes to her. 'Where's the rest?' he demanded.

Lowering the poker, she tilted her head and looked at him blankly. 'Why, 'ow much were yer expecting, son?'

'Much more than this.'

'Well, sorry ter disappoint yer.'

He narrowed his eyes. 'Don't try and convince me this is all your nest egg. It ain't, Mother, it can't be,' he said, advancing menacingly towards her. 'Me and Neil have given you lots more than this over the years besides what you put aside. And don't say it all went towards food and rent and other living expenses 'cos I don't believe yer. You never fed us for a start and the rent ain't that much on this filthy dump.'

Her face barely flickered. 'I'll say it again, I'm sorry ter disappoint yer.'

'You bitch!' he cried. 'You fucking bloody bitch.'

He raised his hand to strike her and simultaneously Evelyn raised the poker.

'Lay one finger on me,' she warned venomously, 'and I'll scream so loud all the neighbours'll come rushing. That's *after* I've bashed yer bloody head in.'

His hand lowered and his fist closed on the notes. 'This money is mine and I'm taking it,' he hissed.

Evelyn sighed deeply. 'Won't be the first time you've stole off yer mother, will it?' She stood aside. 'Don't let me keep yer.'

She watched silently as he pushed past her, listening to his feet thump down the stairs and the front door slamming so hard the rotting window frames rattled. Then, throwing the poker on the bed, she lifted up her skirt and put her hand inside her winceyette drawers. From a concealed pocket inside she pulled out a home-made draw-string bag. Dropping her skirt, she opened the bag and took out the contents. As she looked at what lay in her gnarled hand her face split into a grin and she began to laugh. Her laughter grew louder until she was shrieking hysterically.

'Who's not so clever after all, son?' she said aloud. Laughter finally subsiding, her nest egg of five hundred and thirty-two pounds in folded notes was safely returned to its hiding place.

A while later Eddie stood before the doors of the Grapes and composed himself. His only hope now was that Kelvin would stand him good for the ten pounds he couldn't possibly get until the next lot of spares were sold. He could do that in one day, he had no doubt, would even travel back 'specially to Coventry on the Monday evening to bring it across. Kelvin had to trust him for it, *had to*. Eddie took a deep breath and composed himself.

He searched every nook and cranny of the Grapes but found no sign of Kelvin. Finally he approached Grim Jack. 'Have you seen Kelvin Mason?' he asked, praying that whilst Kelvin was awaiting his return he had been called urgently away on some business or other and had left a message telling Eddie to wait.

Jack shook his head. 'Ain't seen him all night.'

'What? Yes, you did, Jack. He was in here with me earlier. We were sitting over there in the alcove by the toilets.'

'Yer might have bin but I didn't see yer.'

Eddie might have known to expect this answer from Jack, given his close-mouthed reputation. 'Jack, please,' he pleaded. 'I know you don't hear or see nothing but this is crucial.'

'So is serving that man at the other end of the bar before he kicks up a stink. Sorry, mate, can't help yer,' said the publican, moving away.

'Buy us a pint and I'll tell yer?'

Eddie spun around to see a short, scruffy, elderly individual at his side. 'I knows. I 'eard, see.'

'Heard what?' Eddie asked.

'Buy us a pint and I'll tell yer.'

Eddie hurriedly complied, breaking into one of the pound notes he'd taken from his mother.

The man supped on it slowly before he placed his glass on the bar counter and said, 'He left wi' a man about ten minutes afore you came in.'

'Left? With a man, you say? Where were they going?'

The man picked up his pint and supped on it. 'They'd just done a deal.'

'Deal? What kind of deal?'

'Buy us another pint and I'll tell yer.'

Eddie forced himself not to grab the man by the scruff of his neck and shake the information out of him. But should he even lift a finger he'd soon have Grim Jack's boot up his backside, then he'd learn nothing. He purchased another pint. 'Now tell me what deal?' he hissed.

The man downed his second pint before saying, 'Summat to do with a van full of car spares.'

Eddie's face paled alarmingly. 'Are you sure? Doubly sure?'

'No doubts. I was sitting behind 'em and 'eard every word. Fifty quid the man paid fer the lot.'

Eddie's body sagged. The bastard! His mind screamed. Not only had Kelvin got his own hard-earned seventy-five pounds, he now had another mug's fifty as well.

'D'yer wanna know 'ote about anyone else? I knows everything that goes on in 'ere,' the old man rasped gleefully. 'But it'll cost yer.'

Eddie had heard enough. And one more name was added to his vengeance list.

Chapter Eleven

'Are yer seeing Ian tonight, our Frankie?'

She lifted her head from under the bonnet of an old Ford Popular she had just finished replacing a leaking oil seal on and looked across at her uncle who was washing his grease-caked hands under the tap. 'Tonight? Well, I am, but not until about nine. He's just going to pop over for a cuppa. He's revising for an exam he's taking next week. Says I distract him.'

Wally smiled affectionately at her. 'You, me darlin', are so pretty you'd distract a blind man, so I can see his point.'

'Flatterer,' she replied, grinning. 'Why did you ask?'

'Why did I ask what?'

She sighed in exasperation. 'If I was seeing Ian?'

'Oh, I just wondered if you'd lock up for me tonight?'

'What, again? This is the third time this week.'

'So?'

'Well . . . it's just not like you, that's all. You're first in, last out, usually.'

'Yeah, well, that's as it should be. I'm the boss, ain't I? First in to mek sure all me staff ain't late, and last out to mek sure none of yer clock off early,' he said, a mischievous twinkle in his eyes.

'Oh, like that, is it? Well, I think I'd better start looking for a job with a boss who trusts me,' she bantered back, lowering the bonnet of the car. 'And while I'm at it, a job with better pay, more holidays, no men who leave all the washing up for me to do, nor a mucky sink to scrub 'cos they all reckon that's women's work no matter I'm a skilled as they are and . . . and . . .'

'There's more?' an amused Wally asked, trying to keep his face straight.

'Er . . . I'll think of something.'

'Well, if you do get a job with those conditions, let me know and I'll apply as well.'

They both giggled.

She walked across to join him. 'I'll lock up for you, Uncle Wally. Doing anything special?'

He eyed her sharply as he turned off the tap, picked up a grubby piece of towelling draped over the side of the sink and began to dry his hands. 'Anything special? What d'yer mean by *anything special*?'

She looked at him, taken aback by his uncharacteristic abruptness. 'Nothing in particular. I was just asking out of interest, that's all. I'm sorry, Uncle Wally, I didn't mean to pry.'

His face fell. 'It's me that should be apologising, me darlin'. I don't know what made me jump down yer throat like that. Anyway, to answer yer question, I'm doing n'ote special. Being's we ain't busy I just thought I'd . . . er . . . catch up with a few chores at home while I've got the chance.'

'Well, as I'm not doing anything until nineish, I'll come and give you a hand with your cleaning?' she offered.

He gave a sardonic chuckle. 'Who said anything about cleaning?'

'Oh, sorry, I thought that's what you meant. Well, I could help with whatever else you're doing then.'

'What about young Stella?'

'What about her?'

'Well, she usually calls by to walk home with you, so you could arrange to have a night with her if she's not doing 'ote 'erself.' He frowned, puzzled. 'Come ter think on it, I ain't seen her for . . . must be getting on for weeks now. N'ote happened between yer, has there?' he asked, knowing how close a friendship Frankie and Stella had.

Frankie looked at him. Since their conversation in the pub when Stella had finally confessed that she had been out more than once with that Eddie fellow behind Roger's back, she hadn't seen her friend at all. She had called around to her house several times to enquire after Stella but her friend was apparently either already out or in bed with a headache and it was obvious to Frankie Stella was avoiding her.

Her mind flew back to the last time the four friends had been out together. Going back to the table to rejoin the men, knowing what she now did, was purgatory for Frankie. Acting as though nothing was amiss had been extremely hard, she hadn't liked deceiving Roger one little bit. Ian had noticed something was wrong and once on their own had questioned her. She had had to avoid the truth again. Deceiving the love of her life was far worse than not enlightening Roger and she'd spent several sleepless nights struggling with her conscience on whether to come clean, but she had made a promise to Stella and loyalty to her best friend wouldn't allow her to break it. She hadn't seen Stella since and as far as she was aware Stella hadn't yet done the deed with Roger. Frankie had no idea whether she was still seeing Eddie behind his back. She sincerely hoped not.

'Stella's been busy lately,' she replied and quickly changed the subject. 'So do you want me to come and give you a hand with whatever it is you're doing? I could come straight after I've helped Mam clear up after dinner.'

'Don't you see enough of me during the day?' Wally asked, then smiled knowingly. 'Oh, I get it, Frankie, you're at a loose end and think you're going to come and pester me. Well, I've got news fer you, young lady, yer not. I'm having a quiet night in by meself so you go and find someone else to entertain you until nine. That you off then, Taffy?' he shouted across to the big Welshman as he came into the garage dressed for outdoors. 'Oh, flowers, eh? You old softy. Mary is in for a surprise,' he said, replacing the towel. 'That wants a wash, Frankie. Tek it home with yer tonight and bring a clean one in, there's a duck.'

She just looked at him.

Embarrassed, Taffy stared at the wilting bunch of Michaelmas daisies he was holding, then across at them both. 'Well . . . er . . . she's been in a bit of a mood just lately, see.'

'Oh, and this is your way of saying sorry for whatever it is you haven't done, I take it,' said Wally.

Taffy gulped in embarrassment. 'Something like that, boss.'

'I hope you got her chocolates as well, Taffy,' Frankie asked, hiding a smile. 'That sorrowful-looking bunch isn't going to go far in the apology stakes, if you want my opinion.'

He studied the flowers. 'Oh, don't you think so? Oh, well, I'll pop in the corner shop on my way past and get a box of Dairy Milk.'

'I'd do that, Taffy,' said Frankie. 'And a half pound, not a quarter, I know what you men are like when it comes to spending money on us women. Goodnight.'

He gave a half-hearted smile and nodded. 'Goodnight, both.'

Wally waited until the door had closed behind Taffy then said, 'He must be in the dog house if he's bought his wife flowers.'

'And what would you know about annoyed wives, Uncle Wally, being's you haven't got one?'

He grinned. 'Point taken.'

Talking of wives brought to mind her mother's aim of bringing Wally and Hilary together and she felt maybe this was a good time to try and do something towards it as she and Wally were on their own. Not that Frankie and her mother hadn't already attempted several tactful ploys over the last two weeks, but each time it had been a complete and utter failure. Both of them were running out of ideas and getting very frustrated. In desperation Nancy had resorted to the idea of asking them both to a meal but Frankie had something else in mind. Well, it might just work as nothing else seemed to.

'Er . . . Uncle Wally, why don't you go down to the library?' she asked.

He frowned quizzically at her. 'And why would I want to do that?'

'Well, I thought you might like to get a book out. I mean, if you've nothing particular on you could sit and relax with a good read.'

'Listen, young lady, the only print I read is newspaper print. I leave all that lovey-dovey stuff to you women.'

'Not all books are lovey-dovey. I'm reading an Agatha Christie at the moment and I'm learning some very interesting things.'

'Really. Such as?'

Face straight, she looked him in the eye. 'How to poison an irritating uncle.'

He held her gaze and asked seriously, 'I don't suppose there's anything in that book on how to deal with annoying nieces, is there?'

She couldn't help but giggle. 'I haven't got to that chapter yet. Er . . . but if you do go to the library, I've a couple of books you could return for me.'

'Frankie, if you want your books returning, you can do it yourself.'

'Okay,' she said. Another failure she thought. Maybe this was all a waste of time and her mother and she should just leave matters in the hands of fate. If Uncle Wally and Hilary were meant to meet, they would. Then she remembered her mother had again requested her to try and get Wally to agree a firm time to come to dinner so she could coax Hilary to pop in on some pretext or other whilst he was there.

'Oh, Mam asked me to ask you to dinner on Saturday. Just come,

Uncle Wally, she's fretting you haven't had a hot meal since the last time you came and that was weeks ago.'

'I had egg and chips last night and that was hot. I've got a burn on me tongue to prove it,' he said, sticking it out to show her.

'Mam means a *decent* hot meal, Uncle Wally. Meat and veg.'

'Tell yer mam I had meat and veg on Sunday. A pork chop and peas. I wish you and she'd stop fussing over me. I'm quite capable of looking after meself, thank you.'

'Oh, in that case, do you want me to stop bringing those pies and casseroles from Mam and will you manage your own washing now?'

He eyed her worriedly. 'That's being a bit harsh, our Frankie. I mean . . . Well, yer mam might tek offence if I refused what she did for me. I wouldn't hurt her for the world, yer know that.'

She gave an infectious giggle. 'Oh, you should see your face, it's a picture. Don't worry, nothing will change. And for your information we only fuss over you 'cos we love you, Uncle Wally.'

He smiled broadly, his eyes tender. 'Oh, and don't I know that, me darlin'?' Then he added, 'But I've a feeling on me just lately it's more than fussing that's going on.'

She gulped guiltily. 'I'm sorry, I've no idea what you're talking about?'

His eyes twinkled mischievously. 'If you say so, Frankie.' He looked up at the wall where an old round clock was ticking merrily away. 'God, is that the time? I'd better dash. You know where the keys are, Frankie. Tell Bernard to leave the stacking of the rest of those old tyres until tomorrow. He's worked hard today for a change so he can go home sharpish tonight too.'

'Bernard always works hard every day, Uncle Wally, stop being so hard on him.'

'I was just having fun, I know he does. I've got a grand work force, couldn't ask for better.'

'I'm glad you realise that. Er . . . as a matter of interest are you ever going to do anything proper with the building at the back? It's hardly been used for years and it seems a shame just to stack junk in it.'

'Old tyres aren't junk, neither are the salvaged parts I keep in the building or the junk on the scrap heap come ter that. It all comes in handy. Anyway that building is easily cleared out, which it will be when I finally persuade yer dad to move in there. I haven't given up hope of that, yer know.'

'You've been trying since the day you bought this place ten years ago, Uncle Wally. But he loves working in the back yard and being so close to Mam.'

'Yeah, well, it wasn't too bad before but I worry so much for him since we nearly lost him through that 'flu.'

'And you know as well as I do what a stubborn bugger my dad is. He's quite happy where he is and won't budge.'

'That's as maybe but I still won't give up hope. Now give Bernard me message, get locked up and get yerself off home, so you can curl up with one of those Aggiwhatsit books you've told me about. And if you find a way to do me in, mek sure it's painless, gel.'

She laughed. 'Not on your Nelly! I want to know you've suffered as much as I have, working for you for all these years.'

She watched tenderly as her uncle grabbed his outdoor things and departed. Now where was he rushing off to when he'd said he was having a lazy night by himself? she thought. Somehow she felt he wasn't being quite truthful with her and wondered what he could possibly be hiding.

'Uncle Wally knows,' she whispered to her mother as Nancy was bustling around dishing up the dinner an hour later.

Flustered, Nancy turned and looked at her. 'Knows what?'

'Oh, Mother,' Frankie scolded. 'That we're up to something. He hinted as much today. He's not daft, you know, and we have made it pretty obvious.'

'You might 'ave but I've not,' Nancy whispered back, giving her daughter an accusing look. 'Anyway I don't care if he knows or not, I just know those two are made for each other and I ain't giving up until I at least get them face to face. Then I'll leave the rest to them,' she said, spooning a mound of Savoy cabbage on to a plate. 'Is that enough for you or d'yer want more? I've plenty.'

'No, that's fine, Mam, thanks. And one sausage, please.'

'One! Oi, you're not on one of those silly diet things, are yer?'

'No, Mam, but them sausages are huge.'

Nancy looked into the frying pan where ten fat sausages, all golden and crispy, were sizzling merrily away. 'Mmm, they are a good size. I got 'em from Walker's in town this time as I wasn't particularly keen on the ones I've bin getting lately from Worth's round the corner. The last lot of stew I had was more fat than meat, and it were tough. I reckon old Worthy's trying to palm us off with old bullocks to up his profits. Well, he ain't gonna get rich on me. He might fool his other customers but I ain't that daft.' Her voice lowered again. 'Did yer get Wally to make a definite date for dinner on Sat'day?'

'I'll have Frankie's other sausage if she dun't want it, Nancy, and who's coming fer dinner on Sat'day?' Sam's voice called out.

'Oh,' Nancy fumed. 'Yer dad might not have the use of his legs but he's ears on 'im like radar. Two sausages is enough fer you, yer fat enough as it is, and it's Wally I asked Frankie to get to come on Sat'day.' She addressed Frankie, her voice low enough for Sam not to overhear this time. 'Well, did yer?' she asked eagerly.

Frankie shook her head. 'No.'

Nancy frowned, disappointed. 'Well, ask again tomorrow. Mind you,' she said a mite worriedly, 'I think I've upset Hilary, though God knows how.'

'What makes you think that?' Frankie asked, giving the delicious-smelling thick brown gravy a stir in the saucepan which was bubbling away merrily on the old gas stove.

Nancy stopped what she was doing and looked thoughtfully at her. 'Well, only that I saw her today when I got off the bus in town. She musta bin on her dinner hour. Anyway, I waved to her and she waved back and I went to cross the road to have a natter and just waited 'til the bus pulled off so I could see if 'ote wa' coming the other way, then the next thing I knew she'd disappeared.'

'Oh, Mam,' Frankie tutted. 'I can't see for the life of me how you make out she's not talking to you, going on that. She was probably in a rush.'

'I appreciate she might have been, but she usually stops for a chat whether she's in a rush or not.'

'You're making too much of it. Guilty conscience, I suspect, trying to manoeuvre her and Uncle Wally together.'

'Is there any action goin' on in that kitchen?' Sam's voice boomed. 'A man could die of starvation the time it's took you two to dish up.'

Nancy tutted loudly. 'Tek yer dad's dinner through, Frankie, me duck,' she said, thrusting a piled plate in her direction. 'I'll just finish plating yer granddad's and you can tek it down to him after you've finished yours. Eh, and give yer dad a message from me. Tell 'im if he can do it any quicker then he can do it his bleddy self.'

Frankie giggled.

'Is there anything wrong?' she asked Ian in concern much later that night as the two of them sat side by side on the settee in the parlour. 'Only you're very quiet. Is it the exam next week? Is it worrying you? 'Cos don't let it, Ian, you'll pass, you'll see. You've studied hard enough for it.'

Ian had a lot on his mind but it was nothing to do with his forthcoming exam. That morning he had received a letter informing him his application for the job had been received and he'd been given a date for an interview. He was excited, sure that if he could get this job not only was the career change perfect for him but it would mean he would be in a position to ask his beloved Frankie to marry him. It was taking all his will-power not to share this with her. But on the way home from work this evening he had been waylaid by Roger. His friend had looked to be in a bad way, and what he'd told Ian had shocked him and caused him to be unusually quiet tonight.

He fidgeted uneasily for a moment, then taking a deep breath he turned his head and looked at her questioningly. 'You'd never do anything behind me back, would yer, Frankie?'

She stared at him aghast, his question coming as a total shock. ''Course I wouldn't. What on earth made you ask that?'

He exhaled forlornly. 'I saw Roger tonight. Yesterday he made Stella tell him what was wrong with her. She's met someone else. Been seeing whoever it is behind Roger's back. He's broken up, Frankie. I've never seen a man so . . . so cut up before.'

'Oh,' she uttered.

His eyes flashed to her. Brow furrowing deeply, he stared at her quizzically. 'Did you know about this, Frankie?' he demanded.

She gulped, guilt-ridden, and her face drained of colour. 'Well . . .' Her voice trailed off.

He eyed her searchingly. 'You did, didn't you, Frankie?' He spoke accusingly. 'You knew what was going on and you never said anything. Frankie, how could you? Stella's being making a fool of Roger for God knows how long yet you never said a word. I can't believe it of you.'

She took a deep breath and wrung her hands tightly. 'Ian, please understand, Stella's my best friend. She made me promise not to say anything until she'd spoken to Roger.'

'*I'm* your boyfriend, Frankie. And Roger is *my* best friend. If nothing else you should have mentioned something to me.'

'Yes, I know, but . . .'

'There's no buts, Frankie. You *should* have said something so I could at least have warned him . . . anything but have him find out like this. You should have been there when he told me, Frankie. It was awful, I didn't know what to say to him.' Ian shook his head sadly. 'And the state he's in. He never went to work today and hadn't washed or shaved.'

'I'm sorry,' she uttered, ashamed.

'Sorry? Is that all, Frankie?'

'Ian, I've given you my reasons for keeping quiet. I had no choice. You have to try and understand the position I was in.'

'No, *you* have to understand the position *I'm* now in. I told Roger you knew nothing about this. That you couldn't have else you'd have told me. I lied to him, Frankie. I lied to my best friend.'

'No, you didn't, Ian. At the time you didn't know I knew.'

He eyed her searchingly. 'But I do now, Frankie, and it makes me wonder . . .'

She frowned quizzically. 'Makes you wonder what?'

'If . . . well, if you want to know . . . if you're being completely honest with me now.'

'And what do you mean by that?' She was horrified. 'Oh, I see. You mean if Stella can do it, so might I. Is that what you're thinking, Ian?'

His face grew grave and as he looked at her Frankie saw an expression in his eyes she'd never seen before. It was uncertainty. Her heart began to pound. 'You don't trust me, Ian? You don't, do you?' she whispered, mortified.

He averted his gaze, shifting position uneasily. 'This has all knocked me for six and if yer want the truth, Frankie, right at this moment I don't know what to think. I never thought Stella had it in her to do something like this.'

'And because she has, you're accusing me too.'

'No, no . . . it's not that at all.'

'Then what are you trying to say? Oh, Ian, just because I stood by my friend you're thinking I'm a liar and cheating on you?' she said, deeply hurt, dreadfully offended.

He lowered his head to study his hands. Ian was feeling very confused. Witnessing his best friend in such torment was still telling on him greatly and now he'd found out the woman he loved and trusted, a person he'd thought he shared everything with, had known what was going on all the time. Worse, by her willingness to stick by Stella, she appeared to Ian to condone her friend's actions, making him have doubts about Frankie herself.

He knew deep down, though, he was being stupid, knew without a doubt Frankie would never do anything like Stella had done. He ought to apologise to her, beg her forgiveness for what he'd just implied. He opened his mouth but Frankie got in before him.

'I think you'd better go, Ian.'

'What!' He was stunned. 'Look, Frankie . . .' he blurted, attempting to take her hands.

She pulled them away, jumping up. 'Please, Ian, just go home. I think you've said enough for one night. And I'm tired.'

Face stricken, he jumped up to join her, attempting to take her in his arms. 'Frankie, please . . .'

She stepped away from him. 'Ian, please, just go.'

'Did I hear the front door just then?' Nancy asked Frankie a minute or so later as she popped her head around the back room door. Her father, who was completing a complicated jigsaw puzzle on a board balanced across his useless knees, looked up and smiled at her then resumed what he was doing. The look on her daughter's face which Frankie was trying her best to hide registered with Nancy. Laying down her knitting in her lap she asked, 'Anything wrong, lovey?'

'No,' she answered lightly. 'I'm just tired and so is Ian. We decided to have an early night.'

'Oh,' Nancy mouthed, unconvinced. 'So it wasn't words I heard you having just now then? And it's not like him ter leave without saying goodnight.'

'Words . . . no, no. We were just having a discussion, Mam, and it got a bit heated. It was about nothing in particular. He told me to say goodnight to you both as he wanted to get back and do some more revising for his exam. He didn't manage to do as much as he'd hoped before he came around.' Frankie did not like evading the truth like this but if she told Nancy what was really the cause of their heated exchange, Stella's behaviour would have to come out and that would mean Frankie would have broken her promise. When she'd agreed to keep her friend's secret that night, little did Frankie realise what dreadful repercussions it would have.

All right, lovey, if yer say so,' Nancy said, unconvinced, knowing the raised voices she'd heard were caused by more than nothing in particular. But from Frankie's tone at the moment it was better not to probe further. She attempted to rise. 'I'll heat the milk fer yer cocoa.'

She shook her head. 'I don't fancy any tonight, Mam, thanks. I've just popped my head in to say goodnight.'

'Oh! All right, then. Goodnight, lovey, sleep well.'

Frankie didn't, far from it. This was the first time she and Ian had had cross words in all the time they had been courting. But what was upsetting Frankie so greatly was that the man she loved actually considered she might cheat on him. Knowing this, what sort of future could they possibly have together?

Chapter Twelve

Earlier that evening a miserable Stella had perched on the edge of her bed, staring blindly into space. The loud confrontation resounding from below caused by her parents' rowing, and sounds from outside of babies crying, playing children shrieking and their mothers shouting them to get inside, did not register. She sighed forlornly. How dramatically her life had changed in three short weeks, and it was all down to meeting Edwin Taylor. How much she had given up in her total belief that he had fallen for her as deeply as she had for him, but now she was beginning to doubt he'd cared at all as she hadn't seen a glimpse of him for over a week.

A vision of Roger rose before her and she shuddered at the memory of his total devastation when she had finally given into his constant nagging to tell him what was troubling her. She hadn't enjoyed hurting him, but then it was all his own fault, he shouldn't have demanded she tell him. As the news of their break-up and the reasons why had travelled, no one was talking to her. Her own parents, his mother – Roger's father having been killed in the war – and three sisters had all taken Roger's side, not appreciating Stella's at all. She supposed she should make the effort to go and see Frankie to tell her she could relax as Stella had now come clean with him, but the effort of doing that at this moment was far too great. She suspected Ian wouldn't be very accommodating towards her either as he was Roger's best friend. Still, at the moment none of that was important. The fact she hadn't heard from Eddie was. It was all she could think about and as the days passed his bewildering absence was having a terrible effect on everything she did.

All sorts of excuses to justify his absence raced around her head. He'd had a dreadful accident; been called away urgently on business; a member of his family was ill – but never once had it crossed her mind that his lack of contact could simply be because Edwin Taylor was a selfish man who hadn't given her another thought since he'd said goodnight to her seven nights before after making arrangements to meet her outside the Belgrave Cinema two nights later. He would have met her sooner, he had said, but he'd to go away to finalise a big business deal. They'd celebrate his success when he returned.

She had been so excited and had dressed particularly carefully to look her best for Eddie, buying herself a new frock which she could ill afford, and nervously waited outside the cinema at ten minutes before the appointed time. And she had waited and waited. Finally at nine-thirty she had tearfully accepted the fact that Eddie wasn't coming and had returned home where she had sobbed herself to sleep.

A loud crash, followed by a thud then a scream jolted her out of her stupor and her face screwed up in disgust. Her parents' row was turning violent, which was nothing unusual. Why didn't they just kill each other and be done with it? she thought unkindly. No wonder her brother had been jubilant to get that job digging the foundations of the new M1 motorway. If nothing else it had got him away from here, albeit temporarily, and she felt her brother was lucky.

Suddenly the four walls started to close in and she jumped up as an overwhelming desire to be out of this house overwhelmed her. Creeping down the stairs, she deftly unhooked her coat from the wall rack just inside the front door and left.

Across town Eddie Taylor was a very worried man but he did not let this show one iota as he gave his elderly landlady one of his charming smiles as she placed a plate of egg and chips down in front of him on the frayed, stained tablecloth. The egg was swimming in fat, the yolk broken, spreading out all over the undercooked white, and the chips were burnt. It looked disgusting but was regardless better than anything he could remember his own mother putting before him. And most importantly to Eddie this meal, the same as all the rest his landlady had served him since his return to Leicester after his fateful trip to Coventry, was free to him, although the aged dirty creature who had cooked it wasn't aware of that yet. He had only five pounds left of the ten he had stolen from his mother of which in truth he owed all but a few shillings to Mrs Herbert for his board and keep, but he had no intentions of giving it to her. He knew in order to survive he'd need to lift a wallet or two and pray the cops didn't spot him.

'My lodgers don't normally eat in,' Mrs Herbert cackled as she fussed around, passing him the salt and pepper. I'm not surprised, he thought, as he began to tuck in. 'So it's nice for me to cook a meal fer a lovely gentleman like yerself. I don't get many like you, yer know. Yer'd never believe how some of 'em leave their rooms, and the state of the sheets . . . well, I'll leave that to yer imagination. A slice of bread and butter?' she asked.

The bread would be stale and the butter was in fact cheap margarine. 'Two would be lovely,' he said giving her a suggestive wink. 'And another cuppa?'

She gave him a broad, rotten-toothed grin. 'Comin' up.'

Surprisingly the food was quite palatable and he wolfed down the lot and eyed her expectantly when he had finished, hoping for a pudding. He was disappointed then alarmed as, clearing his empty plate, she gingerly lowered herself down on the rickety chair opposite and he instinctively knew she was expecting a cosy evening of chatter. Sitting in his dire room alone or traipsing the streets was a far better prospect than listening to her going on all night. He quickly chose traipsing the streets, aware of his urgent need to make definite plans for his future, which so far since his return from Coventry had eluded him. The thought of going back to legitimate work held no appeal. Besides, he doubted very much that he'd get a job without a reference.

Hurriedly scraping back his chair, he rose. 'Well, that were grand, Mrs Herbert, but I must dash, I've a business appointment.'

'Oh, business appointment, eh?' she said, impressed.

If only I had, he thought ruefully as he made a quick exit.

Hands dug deep into his coat pockets, mind churning, he walked aimlessly until he spotted a deserted children's playground – a black tarmac area with a few rusting swings and a frail-looking roundabout, closed in by metal railings – at the end of a run-down terraced street. Slipping through the gate, he gratefully sank his weary body down on a swing, absently rocking it backwards and forwards as he continued deep in thought.

Damn and blast Kelvin Mason, he fumed. If it wasn't for his double dealing Eddie would be well on his way to making a fortune by now. His hard work in getting all those backstreet garage owners desperate to do business with him had been a total waste of time. And all for the lack of a paltry twenty pounds! There was no getting away from it, he was at the bottom of a black hole with no apparent means of climbing out. To use one of Kelvin Mason's expressions, he was up the Swannee without a paddle, but worse still he had a hole in his boat and was sinking rapidly.

A great hatred consumed him for all the people he felt had ruined his life: Kelvin, Amanda Sutton and her father, his mother. What were they all doing now? he wondered. All sitting pretty, he guessed, with not a care or a thought for what they had done to him. His resolve to deal with them grew in intensity until it burned so fiercely it felt as if it was branding his very soul. He made a solemn promise to himself. He didn't care how long he sat on this swing, he wasn't getting up until he had thought of a way to revenge himself on those responsible for his dire situation.

A desolate Stella suddenly realised she was very cold. It was dark and she stopped abruptly to get her bearings. A surge of horror filled her when, looking around, she realised she was the other side of town. She guessed she had been walking for at least three hours, possibly more, and every second of that time her thoughts had dwelled on one thing or one person alone. Edwin Taylor. She had a dreadful feeling she was never going to see him again. She had made a complete fool of herself over him and through her own stupidity had lost everything she had once held dear, but the trouble was she couldn't accept the fact. Her walk hadn't helped. All it had achieved was to make her even more miserable than she was when she'd left the house three hours before, it that were possible.

Despair overwhelmed her at the thought of never seeing Eddie again. Life without him in it would be utterly pointless. She would kill herself, it was the only answer, because certainly now she had nothing to live for.

The eerie sound of a creaking swing nearby froze her rigid. Sensing danger in this deserted, unfamiliar street, her eyes darted around to see what had caused it.

Then she saw him. It was him, sitting on a swing, she'd know him anywhere. Her heart thumped painfully. The chill in her bones vanished as a warm glow filled her, misery replaced by a surge of great joy.

Slipping through the gate, she walked quietly across to lower herself down on the swing to the side of him. 'Hello, Eddie,' she said.

Shaken out of his concentration, his head jerked up to look at her. Annoyance reared within him. Her sudden appearance had interrupted his train of thought. Not that he was getting anywhere, but all the same she had dared intrude. 'Oh, it's you,' he finally said.

Her heart plummeted, his tone of voice making her very aware he wasn't pleased to see her. She gulped. 'Er . . . are you all right, Eddie?' she tentatively asked.

'I'm fine,' he snapped. 'Why?'

'Oh, er . . . nothing, you just look very worried. Are yer sure there's nothing wrong? Look, I don't mean to pry. I'll . . . er . . . go and leave you to it,' she said awkwardly, standing up, the squeaking of the rusting swing splitting the late-night silence.

'Yeah, ta-ra,' he said dismissively. Then it suddenly struck him that in reality Stella was the only acquaintance he had in this Godforsaken city and if he offended her, sent her away, he'd have no one. She was better than nothing. 'Look, I'm sorry, sit down,' he told her. 'I didn't mean to be off with you, it's just that I've had a bad few days.'

'Oh,' she mouthed in relief as she sat back down, glad that whatever was wrong it had nothing to do with her. 'Is that why you stood me up?'

'Eh?' He frowned quizzically. Stood her up? What was she prattling on about? Then a memory struck him. He'd arranged to meet her, his intention being to have someone with whom to share a toast to his lucrative future on doing business with Kelvin. After what had transpired he'd completely forgotten, which he felt was quite understandable in the circumstances. 'Oh, er . . . yes. I had a terrible shock. My . . . er . . . business partner took off with all our money and it's left me in dire straits if you want the truth. That's why I didn't turn up that night.'

'Oh, that's all right,' Stella cut in. 'I understand completely. It was a terrible thing for your partner to do. I hope the police catch him.' Then she said the only thing she could think of by way of comfort. 'Can I help at all? I could manage ten shillings. It's at home in my purse,' she offered, thinking that it was a shame she and Roger hadn't discussed her getting her share of their wedding savings back but at the time it didn't seem appropriate as he was so upset. If she had she would gladly have given all she had to Eddie.

He snorted scornfully. 'Ten shillings is no good to me. It's pounds I need. Lots of them. Unless,' he said sarcastically, 'you've a rich relative you could introduce me to or better still an inheritance you're going to come into soon that you wouldn't mind donating to me?'

She wished she had, anything to take her beloved's misery away, make amends for what his dreadful partner had done to him. She shook her head. 'No, I haven't.' Then she added wistfully, 'But my friend has,' as an attempt to lighten his mood, expecting him to laugh at the absurdity of her knowing such people.

He eyed her sharply. 'You've a friend expecting an inheritance?' he asked, his devious mind whirling into action. 'Really?'

Stella nodded. 'Yes.' Well, she was telling the truth. Frankie did have far more to look forward to than Stella would ever have.

Eddie stared at her thoughtfully. Stella didn't seem the type at all to have such friends, but then why would she lie to him? People expecting inheritances were themselves well off. They lived in houses which were bound to contain valuable items. Stella could tell him, without even realising it, the occupants' movements so he could pay them a visit when they weren't around. Whatever he made would help him out until something better came along.

'She nearly got it quicker than she thought the other week,' said Stella to add credence to her story.

Eddie's mind was concentrating on planning a robbery. 'Eh? What do you mean by that?'

'Oh, just that her dad had a terrible dose of the 'flu. They really thought he was a gonner one night he was that poorly.'

'Oh, he recovered, did he?' said Eddie, disappointed, his train of thought hurtling towards the possibility that Stella would introduce him to this friend and somehow he could relieve her of her inheritance, but that avenue was closed now if the father was still around.

She frowned quizzically, wondering if she had imagined the disappointed tone in his voice. It was just her imagination, she decided. 'Yes, he did, I'm glad to say. He was lucky, though, 'cos you never know with people like him how long they've got.'

'What do you mean, people like him?'

'He's a cripple. Had a bad accident years ago and was lucky he didn't die then. My mam always says that people who've had something like that happen to them rarely live to ripe old ages, having had their insides knocked about. I always thought she was just being the nasty old cow she is but now I wonder, with how bad Frankie's dad took with the 'flu and how long it took him afterwards to recover.'

Eddie stared at her thoughtfully, not sure where this information was leading, but then one never knew. He decided to pursue it. 'Er . . . as a matter of interest, what line are they in?'

'Line? Oh, I see what you mean. Grease monkeys.' She grinned. 'Sorry, mechanics. Fixing motorbikes and stuff. Mr Champion does really well at it.'

He frowned at her quizzically. Champion? That name rang a bell. Where had he heard it before? 'The name seems familiar,' he said absently, racking his brains.

'It should do,' she said, hurt. 'That's the name of the garage where I met you. Frankie's unc—'

'Oh,' he exclaimed, '*that* Champion. Mmm. It's a decent garage is that,' he said, voicing his thoughts out loud. Off a main, very busy thoroughfare if he remembered right. And his first impression was that it appeared a definite cut above some of the other places he'd come across whilst trying to tout his spares. But Stella wasn't right in her description of Champion's line of business. It was motor cars they mainly fixed. When he had visited he had noticed at least three visible through the wide open front doors, the workers inside seeming very busy. And the cars they were working on were decent ones too. One had been a Humber 3-litre. He could remember thinking at the time that if the owner of the garage was the type to be interested in what he had to offer then good business could be had from his point of view. Then of course he had happened upon Stella and all thoughts of business had left his mind. But anyway, it didn't matter how well this garage was doing, it couldn't be of use to him now he hadn't his spares to sell. Then a thought struck. Or could it?

If this garage and others like it kept stocks of spares, he could relieve them of them then sell on to some of the contacts he had already. He could make a few quid to keep him going for the time being at least, give him more time to plan something better. It could be more lucrative than robbing houses. It was something at least. This friend of Stella's could be of value to him. He could get information out of her on how to get into Champion's Garage and maybe others like theirs that she knew of. He needed to know everything about this Frankie so he could judge what resistance he might face in persuading her. 'Er . . . this friend of yours? Frankie, you said her name was. What's she like?'

'Frankie? Oh, she's lovely is Frankie. She's my best friend. Why do you want to know?'

He gave her a winning smile. 'Stella, if she's your best friend this Frankie's important to you, and as you are important to me,' he lied, 'I just wanted to know, that's all.'

A warm glow lit her. Eddie *did* like her. No, more than liked if he wanted all this information about the type of friends with whom she kept company. She beamed happily. 'You've met her actually.'

'I have?'

She nodded. 'When you came into the garage the night I met you she was behind the counter in her working overalls, looking like God knows what. That's probably why you didn't notice her.'

He planted a charming smile on his face. 'Well, that's not surprising with you around, is it?'

She blushed. 'No, I suppose not,' she gushed. 'But Frankie's not bad when she's done herself up.'

At least she's not ugly, he thought, trying to remember her but as he hadn't even been aware of her, his interest at that time lying elsewhere, he couldn't. 'Has she a boyfriend?'

'Yes, and we could go out in a foursome if that's what you're getting at.' Although, worried Stella, that might be difficult to arrange just yet as emotions were bound to be running high considering her treatment of Ian's best friend.

'That'd be great but not just yet,' Eddie replied. 'I want to keep you for myself for a while. But as a matter of interest, what's he like? What I mean is, will I get on with him when we do all get together?'

'Oh, yes, Ian's all right. Not my cup of tea. He's too quiet for my liking and not exactly good-looking but he's passable, I suppose.' She gave a laugh. 'Frankie's desperate to marry him but Ian has to have everything right before he'll do that. He's good enough company on a night out, so you'll enjoy yourself.'

Eddie was pleased with that information, fully of the opinion that once he arrived on the scene and gave Frankie a taste of a real man, the boring Ian would be history. 'What about brothers or sisters?' he asked, not relishing the harder task of first getting beyond strapping siblings hell-bent on protecting their sister's honour. Not that his interest at this moment lay in dishonouring her.

'I've a brother, but he's working away at the moment.'

He had not meant Stella, the silly cow. 'I'll look forward to meeting him. Has . . . er . . . your friend any?'

'No, she's an only child. Lucky her too. My brother and me used to fight like cat and dog when we were little. We get on great now, though.'

Suddenly the idea of procuring spares from Champion's to sell on faded into insignificance as something grander began to manifest itself. As the idea began to take shape a thrill of anticipation swirled in Eddie's stomach.

This Frankie, he thought, was a woman with a very interesting inheritance, a dad in poor health who could die sooner rather than later; she was an only child so had no one to share the inheritance with and wasn't yet married. A boyfriend wasn't a husband. Slowly Eddie began to see a way out of his black hole of despair. Just a couple of things bothered him which might have a bearing on how well and how quickly he succeeded. And he needed to move fast.

He leaned over and reached for Stella's hand. He looked her straight in the eye and said, 'You're beautiful, do you know that? I'll make up for the other night. Take you somewhere nice.'

'Oh, Eddie, that'd be lovely,' she breathed ecstatically.

He leaned over and kissed her lips lightly. 'Er . . . This Mr Champion, what's he like?' he casually asked.

She frowned, bewildered. 'Which one?'

He fought hard not to look at her as though she was stupid. 'Darling Stella, the one we've been talking of. The man who owns the garage,' he said, his voice husky, leaning over to kiss her cheek.

She giggled. 'Oh, silly me, that one. He's lovely. Dead easy to get on with, as soft as putty. He's always treating me and Frankie to the pictures. But why do you want to know?'

God, this woman was getting on his nerves. Was she really that thick she couldn't see what he was doing? One more question and he could get rid of her. Then he could pull what she'd so innocently told him together and plan his line of attack. 'Just interested, Stella. I want your friends to be my friends.' So this Champion was easy to get on with and according to Stella the generous type? A pushover, he thought, 'And what's his wife like? Is she nice too?'

'Wife? Oh, he hasn't got one.'

Dead, he thought, and the dad dotes on his only child, would do anything for her. But unlike Sutton, he wasn't the nasty type. Eddie wanted to yell for joy. Dear God, he thought, you've answered my prayer. This was all too good to be true. A woman with an inheritance ripe for the picking and all he had to do was win her over with his charm. For Edwin Taylor that was as good as done. The future which had looked so bleak only minutes ago was beginning to turn rosy.

He feigned a yawn. 'Stella, I'm sorry, I'd better get back, I'm bushed.' He inched off the swing and stood up. 'I'd offer to walk you home but . . .'

'Oh, that's all right, Eddie, I can see myself home safe.' She laughed. 'After all, I got here on my jacksie.' She hesitated awkwardly. 'So . . . er . . . when will I see you?' she tentatively asked.

He cupped her face between his hands, leaned over and kissed her briefly on her lips. 'I've a few things to see to over the next few days. But soon, I promise. I'll meet you out of work one night and we'll take it from there. That OK with you?'

'Oh, yes, Eddie, yes.' She spoke with such obvious joy, love radiating so glaringly out of her eyes, it sickened his stomach, 'I'll look out for you.'

You'll have a long wait, he thought as he watched her walk over to the gate where she turned and gave him a cheery wave before she disappeared through it.

Chapter Thirteen

'I'll lock up for you tonight if you want me to, Uncle Wally?'

He smiled gratefully across at Frankie. 'That's very good of yer. I was going ter ask. But isn't it one of your nights for seeing Ian?'

Under normal circumstances it would have been, but the situation Frankie was now facing was anything but normal between herself and the man she loved. It was two days since Ian had intimated so hurtfully to her that he doubted her and she had sent him home. She hadn't seen a sign of him since, hadn't slept a wink, and functioning throughout the days, doing her best to appear her bright happy self was proving extremely difficult. But as no one had commented on that, especially her mother who was usually so astute, Frankie gathered she had been a success.

She had hoped Ian would make an appearance the previous night, but he hadn't come round. Although she knew he was fully aware he was in the wrong, it was Ian's way to think things through and decide in minute detail how to proceed before he even got in touch with her again.

She desperately wanted that to happen, knew that as soon as she opened the door and saw him standing there she'd fall into his arms and it would all be all right between them. But a little part of her was still angry with him for even thinking she could cheat on him and she didn't want to make it too easy for him.

Adding to her mood of depression was the fact that she still hadn't seen anything of Stella. Despite what Frankie saw as despicable behaviour, the absence of her friend was upsetting her greatly and she felt that Stella had no excuse to keep avoiding her any longer now the news of her break-up with Roger was common knowledge.

Oh, bugger them both, she thought. 'No, I'm not seeing Ian,' she replied to her uncle. 'Anyway, I want to finish doing the oil change on the Ford Popular before I finish for the night, so I can make a start first thing in the morning on the Standard that's booked in for a service.'

'If yer sure, Frankie, me darlin', but there's no need to finish off the Pop tonight 'cos the owner ain't calling for it until late tomorrow afternoon.'

'I sooner get it done tonight.'

'If yer sure. I'll secure the front doors before I go, 'cos I don't want any Tom, Dick or Harry waltzing in 'ere, you being on yer own.'

She smiled. 'Thanks, Uncle Wally.'

'The thanks are all mine. I don't know what I'd do without yer, Frankie.' He looked up at the clock. 'It's nearly six so I'll make a move for home then, being's you don't mind.'

She frowned at him curiously. Her uncle seemed keen to get home again at a reasonable time, and that was happening more and more of late. For a man who up until a few weeks before was in the garage from the crack of dawn until very late in the evening, this was most peculiar. She knew she shouldn't say anything; after all it was her uncle's own business what hours he worked, and she remembered the response she'd received the last time she'd commented on his leaving at a normal time. Nevertheless she couldn't stop herself from casually asking, 'Doing anything special?'

He spun round to face her. 'You keep asking me that, Frankie. Isn't it enough that a man finds the comforts of his own home welcoming at the end of a hard day, without you and yer mother making more of it?'

She gulped, guiltily, but before she could apologise the urgent continuous thumping of the brass bell on the office counter made them both jump.

'Someone wants us,' Wally remarked. 'I hope to God it's not a breakdown this late in the day. Bernard!' he bellowed.

'Have you forgotten you told him to go home five minutes ago, Uncle Wally? He's worked like a navvy from the minute he got here this morning, never took his dinner break, and he drove us mad all day going on about that date he's got tonight with a girl he met last week at the youth club. And before you shout for Taffy, you know he wants to be finished sharpish too 'cos he's taking Mary to the pictures as a surprise. Between you and me, she's giving him a right hard time of it at the moment and he's making a real effort to please her. Get off yourself, Uncle Wally, I'll go and see who it is.' And she added with a grin as she made her way over to the office door, 'I'm quite capable of dealing with whatever it is. I was taught by the best, remember.'

She was taken aback to see Taffy's wife standing behind the counter. Even more surprising, she was dressed very smartly in a brand new coat and hat if Frankie wasn't mistaken. 'Hello, Mrs Morgan,' she greeted the woman with a welcoming smile.

'I've no time fer pleasantries, Frankie, me duck.' She spoke stiffly. 'Give this ter Taff,' she ordered, thrusting a covered plate at Frankie, which she automatically accepted. 'And it's the last bloody meal I cook fer that man to let go cold 'cos he's never home on time ter eat it. He's never home, full stop.'

Frankie reddened in embarrassment. 'Er . . . yes, 'course I'll give it him. You . . . er . . . off somewhere nice?'

'It's gotta be, ain't it? Better than where I am at any rate.'

Frankie frowned. 'I'm sorry, I don't understand?'

She sniffed disdainfully. 'No, I don't 'spose yer do, Frankie, lovey. Yer far too young to be understanding these kinda things. But let me give yer a piece of advice. Never believe a man when he tells yer he'll make yer the happiest woman alive, 'cos what they mean is the opposite. I can't deny Taff's been a good husband in his own way, but handing over his unopened pay packet on a Friday night and the odd bunch of half-dead flowers and box of chocolates don't mek up fer me spending nearly all me time on me own 'cos he's practically living in this bloody garage. I've bin telling him fer years he ought ter bring his bed down here, but he didn't take the hint. I'm off, Frankie, I've found meself a bloke who finishes work at six o'clock sharp every night and only does half-day Sat'days. I've left Taff a note on the mantle.'

Frankie was gawking, astonished, having a job to take in what she was hearing. 'You can't mean that, Mrs Morgan? I know Taffy thinks the world of you. He does, really.'

'I know Taff thinks the world of me and that's all well and good, Frankie, me duck, but I want to be shown it and Taff doesn't, it's as simple as that. I've had enough of keeping his house spotless and cooking him meals when all he does is fall asleep in the chair when he does condescend to come home. Sundays he's too tired to go anywhere. I've had enough, Frankie. Now if yer don't mind I've a bus ter catch.' She leaned forward, wagging a finger. 'Just remember me words, Frankie, when yer meet the one yer think is the be all and end all. The man yer courting ain't the same after he gets that ring on yer finger. Ta-ra.'

Plate in hand, Frankie stared blankly at the closed office door after Mary Morgan had left. She couldn't believe what had just transpired. How on earth was she going to tell the lovely Welsh giant of a man that his wife had just been in and said she was leaving him? Taffy adored his wife; was always singing her praises; would do anything for her; was under the impression their marriage was a stable and happy one.

Until recently Mary was right, Taffy had worked all hours. But Frankie knew that was only to ensure he took home a reasonable pay packet with money left over for Mary to spend on herself after all the bills had been paid, and since making the great effort to get home at a decent time he'd worked his dinner hour to make up the shortfall. How many other men, she fumed, were so considerate towards their spouses? The only other one she herself was aware of was her own father. And couldn't Mary have told him face to face, not in a note left propped on the mantle? She felt strongly it was Mary who was the selfish one, not Taffy. And it did cross her mind that maybe the man Mary had gone to earned more money than her husband, meaning she would have more to spend on herself which was her main reason for leaving.

Frankie froze rigid when Taffy appeared ready for home. Quickly she shoved the plate of food out of sight under the counter.

'Well, I'm off, my lovely, so I'll say my goodnights. Don't want to miss the start of the picture. *Rear Window* is what I'm taking Mary to see. She loves Jimmy Stewart, though I'm not that struck by him myself. He talks too slow.' Taffy chattered happily in his dulcet Welsh lilt as he lifted the counter flap and replaced it behind him. As he reached the door, he stopped and turned. 'Oh, and don't work too late tonight 'cos anything you don't manage to get done, I'll give you a hand with in the morning.'

Her mind raced frantically. She must say something to warn him, prepare him for what he was going to face. But before she could find the right words Taffy had left. A great sadness enveloped her for what she knew he was going to suffer in a few minutes' time. His world was going to be completely shattered. All she could do was hope he turned to her then so she could try and help him through it. Retrieving the plate of food from where she had hurriedly hidden it, Frankie returned to the main garage area, scraped the contents into the rubbish bin, then put the dirty plate in the sink along with the rest of the mugs accumulated throughout the day for washing.

Under an hour later she had finished working on the Ford Popular and had also washed the dirty dishes and bleached the stained sink ready for the morning. There was nothing else worth starting until the next day so she decided to go home, not relishing the fact she knew she was going to receive a tongue lashing from her mother for being well overdue. Part of her hoped Ian had called round at her house. Her not being there would hopefully give him the impression she wasn't brooding, make him more determined to put matters right with her and not easily let something like this happen again. If she was honest that was the real reason she had so readily stayed late at the garage this evening.

As she was checking around, making sure all was secure, she found a canvas bag in the office and realised with horror her uncle had gone off without locking the takings in the safe. She couldn't do it herself as she hadn't got a safe key, it being such an old thing when Wally had bought it there was only the one. She shook her head. Obviously her uncle was very preoccupied as this was not like him. With what, though? Still there was nothing for it, she'd have to do a detour on her way home and take the takings to him as it was a better prospect than leaving them unattended overnight.

She was just about to switch out the last remaining light of the six in the high ceiling space that illuminated the garage area when she jumped, startled, as she heard the door to the office opening and the footsteps of someone entering. They echoed dully on the hard concrete floor. She stared across and in the gloom by the door could just make out the silhouette of a tall man.

'I'm sorry,' she called a mite uneasily. 'We're closed for the night.'

'I know that, Frankie,' a deep voice replied as the figure of the man advanced towards her.

She frowned. Whoever it was knew her name but she couldn't immediately identify him. He certainly wasn't a regular customer of Champion's. Then as he drew closer recognition registered and her back stiffened. 'Stella's not here,' she said icily.

Eddie arrived level with her, a puzzled look on his face. 'What made you say that?' he asked.

'Well, it is Stella you're looking for, isn't it?'

He shook his head. 'No, why should it be?'

'Because you're going out with her.'

'Am I? That's the first I knew of it.'

Frankie frowned quizzically. 'But she told me you two had been out several times already.'

He looked surprised. 'If she was out with someone, it wasn't me. I did take her out for a drink like she asked me to. The rest, I'm afraid, is a figment of her imagination.'

Frankie looked confused. '*She* asked *you* to take her out?'

'That's right. The evening I called back here hoping Mr Champion had time to see me about business. To be honest, I hadn't realised the time or I'd have left my visit to a more convenient one. It was after you'd left to find Mr Champion. Stella said she was at a loose end and asked if I fancied taking her for a drink. She was quite persistent about it. I didn't want to hurt her feelings by refusing and as I'd nothing else planned, I agreed.'

Frankie lowered her head, gnawing her bottom lip anxiously. Had Stella exaggerated the way things had happened? She was after all renowned for getting her own way.

'There was another reason for accepting her offer, Frankie.'

She raised her head and looked at him. 'Oh?'

He smiled down at her. 'To find out about you.'

'Me?' she said, shocked.

His eyes drinking her in, he nodded. 'You were standing behind the counter that night and it immediately struck me how pretty you were, but before I could speak to you Stella beckoned me over. I automatically went across to see what she wanted. I have to say, I was quite shocked by her forwardness,' he said in a disapproving tone.

As he was speaking Frankie was thinking she didn't remember the events of that night being anything like he was describing. But then she wouldn't have noticed Stella beckon him over as she herself was staring at him at the time. Regardless, she knew that evening she'd been in the same dishevelled state as she was right now and therefore found his flattering remark about herself barely credible.

'After you'd left to find Mr Champion,' he continued, 'I asked Stella who you were and she told me you were her best friend. By accepting her suggestion of what I myself saw as an innocent drink, I thought I could find out more about you.' He looked worried for a moment. 'I did ask Stella to give you my apologies for rushing off and to tell you I'd call back at a more suitable time. I hope she did?'

Distracted, Frankie nodded. 'Yes, she did, Mr . . . er . . . Taylor?'

'Eddie. My friends call me Eddie.'

Frankie swallowed hard, a perplexing uneasiness slowly creeping through her. This man was extremely good-looking, his eyes like magnets drawing her to them, and the intimate way he was looking at her – as if he knew what she looked like without her clothes on – was giving her goose bumps all over. She could appreciate why Stella had fallen so quickly for him. But, she forcefully reminded herself, she wasn't Stella and fully loyal to Ian. She took a deep breath to compose herself then looked him straight in the eye. '*Mr Taylor*, I only know what Stella told me about that night you took her out but I can assure you she is under the impression you two are a couple. Stella isn't stupid, she must have got that impression somehow,' she said accusingly.

He shrugged his shoulders innocently. 'You have to believe this is news to me. We met, had a drink, chatted about this and that.' He smiled disarmingly at her. 'A lot about you. Then I saw her to her bus. I did say we must do it again, but I can assure you I left Stella in no doubt that I was just being polite.'

Frankie took a deep breath, her bewilderment mounting, beginning to wonder if her first impression of this man had been totally wrong. 'I don't understand. It's not how she sees things at all. Did you know Stella's finished with her boyfriend because of how she feels about you? Roger is devastated. They were going to be married.'

Eddie's face filled with assumed shock. 'I didn't know she had a boyfriend. I would never have accepted her invitation if I had. Oh, God, what a mess,' he exclaimed, apparently horrified. 'The poor girl. I'm sorry she's done what she has in the mistaken belief *we* had anything going.' He eyed Frankie beseechingly. 'What can I say that'll convince you I'm telling the truth?'

He sounded and looked so genuine she felt she had no choice but to believe him. 'It will hurt her terribly but you must put Stella right,' she demanded.

'I would, but how can I when I don't see her?'

How can I when I don't either? thought Frankie. A part of her was grateful that she didn't, not relishing telling her friend that her love for this man, her hopes and dreams, were all, according to him, a figment of her own imagination. 'I see your point,' she said, and eyed him awkwardly. 'You'll . . . er . . . have to excuse me, I was just locking up to go home.'

'Come for a drink with me?'

She stared at him, taken aback. 'Mr Taylor, if you found out so much about me from Stella I'm sure she would have told you that I'm already spoken for.'

'But you're not married?'

'No.'

'Engaged?'

'As good as.'

'As good as isn't the same as actually being officially engaged. As good as wouldn't stand up in a court of law.'

'A ring on my finger would make no difference. As far as I'm concerned Ian and I have an understanding. Now, if you'll excuse me,' she said coldly, making to walk past him to show him the door.

He caught her arm, pulled her towards him, magnetic blue eyes boring into hers. 'I meant what I said.' He spoke huskily. 'You're a beautiful woman. That get up you're wearing and that muck on your face can't hide it. If anything it makes you more attractive.'

Every nerve in her body was jangling, sensations from his grip on her arm sending shock waves through her. How can this man have such an effect on me, her mind screamed, when I don't even like him? She fought with all her might to appear detached and disinterested. 'And I meant what I said. I'm already spoken for and your attempts at flattery won't get you anywhere. Now let go of my arm.'

They locked eyes for several long moments then before she could stop him he bent his head and briefly kissed her lips. He released her arm, turned from her and headed over to the door. Before he disappeared through it he turned back and said, 'Goodnight, Frankie. Sleep well.' Then he was gone.

She stood rigid with shock for several long moments. Then she touched the tips of her fingers to her lips, vigorously rubbing her mouth to be rid of the feel of him that still lingered. The cheek of the man! she fumed. How dare he take such a liberty with me? And she was angry with herself for allowing him to do so. Snapping off the last light, she grabbed her coat, handbag and the canvas bag containing the day's takings, secured the office door behind her and hurried off.

Hidden from view in an entry across the road, the very spot he had stood all day to observe the comings and goings at Champion's Garage, a satisfied Eddie watched Frankie's hurried departure. He put his hand in his pocket and pulled out a pack of Woodbines, lit one then blew a plume of smoke in the air. As he had stood all day and watched the proceedings over the street, a growing excitement had built within him and he had planned in meticulous detail how the garage could be of benefit to him.

But first things first. For anything to succeed he had to win the Champion woman over, then her cripple of a father. His plan of how to do both was already formulated and Eddie was feeling very pleased with himself.

Tonight's encounter had gone so much better than he'd expected. Despite what he'd told her, it had been difficult for him to tell what sort of figure lay hidden inside Frankie's unflattering overalls but he knew she wasn't fat, thank goodness. And her face seemed pleasant enough under all that grime, features he could just about put up with looking at for the duration anyway. He wasn't so sure about the red hair, though, never having had a penchant for it, much preferring dark-haired women, but at least as far as he could tell her face wasn't covered by the millions of hideous freckles red-heads usually suffered from.

Eddie inwardly grinned. For an expert with woman like him, he knew his seduction of Frankie Chapman was going to be easy. She had been reticent at first over the story he was telling her but he knew she had eventually believed his lies about his relationship with Stella. In fact, he felt he had been so convincing he'd almost believed what he was telling her himself. But most importantly the Champion woman had been attracted to him. He'd been very careful not to mention the garage in any way, not wanting her to have any inkling at all that the garage and not her was where his true interest lay. He'd certainly left a deep impression on her, enough to give her a sleepless night, he knew. Under normal circumstances he would have left her to mull over their encounter for a few days before making another unannounced appearance, to catch her off guard. But he hadn't the time for a long drawn out seduction. He would strike again tomorrow.

Stubbing out his cigarette, he emerged from his hiding place and, carefully keeping his distance, followed Frankie, wanting to know what kind of house the Champions lived in, where he himself would live very shortly if he got his way.

He was happy to notice her enter the driveway of a smart, decent-sized semi in a well-kept cul-de-sac off the main Loughborough Road. A palace compared to the crumbling tiny terrace he had shared with his mother and brother. Unlike that house, there'd be no damp in this one or rats or bugs to content with. It gets better and better, he thought. Jauntily he then set off for his dismal lodgings, happy in the knowledge that his stay in such miserable surroundings was rapidly coming to an end.

After dropping off the bag of takings to her uncle, Frankie arrived at the homely terraced house she shared with her parents and stood just inside the back gate for several minutes to regain her composure. Finally she managed to push all thoughts of her unnerving meeting with Eddie Taylor to the back of her mind. Taking several deep breaths, she forced a smile to her face and entered the house.

Nancy was at the sink washing the dishes. Frankie made straight for her and kissed her affectionately on her cheek. 'You look tired, Mam.'

'So would you if you'd bin up ter eyes all day in soap suds and hot water, tackling the weekly wash. Why someone can't invent a machine yer just bung everything in and it does it all for yer beats me, when engineers design aeroplanes that fly around the world.' She flashed her daughter a scathing glance. 'And worrying about you being late ain't helped me none neither.'

'I'm sorry, Mam. I had a few jobs to finish at the garage and lost track of the time.'

'I hope yer uncle sees you right in yer pay packet.'

'Mam, you know he does. Er . . . has Ian been around?' she casually asked.

'No.'

Frankie tried hard not to show her acute disappointment but couldn't help but utter, 'Oh.'

Nancy turned her head and eyed her daughter questioningly. 'You two have had a row, ain't yer? A serious one, it must 'ave bin. You ain't seen hide nor hair of that young man since he left by the front door the other night, so don't tell me them was just words you had, it was more than that, Frankie.'

She sighed. 'All right, so we did have an argument. Do you want me to pop Granddad's dinner down to him?' she asked to change the subject.

'I've already done it. I couldn't leave it any longer and let the poor old dear starve, could I? Anyway he was moaning 'cos he ain't seen you for three or four days. And that's not like you, is it?'

'I've just been busy, Mam. I'll pop in later. What is for dinner?' she asked.

Nancy stared thoughtfully at her, thinking the argument Frankie and Ian had had was obviously serious for him to go off like that and stay away for so long without contact. But she couldn't offer Frankie any comfort or words of wisdom if she refused to speak about it. Hurt that her daughter appeared not to trust her, she resumed her task of washing the dishes. 'Cold shepherd's pie, cold peas and cold carrots,' she snapped. 'The stewed cold tea is in the pot.'

Frankie sighed. 'Oh, Mam, I've said I'm sorry for being late. And I haven't told you what caused our row because . . . well, because it involves Stella and if I told you all about it, it would mean me breaking a promise to her. You've always taught me I should honour a promise, haven't you, Mam?'

Nancy nodded. 'Yes, I have, me duck, and it's commendable of you.' With a wet hand she affectionately patted her daughter's arm. 'You're a good friend to Stella, in my opinion sometimes more than she deserves. Yer dinner's in the oven keeping hot and I'll mash yer a fresh cuppa. Just be quiet when yer take it through, yer dad's fast off.'

Frankie leaned over and gave her mother another kiss on her cheek. 'Thanks, Mam, I do love you.'

'I should bloody think so,' Nancy replied. 'I'm the best mother you're ever likely to get.' Her face softened and she smiled. 'I love you too.'

'So can I get me suit outta mothballs yet?'

Frankie put down the Swiss Army knife she had been fiddling with and eyed the old man sitting opposite her blankly. 'Sorry, Granddad?'

'Frankie, I don't know why yer bother ter come and see me,' Edgar Champion grumbled. 'It's cheerful company I want, not the depressing sort. If I wanted that I'd let Widow Twankey move in.'

'Widow Twankey?' Frankie queried.

'Enid Smart, 'er that's still doing 'er best to get her feet under me table. I keep telling her ter sod off but she's skin like an elephant's hide and don't tek a blind bit of notice. Anyway, young Frankie, yer didn't answer me question?'

'Oh, and what was that, Granddad?'

He shook his head in exasperation. 'Is there a wedding in the offing or not?'

'No, there isn't,' she snapped abruptly. 'And it doesn't look likely there ever will be. Not with Ian at any rate..' Scraping back her chair, she rose. 'I've got a headache, Granddad. I hope yer don't mind but I'm going home.'

Peering inside the back of a wireless set, he gave a screw a slight turn then sat back satisfied. 'That's done it.' He addressed Frankie. 'Yeah, you clear off, me duck, I don't mind in the least, 'cos the mood yer in tonight yer getting on me nerves.

After she had left he gave a sigh. His beloved granddaughter hadn't been entirely truthful with him but he knew she had her reasons. It wasn't a headache she was suffering from. He might be old but he recognised heartache when he saw it. And there was something else bothering her, something he couldn't put his finger on, just instinct prodding him. Still, it would all come out in the wash in its own good time, as his dear mother had used to say.

In bed that night Frankie tossed and turned. The question why Ian was taking so long to come around and make up with her was worrying her witless. Did he after all believe that she could cheat on him? Had he lost his trust in her? But what if he couldn't come around because he was sick? Had an accident? But then, if he had his mother would have let her know by now, surely. Restlessly she threw back the covers, got out of bed and padded barefoot across to the window, pulling the curtains aside to stare out blindly into the dark moonless night.

This situation was dreadful. She loved Ian so much, couldn't bear the thought that their relationship could be finished for good over such a simple thing as doing what came naturally and being loyal to her friend. Blast Stella, she fumed. No, blast Edwin Taylor. If he hadn't come into the office at that time in the evening none of this terrible situation would ever have happened.

Then a memory of his eyes boring into hers, his head bending over her and the feel of his lips on hers, came flooding back so strongly she relived it again. And she remembered the sensations that had raced through her body, how stunned he had left her feeling when he had walked away; her own appalled realisation that she wanted him to come back and kiss her again. She shuddered violently, scolding herself severely. How could she harbour thoughts like this for another man when she loved Ian so much? Oh, God, she was so confused. Clutching her arms around herself she slumped to the floor and silently sobbed.

Chapter Fourteen

'Fer God's sake, Frankie, will yer cheer up? Yer've bin like a misery all day. What on earth's wrong with yer?'

'Nothing,' she snapped, without even the energy to lift her head. She was sitting cross-legged on the garage floor scraping the deposits off the end of a tappet with a razor blade. 'Anyway why are you so cheerful, considering Taffy's not in and Bernard was late?' she asked her uncle. 'I'd have thought you'd be upset 'cos we're behind with the work.'

'Ah, well, there's more ter life than bothering yerself over simple things like work, Frankie, me darlin',' he said. 'Taffy's got just cause to have a few days off, considering that selfish wife of his has done a bunk without the courtesy of giving the poor man any warning, and Bernard's more than made up for his late arrival. By the time we go home we'll have caught up.'

He started to whistle happily to himself and then Frankie did lift her head and glanced quizzically at him. 'What's going on, Uncle Wally?'

He stopped his whistling and looked across at her. 'In what way?'

'With you?' You're acting like yer've won the pools.'

'Are you trying to tell me I'm usually a miserable old bugger?'

'No,' she said, managing to raise a laugh, a difficult task considering how wretched she was feeling. 'I just mean there's something different about you.'

He gave her a mischievous grin. 'Well, maybe there is summat different about me, but then maybe there isn't. Oh, Frankie, you've just reminded me, is that invitation for dinner on Sat'day still open?'

She eyed him in surprise. 'I should think so. Yes, of course. Mam'd be delighted.'

'Do you think she'd mind if I bring a friend?'

'A friend?'

'Yes, I do have some, yer know,' he said, his eyes twinkling. 'Anyway yer mam knows 'em so it ain't like I'm bringing a stranger to the house. About seven, all right?'

'I'll tell her,' she said.

They both continued their work and just after six Wally called out, 'Right, that's it,' and stretched his aching body. 'Down tools.'

'Right you are, boss,' replied Bernard, and before anyone could say another word he had grabbed his coat and galloped off, shouting his cheerios before his boss changed his mind.

'Oh, to be young,' Wally said, smiling to himself as he watched his youngest member of staff rush out of the door. He turned to Frankie. 'Oi, did yer hear what I said?'

'I haven't finished yet,' she answered.

'I don't care, I'm telling yer you have. Now get washed up and off home. I'll lock up ternight. I'm gonna pop and see Taffy on me way, see how he's doing.'

'Well, in that case, I'll lock up and you get off and visit him. Give my best regards to him, won't you Uncle Wally? Tell him I'll come and see him soon.'

''Course I will. And are you sure about locking up?'

'I'm positive,' she replied. 'If you just shut the front doors for me, I'll only be minutes behind you.'

Frankie had decided her plans for the evening. After much soul-searching and deliberation she had decided matters had to be sorted out between herself and Ian. If he wouldn't come to her, she would go to him. She couldn't bear another day like today or another sleepless night.

Several streets away a very nervous Ian was knocking tentatively on the Champions' front door. Since he had walked out of this house three nights before his life had been in turmoil. He'd been so wrong practically to accuse the woman he loved more than life itself of an act he knew she would never contemplate. As soon as the door had closed behind him he had wanted to bang it down and beg her forgiveness. But he had felt so dreadfully ashamed and stupid for the way he had acted he had decided it would be best to let Frankie calm down before making his apologies. He would have come yesterday evening but he'd had an important appointment to attend to during the day and didn't get home until very late, and had wanted to wait for the outcome in case he had good news to tell Frankie. He did have excellent news now which had arrived by post this morning and was beside himself to tell her what it would mean to them both. It was going to change their lives dramatically. He was now in a position to ask Frankie to marry him.

The door finally opened and Nancy beamed a greeting at him. 'Hello, me duck, I was beginning ter think I'd done summat wrong since we ain't seen you for a bit.'

He eyed her awkwardly. 'I've . . . er . . . been studying for my exams.'

'Oh, well, let's hope all yer hard work pays off. Anyway, what on earth are you knocking on the front for? It's the back you usually coming to. Decided the tradesmen's entrance ain't good enough for you any more, is that it?' she said, hiding her amusement.

Ian shuffled his feet uncomfortably. 'Is Frankie in, Mrs Champion?'

'No, she ain't, and if she's late again this week I'm gonna tek the brush to that brother-in-law of mine for working her too hard.' Nancy stood aside. 'She shouldn't be long, come in and wait, you can have a chat with Mr Champion. I know he's missed seeing yer.'

'I won't, if you don't mind. I'll make me way to the garage and meet Frankie.'

'Suit yerself, me ducky. I'll have the kettle boiled ready for when you come back. Have yer had yer dinner? I've enough if you ain't.'

'Thanks, Mrs Champion, but I've already eaten,' he said, though what he'd managed to swallow of what his mother had placed before him tonight could hardly have been classed as a meal. He'd been too highly charged to eat, full of worry about his reception from Frankie and excitement at the news he'd received and couldn't wait to tell her. 'See you in a bit then,' he said, in every confidence that he would.

Nancy had just arrived back in the kitchen when the door was rapped on again. 'Bloody hell,' she grumbled to herself. 'Now who can that be?'

'Like Paddy's market,' Sam chuckled as she passed by him on her way to the front door again.

'More like London Road station on a Bank Holiday Monday. Still I expect it's better than nobody knocking at all. Well, 'ello, stranger,' she said to the girl standing on the cobbled pavement before her.

Stella gulped sheepishly. 'Is Frankie in, Mrs Champion?'

She shook her head. 'Not home from work yet, me duck. How's your Roger?'

'Er . . . fine, I think, Mrs C. We're . . . er . . . not together any more. I've got someone else now.'

Nancy stared in surprise. 'Really? Well, I never. Frankie's not said anything. I must say, I'm shocked. I thought you and Roger were practically up the aisle?'

'Well, it wasn't meant to be.' Stella's eyes lit up excitedly. 'I'm hoping to get my new bloke up there, though, Mrs C. Oh, you wait 'til you meet him. He's a corker. Looks just like a film star.'

'Really?' Nancy replied dubiously, wondering if Stella was doing her usual exaggerating. 'I'll give you me judgement when I get to meet him then. Want ter come in and wait for Frankie?'

Stella stared at her thoughtfully. It had taken much courage to come here tonight, knowing Frankie was bound to be angry with her for her long absence. But since coming clean with Roger and then meeting Eddie two nights ago and receiving his promise to take her out as soon as possible when his business was concluded, her spirits had soared and she felt able to face the world again. She'd even enjoyed work today which was most unusual. The estrangement between herself and Frankie was all her own doing, she knew, and she also realised she'd have much to do by way of making up, but Frankie was worth it. Stella knew regardless of what had happened she would talk Frankie round. Her friend would forgive her.

She couldn't wait now to introduce Eddie to Frankie, show him off to her best friend. Hopefully tonight's reconciliation would go well enough for them to make arrangements to go out together. There was still Ian's loyalty to Roger to contend with but she felt positive Frankie could sort that out. She smiled happily at Nancy. 'I'll walk that way and meet her, come in later for a cuppa when we get back. I hope you've some cake, Mrs C? I've missed your Madeira slab.'

Nancy tutted as she watched the girl walk quickly down the street in the direction of Champion's Garage. Only Stella Simpson could misconstrue a polite request to come inside and wait as an invitation for tea and cake.

Frankie was just switching off the lights when the outer door opened and someone stepped through. Her heart soared, convinced it was Ian. He'd finally plucked up the courage to come and see her and resolve matters between them. Then her excitement died as she saw who it was and her back stiffened. 'What do you want?' she asked the uninvited visitor, in all honesty the last person she'd expected to see.

Eddie walked across to her, his face taut. 'I'm sorry, Frankie,' he said, voice thick with emotion. 'I just had to come.'

'Why?'

'To see you. I haven't been able to get you out of my mind. I never slept a wink last night. Look, I know this is wrong, you've a boyfriend . . .'

'Yes, I have,' she cut in icily. 'And one I'm very happy with, thank you.'

He took a stance before her and looked at her hard. 'I don't believe you.'

She stepped a pace backwards, his closeness unnerving her. 'I beg your pardon?'

'You heard me, Frankie. I don't believe you. If you're so close to this man, how was it so obvious to me that you liked it when I kissed you?'

She gave a sardonic laugh. 'I never asked you to kiss me. You took a liberty. And you're very much mistaken if you think I liked what you did.'

'No, I'm not, Frankie. You felt it too.'

She frowned, perplexed. 'Felt what?'

'The spark between us.'

'I can assure you I did not,' she cried indignantly. 'Now I'd be obliged if you'd just go.'

His face crumpled. 'You don't mean that?'

'Oh, yes, I do. Anyway for your information, even if I hadn't a steady boyfriend, I wouldn't dream of having anything to do with you.'

'Why ever not?'

'In consideration of Stella's feelings. She thinks she's in love with you.'

'And I've already told you that is of her own making, not mine.'

'It doesn't matter.'

He leaned towards her smiling disarmingly, which sent a shiver of goose bumps all down her spine. 'I find it hard to believe an intelligent woman like you would jeopardise her own happiness for the sake of a friend's mistake. Frankie, let me ask you a question. Do you believe in love at first sight?'

She wanted him to go, desperately so. His presence and the way he was acting towards her were having a worrying effect on her. Sensations were whirling in her stomach, ones she knew she shouldn't in the circumstances be experiencing, and she was beginning to feel concerned that she wouldn't be able to find the strength to resist his charms for much longer. Regardless, she was intrigued to know where this conversation was leading. 'Yes . . . no . . .' She shrugged her shoulders. 'I suppose I do. Why?'

'I didn't at all until the night I walked through Champion's door. Frankie, let me tell you that one look at you and my insides turned somersaults. I knew instantly I'd met the woman I wanted to share my life with.'

She stared at him, feeling herself weakening, the effect he was having on her momentarily pushing all thoughts of Ian from her head. 'Really?' she uttered.

Eyes tender, he nodded. 'Oh, yes. Only your so-called friend didn't like not being the centre of attention, so she interfered. I've said it before and I'll repeat it: she's very full of herself that one, isn't she?'

A warm glow of satisfaction was filling Eddie. He knew by Frankie's posture, the look on her face, that he was steadily reaching her. All he had to do was keep this line of attack going and he was home and dry.

But he'd bargained without Frankie's sense of honour and loyalty to those she loved.

It suddenly struck her that she was gawking at him, drinking in his every word, readily believing all he was telling her. A vision of Ian flashed before her and she realised with horror that she was on the verge of fulfilling his false accusations. With all the strength she could muster, she regained her composure. 'I don't want to hear any more of this,' she snapped at Eddie coldly. 'I want you to go and I don't ever want you to come here again.'

He seethed inwardly, a terror of failure beginning to settle upon him. His assumption that the Champion woman was going to be a pushover was rapidly fading along with any hope for improvement in his immediate future. The chance of ever again coming across a situation as perfect as this was slight, he knew.

He couldn't allow this opportunity to elude him. The alternative, returning to Coventry to his old way of life, to his mother, with no means of escape from those miserable streets, was too dire. He could not forget his vow of vengeance on those people he felt were responsible for his dire situation either. He'd sooner be cast down to

Hell for eternity than go back on that. He was facing a fight for his life and wasn't going to give up until the absolute bitter end.

He summoned up a tragic expression, praying his show of dejection would play on her conscience. 'Frankie,' he uttered, his voice choked with false despair, 'accept my apologies. I didn't mean to offend you.'

Any hopes of a reversal of her decision were cruelly dashed.

'Accepted,' she said resolutely. 'Now will you please go?'

He stared at her, stunned. Was this stupid woman really turning him down? Women fought to receive his attentions, would give their right arms to be offered what he was offering to Frankie Chapman. The woman before him was no Amanda Sutton. She was a passable-looking redhead, with a dumpy figure. The only thing going for her in Eddie's eyes was her inheritance of this garage and the living that went with it. 'You don't mean that?'

'I do. Now please go. My boyfriend will be here at any minute to collect me,' she lied to get rid of him.

Eddie realised she was not going to change her mind. An intense rage filled him and it took all his self-control not to put his hands around her throat and throttle the life out of her. Spinning on his heel, he strode away from her and out of the building.

A feeling of doom enveloping him, with no idea what he was going to do next, he thrust his hands into his pockets and was just about to set off when movement across the street attracted his attention and he automatically slunk back into the shadows. From opposite directions a man and a woman were making their way towards him. They suddenly became aware of each other, stopped, looked at each other, then without a word passing between them each resumed their journey. They were definitely both coming in this direction. Eddie suddenly recognised the woman as Stella.

'Shit!' he hissed, she being the very last person he wanted to come across. She had nothing of value to offer him and he wasn't prepared to waste any more time on her. He flashed a glance around him, quickly assessing his only means of escape was down the side of the garage to hide in the dark until the threat of encountering her had passed. Then out of nowhere a thought struck him. The man . . . could he possibly be Frankie's boyfriend? She had said he was calling to collect her. It was him, it must be. Eddie's mind raced into action. A way to turn this failure around had suddenly occurred and filled him with renewed determination. Quick as a flash, he pulled open the door behind him and hurried back inside to the main garage area.

A deeply distracted Frankie was in the process of pulling on her coat. She froze in shock as Eddie bounded towards her. 'You again,' she exclaimed.

Before she could utter another word he had grabbed her in an iron grip, pulling her against him, bent his head and was crushing his lips against hers. She fought with all her strength to get away from him but he was embracing her so tightly it was impossible for her to move. Suddenly she became fully aware of the sensation of his lips upon hers. Ian's kisses had been gently sweet but never had he kissed her with such intimacy. As Eddie explored her mouth with his tongue, she felt her body go limp and could not stop herself from melting against him, all common sense flying momentarily from her.

She was so overcome by his actions, she was totally unaware of the arrival of two people standing only a yard or so away, frozen rigid in shock at the scene before them.

Eddie was very aware, though, he had been listening out and as he heard them enter, slightly turned Frankie around so that whoever was watching could witness him seek her breast, his large hand gently fondling it. When he felt a suitable time span had passed he released her from him, to stare down at her. 'Well, Frankie.' He spoke in husky tones but loud enough for the witnesses to hear, choosing his words very carefully so they would automatically assume Frankie had kissed him and not the other way around. 'For a woman who's supposed to love another man that's quite a kiss to give me.'

Stunned senseless by what had just transpired, and shocked to the core by her own responses, she just stared wildly up at him. Then suddenly a sound startled her and it hit her full force that she and Eddie were not alone. Her eyes flashed over to where the sound had originated and immediately settled on the two people standing by the door. Horrified, she instantly recognised them and gave a groan of despair. 'Oh, God,' she whispered, utterly devastated by what she realised they must both have seen. She made to approach them to attempt an explanation but the horror she saw in their eyes froze her rigid.

She stared helplessly, blind terror filling her, as with faces now wreathed in disgust they both turned and walked out.

All the time this was happening Eddie ensured his back was towards the door, appearing unaware of the visitors, pretending his attention was all on Frankie, feigning bewilderment as to why she was reacting the way she was.

Face ashen, she spun to face him. 'Do you know what you've just done?' she cried.

He smiled tenderly. 'Kissed you,' he said innocently.

'You've just ruined my life. Get out!' she screeched, pointing towards the door Ian and Stella had just departed through. 'Get out. Get out.'

Eddie was quite happy to oblige, smug in the knowledge he had achieved his aim.

Chapter Fifteen

'I don't believe it, I really don't believe it,' Nancy fumed as she plonked several full brown carrier bags on the blue Formica kitchen table and stripped off her coat.

Washing through some clothes in the pot sink, a thoroughly miserable Frankie turned her head and looked at her mother, making a huge effort to appear normal. 'Believe what, Mam?' she asked.

Nancy quickly popped her head around the door leading into the room beyond then looked back at Frankie. 'Where's yer dad?' she whispered.

'Working in the yard. You must have passed him.'

'Is he?' she said, moving beside her daughter to look out of the scullery window. 'I didn't notice. Ah, bless him, look how hard he's working. He's desperate to finish that bike early so he can enjoy tonight.' She sniffed disdainfully. 'T'int surprising I didn't notice him, me mind's so occupied with what I've just found out. I can't believe it, Frankie, I really can't.'

Her face drained. She was terrified that somehow gossip had got out about what had happened to break up Ian and herself. She'd made a limp excuse to her parents about not being able to make up their quarrel. Frankie had not liked being so evasive with the truth but how could she explain and expect them to believe that she hadn't encouraged Edwin Taylor to kiss her? Especially when, despite her heartache over her loss of Ian, she was still having trouble coming to terms with the way she had responded to Eddie's attentions. How she had felt enveloped in his arms. Because of that she was worried that somehow, without herself realising it, she had enticed him to act as he had. She knew how much her parents loved and trusted her but worried that even they were bound to doubt such a story. She hoped they never found out.

As far as Nancy and Sam Champion were concerned Ian and

Frankie hadn't been getting on well at all lately and had decided to end their relationship amicably. Nancy had been very upset at the news, Ian was a lovely lad and as far as she was concerned a better son-in-law she couldn't have wished for. The same went for her Sam, but both parents' allegiance lay with their daughter and as such they had respected without question her explanation for the break-up, it never entering their minds that the reasons for it were other than Frankie had given them.

It had been three long days since that shattering night and she was at breaking point, only sheer will-power keeping her functioning. Visions of that dreadful night came flooding back and she shuddered at the memory of the look in Ian's eyes when she had raced after him and finally caught him up just before his house.

'Ian, please,' she had begged, grabbing his arm. 'It's not what you think, honestly it's not.'

He had wrenched his arm from her as if she had burned him, a frozen look on his face. Eyes that had once looked so tenderly at her now brimmed over with pain and hurt. 'I know what I saw, Frankie.' His cold tone had made her shudder. 'Now please go, leave me alone, you've hurt me enough.' He had given a wry smile. 'You have my best wishes. I hope you and that man will be very happy together.'

With that he had turned abruptly from her and, shoulders slumped, walked away, not once turning back.

She had been around to his house several times since but each time Ian had refused to see her. She was now trying to come to terms with the fact that unless a miracle happened, she had lost him for good. She prayed for that miracle.

Stella hadn't taken the situation quite so calmly. Her door had been flung wide the second Frankie had summoned up the courage to knock, as though Stella had been lying in wait for her. 'You bitch!' she had cried, slapping Frankie hard on her face. 'He was mine – MINE!' she had screamed loud enough for the whole street to hear. 'And you stole him from me. I hope you rot in hell for what you've done. I hate you, you hear? I HATE YOU.'

Without affording Frankie the opportunity to utter a word in her defence, she'd slammed the door shut so hard the windows had rattled, leaving Frankie in no doubt she had better not call again.

She had, though, several times, but Stella had refused to see her or else Frankie was told she was out. Frankie now realised that she had lost her best friend.

To make matters worse, on leaving work each night since, the cause of all her heartache would appear at her side, armed with a bunch of flowers, proclaiming his deep love for her, pleading with her at least to go for a drink so that they could talk. Each time she had been cold and aloof towards him, demanding he leave her alone. Despite her wretchedness over the loss of Ian, she was confused by the guilt she felt to see the hurt Eddie appeared to be suffering at her rejection of him.

Today being Saturday, she had finished at midday. To her relief when she had left work there was no sign of him. At least today she had been spared having to deal with his persistent harassment of her, nor had she been forced to witness the sadness in his eyes when she'd turned him away. Hopefully Edwin Taylor had finally accepted she meant what she said and she wouldn't see him again.

What she couldn't know was that Eddie had been busy at the other side of Leicester lifting a couple of purses for urgent funds.

Dreading that her mother now knew the truth and as about to tackle her with it, Frankie took several deep breaths before turning to face her. 'You . . . er . . . can't believe what, Mam?'

'That after all me trouble getting Wally to dinner, Hilary can't come. She's already got another commitment.'

Frankie didn't know whether to laugh or hug her mother in relief. 'Oh, Mam,' she said. 'Is that all?'

Nancy eyed her daughter, astounded. 'What d'yer mean, is that all? I've gone to a lot of trouble to organise this meal. After you told me Wally was coming I was so excited I've bin like Sherlock Holmes trying to catch Hilary, and when I finally did this morning what does she tell me but that she's already going out? Well, I give up,' she fumed. 'Wally can stay a bachelor for all I care. Here was I thinking I was gonna be preparing an introductory meal for two lovely people, and what do I get? Wally bringing a bloody stranger to me table. I hope whoever he is he likes chicken, 'cos that's what he's getting.'

'I'm sure he will, Mam. Uncle Wally did say you knew him.'

'I probably do. It'll be one of them mates of his he used ter work with years ago in the factory.' Nancy sighed, fed up, then her good nature took over and a broad smile lit her face. 'Oh, never mind, yer dad'll enjoy the company and I will too. I got a couple of bottles of Nut Browns for the men as a treat for after. Right, hurry up wi' that sink. I need ter get cracking if this meal's gonna be ready in time.'

★ ★ ★

'Smile, Frankie, fer goodness' sake. We want to make Wally's friend feel welcome, not scare him off with your miserable face.' Nancy sighed heavily, putting her best china plates on the table spread with her best Nottingham lace cloth – cherished possessions that only saw daylight on highdays and holiday – and then turned towards Frankie, put her arms around her and gave her a hug. 'It's all right, me darlin', I didn't mean ter scold yer, I know yer hurting.' She pulled away and looked at her daughter worriedly. 'You sure about Ian and you not being able to patch things up? It seems funny ter me that such a devoted couple as you two should just decide yer not right for each other. Is there something yer not telling me, Frankie?'

'Leave the gel alone, Nancy. She's old enough to mek her own mind up who's right for her and who's not.'

'Yes, I know that, Sam, but all the same . . .'

'Nancy.'

She flashed her husband an annoyed glance. 'All right, Sam, all right. I was only being motherly.' She turned back to face Frankie, her face softening. 'Yer dad's right, lovey, I shouldn't be questioning yer. You've yer own mind to pick and choose who yer friends with, and especially who yer marry. I just liked Ian, that's all, and I know you did, and I'm having such trouble getting used to you two not being together any more. Anyway, I've said enough and won't mention it again. Now how do I look?' she asked, smoothing her hands over her skirt and patting her hair. 'Reckon I'll pass, do yer?'

'I think yer look grand, Nancy,' her husband said admiringly. 'Could fancy yer meself if I wasn't already spoken for,' he chuckled.

'Thank you,' she said to Sam. 'But it was Frankie I was asking.'

Frankie appraised her mother. Her normal daily working dress and old faded wrap-around apron had been replaced by a blue Crimplene knee-length skirt and crisp white blouse fastened at the neck by a cameo brooch her husband had bought her in celebration of their first wedding anniversary. Her greying hair had been pinned up in curlers all afternoon and was now brushed and styled becomingly. It was obvious Nancy had made a great effort to look her best. Frankie smiled at her. 'You look really pretty, Mam,' she said sincerely.

'Pretty indeed!' she said, blushing at the compliment. 'It's just nice to have an excuse to dress up for a change. Now let's have a look at you.' She glanced Frankie over and nodded in approval. Despite not feeling at all in the mood, Frankie had made a great effort with her attire. The dress she had chosen to wear was one her mother and she had run up on the old treadle with emerald green material brought from Lewis's for two shillings and elevenpence a yard. It had a deep scooped neck and short sleeves, was fitted at the waist, and underneath the full skirt Frankie wore several layers of net petticoats to fill it out. A wide black belt completed the outfit. Ian had loved her in this dress. 'Well, yer do look nice. That dress suits yer, me duck, and the colour is perfect, it matches yer eyes. Don't she look nice, Sam? Sam?'

Head cocked towards the wireless set on a small table to the side of him, pencil poised, a distracted Sam muttered, 'What?'

She tutted. 'Oh, n'ote, just finish doing yer pools.' As Nancy fussed around inspecting her table which had been pulled into the centre of the room and the furniture pushed back to allow space for the extension leaf to be put in the middle, she grumbled good-humouredly. 'Yer dad's been doing them pools for over twenty-five years and we ain't so much as won five bob. Does that look all right, Frankie?' she said, standing back, hands clasped in front of her as she cast a critical eye over her arrangements. ''Cos I don't want our Wally's friend thinking he's got a slovenly family.'

'It looks lovely, Mam,' Frankie said sincerely, leaning over to straighten one of the Sheffield plate knives. 'Do you want me to fetch Granddad or is it too early?'

Nancy looked at the clock ticking away on top of the mantelpiece. 'You'd better. If I know yer granddad he's still sitting at his table, working away, having completely forgotten he's coming here tonight for his dinner. And warn him I want him on his best behaviour. Tell him to put his best trousers on and that new V-neck I knitted him last summer. Not the red one, the green to go with your dress.'

'I'll tell him, Mam,' she promised.

Frankie was not surprised to find her grandfather exactly as her mother had said he would be, sitting at the table, still in his old clothes, unshaven, hair unbrushed, concentrating so intently on a child's toy car he was fixing he did not hear her enter.

'Edgar Champion,' she scolded as she stood, hands on hips, framed in the doorway, 'why aren't you washed and dressed ready for Mam's dinner tonight?'

Tongue poking out in concentration, he finished tightening a minute screw before he slowly turned his head and glanced at her, a merry twinkle sparking in his aged eyes. 'It's granddad to you, young lady. And I hope you're in a better mood than you've bin in just lately or I ain't coming.'

'Yes, you are, Granddad,' she said as she advanced into the room and sat down in a chair next to him. 'Mam's expecting you, and it's chicken.'

'I don't like chicken,' he snapped.

'Is that a recent dislike?'

'Eh?'

'Well, I'm only asking because if I remember rightly it was you who polished off the last scrap of the one we had for Easter Sunday. Dad complained because there was none left for a sandwich the next day.'

He grinned cheekily at her. 'You might be miserable but I'm glad to say you ain't lost yer sense of humour, Frankie, me duck.' He put down his screwdriver, leaned his arms on the table and looked at her intently. 'Now, how's that young man of yours?'

She gave a deep sad sigh, lowering her head. 'He's not mine any more, Granddad,' she said softly.

He nodded. 'So it's true what I heard then?'

Her face paled alarmingly and her head jerked up. 'Just what have you heard, Granddad?'

'That Ian and that young girlfriend of yours . . . whatsername? Tilly?'

'Stella, Granddad.'

'That's her. That they caught you in a bit of a situation with a good-looking stranger in the garage.' The horror on her face was readily apparent. 'So it is true then?'

'Who did you hear it from?' she asked, her worry mounting.

'Enid Smart, who else? Seems your friend Stella's been spouting her mouth off. But I gave Enid what for.'

'You did, Granddad?'

He leaned back in his chair and gave a cackle of mirth. 'Bloody right I did.' Then his face contorted in annoyance. 'I'm not having that wizened, foul-mouthed old creature coming into my house telling me my granddaughter's a trollop. I told her Stella's only spreading these rumours 'cos she jealous that a good-looking man wa' kissing you and not 'er. I told Enid she'd better tell everyone it's spite that Stella's spreading. And I also said that should I hear another word from anyone on the subject, in any way, shape or form, Enid can forget her ideas of getting her hands on me savings.' He gave Frankie a grin. 'I don't think you'll hear any more on the matter 'cos there's only one thing more important to Enid than gossip and that's the thought of getting her claws on what money she thinks I've got. Well, she'll live in hope for a very long time 'cos whatever I've got she's never gonna get her hands on it. And, Frankie, darlin', if yer mam and dad ain't heard whispers about any of this yet then they ain't likely to now so you can stop worrying your pretty head about it.'

Her body sagged in relief. 'Oh, Granddad, thanks,' she uttered.

He patted her hand affectionately. 'One thing I know about you, Frankie, and that's yer no hussy. Now, never mind what yer told yer mam and dad, I wanna hear what really went on.'

He listened intently and when she had finished, said, 'Well, I ain't surprised that young man is smitten by yer, yer a fine-looking gel. It was just a shame Ian witnessed it all.'

'He'll never forgive me, Granddad. I never asked for what happened, please believe me, but Ian won't even listen to my side.'

Edgar patted her hand again. 'He might, in time. He's a man. You've damaged his pride.'

'Do you think he might come around?' she asked hopefully.

'Well, stranger things have happened. God sometimes does answer prayers, yer know, depending what mood he's in. In the meantime, lovey, put a smile on yer face or you'll stay like that if the wind changes.'

She couldn't help but giggle. 'Oh, Granddad.'

He grinned. 'That's better. Now I suppose I'd better do summat wi' meself before yer mam comes around creating blue murder. Did yer say our Wally is coming too?'

She nodded.

'Good. All me family together around the table. I can't think of a better way to spend an evening.' He licked his lips in anticipation. 'What's yer mam made for pudding?'

'You're late. I said seven,' Nancy scolded Wally as he came in the back door.

He ignored her chiding and sniffed appreciatively. 'By hell, that smells good, Nancy,' he said, leaning over to kiss her cheek.

'Flattery won't get you a larger portion,' she replied good-naturedly, and gave him a quick appraisal. 'You don't brush up bad when yer make the effort. New shirt?'

'New suit,' he responded proudly. 'Like it?'

'Not bad.' Then she grinned. 'It's very nice. Pity it's just being wasted on me and our Frankie.' She eyed the brown paper bag he was carrying. 'What's in the bag then?'

'Half a dozen light ales and a bottle of cream sherry.'

She looked surprised. 'Sherry? I hope it's decent.'

'Only the best for my favourite sister-in-law.'

'Huh. You're splashing out, ain't yer?'

He smiled secretively at her. 'We might need it later.'

'What for?'

'You'll see.'

'Hello, Uncle Wally. Dad asked me to pop in and see if it was you that'd arrived. He wants you to check the pools coupon over for him 'cos he thinks we might have won a permutation and get a few bob. Granddad thinks so too.'

'Really? I'd better go through then,' said Wally excitedly.

'I shouldn't get yer hopes up, Wally. Sam thinks he's won summat every week and every week he ain't, you know that as well as I do,' Nancy warned.

Wally laughed. 'Yes, but one of these weeks he just might be right.'

'Well, I live in more hope than anger,' Nancy replied matter-of-factly.

Frankie pulled her uncle aside. 'How was Taffy when you popped around this afternoon?'

He pulled a grim face. 'He's took it bad, Frankie, much worse than I feared. He's talking of going back to Wales.'

'Oh, no,' she said, dismayed. 'Maybe we can talk him out of it. He's got friends here and he's often said that since his parents have gone and his brother's moved to Manchester there's not much back in Wales for him now. If he did go back he'd be so lonely, Uncle Wally.'

He patted her arm. 'It's early days yet. Let's give him time to come to terms with what's happened. He could change his mind but I must say he seemed quite adamant.'

'Wally!' Edgar shouted.

'Just coming,' he replied.

'Oi, before yer go, Wally,' Nancy stopped him, 'where's this friend of yours yer bringing then?'

'They shouldn't be long.'

'Well, I hope not, I don't want the dinner spoiled. Frankie, check the roast spuds are done,' she ordered, flinging the oven cloth across to her.

'It's all ready to be dished up,' said Nancy twenty minutes later.

'Oh, good, I'm starved,' said Edgar, rising from his seat to sit at the table.

'Well, yer'll have ter starve a bit longer, Dad,' she said, agitated. 'I can't very well dish up 'til Wally's friend arrives, so just stay where you are.'

Wally pulled a face. 'I can't understand it. I did say seven.'

'We'll hang on a few minutes but that's all,' Nancy warned. One of the things that really annoyed her was overcooked food and especially when she'd made such an effort to make everything nice. Just then the front door knocker sounded and she smiled in relief. 'Thank goodness! Frankie,' she called, 'start straining the veg. Wally, you go and let yer friend in. Dad, can yer manage to get Sam's wheelchair up the table?'

'I'll do that, Nancy,' Wally volunteered. 'Dad'll 'ave him over.'

'I ain't that old I can't push a wheelchair ter the table,' Edgar said indignantly.

'Excuse me but I can get meself ter the table,' Sam chirped up, looking very smart in a crisp white shirt and blue tie as well as his best suit trousers.

The door knocker sounded again.

'For God's sake,' fumed Nancy. 'Oh, you lot, just get on with it. I'll answer the bloody door, as if I ain't got enough to do,' she grumbled.

Expecting to find a man standing on the cobbles before her she was most taken aback to hear a woman greeting her. 'Hilary!' she exclaimed in delight.

'Hello, Nancy. I hope you don't mind but my evening plans were cancelled so I thought . . .'

'Come on in,' she cut in, beaming, extending a welcoming hand as she stood aside. 'Glad ter see yer.' And she was, the prospect of finally being able to introduce her beloved brother-in-law to this very lovely lady making her want to leap with excitement, though that would never do. 'Yer couldn't have timed it better. I'm just about to dish up. I hope yer like chicken?

'Look who I found on the doorstep,' she announced jocularly as she led Hilary through to the gathering in the small back room. 'This is my friend, Hilary Prestwick. You know my husband already, Hilary.'

'Hello,' Sam smiled.

'Me father-in-law, Edgar Champion.'

'Evening.' He grinned. 'You can sit next to me if you like,' he offered, giving her a cheeky wink.

'You'll sit where I put yer,' Nancy scolded. 'And this is my daughter Frankie,' she said as Frankie came through, a covered dish in her hand which she placed on the table.

'Nice to meet you,' she said, shaking Hilary's hand and thinking her mother was right. Hilary was a very pretty and well-presented woman and Frankie's immediate impression was that Wally and she would go very well together.

'And this is Walter Champion, Sam's brother,' Nancy said proudly, beginning to steer Hilary in his direction.

Wally gave Hilary a brief nod, then turning his back on her, addressed his brother. 'Better luck next time, Sam. Everton and Liverpool drew. You've got the result down wrong,' he said, handing the pools coupon back to him.

'Did I?' groaned Sam. 'Oh! Well, that's the television set I promised you up the spout, me old duck.' He grinned at Nancy.

She though, was shocked at Wally's apparent rudeness to the woman she'd hoped to pair him off with. Oh, well, she thought, the night was still young. 'Er . . . right. You sit 'ere, Hilary,' she instructed, pulling out a chair.

'That's where I usually sit,' said Edgar.

'Well, not tonight. You're sitting there,' she said, pointing to a chair the other end of the table.

'Wally, I've put you there.' She indicated the chair opposite Hilary's.

'If I sit there, Nancy, I can't chat to Sam without shouting,' he complained.

Nancy threw up her hands in despair. 'Oh, all suit yer bleddy selves and sit where yer like.' She added as she stormed off into the kitchen, 'And your friend, when he condescends to put in an appearance, can sit in the coal hole for all I care.'

'It's not going at all like I thought,' she whispered to Frankie as the pair of them arrived in the kitchen later with dirty plates which they stacked on the draining board. Nancy picked up a tin of evaporated milk and the tin opener. 'The bowl of fruit is in the pantry, lovey. I hope Hilary likes tinned pears,' she said, making two holes in the lid for pouring it out. 'They don't seem to be getting on at all. What do you think, Frankie?'

She shook her head. 'I have to agree, Mam. Neither of them seems interested in the other. Shame, they look so suited. I can see why you thought so. Granddad likes her, though.'

'He's not the one I'm trying to pair her off with, is he?' Nancy sighed despondently. 'Anyway, apart from the fact he's far too old he's enough on his plate fending off the attentions of Enid Smart.'

She shook her head thoughtfully. 'I can't believe I was wrong about Wally and Hilary. They'd make a lovely couple, I know they would. He does look handsome in that new suit of his, but Hilary's hardly glanced at him. I don't know what else I can do without making it obvious.'

Armed with the bowl of fruit for pudding, Frankie gave a laugh. 'You've been very obvious, Mam.'

'What do you mean?' she snapped.

'Well, fancy practically ordering Uncle Wally to show Hilary around his garage when she made it very plain she's no interest in cars.'

'That was sheer desperation, Frankie. I'm running out of ideas to get those two together. I've tried me best but even an idiot could see I'm wasting me time.' Then a thought struck her. 'I wonder what happened to Wally's friend who was coming?' she mused.

Despite Nancy's disappointment a very pleasant time was passed. Even Frankie seemed to have cheered up a little as the evening had progressed. At just before ten-thirty, Hilary smiled across at her hostess. 'That was a lovely meal, Nancy, thank you for letting me share it with you. But it's getting late and I ought to make a move.' She glanced around the room at each of the occupants. 'It was nice meeting you all,' she said, standing up.

'Glad you could come and it was my pleasure,' Nancy said. 'Just a shame . . .'

'Shame about what?' Hilary asked.

'Oh, nothing. I'll get yer coat.'

'Er . . . just a minute,' Wally interjected, standing up. 'I've a bit of an announcement to make and you might as well stay and hear it,' he said to Hilary. 'Want to get the bottle of sherry and the glasses, Frankie?'

'Oh, the sherry,' said Nancy. 'I'd forgotten about that. Yes, stay and have a glass, Hilary. You will, won't you?'

She nodded. 'Yes, I'd like that.'

Armed with their filled glasses Sam asked, 'Well, come on then, Wally, what's this announcement you've got to make? Our Nancy is bursting her breeches to know what it is.' He flashed a mischievous grin in his wife's direction.

'Sam,' she scolded. 'But he's right, I am. Is it to do with the garage?'

'No, nothing to do with it at all.' He looked across at Hilary standing by Nancy, a broad smile on his face. 'Come here, my darlin',' he said, extending his arm towards her.

Mouth dropping open, Nancy turned in shock to Frankie who was at the side of her and whispered, 'Did I 'ear right? I'm sure he called her darling.'

Frankie nodded. She too was in shock. 'You heard right, Mam. What's going on?'

Both she and Frankie watched, stunned, as Hilary approached Wally to nestle inside his arm. 'This lady is the reason for my new suit. Do you want to tell them or shall I?' he said, beaming down at her.

'You have the honour,' she replied.

He raised his glass in the air. 'Dear sister-in-law, you got your wish. Me and my friend . . .'

'Friend?' Nancy gasped, astounded as realisation struck. '*This* is the friend you invited for dinner?'

He nodded. 'Yes, it is. I'm sorry to have misled you, but you'll appreciate why in a minute, if yer let me finish. Me and my friend are happy to announce we're officially courting.'

Nancy's eyes bulged. 'Yer getting married?' she cried.

'Now don't jump the gun, Nancy. I said we're courting,' he replied, looking lovingly at the woman at his side. 'We're not ruling that out in the future.'

All her own pain forgotten, Frankie cried ecstatically, 'Oh, Uncle Wally, Hilary, this is wonderful news.'

'You bloody pair of buggers!' Nancy scolded. 'How long 'as this bin going on behind me back?'

Wally grinned. 'What d'yer reckon, Sam . . . Dad? Weeks, I'd say.'

They both nodded. 'Yes, must be,' they agreed.

'You all knew!' she accused. 'And none of yer said a word?'

'Well, Nancy, come on, it's only what you deserved,' said her husband. 'From the minute you met Hilary you made it blatantly obvious you were trying to fix our Wally up with her. Even roping our Frankie in,' he said disapprovingly. 'And it was so funny watching yer both pulling yer hair out over how to get them together.'

'I'll deal with you later,' she warned her husband. 'And you, Dad. Fancy you all watching me mek a fool of meself.'

'You're no fool, Nancy,' said Wally. 'We're all fully aware you only had my best interests at heart. And Hilary's.'

Her face softened and she smiled. 'Yes, I did. And it's lovely to welcome you to the family, me duck,' she said to Hilary. 'So your avoiding me was just an act, was it?'

She nodded. 'I'm sorry about that but Wally and I really wanted to see how we got on together first before we said anything, and when we realised how we felt about each other, well, we just wanted to surprise you.'

'Oh, yer've done that all right. And what a wonderful surprise,' Nancy added. She raised her glass. 'To Wally and Hilary!' she toasted.

'To Wally and Hilary!' they all said in unison.

Chapter Sixteen

Frankie laid down her tools and stretched her aching back. She glanced over at the clock. It was just coming up to one-fifteen. Not surprisingly Taffy hadn't turned in that morning and having to cover his work, the three of them, Wally, Bernard and she, had not even stopped for a mid-morning brew. There was still so much to get through if they intended keeping their promises to customers and Frankie knew that to do so a dinner break too was out of the question.

Despite being gladdened by her uncle's budding romance with the delightful Hilary and his infectiously good mood in consequence, Frankie's own depressed state had not lifted at all. Adding to her misery was her concern for Taffy. She liked the Welsh giant and it saddened her deeply to think he was probably sitting alone in his house now, brooding over what his wife had done to him.

She looked at the car she was working on then back at the clock. She desperately felt the need to pop over and see Taffy, just show him a friendly face, let him know people cared for him. She went over to her uncle, working underneath a vehicle positioned over the pit. 'Uncle Wally,' she called, squatting down.

'Mmm,' he replied distractedly. 'Pass me the spanner, me duck.'

She obliged then said, 'I'm going to take five minutes' breather. Thought I'd pop over and see Taffy.'

'Good idea. Get some cobs, Frankie, on yer way back. I don't know about you 'but I'm starving and I ain't got time to stop. Cheese'll do me. Ask Bernard what he wants too. Take the money out of petty cash. My treat.'

'Will do,' she said, rising.

From his secret hiding place across the street, Eddie saw Frankie emerge from the side door and hurry off down the street. He made to follow her then stopped. She was probably only going to fetch the lunch like she usually did around this time.

One good thing he had observed during his time watching from the shadows was that there was never any evidence of the crippled father. That could only mean, Eddie deduced, that he left the running of the place in the hands of his daughter and the other older man with the fair hair. Eddie smiled to himself. Well, little did that fair-haired mechanic realise that his days working at Champion's were coming to an end, and given a little more time so were Frankie's.

Settling back in the shadows, he resumed his watch.

Five minutes later Frankie was hammering on Taffy's door.

'He's left. Went back to Wales this morning, so he said.'

Frankie jumped and looked up to see the woman next door hanging out of the bedroom window, a cigarette dangling from the corner of her mouth.

'Taffy's left?' she confirmed, hoping she had misheard.

'That's what I said. Gave me the keys and enough to clear any rent owing,' she replied puffing on her cigarette. 'He's left all his furniture. I've no idea what 'e intends to do with it. There's a nice three-piece, too, which I know weren't cheap.'

Frankie could tell what was on her mind and said, 'Well, if he gives us instructions to sell it, I'll let you know how much he wants if you're interested.'

With a heavy heart she made her way back to the row of shops on the main Belgrave Road so she could purchase the cobs before she went back to the garage. Armed with her order, she walked out of the shop and immediately collided with a woman coming in. For several seconds they both stared at one another, stunned. It was the other woman who spoke first. 'Excuse me,' she said icily, making to push past Frankie.

She quickly gathered her wits. 'Mrs Fields,' she addressed Ian's mother, 'please let me explain . . .'

The woman turned and glared at her with loathing. 'Explain? There's n'ote to explain. I ain't in no mood ter listen to any cock and bull from you, young lady. What you did to my son was disgusting.'

'Please, just let me tell you. It wasn't what . . .'

'Oh, wasn't it?' she cut in angrily. 'My son catching you in another man's arms, and doing what you were, wasn't what it seemed? You must think we're stupid. It shocked me to the core. I always thought you a lovely young woman, Frankie, but yer just a harlot. I'm glad my Ian found out the way he did before you got wed, even though you've broken his heart. And it's all your fault what he's gone and done, the stupid boy,' she fumed.

Frankie frowned, bewildered, a deep fear filling her. 'What has he gone and done, Mrs Fields?'

'Gone away, that's all you need to know. 'Cos what my son does is nothing to do with you any more. Now get out me way, I've shopping to do and I'm particular who I speak to.'

With that she pushed past and marched into the baker's.

A desolate Frankie stood rooted to the spot. She couldn't believe that less than two weeks ago she and Ian were happy together, under the impression they would spend the rest of their lives with each other. Then Edwin Taylor had appeared in their lives and because of his mindless actions, Frankie's happiness now lay in ruins. If Ian had gone away it was apparent he had no intention of ever forgiving her and she knew the miracle she prayed for was never going to happen. Oh, Ian, she inwardly groaned in deep despair. Where have you gone? But as Mrs Fields had so forcefully told her, what he did now was none of her business.

Her life in complete tatters, her future seeming to disappear down a never-ending black void, she dragged herself back to the garage.

Wally was most upset to hear the news of Taffy. 'I'll miss that bloke. I really liked old Taffy and he was worth every penny to me and more if I could have afforded it.'

'He might come back, Uncle Wally,' she said, trying to be optimistic.

Wally nodded. 'He just might. I'll give it a week or so before I start looking for someone else to replace him, just in case he does. In the meantime we'll manage between us, eh?'

Forcing a smile to her face she nodded.

'Are they my cheese cobs?' he asked, relieving her of a brown paper bag. Fishing one out and taking a big bite, he suddenly frowned at her in concern, noticing the pain etched on her pretty face, her eyes red as though she'd been crying. 'This business with Taffy has really upset you, hasn't it, me duck? I know you liked the man but even so . . .'

She let her uncle ramble on, preferring him to think her distress was for the reason he assumed.

At seven o'clock Wally ordered them to down tools. 'Enough is enough. What we haven't got through, I'm sure our customers will understand. Bernard, get off. And you too, Frankie. I'll lock up.' He sighed then, remembering he'd still the banking to do, which should have been done earlier but he'd completely forgotten with everything else that needed doing. Then a thought struck him. Hilary was coming round and if he took all the paperwork home he knew she'd volunteer to give him a hand. That thought cheered him enormously. He'd forgotten what it was like to have someone to share his life with and was rather getting to like it, especially with a woman like Hilary.

Frankie had only just left the garage when she felt the presence of someone beside her. She stopped abruptly and turned to face him. 'Please, Eddie,' she begged. 'Will you leave me alone?'

God, his mind screamed, this bloody woman is getting on my nerves.

Why didn't she just give in to his demands like any sensible woman would do? She obviously hadn't got it through that thick brain of hers that he wasn't going to give up so she might as well make it easy on herself and relent now and stop wasting time. He planted a hangdog look on his face.

'You're breaking my heart, Frankie. What do I have to do to prove how I feel about you? Besides, it's my fault you've lost your boyfriend. But it's my opinion he couldn't have loved you, Frankie.' He held his arms wide. 'If he had done, no way would he have let you go just because of a silly misunderstanding. I know I wouldn't. I'd be mad, 'course I would. What man wouldn't, catching his woman in a situation like he did us? I've probably rant and rave at you, even give the man a slapping, but finish with you for such a trivial reason? No, never.' He dropped his arms. 'I think myself that old boyfriend of yours was using what he saw us doing as an excuse to end things between you. Makes sense if you think about it, Frankie.'

She stared at him, flabbergasted. Was that what Ian had done? No, he wasn't that devious. But then she had never thought to hear him accuse her of cheating on him without any just reason. And then he'd taken his time coming to see her and make up. Three long days in fact. If he had loved her, why had he waited so long? She'd thought she'd known Ian inside out. Now she was beginning to wonder if she ever had. 'I don't care what you think,' she snapped, her thoughts racing wildly, not knowing now what to believe and what not.

Eddie leaned over, face inches from hers, and looked deep into her eyes. 'I believe you care very much what I think, Frankie. You just won't admit you feel as deeply for me as I do for you.'

'Oh, I've had enough of this. Just leave me alone,' she cried, making to walk off.

He grabbed her arm, pulling her back, and before she could stop him he had her inside his arms and was kissing her passionately. The surprise of his actions knocked the breath from her body and she felt herself, like before, slump against him. Finally he let her go and took a step backwards. Pushing his face close to hers, he said, 'Now tell me you have no feelings for me?' He gave a wry smile. 'You can't, can you, Frankie? Because you know you have. We were meant for each other. It was fate that brought us together. Since I met you I can't function properly, I can't sleep or eat.' He paused momentarily. Time, he thought, to start bringing his assumed background into play. 'I'm supposed to be setting up a branch of the family business in Leicester and I've abandoned that because I can't concentrate. When my father finds out he's going to be very angry. Now for God's sake stop fighting it. Meet me for a drink at nine in the Griffin. I'll be waiting for you.'

With that he strode off, leaving her staring after him dumbstruck.

Her mind whirled, thoughts all jumbled. Was it possible that this man really meant what he said? That he really did love her? He certainly was persistent in letting her know of it. But then, what did a man like him, coming from what she assumed to be a monied family, see in a working-class woman like herself, when he could have anyone with his good looks and background? His declaration of his feelings seemed so genuine. But how could he love her when he didn't know her and had only ever seen her dressed in her working clothes when she knew she looked a sight? They hadn't even been out together. Oh, it was all so confusing.

Then there was Ian. Oh, Ian, she thought sadly. She had loved him dearly, still did, but after Eddie's shocking interpretation of his actions she was beginning to question if Ian's love for her had ever been genuine, considering how readily he had walked away. She felt the life drain from her body because she knew her musing over Ian's feelings for her didn't matter any more. He was gone. They had no future together. So did she spend the rest of her life mourning his loss or give Eddie a chance? That was what she had to decide. Despite the fact she didn't love Eddie Taylor, if she could make him happy, as he insisted she could, then maybe her life wouldn't be a total waste from now on. She took a deep breath. She supposed meeting him for a drink couldn't do any harm.

'You look nice, love,' her mother said to her a while later. 'Don't she look lovely, Sam?'

He lifted his head from his newspaper and looked his daughter over. 'Yes, yer do, very nice. Going out?'

She nodded.

Nancy smiled. 'I'm glad. I'm getting sick of the sight of you moping around this house. You and Stella have a good time.'

Frankie declined to put her mother right, wondering how she could explain her date with another man so soon after Ian and herself had finished. She knew her mother wouldn't think it seemly, her father neither.

'I'll have yer cocoa ready for when you come in,' said Nancy.

'Thanks, Mam,' she said, leaning over to kiss her cheek. 'I won't be late, I promise. 'Night, Dad.'

Eddie's delighted response to her arrival in the Griffin just after their appointed time was so apparent that any nervousness Frankie was feeling immediately began to ease. She ordered a gin and orange to give her some courage, and while he stood at the bar went to find a seat. The only one she could find was in a dim corner at the back of the room. Around her the lively atmosphere was infectious. The place was packed. Old timers were playing cards or dominoes, groups of people deep in conversation were milling around or sitting at tables enjoying their drinks; several inebriated middle-aged ladies were gathered around a piano that was being played with gusto by the resident pianist, a tiny balding man dressed in a white shirt and red spotted dickie bow. His feet only just reached the pedals. Now and again he stopped his playing to take a large gulp from the pint of beer on top of the piano. The instrument itself was dreadfully out of tune and so were the singing women. Frankie could not help but laugh at their antics.

'You look even prettier when you smile,' Eddie said, coming over to join her armed with their drinks. In truth he'd been pleasantly surprised when she'd arrived in the pub. She was no raving beauty, but he wasn't embarrassed to be seen out with her and she scrubbed up quite well. In the clothes she was wearing – fitted yellow Capri pants and a bright blue three-quarter-length-sleeved shirt – her Titian hair piled up on top of her head, she made an attractive picture. This still didn't make her his type. He liked them more glamorous, more forward, more like Stella come to think of it, but far more worldly wise than she was. That was the type he'd return to in the future, when he'd achieved his aims. It was something to look forward to.

Frankie smiled nervously at him, her uneasiness returning. 'I was just laughing at those ladies over there by the piano.'

'They'll be even funnier later when they've had more to drink.'

Time passed pleasantly and now, mellowed by the several drinks

Eddie had pressed upon her, Frankie was feeling really relaxed in his company. All evening he had been very attentive and flirtatious, making her laugh with his quips, even showing his generosity by buying two very poor-looking ladies sitting close by a couple of bottles of stout. And never once had he looked in another woman's direction. She was now fully convinced her first impression of him had been totally wrong.

Coming back from the bar yet again, he placed their drinks on the table, sat down right beside her and took her hands, caressing them lightly. 'Right, Frankie Champion, don't you think it's time we set a date for our wedding? Will Friday suit?'

Her mouth dropped open in shock. She was wondering if her drink-fuddled mind had heard him right. 'What? I came here for a drink with you, to get to know you a little better. You can't be serious about marriage?'

'Absolutely. I can't see any point in waiting. I love you. Why else do people get married? And doesn't tonight prove how well we get on? I've never enjoyed an evening so much in my life, and it's because I'm with you, Frankie.'

But I don't love you,' she said boldly.

He smiled disarmingly at her. 'Not right this minute, but you will.'

'You're very sure of yourself.'

'If I don't have faith in myself, Frankie, then who else will? One thing my father taught me is to go after what you want because damned sure it won't come to you.' That was true, but Eddie's father had actually said it another way when he had been encouraging his sons to get what they could out of life. 'Boys, if yer don't take what yer want in this world, then people won't give it yer.' 'I want you, Frankie, and I won't give up until I have you.'

'But you don't know anything about me.'

More than you'll ever realise, he thought. 'I know I love you and that's all that matters to me. My mother and father only knew each other a matter of days before they got married and they're still together and happy,' he lied.

'Really?'

He nodded. 'I'm like my father, Frankie. I don't like wasting time.' He leaned over and kissed her lightly. 'I could get a special licence tomorrow morning. We could be married by lunchtime.'

'Oh! Er . . .'

'Just say yes, Frankie. Think of the excitement. Have you never wanted to do anything exciting?'

'Well, yes, but getting married is a life-long . . .'

'Just say yes, Frankie,' he cut in, pressing his fingertips to her mouth to silence her. 'When we're old and grey it'll be something to tell our grandkids. Come on, Frankie, just say yes.'

His persistence was overwhelming, her heart was racing erratically, the several gins she'd had were not allowing her to think straight and before she could stop herself, she said, 'Yes, Eddie. All right.'

He whooped with joy so loudly all the people in the pub stopped and looked over at them. He grabbed her and pulled her close, kissing her fiercely until her lips were bruised and she cried out in pain. 'You've made me the happiest man, Frankie. I couldn't begin to tell you how happy.' But whether you'll be a happy woman after I've finished with you, he thought, is another matter.

Frankie was having trouble digesting it all. Had she really just agreed to marry Eddie? She picked up her drink and downed the dregs.

'Want another?' he asked. 'Because I certainly do to toast our future.'

'I think I'd better.'

She smiled as she watched him swagger over to the bar as last orders were being called. He really cut a swathe and she couldn't help but be warmed by the admiring looks he was receiving from the women he passed. She would have to get used to that, she supposed. Other women admiring her husband. Her husband. The words jangled loudly inside her head. Had she really just agreed to marry him?

He returned and sat down beside her, smiling happily. He raised his glass to her. 'To Mr and Mrs Edwin Taylor. Has a nice ring, don't you think?'

'Mmm,' she mouthed. She had thought Mr and Mrs Fields had a nice ring to it only days ago. No she must not think like that again. 'You must come home and meet . . .'

He held up his hand to stop her. 'After we're married, Frankie, then I'll be glad to meet any of your relatives you wish me to. And I can't wait to introduce you to mine. They're all going to love you, Frankie.'

'After we're married?' she exclaimed.

He nodded. 'Let's do it in secret, then surprise everyone.'

'Oh, I don't know if that's a good idea, Eddie,' she said worriedly, thinking of her parents.

'This is our day, Frankie. If we tell our folks, think what'll happen.

We'll get caught up in big wedding plans, your lot wanting one thing, mine another, and delays are bound to happen. I want you now, without the fuss. We could always have a big do later on if you wanted.'

She felt she was being swept along by a raging torrent, unable to grab a rock to stop herself from tumbling over a waterfall. Did she grab that rock and stop this nonsense or did she take a chance and jump off?

'Frankie,' he urged. 'Make me a happy man. Say yes.'

She saw the desperation in his eyes and before she could stop herself she cried, 'OK, I'll marry you. We'll face the flak after.' And they certainly would. Her parents were going to go mad, that much she did know, let alone his. But Eddie's excitement was so infectious, she was past caring. She felt so light-headed she wanted to giggle at the absurdity of it all.

'Right, finish your drink and we'll go and find a hotel room.'

'What?' she gasped.

He smiled suggestively at her, his magnetic eyes boring deep into hers, his voice seductive. 'Frankie, if you think I'm letting you out of my sight so you can go home, change your mind overnight and devastate me, then you've another think coming.'

'But . . .'

'No buts, Frankie. You've agreed to be mine now. We'll be official tomorrow, I promise you. But tonight . . .' He leaned over and kissed her ear. 'Tonight I make you really belong to me.'

She gulped, a shiver of excitement running down her spine. Things like this only happened in films to beautiful people like Ava Gardner and Audrey Hepburn – princes on white chargers arriving from nowhere to sweep them off their feet to live happily ever after. Was this really happening to her? She picked up her drink and downed the lot, then throwing common sense aside, she grabbed Eddie's hand and pulled him up. 'Come on then,' she ordered.

Chapter Seventeen

'Ah, Eddie, I can't tell yer how good it is ter see yer. I thought . . .'

'Don't think, Neil, I'm here and now I've explained what I've been up to I'm sure you understand why I haven't been before. I'd never abandon you, never. You're my brother. What I'm doing now is not just for me but for you as well.'

Neil stared at him, rubbing his hand backwards and forwards over his chin. 'You married? I can't believe it.'

Eddie gave a sardonic laugh. 'I'm having trouble coming to terms with it myself. But then I think of why I did it and, believe me, the sacrifice is well worth it. Just think, Neil, shortly we'll be the proud owners of a garage.'

'But . . .' He paused momentarily as a guard walked slowly past, the enormous bunch of keys hanging from a chain secured to the belt around his thick waist clanking loudly. The guard scrutinised them before continuing down the row of tables filled with other prisoners and their visitors. Once he was out of earshot Neil leaned forward, his voice low. 'We don't know anything about fixing cars, Eddie. So what good is a garage to us?'

'Have you been listening to me at all? Once the old cripple's out the way, and according to Stella another bad dose of 'flu will do the trick, as her husband what's Frankie's becomes mine. That garage will be a front for whatever else we decide to do.'

'You sure come up with some grand ideas, Eddie. This is far bigger than the car spares scam. You certain you can pull this off?'

'I've got this far, haven't I? Got the silly cow to marry me, the rest is . . .' He nonchalantly shrugged his shoulders. 'Like taking sweets off a baby.' He leaned forward, an excited glint sparkling in his eyes. 'Listen, Neil, once the garage is in my hands I've several schemes in mind for us to make real money. But that comes later. For the time being I've just got to keep me head down and play the game of doting husband.'

Neil smirked admiringly at his brother. 'You've it all worked out, ain't yer, Eddie?'

'Down to the last detail,' he said smugly. 'I must admit the Champion woman gave me a few nasty minutes. She was hard work, believe me, but I cracked her in the end, like I knew I would. And I've that silly cow Stella to thank for giving me the idea. I must think of some way of making it up to her one day,' he said, giving Neil a knowing wink.

'Where does your new wife think you are now?'

A slow smile spread across Eddie's face. 'That I'm breaking the news of my marriage to my *wealthy* family and arranging for her to meet them.'

'Wealthy family?' Neil said, chuckling. 'If this new wife of yours ever met Mam . . .'

'But she isn't going to,' Eddie cut in sharply. 'Anyway she's waiting back in the hotel room for me. Then we're going to meet her father. And that should be interesting.' He glanced around at the austere confines of the visiting room of Coventry Prison. 'I wonder what she'd say if she could see where I really am. What's it like in here, brother?'

'Bloody Butlin's Holiday Camp. Wadda you think? It's hell on earth, let me tell yer. The food's disgusting, I've been given better by Mam and that's saying summat. The screws are thugs, give you a going over for the slightest reason, and the other inmates . . . well . . . let's just say me getting out of here can't come quick enough.'

Eddie put his hand in his pocket and pulled out two pound notes. 'This should help pass the time more pleasantly and I'll get more to you the next time I visit.'

The money was snatched from his hand. 'Oh, ta, Eddie. I can get some fags and soap now.'

'Don't get into any trouble, Neil. Just keep your head down and think of what I'm arranging for you to come out to. You'll have a nice place to live in and a way to earn a decent living. Let's face it, anything's got to be better than we had back home.'

'You can say that again.'

Eddie's face suddenly darkened, eyes narrowed. 'And I'll have found a way to pay those bastards back for what they did to me. I haven't thought how yet, but it'll come – and then they'll rue the day they crossed Eddie Taylor's path.' His expression brightened. 'We could still get rich out of this, Neil. I ain't lost hope of that. What more could you ask?'

He grinned. 'Not a better brother, that's for sure. So what's she like, this Frankie?'

Eddie shrugged his shoulders. 'Nothing for you to get excited about.' He smirked maliciously. 'I couldn't believe she was a virgin.'

Neil's eyes glinted enviously. 'Really? I bet that was a pleasant shock for you. Er . . . considering you don't care much for her, didn't you mind . . . er . . .'

Eddie smirked. 'Making out I'm besotted with her, and when I'm doing the business imaging I'm with Elizabeth Taylor, is a small price to pay for what I'm gaining, don't you reckon?'

'Yes, most definitely.' Neil's face lit up with excitement. 'A bloody garage, eh? Who'd 'a' thought it? I'd best start reading all the car mags I can lay me hands on.'

Chapter Eighteen

Shocked at the terrible news he had just told her, Frankie stared dumbstruck at her new husband who sat on the edge of the hotel bed, cradling his head in his hands. She had woken that morning with not a clue where she was, her head thumping painfully from the excessive amount of drink she had consumed the previous night. She was mortified to find Eddie asleep beside her, his arms tightly entwined around her own naked body.

And then it had all come flooding back. She had agreed to marry him and may have been fuddled by drink but had nevertheless willingly marked her commitment to him last night by giving him the very thing she held sacred, something she had been keeping until she was married, as she had once thought to Ian: her virginity. She felt disgusted with herself but nevertheless, as far as Frankie was concerned, doing what she had made her as good as married. The official ceremony later that morning was just a formality.

She twisted the thin gold band on her finger, the one Eddie had chosen for her from Green's the Jeweller's on Churchgate early that morning on their way to the Register Office on Pocklingtons Walk. He had made her wait outside while he'd gone in to get the special licence and she had nervously paced up and down, wondering how on earth she had allowed herself to get into this situation. A large part of her hoped he'd be denied the licence for some unforeseen technicality, but the other part of her told her that marriage with Eddie was now inevitable, so if it happened today or tomorrow or next month, what did it matter? The fact that her family were not with her did matter, she felt very sad about that.

Half an hour later Eddie emerged from the building brandishing a special licence, jubilantly informing her that in under an hour they would be legally united.

Both dressed in the crumpled clothes they had worn the night before, the ceremony had been hurried and impersonal. Before very long had passed Frankie was back outside. They had celebrated their union with a cup of tea at a nearby café and Eddie had then left her to catch the train to Coventry to break the news to his family and arrange her introduction to them. When he returned they would go and see Frankie's family.

She hadn't been expecting his parents exactly to jump for joy at their son's unexpected marriage but never had she expected them to react like this.

Sitting down beside him, Frankie put her arms around him and pulled him close. 'Here's me been worrying myself witless about what my family is going to say when all the time you've been going through this. Oh, Eddie, I don't know what to say. I'm so sorry. We must have been out of our minds to do . . .'

His head jerked up and he eyed her intently. 'Never say that. Marrying you is the sanest thing I've ever done. I'll never regret. Never.'

'But you've lost your family,' she uttered, feeling sick with guilt.

'The loss is theirs, Frankie.' He turned from her to cradle his head in his hands again, his body sagging in total despair. 'I'm not surprised by my father's reaction but my mother's . . .' He sighed. 'She was livid with me, Frankie. She acted like a woman gone mad. She was raving like a lunatic.'

Frankie tightened her arms around him. 'She'll come around, Eddie, give her time. So will your father, I'm sure.'

He shook his head. 'No. What they said to me was final, they left me in no doubt of that. My father wants nothing more to do with me. He threw me out when he realised I wasn't going to change my mind, and as for my inheritance . . .' He gave a deep, sad sigh. 'Well, I can forget about that. He's cut me off without a penny to my name, Frankie.'

She was horrified. 'But why be so harsh, Eddie? I know our marriage must be a terrible shock to them but even so . . .'

'You don't understand.'

'Understand what?'

He sighed forlornly and lifted his eyes to hers. 'I didn't really want to tell you this, Frankie, but you're my wife now and there mustn't be any secrets between us.' He swivelled round to face her and took her hands, squeezing them tightly. 'Frankie, by marrying you I've caused my family a great deal of embarrassment and lost them a lot of money.'

'What?' she gasped. 'But how?'

He exhaled loudly, his voice lowered to barely a whisper. 'I was engaged to be married to someone else.'

Her face paled and her mouth dropped open in shock.

'It wasn't love, Frankie, believe me, I never loved . . . er . . .' he fought to think of a suitable name, '. . . Susan. I was only going ahead with it to please my family. My father is a self-made man, what people call an . . . an . . .' Oh, hell, he thought, can't think of the word.

'An entrepreneur?' Frankie suggested.

'Yes that's it,' he said, relieved. 'Sorry, I'm so upset about all this my brain's not working properly. When he was a kid his family had nothing but he was determined to make something of himself. He started with a borrowed barrow selling apples. When he'd saved enough he bought the barrow. Now he owns the fruit wholesaler's he bought those apples from, amongst lots of other businesses. He brought me and my brother up without any doubt we had to earn every penny we received and there were no privileges for us. We went to ordinary schools and had to work for our pocket money. My father was determined we should have no better start in life than he did. He wanted us to learn the hard way, just like him. He might be my father, Frankie, but he's a hard man, let me tell you. And my mother sides with everything he said. She came from the same sort of background and felt it right that we worked hard for what we got, the same way they did.

'My father's latest idea was going into the car spares line. That's what I was helping to set up in Leicester. He'd ploughed a lot of money into setting up a business, with the help of Susan's father who's connected to the Rootes family who own the car factory in Coventry. Of course, that won't happen now.'

'Oh!' Frankie exclaimed.

'And not only have I wrecked this business deal but, by marrying you, I've humiliated a member of the Rootes family which will never be forgiven. They'll make sure my father's name is mud in Coventry, believe me. The Rootes are very powerful people. So you can imagine why he's so furious.'

She nodded gravely. 'Yes, I can.'

A rush of satisfaction filled Eddie. He couldn't believe how readily she was believing his fabricated story.

Frankie meanwhile was feeling wretched as the full extent of what he had given up for her hit her full force. He must love me very much indeed to shoulder the loss of all he had, she thought. 'Oh, dear,' she uttered. Her mind whirled frantically but the solution was obvious. 'Eddie, we could always . . .'

'Always what?'

'Get an annulment.'

He grabbed her to him, crushing her tightly. 'I'll tell you the same as I told my father – the answer is no. Don't ever talk like this again, Frankie, you hear? They've made their decision, I've made mine. You're my wife and if they can't accept you as that then they've lost their son.' He released her and stood up. 'I'll get a job. Of course I've only ever worked for my father, but someone will take me on. Lewis's have a men's department . . .'

'Oh, Eddie, you'd hate it!' she cried. 'Someone like you being reduced to selling men's clothes.'

'It's a job, Frankie, until I find something better. I know a bit about cars,' he added casually, throwing her the bait.

'Do you?'

'Enough to know where an oil filter goes.'

She stared at him thoughtfully. 'We've just lost a mechanic at the garage and it doesn't look like he's coming back. I can't promise anything as it's a fully skilled man we need to replace Taffy but I'll ask my . . .'

'I'll take anything, Frankie,' he interrupted. 'I don't care what as long as I'm bringing in something to help keep us. I can always find something better paid after. I'd soon pick it all up, I'm a quick learner.'

She was warmed by his eagerness to do anything to provide for her. Working in a garage was going to be a big come down for him. If her uncle did agree to give him work, the pay wouldn't be that great. But as Eddie said, it was just a breathing space until he found something more suited to him. It surprised her to realise that her feelings for him were growing warmer. As Eddie said, maybe it wouldn't take long for her to fall totally in love with him. She certainly liked everything she had learned about him so far. And in bed last night, he'd made her feel very special indeed. A thrill ran down her spine at the memory. 'I'll see what I can do. And we have to find somewhere to live, Eddie,' she said. Taking a deep breath, she sighed heavily. 'But first it's my turn to face my family. I'm not looking forward to this, but one thing I do know is that whatever their reaction, I won't be disowned. And as my choice of husband, you'll be welcomed into the family.'

He was glad to hear that. 'I'll come with you,' he offered, inwardly hoping she'd decline. Let her smooth the way first, he thought, then he'd win her father over with his charm.

'Thanks, Eddie, but I must do this on my own, like you had to do.' She smiled at him wanly. 'Besides, I think you've been through enough trauma for one day.'

'I'll wait for you here, shall I?' And while she was away, he thought, he could collect his belongings from his lodgings. If he was lucky old Mrs Herbert would be out and he could get away without paying what was due to her, put it with the few pounds he had left from the last lot of wallets he had lifted to fund his future.

Frankie reached up and kissed him on the lips, nodding. 'I'll try not to be long.'

She had reached the door when he called across to her. 'Oh, Frankie?'

'Yes?'

'You must promise me you'll never try to approach my family in any way. I'd never forgive you if you did.'

'No, of course I won't.'

He nodded, relieved. 'Good. Because I've finished with them and that's final.' Then he eyed her uncomfortably. 'I've . . . er . . . no money, Frankie. Well, not enough to settle the hotel bill, only for my lodgings. It's a nice place, didn't come cheap, but then when I booked in little did I know the situation I'd be in. My father has already put a stop to my drawing money from the family account. To be honest, Frankie, I've only got a couple of changes of clothes to my name, all I brought with me for this business trip. My father wouldn't allow me to get any of my things. Sent me out the same way I came in, to use his words.'

'Oh, I see. Well . . . I should have enough to cover the hotel bill in my savings account. I'll draw it out and settle up when I come back. As for everything else . . .' She gave him a smile of encouragement. 'We'll manage.'

'I'll make it up to you, Frankie.'

He looked so dejected she automatically ran back, threw her arms around him and hugged him tightly. 'It'll be all right, Eddie. Anyway, we're married now and what's mine is yours.'

My sentiments exactly, he thought.

Chapter Nineteen

'Oh, Sam,' Nancy wailed. 'Our little girl married, without even telling us! I can't believe it, I really can't.' She looked across at Frankie, her eyes blazing with anger. 'And have you any idea, young lady, what yer put us through last night by not coming home? I was frantic, Frankie. I was getting to think you'd bin murdered or summat.'

'I'm sorry, Mam,' she said remorsefully.

'Sorry? Is that all yer've got ter say for yerself?'

'Now come on, old girl,' Sam soothed. 'As long as our Frankie's happy, what does it matter? She's explained how it happened and . . . well . . . we have to accept it.'

'Oh, what would you know?' cried his wife, dabbing an already sodden handkerchief to her tear-filled eyes. 'A mother dreams about her daughter's wedding from the minute she's born. How could you do this to me, Frankie? How could you?'

Head bowed, Frankie's face was filled with shame. 'I didn't mean to do you out of a wedding, Mam. As I told you, it just happened. Eddie said he couldn't see the point of waiting . . .'

'Frankie,' she erupted. 'There's waiting and there's waiting. You could have waited long enough to introduce us to him, surely? Only days ago you were moping around over Ian, and now you're married to someone else.' A thought struck her. 'You've married this man on the rebound, that's what you've done. You could get an annulment. She could, Sam, we could . . .'

'Mother, I didn't marry Eddie for any other reason than because . . . because . . .'

'Because she loves him, Nancy,' Sam gently cut in. 'That's why our gel has married this man, and why else would he want to marry her unless it's for love? It's not like we've money or anything of value that he's marrying her for, is it?'

Nancy sniffed. 'No, I s'pose not.' She sniffed again, patted her wet face and chirped, 'Not unless he's after yer inheritance, Frankie.' She joked, giving a half-hearted laugh.

'Oh, Mam,' Frankie laughed, glad that the tension was broken.

Sighing deeply, Nancy shook her head, then held out her arms to Frankie. 'Come here and give us a hug.'

Frankie shot over to her and Nancy embraced her and kissed her forehead. 'This'll tek some getting used to. But I suppose over the years I've had to get over worse.' She pulled away from Frankie and smiled affectionately at her. 'Now you'd better fetch this new husband of yours so me and yer dad can give him the once over.'

After Frankie had left, Sam patted his wife's arm. 'I'm proud of you, Nancy.'

She breathed in deeply, and clasped his hand. 'I'm proud of meself, Sam. This has broken my heart. But then yer right, my old darlin'. If this man makes our Frankie happy then so should we be. From what she sez he's given up everything for her so the least we can do is try and do a bit of making up by welcoming the lad into our family.'

'What! I've heard of some excuses for taking a day off without notice but never this one, Frankie Champion.'

'It's not an excuse and it's true, Uncle Wally. And I'm Francine Taylor now.'

Wally stared at her searchingly, the shock of what Frankie had just told him still showing on his face. 'Seems only five minutes ago since I paced yer backroom with yer dad while yer mam was upstairs giving birth to you. And here you are, married.' He looked at her fondly. 'I ain't surprised this man fell head over heels for yer, Frankie, me darlin', 'cos yer as pretty as a picture and with a lovely nature too. If I wasn't yer uncle and old enough ter be yer dad, I'd have snapped yer up meself. Yer mam and dad took it all right then?'

She gave a wan smile. 'They're very upset but they've been great about it all, Uncle Wally.'

'Not much else they can be, Frankie. They love you too much to boot you up the backside and out into the street, which is what you deserve, young lady.' He took a deep breath and shook his head. 'I don't mean that. I just know they'll both be so upset not to have seen you married, especially yer mam, and I expect we'll suffer a few jibes for the next few months 'til she gets over it. If she ever does, that is. Now come on, tell me about this new husband of yours?'

A while later he nodded thoughtfully. 'He must love you, Frankie, to give up what he says he has for you, that's all I can say.'

'Could you find him something, Uncle Wally? Please, he'll do anything.'

'It's a trained mechanic I need, Frankie. I couldn't pay much for someone who's hardly more than a labourer. Oh, take that stricken look off yer face. I'll talk to him, but more than that at the moment I ain't promising.'

She leapt over and hugged him. 'Thanks, Uncle Wally.'

'Ged off, yer daft bugger,' he said, chuckling and playfully pushing her away. 'Now, to more important matters. Where are you going to live?'

She shrugged her shoulders. 'That's a worry, isn't it? It's something that doesn't cross your mind when you're getting carried away by everything else. I'm hoping Mam and Dad will let us stay in my room for the time being.'

'Well, I've a better offer.'

'You have?'

'Taffy's old house is probably still going begging. I'll see if I can secure it for you and as a wedding present pay the first couple of months' rent. How does that sound?'

'Oh,' she cried joyfully, 'Uncle Wally, that would be wonderful!'

'It'll give you a start.'

'Taffy left all his furniture according to the woman next door.'

'Then ain't you a lucky bugger?' Wally grinned. 'Most young couple start with n'ote. I'm sure Taffy would be delighted to know you're getting some use out of it.'

'I hope he's all right,' she said, her face filling with sudden sadness. 'Taffy, I mean.'

'I'm sure he is,' said Wally reassuringly, patting her hand. 'Anyway, he knows damn' well where his friends are if not. Right then, Miss Cham— Mrs Taylor,' he corrected. 'You'd better go and fetch that husband of yours. After the reception he got from his own family I bet he's pacing the floor in case you get the same. I'll come around to yer mam and dad's after work and have a chat with him.'

She grinned at him cheekily. 'You're giving me the rest of the day off, Uncle Wally?'

He laughed. 'It's a good job you're a married woman or I'd scalp yer arse! Anyway the day is practically over so it ain't worth making you work the rest of it. You'll make up for it tomorrow, though,' he warned. 'Now go on, get off back to that old man of yours before I change me mind. Bernard!' he shouted. 'Sorry, lad, yer date's off, yer working late tonight.'

★ ★ ★

The lodging house appeared empty when Eddie arrived. He deftly let himself inside. Immediately the smell of stale cooked food and years of neglect greeted him and he wrinkled his nose in disgust. He remembered the clean and tastefully decorated hotel room with its comfortable bed, spotless sink and fresh towels. He'd had a taste of luxury and he liked it. Frankie's father's house was bound to be nicely furnished though, him having his own business, and they more than likely had a woman in to clean. Eddie smiled smugly to himself. This was the last time he was ever going to stay in a place so dire. From now on he was on his way up.

Leaving the larger of the suitcases still filled with a few spares he and his brother had stolen from Rootes for the landlady to do as she wished with, he packed the smaller one with the new clothes he'd added to the first lot he'd stolen when he arrived in Leicester and crept down the stairs again. He had just reached the bottom when out of nowhere a big lump of a man dressed in a policeman's uniform stepped before him, blocking his route.

He pulled out his truncheon and waved it at Eddie. 'Not leaving wi'out settling yer bill, are yer, Mr Taylor?' he demanded.

Eddie stared at him, paralysed in shock. 'Er . . . I'm not leaving at all, Constable, I was just going out. I'll be back later.'

'It's Sergeant,' he corrected. 'And if yer not leaving, why have yer got yer suitcase with yer? We might look it, but we ain't daft, a' we, Mam?'

Mam? Mrs Herbert was this policeman's mother? Oh, shit!

The aged landlady appeared next to him. 'Five pound ten shilling you owe me, Mr Taylor,' she said, holding out a gnarled hand.

'How much?' Eddie exclaimed, dumbfounded.

'Three weeks' board, food, and interest fer late payment.'

'You must be joking,' he scoffed.

'Oh, we don't joke,' she cackled. 'Now either yer pay up voluntary or me son will make you wish you had. Won't yer, me ducky?' she said, beaming up at him.

'Love to, Mam,' he sneered, poking the truncheon in Eddie's stomach.

He had no choice but to pay what they demanded and he knew it. Putting down his suitcase, he grudgingly pulled out his wallet from his inside coat pocket and counted out his dues. Face as black as thunder, he thrust it at Mrs Herbert.

'Would yer like a receipt?' she chuckled, snatching it.

'Fuck off,' he hissed as he grabbed his suitcase and, with only a few pounds left to his name, made to march from the house.

'Just a minute,' the policeman called after him.

Eddie stopped and turned. 'What is it now, Sergeant?'

He held out three wallets and flapped them at Eddie. 'Just a matter of these?'

Eddie eyed them, recognising them as ones he had stolen and which he had thought he had disposed of. He raised his eyes to the policeman. 'What about them?' he asked innocently.

The man smirked. 'Mother saw you put them in the dustbin. That right, Mother?'

'That's right, son. Late at night it was when you thought I was sleeping,' she said, grinning at Eddie.

'Now what man in his right mind would throw away three good wallets? And don't try and give me any cock and bull, Mr Taylor. I reckon you've been a naughty boy. What do you reckon, Mother?'

'Oh, definitely, son. I can spot a thief a mile off and this one's got all the hallmarks.'

Eddie gulped, a vision of jail looming. 'What do you want?' he worriedly asked.

The policeman's smirk widened. 'It's your lucky day, boy, 'cos I'm a reasonable copper, me. I'll give you a choice. Pay me to keep quiet else I'll march you down the station and make sure they lock you up for a very long time.'

Edie was cornered and he knew it. Reluctantly he once again pulled out his wallet, extracting the last of his stolen booty.

The policeman snatched the notes off him and counted them. 'This'll do nicely.' He leaned forward and with his truncheon prodded Eddie hard in his chest. 'I'll be watching out for you in future and I'll be warning all me colleagues too. Step outta line and you'll bloody wish you hadn't. Now get lost before I change me mind.'

Eddie didn't need another telling. Spinning on his heel, he bolted from the house.

Mother and son turned and faced each other. Mrs Herbert held out her hand. 'Fifty-fifty,' she demanded.

Her son scowled. 'Yer a bloody villain, you are, Mother.'

Mother and son looked at one another and burst into fits of laughter.

'Oh, son,' Mrs Herbert giggled, eyeing him. 'That bleddy uniform you got from the fancy dress shop don't half come in handy.'

The fear of God on him, Eddie fled all the way back to the hotel. He stood for several moments outside looking worriedly up and down the street in case the policeman had followed him. Satisfied he hadn't, Eddie took several deep breaths to compose himself before walking inside to check if Frankie had returned. As he crossed the foyer towards the lift, the hotel manager approached him. 'Will sir be needing the room another night?' he politely enquired.

Still smarting from his confrontation with the Herbert's, he snapped, 'No, *sir* won't.'

'Oh, well, in that case, sir, it is the hotel's policy that guests should vacate their room by eleven so our chambermaids can get it ready for the next guest's arrival.' He looked at his watch. 'It's now after four, sir.'

'Do I look like I can't tell the time?' Eddie sneered.

'Not at all, sir, It's just . . .'

His face clouded darkly. 'Oh, I get it. You think we're going to do a runner.'

'A runner, sir?'

'Don't come the innocent with me.' Eddie leaned towards him, his expression thunderous. 'Now you listen to me, you jumped-up clerk. My father could buy this hotel ten times over and still have change. I'll vacate the room when I'm good and . . .'

'Anything wrong?' Frankie asked worriedly as she came up to join them.

Eddie spun round to face her. 'Oh . . . hello, darling,' he greeted her, remembering to act the fond husband by planting a kiss on her cheek. 'The hotel clerk,' he said, purposely demoting the man, 'was just enquiring if we needed the room for another night.' He eyed her intently. 'Do we need it for another night, Frankie?'

She secretly smiled. 'No. Everything's fine, Eddie. And don't ask me anything more because I want it to be a surprise.' She beamed happily. 'You deserve something nice after what you've been through.' Discreetly she slipped a five-pound note she had withdrawn from her savings account into his hand, an amount it had taken her weeks to save and, as she had thought at the time, towards her marriage to Ian. 'If you want to settle up, we can go.'

He felt excited. From what Frankie had told him he could only deduce she had won her father over. She was going to surprise him, she had said. His heart leapt. A partnership in the garage as a wedding present? It had to be something momentous to account for the radiant smile on Frankie's face. At any rate, if they weren't needing the room again, they were being offered somewhere to live. Maybe that was it. The father was going to buy them a house as well as give Eddie a partnership. He looked cockily at the manager. 'As you heard my wife say, we won't be needing the room another night. Lead the way, my good man, and I'll settle the bill.'

Chapter Twenty

Eddie was most surprised when they got off the bus several streets away from where he knew Frankie's house was – the immaculate-looking semi he had followed her to a few nights previously – and she then proceeded to guide him down several terraced side streets. Must be a short cut, he assumed. Then he frowned, bewildered, when she suddenly said, 'Here we are.' She stopped and turned to face him. 'Are you all right?' she asked.

'Er . . . yes, fine,' he answered.

She smiled encouragingly. 'Come on then, they're expecting us.'

His mind whirled. They?

Before he had time to question her she had turned into an entry separating two flat-fronted terraced houses in the middle of a long row of the same. His bewilderment mounted when he hurriedly glanced around the small yard they entered which was strewn with all manner of motor parts. A half-dismantled motorbike was propped up on bricks by the outhouse and two older-looking bikes were lying against the perimeter wall. But before he could question Frankie the back door burst open and a homely-looking woman stood on the threshold, beaming at them.

'There yer are,' she exclaimed, arms wide in welcome. 'We was beginning ter think yer'd got lost. Come on in,' she beckoned.

Frankie turned to Eddie. 'See, I told you everything was all right. Put your case down here a minute and come and meet my mam and dad.'

Mam and dad? Eddie's thoughts whirled even faster. Had she really said, *mam* and dad? No, he must have heard her wrong. Frankie didn't have a mother surely?

Following her into the tiny backroom he was most perturbed to find that as well as a man in a wheelchair by the fire – obviously Frankie's father – there was another sitting in the armchair opposite. Eddie immediately recognised him as the fair-haired mechanic he'd observed from his hiding place across the street from the garage. What was he doing here?

Frankie turned to Eddie, smiling. 'This is my dad, Samuel Champion,' she said proudly.

Sam held out his hand in greeting. 'Hello, son. Nice ter meet yer.'

Automatically Eddie shook his hand. 'Nice to meet you, Mr Champion.' He hoped he sounded suitably respectful.

'My Uncle Wally,' Frankie said, smiling warmly at the fair-haired man.

His hand outstretched, Wally stood up and walked towards Eddie. 'Welcome to the Champion family. I hope you know what you've let yerself in for,' he added, a twinkle in his eye.

Uncle! Eddie fought to keep his composure as slowly a feeling of foreboding began to niggle in his stomach. He automatically accepted Wally's hand.

'My mother, Nancy Champion,' Frankie then said, turning to Nancy.

Mother! So he hadn't misheard Frankie. Eddie's heart thumped painfully. This was all wrong. Stella had said Frankie had no mother and she had never even mentioned the existence of an uncle.

'Welcome to the family, Edwin.' Nancy smiled also, stretching out her hand in greeting. 'I hope yer like cottage pie?'

'Eh?' he answered deeply distracted.

'Cottage pie. For yer dinner. Well, it was short notice, you have ter agree. We'll have a proper celebration meal soon, though, I promise yer. Now, you tek yer coat off and mek yerself comfortable. Have a nice chat with Frankie's father and Uncle Wally while we'll see to the dinner. Come on, Frankie,' she ordered.

'Well, he's a good-looking fella,' Nancy whispered, impressed, when they were out of earshot. 'Nearly as good-looking as yer dad was when he was that age. I just hope he treats yer as well, that's all I can say, Frankie, and yer both as happy as me and yer dad have bin.' Tears welled up in her eyes and she sniffed. 'Oh, don't mind me, me duck, this is all a bit too much.'

'Oh, Mam,' she said, throwing her arms around her and hugging her tight. 'I've not quite taken it in myself but I can only thank you for how you're all being.'

'Well, as yer dad said, what's done is done and we just have ter get on with it.' Nancy smiled encouragingly. 'Now, the dinner's all prepared, we're just waiting for it to finish cooking.' She checked two pans bubbling merrily on the stove. 'We'll leave the men to it for a bit so how about I mash a cuppa? I bet you could do with one.'

In the backroom Eddie was staring at the two men facing him, his heart sinking rapidly as the truth of the situation dawned.

'So, our Frankie bowled you over and you couldn't wait to get that ring on her finger?' Sam was saying.

'Pardon? Oh, yes, er . . . that's right,' he answered, shifting position uneasily.

'Well, I can't say that her mother and meself are exactly jumping with joy but we love our daughter and we'll do our best to welcome you into the family, lad.' Sam's face grew grave. 'Our Frankie's explained the reception you got from yer own folks. Still, give 'em time, lad, they'll come around, I'm sure.' He gave a sudden grin. 'Tek that look of doom off yer face, we ain't gonna bite yer. I expect this is daunting for you, meeting Frankie's folks, especially after whisking her off her feet like that. If it meks yer feel any better it's as bad for us meeting you. Now we can't do much by way of helping yer out money-wise but we can offer you both a roof over yer head 'til yer get yerselves sorted, so you needn't worry about that.'

A knot tightened in Eddie's stomach. A room in Frankie's parents' house was not the kind of accommodation he had been expecting to be offered. Nevertheless at this moment he couldn't afford to appear ungrateful. 'That's very good of you,' he said.

'Yes, well, talking of that,' Wally piped up. 'I don't know whether our Frankie's mentioned anything to you but I know of a house that's going for rent. It's not a bad little place. I popped around to see the landlord on my way here and I hope yer don't think it presumptuous of me but I secured it for you before anyone else got in. I've paid two months' rent as my wedding present. You can move in at the end of next week. I hope that's to your liking?'

A house was a far better prospect than a room with her parents. 'That's very good of you,' said Eddie.

Wally smiled. 'Well, it's somewhere of yer own and newly marrieds need their own place.'

'Yes, they do,' chipped in Sam. 'When me and Frankie's mam married we lived for quite a while with my folks. I can't fault them for how welcome they made us but, well, it's not to be recommended unless there's no other choice.'

'As to work,' said Wally, 'Frankie said you've been working for your dad?'

Eddie cleared his throat. 'Yes, er . . . that's right. Mainly helping him to set things up. His businesses, that sort of thing.'

Wally nodded, impressed. 'Teks brains to do that. Successful, was he?'

Eddie prayed he wasn't about to be interrogated on his fictitious father's means of acquiring his equally as fictitious wealth. 'Yes, very. It's a dreadful blow to me how he's cut me off. Look, er . . . please don't think it rude of me but what happened this afternoon . . . well, it's upset me.'

'Oh, yes, Eddie, we understand. 'Course yer upset,' cut in Sam. 'We didn't mean to cross examine you.'

'No, no, we didn't, not at all,' said Wally, and hurriedly changed the subject by asking, 'Frankie said you know a bit about cars?'

I should do, Eddie thought scathingly. Having worked in that blasted car factory for all those years. But why was the uncle asking him all this, as though he was conducting an interview and not Frankie's dad who owned the garage? And he wished they would both stop addressing him as 'lad'. It was really annoying him. 'My father has had several and I liked to tinker around with them.'

'That tinkering might have held you in good stead then, lad,' Wally replied. 'I'm not sure yet what I can offer you until I see what you can do, but d'yer fancy coming down to the garage with Frankie termorrow and we'll take it from there?'

Eddie looked at Sam keenly. 'You could offer me a job until I get something else, Mr Champion. I'd be most grateful, I must say. I intend to look after your daughter as best I possibly can.'

'That's very gratifying to hear,' Sam replied. 'And I hope I don't need ter tell you that should you do otherwise, you'll have me and her uncle to deal with. But as to me offering you a job, well, much as I'd like to my little business only just supports Mrs Champion and myself.'

Eddie eyed him, mystified. 'I don't understand, Mr Champion?'

Sam grimaced. 'What don't you understand?'

'Well, you've just offered me a job of some sort in your garage and now you're saying it only just supports you and Mrs Champion?'

Sam chuckled. 'My little backyard can hardly be classed as a garage. It's Wally that's offering to try and do something for yer, not me.'

Eddie paled. 'Wally?'

Sam nodded. 'He owns the garage.'

Eddie's face drained. 'Oh! But I thought . . .'

'Thought what?' Wally cut in, frowning. Then he eyed him in concern. 'Is there anything wrong, lad? You've gone all white.'

Eddie was reeling from the shock of his discovery. His conversation with Stella flooded back to him and he saw now all the clues he'd failed to spot at the time. Oh, God, this terrible situation was all his own fault. What a fool he'd been not to realise there were two Champions, not one. It was the uncle's garage, not the father's. Oh, hell, his mind screamed. What have I done? His whole body sagged as the vision of his bright new future began to fade then die. He'd just been stupid enough to marry a woman he didn't care a jot for in the mistaken belief that their marriage would be his salvation, the springboard which would catapult him to a lucrative life. Now he'd no money, nowhere to go, and the added dreadful fear that the police were watching him in Leicester as well as Coventry. To make matters worse, if that were possible, he'd solemnly promised his brother a roof and a living when he'd got out of jail.

He felt a desperate desire to jump up, grab his belongings and make a run for it, but he couldn't. His dire circumstances dictated he was stuck with this situation for the immediate future. All he could do for the time being was make the best of it while he planned a way out. Swallowing hard, he placed a charming smile on his face. 'I'm sorry, it just after all that's happened today, I'm so confused.'

Sam nodded in understanding. 'That's all right, son, we can appreciate how yer must be feeling. Let's talk about other things, eh? But just let me ask first if you're happy with what Wally's offering because if yer'd sooner get summat yerself then we'd understand, wouldn't we?'

'Oh, yes,' Wally said, embarrassed. 'I'm only trying to help, that's all.'

'What you're trying to do is much appreciated,' Eddie cut in hurriedly. 'I think you're being most generous, Mr Champion, and I'd be delighted to come down tomorrow and show you what I can do.'

Wally smiled, relieved. 'Good, then that's settled. Nancy,' he shouted, 'are we getting any dinner tonight or does a man die of starvation in this house?'

Much later that night Frankie perched on the edge of her bed, dressed in her best cotton nightdress – wishing she had something a lot more fitting for a new bride to wear – and watching Eddie as he got undressed. Without warning a vision of Ian rose before her and a sudden wave of sadness enveloped her for her loss of him. For a fleeting moment she wondered what he was doing. If he thought of her at all. If he missed her like she did him. Then feeling guilty and disloyal to her new husband she pushed all thoughts of Ian to the back of her mind, knowing that was where they must stay. She was married to Eddie now. To quote her mother, she had made her bed and she must lie on it.

'This must all be very strange for you?' she said to him softly.

He stopped unbuttoning his shirt and looked across at her. 'What do you mean?'

She sighed. 'I mean that where I live must be . . . well, very different from what you're used to.'

Despite the wretchedness he was feeling at the terrible blow he'd suffered, he wanted to laugh at the absurdity of Frankie's assumptions. There she was feeling remorse for the fact that these surroundings were so below him when in fact the opposite was the truth. This house could not compare to anything someone with means would live in, but compared to what he was used to it was indeed a little palace and the occupants more than a cut above the people who had been responsible for giving him life.

He looked as though he was making a great sacrifice. 'I'll get used to it, Frankie. Losing a few home comforts is a small sacrifice to make for what I'm gaining.' He smiled winningly at her. 'And to be honest, I was getting tired of working for my father. He wouldn't give me any proper responsibility.' He heaved a sad sigh. 'Being cut off from my family has shocked me rigid, Frankie, I can't deny that, but all the same it's about time I stood on my own two feet. I'm looking forward to working for your uncle,' he lied.

A warm glow filled Frankie on hearing his words. She went to him and hugged him tightly.

He inwardly groaned, wishing she would leave him alone. It irked his male pride to know that Frankie did not love him, but she was growing very fond of him, that much he did know. Quite naturally she would expect him to make love to her tonight but that was the last thing he felt like doing. She aroused no feelings of that sort within him. He had quite easily faked it last night, driven by the mistaken belief it was a means to an end. But that drive was gone now. Much to his annoyance, though, he still needed to act the husband towards her for the foreseeable future. He bent his head, kissing her lightly on her forehead. 'You know I love you,' he lied.

She smiled up at him, eyes tender. 'Yes,' she whispered, having no reason to believe otherwise and wishing wholeheartedly she felt the same towards him so she could respond accordingly. But if the feelings she was beginning to experience now were any judge, she'd soon be able to.

His face grew troubled and he looked towards the bed then back to her. 'I want you, Frankie, so much it's like a fire within me. But I couldn't, not with your parents so close.'

She took a deep breath and smiled wanly. 'Oh, of course, I understand, Eddie. Not to worry, we're moving into our own place soon.'

He nodded, kissing her lightly on her forehead again. 'I can't wait,' he lied.

In the room next door Nancy heard the springs on Frankie's bed creak as the pair got into bed. She turned over, pulling the covers over her head.

Sam, sensing her discomfort, reached out and placed a reassuring hand on her arm. 'You all right, old gel?' he whispered.

Nancy grunted and turned over to face him. 'No, I ain't. I can't get used ter the fact that our little girl is a married woman, and I can't say as I feel comfortable knowing they're both next door. It wouldn't bother me so much if I knew Eddie better but it's like our Frankie's just got into bed with a stranger, if yer understand my meaning.'

Sam sighed. 'I understand love, I'm having the same trouble. You like Eddie well enough, though, don't yer?'

'Yes, I've got to admit I do. It's teking all me strength not to go and find that family of his and try and mek them see reason, but as Frankie's promised Eddie she'll never do anything like that, I can't either, can I?'

'No, yer can't,' Sam insisted. 'All we can do, Nancy, is try our best ter be good to him. Of course we'd never replace his own mam and dad but let's hope in the future they'll both mellow and want to make amends.'

'Yes, let's hope. I have ter say, Eddie's left me in no doubt how much he loves our Frankie and that's the main thing. And I can't deny he's a good-looking chap all right. I just hope ter God the difference in their backgrounds won't cause any problems. He seems to have his head screwed on so I've no doubt he knew what he was doing. It's our Frankie that bothers me,' she said thoughtfully.

'What d'yer mean by that, lovey?'

'Oh, I dunno really, Sam, just summat niggling me. Frankie's done her best to convince me she's not married Eddie on the rebound, but I'm not so sure. Still, she *has* married him and whether she's still harbouring feelings for Ian or not, she'll have to get on with it. You like Eddie well enough, don't yer, Sam?'

'Yes, I do. And he seems very willing to do any kind of work to support our Frankie, so I can't fault that. Pity I can't offer him summat meself. Let's just hope our Wally can. Anyway, me darlin',' he said, tenderly running his hand down the side of her face, 'in a week or so the youngsters will be moving to their own place and if I know you, you'll be in your element helping them get settled in. Sounds a nice little house.'

'Yes, it does,' she mused. 'And the furniture that's bin left will help.' She giggled as a memory struck her. 'Remember when we moved into those rooms after we left your mam and dad's? We were so chuffed at having our own place but we'd hardly 'ote to our names. We slept on that old settee Aunt Flo gave us for months, do you remember?'

'I do, Nancy, how could I forget? My backside still bears the scars of those springs. And you trying to cook on that old range! You could never get the fire going in it properly. Some of the dinners you dished up and expected me to eat defied belief.'

Nancy laughed too. 'Well, at least our gel won't have to suffer anything like we did. She'll be all right, won't she, Sam?'

''Course she will. Besides, we're hardly four streets away, you can check for yerself that she is. Eh, but not too often, Nancy. I don't want you turning into an interfering mother-in-law.'

'As if I would,' she said indignantly, and leaned over and pecked him on his cheek. ''Night, Sam.'

''Night, night, me darlin'.'

Chapter Twenty-One

Eddie smoothed his hand over the bonnet of the black Triumph TR3 sports car, gazing at it enviously. What a beauty it was, and what he'd give to own a car such as this. He gave a dissatisfied sigh. As matters stood, some hope he'd ever have of owning a pushbike, let alone a car. The money he was paid for his labours hardly covered the rent, let alone luxuries. He supposed he was being unfair. The four pounds a week Wally paid him was very generous considering his lack of experience, and he was also training him as a mechanic. Eddie being Eddie was a master at making people believe he was working hard when in reality he was hardly doing anything at all, so in truth he was being paid well over the odds. And they had Frankie's wages too, more than some young couples had to manage on, but both put together still didn't amount to much when bills had to be paid.

He glanced across at Frankie, her head stuck under the bonnet of a Singer Vogue, seemingly so happy in her own little world she was oblivious to anything that was going on around her. He felt no affection for her. Many men would give anything to have what he possessed, but not Eddie. As far as he was concerned he had a boring job, was married to a boring little housewife, and they lived in a dreary little house in an equally dreary street. Their social life consisted mainly of a visit to the pub on a Friday evening, the odd time by himself during the week, the occasional visit to the pictures, money permitting, and tea round at her parents' every other Saturday afternoon. A far cry from the life he had expected when he had married her.

For nearly a year he'd been in this dire situation. For almost twelve long months he had not put a foot wrong, faultlessly acting the part of the doting husband, dutiful employee, courteous son-in-law, always acutely conscious of the need not to give anyone a reason to become suspicious of him, especially the police. He knew he'd fooled everyone into believing he was a thoroughly decent man and that was the main thing as far as Eddie was concerned.

And his twelve months of patience hadn't been entirely wasted. Eddie now knew what he would do when his brother was released from jail. He and Neil would go to another town and start up a second-hand car sales business. Financing it was going to be easy. Before he left Eddie planned to help himself to Champion's takings. It would be simple. All he had to do was keep his head down until the day Neil was released.

Of course his brother knew none of this, Eddie not having had the opportunity of going to see him since the one and only time he had, on the day he married. His brother, he knew, would be disappointed that the garage plan hadn't come to fruition but once he heard Eddie's idea of selling cars and saw the stolen money his disappointment would quickly vanish.

Eddie eyed the car again and imagined driving in it along a deserted country road, a gorgeous brunette reclining in the passenger seat, looking at him adoringly. He'd be seeking a secluded spot where they could eat their picnic lunch from a hamper of delicacies from Simpkins and James, washed down with Champagne, then for afters they'd make passionate love until she begged for mercy.

'I bet I can guess what you're thinking.'

Eddie jumped and turned to find Wally at the side of him. He secretly smiled. I bet you can't, he thought.

'She's some car,' said Wally. 'Wouldn't mind one meself. The owner is one of those young upstarts who works in the city in some finance company and has a rich daddy to boot. A customer of ours recommended he try us to do the service as his usual garage couldn't fit him in. With a bit of luck he'll be happy with us and tell his posh chums and then we'll get their business too.' He glanced over the car again and said, 'I've always bin a motorbike man meself but I think it's about time I got meself a car.'

Eddie looked at him. 'You do?'

Wally nodded. 'Nothing grand, just something small to take Hilary out in for a run in the country.'

Eddie fought to hide the disdain he felt for the man standing next to him. He owned a garage, for Christ's sake. A busy one at that. Eddie couldn't understand why his employer had never had his own car before, and surely he could afford to buy himself a decent one. 'That'll be nice,' he said flatly.

Wally ran his hand lovingly over the bonnet of the Triumph. 'A car like this makes a statement, though, doesn't it? It tells people you are somebody. But another garage is top of my list before I ever contemplate such an expensive toy.' He took a deep breath. 'Maybe one day, eh? Until then it's back to the grindstone. Have you finished doing that oil change, Eddie?'

'Near enough,' he replied matter-of-factly.

'Right, well, when you have, if you want to join me down in the pit you can help me take a gear box out then we can go over it together to find out what's wrong.' He slapped Eddie on his arm in friendly fashion. 'Let's hope it's fixable or the owner is in for a bit of a shock, poor chap.'

As Wally crossed over to the pit, Eddie looked over at the car again, Wally's words returning to him. He was so right, he thought. A car like this was a statement. It told people so much about you, that you were someone important – someone with money at any rate. He suddenly wanted this car so badly he felt his insides burn with longing.

'You all right, Eddie?'

He turned his head to see Frankie approaching. As usual she looked dreadfully unattractive to him in her baggy working overalls, her face and hands all caked in grease, nothing like the brunette he had just visualised in the car beside him on their imaginary outing. And being with his wife every minute of the day he seemed never to be free of her, inwardly likening her to a jailer. 'I'm fine, why?' he said shortly.

'Oh, nothing. You looked miles away, that's all.'

'And who wouldn't, looking at a car like this?' he answered distractedly.

'Yes, it is nice, isn't it?' she said, appraising it. 'Pity we can't afford one. I can just see me and you whizzing along country lanes, the wind in our hair and not a care in the world, with some tinned salmon sandwiches and a flask of tea for a picnic lunch. Be wonderful, Eddie, wouldn't it?' she said, looking at him longingly.

His own vision rose before him again, more vivid this time. The brunette and he were speeding along, she looking stunning in a tight red dress, the skirt having ridden up exposing her shapely legs, her full breasts overspilling the low-cup top. She was staring at him seductively, licking her lips in anticipation of what was to come. He could feel a heaviness in his breast pocket and knew it was the weight of a wallet stuffed with money.

A sudden surge of desire to get in this car and drive away raged within him and before he could stop himself his frustration boiled over and he hissed, 'Some fucking hope we've got of ever owning a car like this!'

Frankie gawped at him, shocked at the savageness of his tone. 'What did you say, Eddie?'

He glared at her, then it suddenly hit him what he had blurted out and he forced his face to soften. 'Look, I'm sorry.' He apologised with great difficulty as it was the last thing he felt like doing. He ran his hand over his forehead. 'I've got a flipping awful headache. It must be all those oil fumes getting to me.' His need to get out of the garage, away from Frankie to clear his head, overtook all else. 'I'm . . . er . . . just going to pop out for a bit of fresh air and I need to go and get some ciggies. I hardly had a dinner hour today so I'm due some time. Tell Wally I won't be long.'

'I could get your ciggies on the way home as I've to do some shopping anyway,' she offered.

God, this woman was getting on his nerves. Before he could stop himself he'd spun round to face her, eyes blazing. 'For Christ's sake, Frankie, do you have to scrutinise everything I do? I'm quite capable of going to the shops and buying my own cigarettes. You're not my mother.'

Stunned speechless by his outburst, she watched open-mouthed as he stripped off his grimy overalls, dropping them in his wake, and stormed out of the garage.

The walk to the shops did nothing to improve Eddie's mood and by home time he was ready to erupt in pure frustration at what he saw as his claustrophobic situation. He was in the office collecting a fresh tub of engine grease from the stock under the counter when a man burst in.

'Is my car ready?' he demanded, pulling out a wallet from his inside jacket pocket. 'Only I've got to get to the station and catch a train to London in less than thirty minutes. If I don't get that one I'll miss an important meeting and my boss won't be happy. It's the Humber with the broken fuel pump.'

Eddie glanced him over. He was smartly dressed in an immaculately cut dark blue suit, a trench coat over his arm, a fawn Homburg pushed back jauntily on his head. Obviously a successful businessman. He felt a surge of envy for the man's status, thinking it should be himself standing the other side of the counter demanding his car, not this man. Well, when he got his car sales business up and running it would be. 'I'll go and check,' he grunted surlily.

'Chap in the office come to collect the Humber.' He addressed

Wally's size nine boots, the rest of him being hidden under the car he was working on.

'Oh, bugger,' came the response. 'Can Frankie see to him? I'm wrestling with a stubborn bolt at the minute. The bloody thing is welded on, I think.'

'She's gone to road test that car she finished working on. Left ten minutes ago.'

'Oh. Well, you can manage, Eddie, can't you? Mr Wallace's bill is on the hook in the office along with his keys. The bill's self-explanatory. We replaced his broken fuel pump, tell him the car's purring like a kitten now.'

After nearly a year working here you're actually trusting me to take money, Eddie felt like saying. 'Yes, sure, Wally, leave it to me.'

He returned to the office and handed the customer his car keys and the bill, giving him Wally's message.

'Ah, good,' he said, gratified. 'Don't take offence but hopefully I shan't be seeing you for quite a while.'

He handed over a white five-pound note and Eddie unlocked the cash drawer to put it in and give him his change. Immediately his eyes fixed on the day's takings inside. There was at least thirty pounds, he quickly calculated, in notes and loose change. What he could do with that! Resisting his natural instinct to help himself, having no doubt that any theft would immediately be discovered and attributed to him, he quickly counted out the correct change and made to hand it over. Suddenly an idea struck him. He quickly weighed it up. It was brilliant. Too good an opportunity for the likes of Eddie to pass up.

'Can I just take a look at your bill, Mr Wallace?'

'Yes, sure,' he said, handing it back over. 'Is there a problem, only I've got to dash?'

Eddie pretended to scrutinise it. 'Ah, it's as I thought. Frankie hasn't added the extras.'

Frowning, Mr Wallace glanced worriedly at his wrist watch. 'Extras?' he questioned, bringing his eyes back to Eddie.

'Yes. After she'd finished fitting your fuel pump she noticed the spark plugs needed replacing as well as . . . er . . .' his mind raced and he blurted the first thing he could think of, hoping the man knew nothing about engines '. . . an adjustment to the rocker cover, which meant it had to be dismantled and put back together. Very time-consuming job that. Did you not notice a sort of clanking noise when you were driving along, Mr Wallace?' he asked, hoping the rocker cover did make such a noise though with his own limited knowledge he wasn't quite sure.

The customer's frown deepened. 'No. Can't say as I did.'

'Well, you soon would have. According to Frankie it's a wonder it hasn't caused you serious trouble before now.'

'Oh, I see. Well, trust her to spot it. And if she says it needed adjusting then I have no problem with that. Along with her uncle she's done me proud over the years, I've no complaints. Look, is there anything else only I really must be off or I'll miss that train,' he urged.

Eddie sighed with relief. Mr Wallace had fallen for his lie. 'Well, it's just a matter of payment. Frankie's been up to her eyes all day and she forgot to adjust your bill.'

'Oh, I see.' He hurried pulled out his wallet again, extracting another five-pound note. 'How much do I owe you?'

Eddie's answer was purposely slow in coming. 'Three pounds will cover it,' he eventually said.

The man frowned in surprise. 'That seems a bit steep.'

Eddie shook his head. 'Garage I used to work in before I came here would have charged you double that, let me tell you.'

'Really? Oh, well, my apologies. I shouldn't have questioned it. Mr Champion is more than fair with his charges,' he said, thrusting the money at Eddie.

Hiding a thrill of excitement he calmly took the note and split it into five single pound notes from the cash drawer. He gave two in change to Mr Wallace and with practised sleight of hand slipped the other three into his overalls pocket. He closed the drawer afterwards and locked it, hiding the key in its usual safe place where customers couldn't get to it.

'Hope you catch the train in plenty of time,' he called to Mr Wallace as the man ran out of the door. In fact Eddie didn't care a damn whether he did or he didn't.

'Satisfied customer?' Wally asked when Eddie returned to the garage.

And employee, he thought smugly, wondering how he could make such easy money again. 'Delighted, told me to tell you so.'

Chapter Twenty-Two

Despite still being upset by Eddie's rudeness to her earlier, nevertheless Frankie looked at him in concern when they were preparing to go home. 'You look really tired,' she said, not paying any heed to her own fatigue after a hectic day. 'I tell you what, when we get home, you put your feet up and relax while I'll cook you a nice meal.'

Eddie was far from tired. He had already made his mind up he was going out to have some fun with the money he'd stolen, and that fun certainly did not include Frankie. He knew exactly how to get out without her tagging along. He eyed with distaste the plate of food she put before him later at home. 'What's that?' he snapped, looking at it in disgust.

'Corned beef hash,' she said, sitting down opposite.

He pushed it away. 'I hate corned beef hash.'

She eyed him, surprised. 'But you've always said you love it, Eddie?'

'I lied,' he announced. Then added as an afterthought, 'I didn't want to hurt your feelings.'

'Oh!' she exclaimed, hurriedly scraping back her chair. 'Then I'll get you something else. What about egg and chips?'

'Egg and chips! I'm a man, Frankie. I've done a hard day's graft and I need a decent meal in my stomach.'

Her face crumpled. 'I know that, Eddie, and I do my best, but until we get our pay and you give me my housekeeping money, that's all we have in the pantry.' She eyed him worriedly. 'Has something happened, Eddie?'

'What do you mean?' he demanded.

'Well, to put you in such a mood. I've never seen you like this before. You've already had a go at me today and I'm not sure why. Is it something I've done?' she asked worriedly.

Being born to the wrong Champion is what you've done wrong, he wanted to shout at her. Slyly he glanced her over. He supposed many men would find her attractive, she had a nice shapely figure, but their months spent closeted together had done little to recommend her to him, he resented her too much. Resented the fact that through his own stupidity, which he'd never admit to anyone, he was saddled with her. The only thing he did appreciate, if appreciate was the right word to use, was how she looked after him. Not that he often thought to praise her, but he couldn't fault her housewifely abilities. After his years of doing everything for himself, being looked after was pure luxury to him and the only thing he would miss about Frankie when the day finally dawned when he could walk away from her.

At this moment, though, all he could think of was the three pounds burning a hole in his pocket and all he wanted to do was get out of this house alone to spend it. 'It's nothing you've done, Frankie,' he said, purposely sounding miserable. 'Don't ever think that.'

'Then what is it? I'm your wife, Eddie. If you can't talk to me, who can you talk to?'

You don't need to remind me of that, he inwardly fumed. He took a deep breath. 'It's nothing, I've told you. I've had a hard day and I'm bushed. I was thinking of going for a pint. You don't mind, do you?'

If it would improve his mood she didn't mind at all. 'No, of course I don't.' Then she frowned, bothered. Seeing him like this was upsetting her greatly. 'Eddie,' she began tentatively, 'I know what you've said in the past, but what about going to see your father and making amends with him?'

He flashed a black look at her. 'That's out of the question,' he snapped abruptly.

'Yes, I know, but . . .'

'No buts, Frankie. How many times do I have to tell you? What my father said to me was final, what I said to him was final. As far as I'm concerned I have no family.'

His answer didn't surprise her, she'd heard it before. 'Eddie, you aren't regretting our marriage, are you?'

'No, not for one minute. How many times do I have to tell you that too, Frankie? In fact, I'm getting tired of telling you.'

'I'm sorry, just I asked in case anything had changed, that was all.'

He picked up his coat from the back of the chair where he had slung it earlier. 'I'll see you later,' he said tonelessly.

She watched thoughtfully as he went out of the door. Despite her own attempts to appear satisfied, in truth she was disappointed with her marriage. From almost the moment they had retired to her bedroom to spend their first night as man and wife, Frankie had noticed a change come over Eddie. He had become distant towards her and she couldn't understand for the life of her why, considering he had pursued her so relentlessly, proclaiming undying love for her, and how special he had always striven to make her feel.

Eddie treated her well enough, she couldn't deny that, but she no longer felt special or that he made any effort to make her feel so. The closeness she'd expected to share with her husband wasn't there.

And there was the glaring fact that their love-making had nothing like the uninhibited passion she had envisioned it would after that first night spent together in the hotel room. That was now a long-distant memory and if Frankie didn't know better she could almost believe she had spent the night with a totally different man. Their intimate times together were frequent enough but hurried. Despite trying to please him to the best of her endeavours she felt by his responses she had failed miserably. For her their love-making was unsatisfying. It did seem that Eddie's only aim nowadays was to satisfy his own bodily needs without a thought for hers.

Wearily she glanced around. Not that she expected much but Eddie didn't lift a finger in the house and was the most exasperatingly untidy person with many annoying bad habits. Almost all her spare time was spent clearing up after him and catching up with the housework. Sometimes she felt she was no more than an unpaid housekeeper.

Just then a tap sounded on the door and her mother appeared. 'Hello, Frankie, lovey. Yer dad's having a snooze so I've just popped in for a minute to see how you are.'

She smiled warmly in greeting. 'Come in, Mam. There's tea in the pot, fancy one?'

'Never say no to a cuppa, you know me, me darlin',' said Nancy, sitting down in the chair Eddie had just vacated. 'You look tired,' she said, concerned.

'Yes, I am a bit. It's been a long day.'

'Where's Eddie?'

'He's just gone out for a pint.'

'Well, it'll do him good after a hard day's grind. There's one thing I never begrudge yer dad and that's a pint or two. Although in his case it's difficult with being in a wheelchair unless Wally takes him. But it's a man's thing, is going for a pint. Good job us women don't have that need or nothing 'ud ever get done. Although I have ter say,' she added, casting a critical eye across the table, 'Eddie could have given you a hand with the pots before he went. I'll help yer then you can put your feet up after I've gone.'

Frankie smiled gratefully at her. 'Thanks, Mam.'

'No bother, love, that's what mams are for.' Nancy glanced around the room. 'You've made this lovely, Frankie. A right little palace. Those curtains we ran up last week do look a treat.'

Frankie glanced around also, smiling warmly. 'Yes, they do, don't they? But having Taffy's furniture has helped enormously.' She suddenly gave a wistful sigh. 'I wonder how he is?'

'I expect he's doing okay, Frankie, or he'd have been back by now.'

'I do hope so. I miss him, Mam. He's a lovely man. Still, I suppose things have a funny way of working out because if Taff's wife hadn't done what she did then me and Eddie wouldn't be living here and nor would Uncle Wally have been able to offer Eddie a job.'

'Yes, life's very strange, Frankie. One man's downfall is another's making. It's very gratifying to me and yer dad ter know you and Eddie are so happy together, Frankie. I have ter be honest and say at first I didn't think it'd last five minutes with how quickly it all happened, but I'm glad to say I was wrong. The only regret I feel is that somehow Eddie can't seem to find it in himself to try and make things right with his family.'

'It's no good wishing for that, Mam, he flatly refuses to talk about them. Says they're all dead as far as he's concerned.'

Nancy shuddered, pulling a grave face. 'Seems very harsh, Frankie. I hope ter God I never do anything so bad you think that of me or yer dad. Still, on the bright side, Wally and Hilary seem to be getting on famously and I wouldn't be surprised if a wedding announcement was made soon. And don't look at me like that, Frankie. No matter how much I want this wedding, I ain't gonna say or do anything that could ruin things for that pair. Wally's waited long enough ter meet someone like Hilary and I'd never forgive meself if I put me foot in it now.' She slid over her cup and saucer. 'See if yer can squeeze another cuppa out of the pot, then I'll wash up and go. Your dad'll wake up and think I've left home, bless him.'

Chapter Twenty-Three

As Eddie neared his local pub a woman coming in the opposite direction caught his eye and he stopped abruptly. She was wearing a red dress, something very similar to the one he had visualised the brunette wearing on his imaginary drive in the Triumph TR3 earlier that afternoon. Then he froze as he recognised the woman. It was Stella.

Oh, hell, he thought, she being the last person he wanted to come face to face with, knowing it was bound to lead to a confrontation when all he wanted tonight was to enjoy himself. But as he hurriedly glanced her over he had to admit she did look stunning. Such a pity Stella wasn't Sam Champion's daughter instead of Frankie; he could have tolerated the situation far better with Stella's shapely body arousing him in bed. Unable to stop himself, he caught her arm as she made to walk past. 'Don't you speak to old friends then, Stella?'

She stopped to stare at him in amazement, Eddie Taylor being the very last person she had expected to bump into, or ever wanted to for that matter. 'You're no friend of mine,' she hissed, finding her voice, 'and if you don't mind I'm very choosy who I speak to.'

Her apparent anger was amusing him. 'Come on, Stella, there's no need to be like that.'

'Isn't there?' Her voice was rising. 'You run off and marry a woman I thought was my best friend and you think I should have sent you a congratulations card, is that it? You're a bigger bastard than I thought you were, Eddie Taylor. And that's nothing compared to what I think of Frankie. Now get out of my way,' she demanded, trying her best to loosen his grip on her arm.

He made to do so, then stopped, a thought striking him. He fancied a bit of fun tonight and Stella was just the person to have some with. And added to that excitement was the knowledge that she had once been Frankie's best friend. Because of him they were now arch enemies and he found that state of affairs hilarious.

His grip tightened. 'You've got it all wrong, Stella.'

'And just what have I got wrong?' she demanded. 'You trying to tell me I was seeing things in the garage that night? Hallucinated did I?'

'Not at all. But what you *think* you saw wasn't *really* what you saw, that's all I'm trying to say.'

'You ain't making sense. Now let me go, I've a bus to catch.'

'Where are you going?' he asked.

'That's none of your business.'

He heaved a sad sigh. 'It would have been, though, if Frankie hadn't done what she did.'

She frowned at him questioningly. 'What do you mean, if Frankie hadn't done what she did?'

'Well, if you must know, I went to meet you out of work that night and thought I'd missed you as I couldn't spot you anywhere. I went along to the garage because I knew you used to meet Frankie from work so you could walk home together. As soon as I arrived she made a pass at me.'

Stella frowned, bewildered. 'She what?'

'She made a pass at me,' he repeated. 'She told me how good-looking I was and how she thought a bloke like me was wasted on you.'

Stella grimaced. 'Frankie said that?'

'Yes, she did. Then the next thing I knew she had thrown herself at me. What you saw wasn't me kissing her, it was the other way around. Only I didn't know you were there at the time, or her own boyfriend. Frankie very smugly told me so after you'd both left.'

Stella was gawping at him, astonished. 'I know Frankie very well, Eddie Taylor, and I can't believe she was the one to proposition you.'

He gave a sarcastic laugh. 'Maybe you never knew her as well as you thought, Stella. I've realised to my cost that Frankie will do anything to get her own way.'

She laughed scornfully. 'I'm sorry, Eddie, but you must be talking about someone else. Frankie hasn't got that in her. Out of the two of us, it was me who was the selfish one. I wouldn't admit that to anyone else, though. So you can stop trying to make out that it was her that threw herself at you, when I know it was the other way around. Anyway, I don't know why we're having this conversation. You and Frankie are married and I want nothing more to do with either of you.'

She stared at him for a moment, her eyes blazing furiously. 'As a matter of interest, Eddie Taylor, did it ever cross your mind at all how much hurt you caused me? I really liked you. I gave up a serious boyfriend for you. It took me ages to get over what you did and now I have, so piss off and leave me alone. I'm back with my boyfriend now and happy with him. So go back to your little wife 'cos to be perfectly honest I don't give a toss whether you're happy together or not. As far as I'm concerned you can both rot in hell.'

He planted a sorrowful look on his face. 'I'm pleased you're back with your man, Stella, and I'm not surprised you feel about me the way you do, but you have it all wrong. You must listen to me,' he begged. 'Believe me, what I've told you is the truth. You've no idea how Frankie's lies have ruined my life.' He pulled her to him, his face inches from hers. 'After I realised you'd seen me with her I was so devastated I wasn't thinking straight and I admit I had sex with her. It wasn't nice, Stella, it was there and then on the garage floor. But let me tell you, after it was over I was thoroughly ashamed of myself and left intending never to see her again. I wanted to make things right with you but I never got the chance.

'Frankie hounded me, Stella. Everywhere I turned she was there. I tried to reason with her but there was no talking to her. She'd got it into her head that I was madly in love with her. Then three or four weeks later she told me she was pregnant and threatened that if I didn't marry her, her father and uncle would make sure I did. I might be some things, Stella, but I'm an honourable man. Frankie's pregnancy was my doing and I'd no choice but to stand by her.'

Stella was staring at him, stunned. 'I can't believe this,' she uttered, flabbergasted.

'It's true, every word. Though if you questioned her, I know she'd deny it. She's jealous of you, Stella.'

'Jealous of me?' she exclaimed.

'Why else would she do this?'

Stella sighed. 'I suppose you're right. I am better-looking than her. But all the same, I'm having trouble believing that Frankie would do something like this out of jealousy.' She exhaled loudly. 'I was devastated when I heard you were married but I didn't know you'd had a baby.'

'We haven't, Stella. Frankie . . . er . . . well, she had a miscarriage a few weeks after we were married. It was terrible . . . the blood . . . I've never seen anything like it. She was ill for days, weeks really. In fact, I don't think she's ever recovered from it.'

'Oh, Eddie,' she cried, shocked. 'I'm so sorry.'

He gave another deep sigh, his face the picture of misery. 'I'm sorry for myself, Stella. I'm saddled with a woman I don't love or want to be with and there's nothing I can do about it. I can't blame anyone but myself. I fell for the oldest trick in the book and I've suffered ever since, believe me. My family have cut me off without a penny and I'm stuck in a dead end job with that uncle of Frankie's so she can keep an eye on me every minute of the day.'

'Oh, Eddie,' Stella cried sadly. 'I had no idea, really. I thought it was all your doing.'

'Well, now you know the truth.' He leaned closer, his eyes boring into hers. 'It was you I wanted, Stella. I fell for you the first time I saw you. "That's the woman I'm going to marry," I said to myself.'

'You did?'

He smiled at her winningly. 'Oh, yes. I lie awake at night and think of nothing but you.'

'You do?' she whispered.

He nodded. 'I can't change the way I feel, Stella. I'm angry at how things have turned out. I keep thinking, if only I hadn't walked into Champion's that night. But I did, and I just have to grin and bear it, don't I?'

'You could leave her?'

He shook his head remorsefully. 'Don't you think I've tried, Stella? But she threatens she'll kill herself and I couldn't have that on my conscience. I will leave her one day, though, but it's too late for me and you, isn't it?' He stared at her longingly. 'Still, I'm glad I've had this chance to put things straight and I hope you'll not think so badly of me in the future. I'm just sorry to have to open your eyes to how Frankie really is, that's all.' He smiled at her wanly. 'You'd better go, hadn't you, or you'll be late.'

Heart racing frantically, she gave a shudder, wishing Eddie wouldn't look at her like that, like he wanted to devour her. It was unnerving. A vision of Roger rose before her. Dependable, pleasant-faced, unadventurous Roger. He'd be waiting for her as they had arranged outside Timothy White's. Having long ago forgiven her for her dalliance with Eddie, Roger was taking her for a meal at the Turkey Café tonight and Stella had a feeling he was going to insist she agree to set a date for their wedding. But Eddie's declaration of his feelings for her was having a worrying effect on her. Marriage to Roger was the last thing she was thinking of.

Since the moment she had met him, Eddie was the one she'd wanted to be with, and despite all that had happened, all the pain she had suffered when he married her friend, the lure of him had not waned in the slightest. If anything, because of his terrible plight, it was stronger. She suddenly felt a great urge to lash out at Frankie for all the pain she had caused through her selfishness. But as Eddie had said, she would deny everything if Stella confronted her and she could possibly make life for Eddie worse which was the last thing Stella wanted. He had suffered enough. She fixed her eyes firmly on his. 'It's not too late for us,' she said with conviction.

'It isn't, Stella?'

She shook her head. 'I've never stopped loving you.'

He smiled winningly at her, pulled her to him, bent his head and kissed her fervently.

She felt her whole body weaken. 'Oh, Eddie,' she uttered breathlessly when he finally released her. 'How I've missed you.'

'Me too,' he lied. 'So what do we do?' he asked her lamely.

She sighed deeply. 'I don't know.'

'We could . . .' he began.

'We could what?' she urged.

'Nothing, Stella. It wouldn't be fair on you.'

'Let me be the judge of that, Eddie. Tell me what you were going to suggest?'

'Well . . . we could see each other.'

Fighting her conscience, she stared at him. It would be so wrong of her to see him, after all he was a married man, but it was something she wanted so desperately. Besides, she felt that by seeing Eddie she was really doing nothing wrong. He had been hers in the first place. It was Frankie who'd been in the wrong by stealing him off her so diabolically. 'I'd like that.'

He managed to hide a smirk of satisfaction. 'You know it'll be difficult, Stella? And we'll have to keep it between ourselves?'

'Yes. But it won't be for long will it, Eddie? You will leave Frankie?'

'You have my word, my darling. But at the moment, I can't promise when.'

'But when you do, we'll be together?'

'I want nothing more,' he lied.

'Then I'll wait for you,' Stella said softly.

You'll have a long wait, he thought maliciously. He was about to ask her to accompany him for a drink when suddenly his daydream of earlier returned full force. Before him stood the woman in the tight red dress even down to the full breasts overspilling the low-cut front, albeit her hair was blonde and not brunette. But that was a minor flaw he could live with. The car in his daydream was still in the garage. He knew where Frankie kept her set of keys and they were easily obtained without her knowledge. He looked at Stella, his eyes full of devilment. 'How do you fancy a ride in a fancy car?'

'A car? A fancy car? You've got one?' she asked, awed.

'The use of one. So what do you say?'

All thoughts of Roger flown from her mind, she nodded excitedly.

'Wait here.'

Twenty minutes later, he drove up to where Stella was waiting for him in a secluded spot down a side street, leaned over and opened the passenger door.

She stared at the car. 'Wow,' she mouthed.

'Get in,' he said, grinning. 'Let's have some fun.'

Frankie was relieved to find Eddie in a much better frame of mind when he returned home that night. He was whistling when he came through the door, which was most unusual.

'I thought you'd be in bed,' he said, crossing over to the armchair where she was curled up reading a book to peck her lightly on her cheek. He then stripped off his coat and slung it over the back of a dining chair.

'I wanted to wait up for you. Isn't that what wives do?' she said, smiling, happy to see him.

'I suppose, but you didn't have to.'

She was taken aback by his toneless response. 'As I said, I wanted to. I was . . . er . . . getting a bit worried, though.'

'Worried? In God's name why?'

'Well . . . it's after eleven-thirty, Eddie.'

'Oh, timing me now, are you?'

'Not at all. I was just bothered something had happened to you.'

'Oh, Frankie, for God's sake, such as what? I was down the road having a quiet pint and I got chatting to a bloke. That's all.'

She closed her book and rested it on the arm of the chair. 'I didn't mean to sound as if I was questioning you, Eddie.'

'I should hope not. Anyone would think you didn't trust me.'

She rose to join him, looking him in the eye. 'Of course I trust you. Why shouldn't I?'

More fool you then, Eddie thought. 'Are you spoiling for a fight?' he asked.

She frowned, mystified. 'What? No, of course not.'

'Well, it feels like it. First you question the time I come in then you insinuate I've been with someone else.'

She gasped. 'Oh, Eddie, I didn't. If you thought that I'm sorry.'

'Huh! Okay, apology accepted. But don't let it happen again, Frankie. It isn't nice to be accused by your wife of something you haven't done.' He gave a deep sigh. 'You've spoilt my night now. I really enjoyed my pint and was looking forward to coming home to you but I never thought for a minute you'd be in such a mood.' He paused. He had enjoyed intimidating her, making her feel guilty for something she hadn't done, it had given him much pleasure. He felt like carrying on but thought better of it. He'd had an enjoyable evening with Stella which had left him in no doubt of better things to come from her, and very soon if he was not mistaken. Now his libido was screaming for satisfaction and Frankie was the only woman available to him at the moment. 'Are you coming to bed?' he said to her meaningfully.

He hadn't made advances towards her for weeks and, still hurt from his unwarranted treatment of her, making love was the last thing she felt like doing, but he was her husband so how could she refuse? She nodded.

'Hurry and lock up. I'll be waiting for you.'

Chapter Twenty-Four

'You look tired, Frankie. After you've cleared up, why don't you make yourself a nice cup of tea and put your feet up? Give the pub a miss for tonight, if you like.'

After the day she'd had the thought was a very welcome one but it was Friday night and usually she and Eddie went for a drink down the local pub and had a game of Bingo, or just soaked up the jovial atmosphere. She didn't like to disappoint him. Just for a change she would sometimes have loved to have gone dancing or to a pub in the town where people of their own age went, but whenever she had suggested it Eddie never seemed keen to take her. As the easygoing person she was Frankie hadn't pushed it, eventually keeping her preferences to herself. The fact he had noticed her fatigued state this evening came as a nice surprise considering she had been tired many times in the past and he hadn't appeared to notice, let alone be willing to sacrifice a night out so she could rest.

But there was another reason for her being glad of his suggestion they stay in. She had something to tell him. Something she had suspected for several weeks and had had confirmed by the doctor today. She wanted to pick her moment to break the news to Eddie that he was going to be a father. She wasn't sure what his reaction would be. It had shocked her to realise after the doctor had confirmed her condition that the arrival of children had never been discussed, or mentioned even, during their fifteen months of marriage. The topic just hadn't arisen.

As an only child herself Frankie had always wanted several and hoped Eddie felt the same. This news was bound to come as a shock to him, just as it had to her own father, but she hoped Eddie didn't react in quite the same way as Sam had when Nancy had broken the news of Frankie's own impending arrival. Apparently he had been so stunned he had fainted and in the process crashed into the table and sent everything on it flying. The incident had since been the topic of many an amusing recollection. Frankie, though, was secretly hoping this baby would bring about the closeness she'd always felt was lacking between herself and Eddie, and even be the incentive to bring him and his estranged family back together again.

She smiled warmly at him as she rose from the table and began to gather the dirty dishes together. 'I am tired, Eddie, it's been one of those days when I thought hometime would never come. A relaxing evening sounds wonderful.'

For the next half an hour she happily busied herself tidying up after their evening meal and had just come back into the living room armed with two cups of fresh tea when simultaneously Eddie came through the door leading upstairs.

She stopped dead, eyeing him in astonishment. While she had been busy in the kitchen she hadn't noticed him slip upstairs. Washed and changed, he now looked very spruce in a fashionable pair of tight blue trousers and matching jacket, black velvet trimming the collar, his dark hair slicked back with Brylcreem. The fragrance of the Old Spice aftershave he had slapped on liberally filled the room.

'Do you like it?' he said, parading before her. 'I thought I'd treat myself.'

'Oh! Er . . . yes . . . you look very nice.'

'Nice? Is that how you describe your husband. What about handsome, Frankie?'

'Well, yes, you do look handsome, Eddie. It's just that . . . well, that outfit must have cost a bit.'

He pulled a condescending face. 'It's quality that counts, Frankie, not the cost. People look at you in a good bit of cloth and know you are somebody. Don't worry, I used my bonus to pay for it. Oh, and I borrowed some of yours,' he added casually. 'I needed shirts too. You don't mind, do you?' It wasn't a question so much as a statement.

But she did mind. That was her bonus, hard-earned. She had been overjoyed when Wally had surprised them all with their pay packets just before dinnertime and she had discovered an extra ten pounds inside. She had spent the rest of the afternoon planning what she would do with it which had been to discuss things with Eddie first, then hope he'd agree that she should put a third away to save, use a third on something for the house, and the rest on a pair of much-needed shoes for herself and one or two bits for the coming baby.

He noticed the look on her face and misconstrued hurt for annoyance. 'Nothing wrong, is there?' he asked, eyes narrowing. 'Only you're looking at me like I've stolen your life savings.'

Her jaw dropped. 'Oh, Eddie, of course I'm not. I don't begrudge you anything, you know that. It's just that . . . well, I had plans for my bonus, that's all.'

He gave a disdainful click of his tongue. 'Things for the house, I bet.'

'Some of it, yes, as a matter of fact.'

'And you don't think we've enough clutter?'

'Well, no, not what I'd call clutter. Most of what we have has been given us, Eddie, one way or another and I wanted to get just a few bits of our own together. And I needed a pair of shoes. I've holes in the sole of my others.'

'Well, not to worry, you can get them next time Wally is generous enough to pay us a bonus.'

'Yes, I suppose I'll have to,' she said, unable to keep her annoyance from her voice. 'And, Eddie, Uncle Wally is as generous as he can afford to be,' she said defensively, thinking his comment very unfair. A thought suddenly struck her and she eyed him quizzically. 'Are you going out?'

'Yes, thought I might, that way I'll give you a bit of peace. You don't mind, do you?'

Yes, she did, very much so. She desperately wanted to tell him about the baby but knew now wasn't the best time. Never one to hold grudges, she realised in an hour or so she would have got over what he'd done so unthinkingly, and once in a better frame of mind she could tell him their wonderful news. 'I'd quite welcome a bit of peace and quiet,' she agreed.

Eddie inwardly grinned. He had been bold in arranging to meet Stella on the one night of the week he normally took Frankie out as a token gesture. When he had made the arrangements with her it had been like a dare to himself. If the mental bet he'd made that he could get away without arousing his wife's suspicions had been in actual money, he'd have won a fortune. He felt a thrill of excitement rise. Not only was he sporting a brand new set of clothes that had cost far more than Frankie would ever know, but in the garage there was a very nice Standard Vanguard, all ready serviced and waiting for its rightful owner to collect it in the morning. It had a big back seat.

Several times now he had taken a car out and no one had noticed anything amiss and Eddie thought himself very clever. Having his illicit fun with the very willing Stella, with the added bonus of taking a car for a spin whenever the opportunity presented itself, was making his life much more bearable. He now had at the most another nine months before Neil's prison sentence was up, and in turn his own sentence. He was determined to make the best of it meantime.

He smiled at his wife winningly. 'Well, if you insist you don't mind, I'll go. I won't be long.'

He turned and went into the kitchen where he quickly checked to make sure Frankie wasn't looking and made to snatch her set of garage keys off the hook by the back door. Then he gasped, shocked. They weren't there. Frantically his eyes flashed around. No sign. A surge of panic filled him. He had promised Stella an exciting night and was going to look so foolish when he could not fulfil his promise. What had Frankie done with those bloody keys? She always came in and put them straight on the hook for fear of losing them. But for whatever reason, tonight she had not followed her usual routine. Eddie was looking forward to having some privacy with Stella. If he wanted to get his hands on the car he had no choice but to ask Frankie where the keys were, and without arousing any suspicion.

'Er . . . Frankie,' he casually called. 'As a matter of interest, where are your garage keys? I just happened to notice they're not on the hook.'

'I haven't got them,' she called back. 'I forgot to pick them up when I left the garage tonight.'

His plans for that evening faded before him, his fists clenched in anger and before he could stop himself he spat, 'You dozy cow!'

Seconds later she appeared in the kitchen doorway, a frozen look on her face. 'What did you call me, Eddie?'

He stared at her, stunned rigid by his own outburst even though he felt it was warranted. 'Eh? Oh, I . . . er . . . just asked *how*. Why, what did you think I said?' he demanded.

'Oh . . . er . . . nothing.'

He stood staring at her, his mind searching frantically for an excuse, anything would do, to get those keys. But nothing feasible would come to mind. Through Frankie's stupidity his whole evening lay in ruins. He felt like slapping her.

'Is there anything wrong, Eddie?'

'What?'

'I asked if there was anything wrong? You look like . . . well . . . really annoyed.'

'Annoyed? No, no, I'm just bothered those keys are lying around for anyone to pick up. It really is careless of you, Frankie. Maybe in future I should take care of them so this sort of thing doesn't happen again.'

She gave a laugh. 'Oh, Eddie, don't be silly. This is the first time I've ever forgotten them in all the years Uncle Wally has trusted me with them. Surely I can be forgiven for one lapse? I just forgot them, that's all.' And she wasn't surprised, considering what she had occupying her mind. 'Uncle Wally will have locked up safely with his set and if we arrive before him in the morning we'll just have to wait for him, that's all. If it makes you feel any better I'll promise not to let it happen again. Now hadn't you better go or it won't be worth it. I'll see you later, all right?' she said, stepping over to him, reaching up and kissing his cheek.

He didn't respond to her display of affection and the fact did not go unnoticed.

Eddie was fuming. There was nothing he could do about this situation. With a grunt, he turned from her and left the house.

Thoughtfully, she stared after him. Despite his plausible explanation she could have sworn Eddie had called her a dozy cow.

She had not long settled back in her seat when the back door was tapped upon and Hilary came through. Putting down her book, Frankie smiled happily at her in greeting. She and Hilary had become very good friends since their introduction almost fifteen months ago. Although many years older than Frankie, Hilary was a blessing to her, steadily becoming a very dear and trusted friend. No one could entirely replace Stella, their history spanning years and going too deep, but Hilary had qualities that Stella didn't possess. She was wise, considerate of others, and hadn't a selfish bone in her body.

Frankie quickly appraised her as she walked in. She always looked so well presented. Tonight she was wearing a flattering cream-coloured wool skirt and a turquoise twinset. A pearl necklace and tiny matching earrings finished off the outfit. Her hair was cut short and waved naturally to frame her attractive face. Frankie became aware of how she herself was dressed. She knew she looked very respectable but her jumper and slacks were far from new, and although not for one minute did she begrudge him she still felt Eddie could have been more considerate when he had spent all that money on clothes for himself. Still, what was done was done, and Frankie had to admit her husband had looked very handsome in his choice of clothes.

'I'm on my way to meet Wally and saw your light on so I thought I'd pop in and see how you are,' Hilary said. 'I promised to help him do the monthly accounts tonight.' She added with a laugh, 'It's not a task I enjoy but I feel it's better than the haphazard method he had before.'

'You're doing wonders for my uncle, Hilary, in more ways than one.'

She beamed at the compliment. 'Where's Eddie?' she asked, sitting down in the armchair opposite.

'You've just missed him. He's gone for a pint. I didn't feel like going.'

'Oh.' Hilary looked concerned. 'Nothing wrong, is there? I've not known you miss your Friday night out with Eddie before.'

'No, nothing's wrong, just a bit tired, that's all.'

She frowned. 'Wally's not working you too hard, is he?'

Frankie grinned. 'You sound like my mother. No, not at all. We're busy, I'm glad to say, but Uncle Wally never takes advantage of his staff. Despite the hours he works himself, it's always his workers' choice whether they stay late or not.'

Hilary smiled. 'He's a good man?'

Frankie eyed her. 'You love him, don't you?'

'Oh, yes,' Hilary replied without hesitation. 'I was very happy with Frederick. He was a decent man, Frankie, and I loved him very much. I was devastated when he died so young, then when I met Wally I felt so guilty about the feelings I was having for him, like I was betraying Frederick's memory and all we'd shared between us. And I compared them too. Then I realised I shouldn't be doing that comparing them. No one could replace Frederick. He was himself and Wally is Wally. Two different people I'm sharing my life with at two different times. I know I'm very lucky, Frankie. Not many women get two chances like I have. I have to say, though, that the love I have for your uncle is very different from what I had with Frederick.'

'Different? In what way, Hilary?'

'It's hard to put into words really but Wally just has this way of making me feel so special, Frankie, which Frederick didn't, and we have this bond between us, a closeness that's hard to describe. I see him most days yet when I'm away from him I feel part of me is missing. I never quite felt that with Frederick. I didn't know about it at the time, not until I experienced it with Wally. You know what I mean, Frankie, just like you feel for Eddie.'

Although she knew she gave that impression, that was just it, Frankie didn't feel like that – not with Eddie. She'd had that special bond with Ian, though. Ian. Funny, she hadn't thought of him for a while. It was as if she had put her special memories of him in a little box at the back of her mind and shut the lid, afraid to open it because his loss was too painful to bear even now. She just hoped wherever he was and whatever he was doing and whoever with, that he was happy, and if he thought of her at all, it was fondly despite what she had done to him.

Frankie gave a sigh. 'Yes, I know what you mean.' She hurriedly changed the subject. 'Have you time for a cuppa before you go off and tackle those dreadful books? I have to say, sooner you than me. I'd rather fix ten cars than make up the firm's ledger.'

Hilary laughed. 'Uncle and niece are so alike. You two are only happy when you've a spanner in your hands. I've always time for a cuppa, Frankie, but you sit where you are, I'll make it.'

'We'll both make it,' Frankie said, rising to join her.

Armed with their cups of tea and plate of arrowroot and fig biscuits the pair had spent the next twenty or so minutes happily chatting about nothing in particular when without warning Hilary suddenly looked at Frankie quizzically and asked, 'Are you all right?'

She stared, completely taken by surprise. 'Yes, of course, why do you ask?'

'I don't know. It's just a feeling I have. It's . . . well, it's not what you say, Frankie, it's what you don't say.'

She looked bewildered. 'I don't understand?'

A look of shame clouded her friend's face. 'Look, I'm sorry, just forget what I said.'

But Frankie couldn't. Why had Hilary asked her that question? And what did she mean by what Frankie didn't say? 'Please, tell me why you asked if I was all right? I mean, do I look miserable or something?'

'No, not at all. I really don't know why I asked, Frankie. It's just a feeling I have that . . . well . . . all is not right, that you're holding something back. I'm sorry if I'm speaking out of turn, please forgive me.'

'Forgive you? Oh, Hilary, there's nothing to forgive. You're asking me because you care, I know that.'

Hilary smiled. 'I do care, very much so. I care for all your family, but especially for you, Frankie. You're like the sister I always longed for. I can't thank you enough, and your mother and father too, for the way you've all treated me. I felt part of your family from the minute Wally announced we were courting. For someone like myself with no family left it's been such a blessing. You've all come to mean so much to me. That's why I take an interest in you all.'

Frankie stretched her hand across the table and grasped Hilary's affectionately. 'We're all delighted about you and Uncle Wally and none of us could have wished him to have chosen anyone else. I love you as much as I would a sister too.'

'Oh, Frankie,' Hilary uttered, tears welling in her eyes. 'That's the loveliest thing anyone has ever said to me.'

'Don't be so daft,' she said, smiling knowingly. 'The loveliest thing ever said to you was by my Uncle Wally when he asked you to marry him.'

Hilary gasped. 'How did you know?'

Frankie giggled. 'I didn't. Just intuition. There's been something different about you for a week or so now. A glow, that's all I can describe it as. And don't worry, I shan't mention a word to my mam until you've told her yourself. But I warn you, be prepared. My mother is going to be uncontrollable with excitement. Her sole aim in life is to see Wally happily settled.'

'Oh, he'll be happy all right, Frankie, I shall make sure of that.'

'I've no doubts, Hilary. None at all.'

Hilary took a deep breath and eyed her searchingly. 'So, Frankie, are you all right?'

'Yes, of course, I've already told you I am.'

'I know, but as I said before, it's not what you say, it's what you don't say.'

Frankie looked at her. Hilary was right. She was very good at being evasive when she wanted to be. She supposed she didn't want to spoil her family's illusion that she was deliriously happy, worry them and then have them probe and not really be able to explain her reasons for feeling as she did. But after Hilary's words of tonight Frankie was questioning herself. Like Hilary she'd compared two men, and felt guilty for not feeling exactly for Eddie as she had for Ian. Confusing, she knew, but it made sense. And she also realised that special closeness between couples sometimes didn't happen instantaneously.

As a relationship built so did everything else, and Eddie and she hadn't had any courtship time to get to know how each other ticked. Eddie had had such a lot to contend with himself with the unexpected loss of his family and his livelihood, all in all such a drastic change in his circumstances when he had married her, it must have been very difficult for him to deal with. No wonder he was tetchy with her sometimes without apparent reason.

Suddenly she began to feel better and to view the future much more brightly. She felt a great urge to share her exciting news about the baby. She would have preferred to tell Eddie first but knew her secret would be safe with Hilary until she had. 'Can you keep a secret?'

'A secret? Well, that depends what it is,' she said, grinning mischievously. 'If you're going to tell me you're having an affair with the chap next door then I'm sorry, but I'll have to tell his wife.'

'Hilary, stop it,' Frankie scolded. 'I'm being serious.'

'I should hope so,' she said, giving a merry chuckle. 'The chap next door is old enough to be your father and I've seen better-looking men at his age.' She leaned her elbows on the table and eyed Frankie keenly. 'I promise I won't tell a soul, so come on, out with it?'

Frankie took a very deep breath and clasped her hands, a smile of pure delight on her face. 'I'm going to have a baby.'

Hilary's jaw dropped. 'Baby?' she whispered, utterly shocked. Then her whole face lit up and she cried delightedly, 'A baby! Oh, Frankie, that is such wonderful news. I bet Eddie is beside himself?'

'He doesn't know yet.'

'He doesn't?'

'No. I haven't had the right moment to tell him. I only found out for sure myself this morning. Uncle Wally and Eddie thought I was popping to the shops and got stuck in a queue but really I was at the doctor's. I'm actually still getting used to the idea myself but I'm so thrilled. I just hope . . .' Her voice trailed off and she frowned.

'Hope what, Frankie?' Hilary urged.

Her face was worried now. 'That Eddie is too.'

'Of course he will be,' Hilary said, astounded. 'Whyever shouldn't he be?'

She shrugged her shoulders. 'It sounds odd, I know, but we've never actually got around to discussing having children so I don't know what he feels about them or what his reaction will be.'

'Wally and I haven't discussed having children either but I know that if we ever were blessed he'd be delighted. You're worrying over nothing, Frankie. Eddie loves you dearly and will jump for joy when you tell him.'

Despite her reassuring words Frankie still felt a niggle of doubt. 'I suppose I'm just worried that he might feel we're not ready for a family.'

'I doubt any couple is ever ready, Frankie. The baby's coming so you'll just have to be.' She leaned over and patted Frankie's hand. 'You'll make wonderful parents.'

Frankie smiled. 'Thanks, Hilary. I'm being silly and you've put my mind at rest.'

'You're pregnant, Frankie, and expectant mothers have all sorts of fanciful ideas. You're no different from the rest but you'll get through. Oh, just think,' she exclaimed, beaming happily. 'When I marry your uncle I'll become a great-aunt. How wonderful! Your mother is going to be over the moon at becoming a grandmother.'

Frankie chuckled. 'Yes, she is, isn't she? I can't wait to tell her.'

'And I can't wait to start knitting. Between me and Nancy this baby will want for nothing, let me assure you. So hurry up and tell Eddie then you can tell your mother and we'll get down to discussing patterns.' Hilary suddenly realised the time and jumped up. 'I'd better get going or Wally will think I've deserted him.' She went over to Frankie and threw her arms around her, hugging her tightly. 'Congratulations,' she said, kissing her affectionately on her cheek. 'And don't worry, your secret is safe with me.'

'Thanks, Hilary.'

'Don't get up. I'll see myself out.'

As she listened to the click of the back door a warm glow filled Frankie. Eddie would be delighted when she told him. Her own doubts over how he would receive the news were being caused by her condition, that was all.

Having made herself a fresh cup of tea she settled back in her chair, tucked her feet comfortably under herself and picked up her book. She had only read a few words when she heard the front door knocker. So much for her couple of hours of peace and quiet, she thought, getting up to answer it.

She was most surprised to find Roger on her doorstep.

'Roger!' she exclaimed. 'How lovely to see you, it's been such a long time.' It was then it struck her how deeply upset he looked. His face was the colour of parchment and it was obvious he'd been crying. 'What on earth is the matter?'

He swept his hand over his hair and shuffled his feet uncomfortably. 'Can I come in, Frankie?' he asked. His words came out in a choked voice.

'Yes, of course,' she replied, grabbing his arm and pulling him inside.

Sitting him down in the armchair Hilary had just vacated, she sat opposite and eyed him worriedly. 'What's happened, Roger? Has . . . has someone died, is that it?'

Perched on the edge of the chair, wringing his hands so tight his knuckles cracked, he sighed loudly. 'Worse than that, Frankie.'

'Worse!' Her mind whirled frantically. Whatever could be worse than someone dying?

He fixed his eyes on hers. 'I don't know how to tell you this.'

Her heart thumped painfully, a feeling of foreboding filling her. Whatever was wrong with Roger was in some way connected to her. Oh, God, her mind screamed. Whatever could it be that was so terrible it was worse than death? 'Just tell me, Roger,' she demanded.

His bottom lip quivered. 'It's . . . it's Stella and Eddie.'

She frowned, bewildered. 'Stella and Eddie? I'm sorry, I don't understand?'

'They've been seeing each other, Frankie.'

Her face paled and she shook her head in denial. 'Seeing each other? No, you've got it wrong, Roger.'

He swallowed hard. 'I ain't, Frankie. I don't know how long it's been going on but I know they're together tonight.'

She shook her head. 'You're mistaken. Eddie's gone for a pint, he'll be back soon.'

'He's with Stella, Frankie. They're in the Rose and Crown on Carts Lane and have been for the last hour or so. I followed them. I've known something wasn't right for a while. Stella's been acting funny again and when she made up such a daft excuse for not seeing me tonight, I knew summat was going on. So I followed her. She stood in a dark alleyway, Frankie. She was waiting for him and when he arrived she ran up to him.'

Frankie looked at him, horrified, trying to find a reason to excuse what Roger had just told her. 'Just because she ran up to him doesn't mean anything. She could have . . . could have . . . thought he was someone else. It is dark outside.'

'They kissed when they met, Frankie. And it wasn't just a peck on the cheek.'

'Kissed!' The life seemed to drain from her and her whole body slumped. 'No, please tell me this is a joke of some kind? Eddie wouldn't do this to me. He wouldn't!'

'Oh, Frankie, do you think I'd joke about something like this? It's tearing me apart. I love that woman more than life itself. I'd do anything for her. I can't believe she would do this to me again. She promised me faithfully it was over between her and Eddie. She told me she'd made a dreadful mistake and begged me to forgive her. Anyway, he's married to you so I didn't see any danger.' Roger looked at her, his eyes desolate. 'I don't know what to do, Frankie. Please tell me what to do? I can't bear to lose her, I really can't.'

Her head was pounding, thoughts flashing wildly. 'I can't tell you what to do, Roger,' she said, utterly bereft. 'I don't know what to do myself. I can't believe this, I really can't. You couldn't have been mistaken, could you?'

He shook his head. 'No, Frankie, I know what I saw.'

She sagged back against the back of the chair and put her head in her hands. 'Oh, God,' she groaned. 'I'm so sorry, Roger.'

'*You're* sorry, Frankie? This isn't your fault.'

'I feel that it is. He's my husband.'

'Stella's my girlfriend. It's they who are at fault. Why is she doing this to me, Frankie? I treat her well, take her out wherever she wants to go, make a fuss of her. What more does she want?'

It seemed to Frankie that if Roger was correct then Stella obviously wanted another man. Her husband, Eddie. Did he want Stella? That question was far more important to Frankie. 'I don't know,' she whispered. She lowered her hands and took a deep breath. 'I'm sorry, Roger, I really need to be on my own. What you have told me has knocked me for six. I can't think straight.'

He stood up. 'Are you going to tackle Eddie?'

She took a deep breath. 'I'll have to, won't I? Though God knows what I'm going to say. If you have this all wrong . . .'

'I haven't, Frankie. You have to know I didn't come to you lightly with this, I just had to.'

She nodded. 'I understand.'

'I've always liked you, Frankie. In a way I always wished Stella was more like you.' He gave a wan smile. 'Don't get me wrong, I love Stella, worship the ground she walks on, but she's got this side to her and she can be so selfish sometimes. Whereas you . . . well, Frankie, you're lovely, you are. You've just got something about you that . . . I dunno . . . makes people like you. I was so shocked when all that came out about you and Eddie in the garage. I couldn't believe you would actually do something like that. I know Ian and Stella saw you but I still had a feeling on me that you were innocent somehow, that maybe they'd got it wrong. I wanted to come and talk to you about it but Ian's my best friend. I had to stand by him, Frankie.'

She shuddered at the mention of her lost love's name. 'I know,' she whispered. 'But I can't think about the past, Roger. It's what's happening now that bothers me.'

'Yes, me too. I'll go then.' He made to turn, then stopped. 'I'm sorry, Frankie, really I am.'

She gave a watery smile and watched blankly as he left. As the front door closed her self-control gave way and the tears came then. 'Oh, Eddie,' she wailed. 'Why? Why? And with my best friend too.' Because although Stella and she were estranged Frankie still somehow looked on her as such.

The house was in darkness when Eddie let himself in several hours later. He was drunk, very. Considering its awful start, his evening hadn't gone too badly. Stella, under the mistaken illusion that Eddie could help himself to whatever car was available in the garage at the time, had been disappointed she wasn't getting a ride out, but had quite readily accepted the excuse that there wasn't a car good enough for either of them to be in and had happily settled for a night in the pub. So long as it was with Eddie himself she didn't care what they did. Eddie hadn't been so happy, though. He was dressed in expensive new clothes and wasn't about to ruin them by a romp on the canal bank, however much he needed his manly urges satisfied. And it was all Frankie's fault for carelessly leaving her keys behind. As the evening had progressed his mood had darkened, helped along by the number of drinks he had consumed, at least five pints of bitter and several whiskies.

As he came through the door he stumbled in the darkness and swore loudly.

Frankie, who had spent a dreadful few hours waiting for him to return home, worrying herself witless as to how she would approach him with what Roger had told her, had dozed off through sheer mental exhaustion.

His profanities awoke her sharply and she called, 'Is that you, Eddie?'

He swore again, under his breath this time. He'd been hoping Frankie would be in bed. 'Who the . . .' He abruptly stopped and corrected himself. 'Yes, it's me,' he slurred. 'Why aren't you in bed?'

She appeared in the kitchen doorway and switched on the light, his inebriated state registering. For a fleeting moment she wondered if the rest of her bonus had been what had paid for it. It took all her strength to be civil to him. 'I was waiting up for you.'

He blinked rapidly, accustoming his eyes to the sudden brightness. 'Well, you needn't have bothered,' he said off-handedly. 'I'm quite capable of seeing myself to bed.'

'Did you have a good night?' she asked lightly.

'So, so,' he muttered trying to keep his balance while he kicked off his shoes.

'Did you go to the local pub?'

'That's where I usually go, isn't it?' Slumping heavily against the back door he frowned, eyes darkening. 'Why all the questions?'

Her heart was pounding, not liking this situation one little bit. But he was her husband, she was having his baby, and if, God forbid, it was true he was seeing Stella she wanted to know, despite the grief it would cause her and not knowing what she would do about it. 'Er . . . just interested, Eddie, that's all.' She picked up the kettle, filled it, then turned to face him, her heart thumping painfully now. She took a very deep breath and steeled herself. 'And as a matter of interest, did you . . . er . . . see Stella at all?'

He stared at her. In his drink-fuddled brain thoughts were whirling madly. Why had she asked that? Did she somehow know what he'd been up to? But she couldn't possibly. She hadn't left the house all night that he was aware of, and besides he and Stella had been so careful not to be seen. If only he wasn't so drunk he could handle this situation better. He gave a shrug of his shoulders. 'Stella? I don't know any Stella.'

She was studying him intently. He seemed so convincing even though this was a blatant lie. She took another deep breath to try and calm her quaking nerves. 'What a short memory you have, Eddie. Stella was my best friend. You took her out. Surely you remember her?'

He gave a loud belch and a spark of merriment lit his eyes when he saw her flinch in disgust. 'Oh, that Stella,' he said flippantly. 'God, I'd forgotten she even existed. No, I didn't see her, I doubt I'd recognise her anyway. Don't bother with tea for me, I'm going to bed.'

Before she could stop him he had pushed past her, stumbled across the back living room leaving his new clothes scattered in his wake, and was mounting the stairs.

She froze for a moment, a huge part of her not wanting to address this any further, the other part knowing she had to or she'd never rest easy. She just prayed, though, that somehow Roger had got this all wrong. Face set in determination she followed him.

She found him in the bedroom, not an attractive sight. Naked now, he was desperately trying to put his pyjama trousers on without losing his balance.

Spotting her, his lip curled. 'For God's sake, don't just stand there, woman, give me a hand.'

His insulting manner offended her. 'If you hadn't drunk so much, you wouldn't be in such a state as not to be able to dress yourself.' She eyed him hard, wanting to get this over with before she lost her nerve. 'Eddie, I had a visitor tonight. Roger came to see me. In case you don't know who I'm talking about, he's Stella's boyfriend. He told me you two have been seeing each other. Have you, Eddie? Have you been seeing her?'

Hell! His mind screamed. She knew. A surge of panic filled him, mingled with outrage that he'd actually been caught. His eyes darkened. Temper flaring, he reared back his head and before he could stop himself, blurted, 'If you weren't such a miserable cow, I wouldn't have. It's all your fault!'

She gasped in shock. 'You *have* been seeing her?'

He was so incensed now he couldn't stop himself. 'Yes,' he shouted, advancing towards her to push her hard on the shoulder. She stumbled backwards out onto the landing at the top of the stairs. He followed her, pushing her again. 'And do you want to know something else, Frankie? She's a better fuck than you are.'

With that he went to push her again. Despite her shock at what he had so blatantly confessed she automatically stepped backwards to avoid him. The next thing she knew she was tumbling down, crashing hard against every step on her journey, her screams of terror rending the air. She hit her head with a thud on the unyielding floor below, then everything went black.

Chapter Twenty-Five

Through her hazy state, Frankie knew someone was holding her hand, but she didn't know who or why. Her head was hammering relentlessly, shooting excruciating pain through the whole of her body. She tried to speak but her throat was dry. Panic-stricken, she tried to open her eyes. They seemed to be glued together. Finally she won the struggle but the dazzlingly bright glare made her snap them shut.

She heard a voice in the distance. It was calling her name. Was that her mother? She swallowed several times to lubricate her throat, simultaneously blinking her eyes to accustom them to the light.

'Is that you, Mam?' she managed to croak, eyes half open.

The voice was louder now, nearer. 'Oh, Frankie, love, yes, it's me. Mam. I'm here, me darlin', don't try to move. Nurse . . . NURSE! She's awake.'

She was in hospital? 'Mam . . .'

'Shush, Frankie, don't try to speak,' Nancy soothed, gently squeezing her hand. 'Yer in 'ospital, lovey. You had an accident. Fell down the stairs. NURSE! Where's that bleddy nurse? Oh, there yer are,' she cried in relief to the sister who bustled over. 'She's awake. My Frankie's awake.'

'All right, Mrs Champion,' she said matter-of factly, looking hard at the patient, picking up her hand to feel her pulse which she timed with the watch pinned to her chest. 'Try to keep calm or you'll panic the patient. I'll fetch the doctor,' she said, laying Frankie's hand gently back down.

'Thirsty, Mam,' uttered Frankie.

'Can I give her a drink?' Nancy asked the nurse.

'Just a sip of water. Use a spoon. Nothing more until the doctor's seen her,' she said, hurrying away.

Although she spluttered when she swallowed it, the welcome sip of water eased Frankie's throat just a little.

'Eddie's here, lovey,' Nancy said. 'He's just outside having a ciggy. I'll go and fetch him.'

'No,' she uttered. 'Not now.' Why had she said that?

The doctor arrived, a frosty-looking elderly man. Despite his severe features he smiled kindly at her. 'How do you feel?' he asked.

'Dreadful,' she croaked. 'So much pain.'

'Well, that's understandable, my dear. Some tumble you took. You've a broken leg and two ribs, you've badly bruised your back and had a nasty knock to your head. And of course you'll feel sore from the surgery but Sister will give you some pain relief for that.'

She looked at him questioningly. 'Surgery?' she asked, worry mounting.

The doctor looked at Nancy. 'You haven't told her?'

Face grave, she shook her head.

The doctor pulled a chair forward, sat down beside Frankie and took her hand. 'I'm sorry, my dear, we had no choice. The way you fell must have caused internal damage which we couldn't repair. We had to give you a hysterectomy.'

Through bloodshot eyes, she eyed him blankly. 'A what?'

Nancy gently squeezed Frankie's other hand again. 'What the doctor's trying to tell you, Frankie, is that they had to remove yer women's bits. Yer womb, lovey,' she said, her voice full of emotion, eyes streaming with tears. 'But yer alive, me darlin', and that's the main thing.' She swallowed hard to try and rid herself of the lump of grief forming in her throat.

Frankie lay for several long moments, numb with shock, trying to digest what she had just been told her. 'My womb,' she whispered. 'They took my womb?'

'They had to,' Nancy said gently.

Tears of devastation poured down her face. 'My baby . . .'

'I'm sorry, Mrs Taylor. There was nothing we could do,' the doctor reiterated.

Agony so great it overwhelmed the almost unbearable pain of her injuries flooded through her. 'Oh, Mam,' she sobbed.

Nancy looked at the doctor. 'Can't yer give her something? This is all too much.'

He nodded. 'I'll see to it.'

Frankie was floating through a brilliant blue sky, fluffy white clouds sailing gently by. On each cloud sat a baby with pink chubby angelic features. On their backs grew tiny feathery wings. As each baby slowly passed her they called to her, 'Mamma, Mamma.' Each time she reached out to grab one but as she did so the baby gurgled with laughter then faded away, her hands enclosing thin air.

Her own screams woke her. She was sweating profusely.

'Shush,' a voice soothed. 'Go back to sleep, Mrs Taylor.'

'My dreams,' she wailed. 'Oh, my dreams are so horrible.'

The pretty face of the night nurse attending Frankie clouded in sympathy. 'They'll pass in time, Mrs Taylor,' she soothed reassuringly, but after what this poor young woman had suffered, her nightmares would probably last many months yet before they started to ease. If, in fact, ever.

Chapter Twenty-Six

'You look better today,' Eddie said, leaning over to peck Frankie's cheek.

Propped up by pillows, evidence of the severe bruising she had suffered two weeks previously still showing, she managed a thin smile. She wished she felt better.

He put a brown paper bag down on top of her locker. 'I brought you some apples.'

'Thank you,' she said, knowing she wouldn't eat them as she'd hardly any appetite, despite the nurses' insistence she must eat or she'd never get well. She waited for a moment while he unbuttoned his coat and made himself comfortable. 'Eddie, please tell me what happened again?'

He sighed. 'Not again, Frankie. I'm sick and tired of going over this.'

'Please, Eddie.'

'You still don't remember?'

'No,' she whispered.

Thank God, he thought. Unrepentant for the part he had played, he just prayed she never remembered. Well, at least until after he had left, then he didn't care what she remembered and what she didn't. Just another few months, that was all the time he needed, and he could be done with this pretence. To the loss of their baby, or of the fact that his brutal actions meant she could have no more, he gave no thought. It made no odds to him. Children didn't figure at all in his future plans and neither did Frankie. 'All right, if you want me to go over it again. But I don't know why you just don't forget it, Frankie, and concentrate on getting better.'

'How can I?' she whispered, voice choked with emotion. 'I lost our baby and any chance of having another, and I don't know how it happened.'

He emitted a loud sigh. 'You were tired and didn't want to go out but insisted I did. I was late back because I got chatting and you had a go at me.'

That part didn't make sense to her. Why would she have a go at him? She had never been in the habit of doing so before, so why that night? Had her condition caused that, her changing hormones? It must have. What other reason could there have been?

'I've no idea why but you were in a dreadful mood, Frankie,' he continued. 'But I managed to calm you down and we went to bed. You came up behind me as you insisted on locking up. I was in the bedroom, I heard you coming up the stairs and the next thing I knew you were screaming blue murder and I heard the crash as you hit the bottom. As I told you before, you obviously missed your footing. That's what the doctor said too.'

Eddie's explanation of events sounded plausible. Frankie didn't understand why but something still didn't seem right, though. Two whole weeks she had lain in this bed and thought of nothing else and still she couldn't remember. The last thing she did recall of that night was saying goodbye to Hilary and settling down to read her book.

Eddie grasped her hand, his face suddenly grief-stricken. 'Oh, Frankie, it was so awful. I thought you were dead. I got the ambulance as quick as I could and we brought you here. Now, please, please, can we not talk of this again? I'm just so thankful that you're alive.'

'And it doesn't bother you that I can't have any children?'

'I've told you before, Frankie. No. You're what matters to me. As long as we have each other, that's all that counts.'

He stood up. 'Your granddad's outside and I promised him I wouldn't stay long so he could have a natter with you.'

'My granddad?' He's come all this way to see me? Oh, bless him,' she said, delighted.

Eddie himself was pleased as it gave him an excuse to leave early, wanting to catch the pretty nurse he had his eye on on his way out. He meant to ask her out for a drink on her next evening off. She fancied him, he knew by the way she looked at him. He'd never been out with a nurse and wanted to see if the rumours were true and they were free with their favours. He leaned over and pecked Frankie's cheek lightly. 'I'll see you tomorrow.'

She nodded, smiling. 'Oh, before you go, Eddie. The garage? How's it doing?'

'Fine. We're managing all right. Wally's thinking of getting a temporary mechanic in until you're fit enough to return to work. Oh, that reminds me, he told me to tell you he'd pop in tomorrow lunchtime. He'll tell you all the news himself then. Right, I'm off or your granddad won't have any time left.'

Edgar arrived moments after Eddie had departed, hobbling slowly down the ward, obviously in pain.

'Your rheumatics playing up?' she asked after he had awkwardly bent over to kiss her.

'No more than usual,' he said gruffly, easing himself down on the chair Eddie had just vacated. 'And considering what pain you must be in, lovey, I've nothing to complain about. I didn't know what ter bring yer, me ducky, so I didn't bring n'ote.'

'You brought yourself, Granddad, and that's what counts. It's lovely to see you,' she said sincerely.

'It's good to see you, me darlin', but not like this. So what happened?'

'Mam must have told you I fell down the stairs?'

'She did, but it's not like you to be so careless, Frankie. Clumsy sometimes but not enough to cause such damage to yerself.'

'I missed my footing, Granddad, and fell headlong, hitting every step on my way down. I knocked myself out at the bottom, simple as that. But I can't for the life of me remember anything about it.'

'Well, maybe yer've blanked out whatever happened to cause it 'cos it was so 'orrible?'

'Oh!' she exclaimed. She hadn't thought of that. Had something happened prior to her fall that she couldn't remember? But then, if it had, Eddie would have told her, surely.

Edgar's face grew grave and through rheumy eyes he looked at her sadly. 'I'm sorry about . . . well, you know what.'

She took his gnarled hand and squeezed it. 'Thanks, Granddad. I don't know whether I'll ever get used to the fact that I can't have children,' she whispered, tears pricking her eyes.

'There's more ter life than having kids, Frankie. You're alive and getting better, and that's the main thing to all of us.'

She forced a smile. 'So what's happening in the big wide world.'

'Not much in my part of it.'

'Oh, come on, Granddad, surely something is?'

Lips pursed, he paused for a moment thoughtfully then announced. 'Oh, I finally stopped Widow Twankey from popping in.'

'You did? How?'

'Told her straight. Stop bothering me, yer getting on me nerves, and the next time you come in, I'll get the police on yer fer trespass.'

If her injuries hadn't still hurt so much Frankie would have laughed. 'Oh, Granddad, you didn't?'

'Bloody did. Anyway, can't have her traipsing in willy-nilly now Nelly Dawson is living wi' me, can I?'

Frankie stared at him aghast. 'Nelly Dawson? Living with you? But, Granddad, she's married.'

A mischievous twinkle in his eyes, he replied, 'So she is, Frankie. But she saw sense at last, left that cretin who had the nerve to call 'imself 'er husband and came to live with me.'

'You're living in sin! Oh, Granddad, the shame.'

'Sod the shame. I'm far too old to turn down a bit of happiness, Frankie, just because of what the bleddy neighbours might think.'

She could see the wisdom in that. 'Well, good on you, Granddad, and give my best to Nelly. Does my mam know?'

'Not yet, but she will termorrow. Me and Nelly are going to see her.'

'She'll be happy for you, Granddad.'

'Yes, I think she will.'

'What a fine old chap your granddad is,' said the pretty young nurse later as she stuck a thermometer in Frankie's mouth just after Edgar had left. 'And a good-looking husband too,' she added. 'Such a gentleman, not at all the sort we see so many of here. Take us nurses for granted, think they can order us about. But not your husband, Mrs Taylor. Chats to all of us. Even brought us chocolates too. Said it was by way of thanks for looking after you. Need a bed pan?' she asked, picking up Frankie's wrist to check her pulse.

Eddie's luck wasn't in that night. There was no sign of the pretty nurse as he left the ward. Thinking that she'd keep for another time, he made do with Stella. They were huddled together now in a secluded area behind a clump of bushes on the canal bank, Stella looking at him adoringly.

'I still can't believe what you did,' she said, giggling. 'Fancy chucking stones up at my bedroom window to get my attention.'

'Well, I couldn't very well knock on your door, could I?'

'No, not really. But you will one day, though, won't you, Eddie. And soon?'

He pulled away from her, scowling fiercely. 'Oh, don't go on about me leaving Frankie, Stella. For God's sake, the woman has just been injured. I can't very well walk out on her 'til she's better, can I?'

She inwardly scolded herself, knowing she had gone too far. It was unforgivable of her to expect Eddie to walk out on Frankie while she was in such a bad way, even if she had caused it herself. Stella was so desperate to be with him though that the news of Frankie's accident had come as a devastating blow. It delayed Eddie's departure indefinitely. But if she wanted Eddie, which she did above everything, couldn't visualise her life without him, then she'd have to have patience. 'No, I suppose not. But as you said, she brought it all on herself. I can't believe Frankie's changed so much.'

'Well, believe it, Stella, she has.'

'Oh, Eddie, this is so unfair on you. And me,' she added. 'It's not enough that she stole you from me in the first place, then lied to get you to marry her, now she does this on purpose to stop you leaving her for me. It's criminal, it is.'

'She wants locking up, Stella, believe me. She told me she'd try and kill herself if I threatened to go but I didn't think for one minute she would.' He looked at her, smiling charmingly. 'Rest assured, my darling, I will leave her as soon as I possibly can and then me and you will go away together and start afresh,' he said, slipping his hand inside her blouse to caress her breast. 'But that boyfriend of yours . . .'

'Oh, I've finished with him, Eddie.' Stella snuggled closer to him. 'I should have done it when we started seeing each other. It's just that he looked at me so pathetically when I tried, I couldn't bring myself to at first. And he was someone to go out with on the nights I wasn't seeing you. I'm so angry he went and told Frankie me and you were seeing each other.'

Eddie gave a callous laugh. 'I can see his point, Stella.'

'Yes, I suppose. Anyway, Roger and me are history as far as I'm concerned. I couldn't believe it when he said he'd wait for me to come to my senses. I think he really must love me,' she said distantly. 'Still, that's his problem, not mine.' She moved her body even closer. 'Eddie, while Frankie's in hospital we'll be able to see each other more often, won't we?'

'Have more sense, woman,' he snapped, looking at her hard. 'Apart from the fact I have no choice but to show my face at the hospital every night, I have to be careful her family don't suspect anything until I'm ready to leave. I'm trying to get some money together for us, Stella,' he expertly lied. 'One word of this getting out and I could lose my job, and then where would we be? I've already lost my family and inheritance through Frankie, I can't afford to lose any more.' His voice lowered seductively. 'Just be happy with what we have now, Stella. We'll be together soon enough, believe me.' He kissed her long and hard and while she was still reeling from his passion he pulled away slightly and whispered, 'Have you any money you can loan me, only I'm a little short at the moment?'

''Course, Eddie,' she murmured. 'I've ten shillings in my purse.'

'You couldn't make it a pound, could you?'

'Oh, er . . . I could draw it from my savings out of what I was putting by for when we get our house together.'

He pulled her close, caressing her more urgently. 'I'll have plenty of money by then myself so you needn't worry about saving, my darling.'

'Oh, okay then, Eddie, I'll get it out for you tomorrow.'

'I'll meet you outside your work at dinnertime and you can get it then.'

His hand sought her inner thigh and stroked it suggestively.

'Have you brought some protection?' she asked him.

As if she need ask. The last thing he wanted was for Stella to get herself pregnant. What a stink that would cause! ''Course I have,' he answered. Then like a bolt from the blue an idea struck him. God, it was so simple, but so clever. *That's* how he would get his revenge on Amanda and her father. Providing she wasn't married by now, which he doubted she would be, he would get her pregnant then dump her. Amanda would be destroyed, being abandoned with a child on the way and no hope of its father marrying her, and as for Sutton, not only would it show him what a slut his daughter really was, but his social standing in the community would be drastically reduced, let alone at work. The gossips would have a field day and it'd be many a long day before he'd hold his head up again.

Eddie was ecstatic with excitement. 'Come here,' he said to Stella, pushing her backwards on the grassy slope. He rolled on top of her and Stella giggled.

The next night Frankie was propped up in bed at visiting time, not sure if Eddie would manage to come but hoping he would.

The bell sounded and at the bottom of the ward, the doors burst open and a stream of visitors poured in.

'Oh,' she exclaimed when she recognised the young man heading towards her. 'Roger,' she said, smiling when he arrived at the side of her bed. 'How lovely to see you.' Suddenly her hopes soared. 'Is Stella with you?'

He frowned quizzically. 'No.'

'Oh. I was kinda hoping she was. I hoped you and she were back together. But it's great to see you, Roger. I'm so glad you came. To be honest after what happened in the garage . . .' Her face fell and she gave a sad sigh. 'Well, I thought none of you would ever speak to me again.' She brightened. 'But anyway, I hope your being here means that's all past history? Sit down,' she invited, indicating a chair at the side of the bed. 'You must have so much news to catch me up on.' She suddenly frowned questioningly. 'How did you know I was in hospital, Roger?'

He stared at her uncomfortably. There could be only one reason Frankie was acting so strangely. He knew she had suffered a bad blow to the head and now she obviously didn't remember his visit to her house or anything he had told her. What did he do? Did he remind her? Oh, but she looked so poorly. Some fall she must have taken to inflict such damage. He just prayed it wasn't what he had told her that had upset her so much it had caused her to have her accident. His mind raced, deliberating what best to do. He'd not mention anything. Not just now anyway. Her memory might come back naturally. 'The neighbour told me when I called around ter visit you at your house,' he said, thrusting a bunch of flowers at her. 'I brought you these.'

'Oh, they're lovely,' she said, gratefully accepting them. It was then that she spotted Eddie arriving. 'Oh, here's my husband. Eddie, this is Roger,' she hesitated, not knowing how to introduce Roger, unsure whether Roger and Stella were back together again or not. She decided to play it safe in order to avoid any upset. 'He's an old friend of mine.'

The two men looked at each other.

Roger weighed Eddie up, thinking, So this the bastard who seduced my girlfriend then discarded her to steal my best friend's woman and marry her. And as if that isn't bad enough he's now betraying Frankie by seeing Stella on the sly. Roger had to fight an urge to take a swing at the man. He only stopped himself because of where they were.

Eddie meantime was eyeing him coldly. So this was the swine who'd spilled the beans to Frankie. Thank God they were in a hospital or he'd make Roger very sorry for that.

Roger was fully aware of the meaning behind the black look Eddie was giving him. 'I'd . . . er . . . best be off, Frankie,' he told her.

'Oh, don't go, Roger,' she said, disappointed.

'I only popped in quickly, just to give you my best when I heard how poorly yer were,' he said uncomfortably. 'I'm sorry about yer accident, Frankie. I hope you get better soon. You take care.'

As Roger walked off down the ward, Eddie glanced after him. 'I'm just going to catch the nurse and get a progress report,' he told Frankie.

'Oh, there's no need for that, Eddie. I can tell you what the doctor said when I saw him this morning.'

'Now you know what your memory is like,' he said condescendingly. 'So I'd best check for myself and make sure I get the right story.'

He caught Roger up outside in the corridor. 'Oi, you!' he shouted.

A passing nurse eyed him disapprovingly. 'Shush,' she said. 'Please remember where you are.'

Eddie smiled apologetically, then grabbed Roger's arm, pulling him to a halt. 'Don't ignore me,' he hissed.

'I've got nothing to say to you,' Roger said, looking at him disdainfully.

Eddie smiled wickedly. 'Well, I have to you.' Grabbing his coat lapels, he pulled the other man close, pushing his face into his. 'Now you listen good. Stay away from my wife. Let me hear you've been within an inch of her, or one word of gossip about anything to do with me, and I'll make you wish you'd never set eyes on me. This is no idle threat, it's a warning, mate.' His voice lowered nastily. 'And another thing. Stella wants nothing to do with you, so stay away from her as well. Now fuck off and don't let me catch sight of you again.'

'Excuse me, gentlemen, is anything wrong?' a passing doctor asked in concern, looking at them both in turn.

Letting go of Roger, Eddie shook his head. 'Everything's fine, thank you, Doctor. We were just having a private discussion, getting a few things straight. That right, Roger?' he said, eyeing him meaningfully.

Gulping, the other man nodded.

Chapter Twenty-Seven

'That's odd,' remarked Wally, coming through the office door into the main garage. 'That's the second complaint I've had this week.'

'Complaint about what?' Eddie asked, pouring himself a mug of tea. He took a sniff at the milk bottle, pulled a face at the rancid smell and grimaced, annoyed, realising he'd have to drink his tea black, which he didn't like. Frankie did have her uses, he thought, like getting the tea things straight and making sure they never ran out. Since her accident they were always running out of tea, sugar, and especially milk. 'The milk's off.'

'Is it? Oh! Well, go and get some then or send Bernard.'

'Bernard!' Eddie shouted. 'Go and get some milk, and hurry up before my tea goes cold.' He returned his attention to Wally. 'You were telling me you've had two complaints this week?'

'Eh? Oh, so I was. Well, the first customer who complained was Mr Sims when he collected his Ford V8 Woodie. He said there was a discrepancy in his mileage, over forty miles more on the clock than there was when he brought it in.'

Eddie knew exactly how that forty miles extra had been added. 'He's just mistaken, that's all. Going ga-ga in his old age.'

'Mr Sims is younger than I am, Eddie. But I have to agree with you that he must have made a mistake because I fixed his rattling gearbox and only did a mile or so when I road tested it. As for the other complaint, well, that's a bit more puzzling. Mr Robinson came in to ask me to check his car over, which I did, and I told him he needed a new gasket.'

'So, what's his problem?'

Wally thoughtfully stroked his chin. 'Well, he said we'd already put him a new gasket in when he brought his car in the other week for a puncture repair and a new fuel pipe. He said Frankie noticed he needed a new gasket and did it, which we charged him for, but according to him we forgot to add it to his bill. Well, apart from the fact we're not in the habit of forgetting to put exactly what we're charging for on the bill, I would have noticed that the receipts and money didn't tally up when I totalled the daily takings. That's no new gasket in his car, it's the original one. Odd, in't it?'

'It's plain to me,' said Eddie matter-of-factly, knowing exactly what had happened to the money for the supposed new gasket. It was long spent, by himself, and he had enjoyed every penny of it. 'He's trying it on. Trying to get you to do the job without paying.'

'Not Mr Robinson, Eddie. I've been dealing with the chap for years and he's as straight as a die. Actually,' added Wally, looking at Eddie quizzically, 'he said it was you who told him what Frankie had done and took the money from him.'

His heart beat quickened. 'Oh, yes,' he said. 'I remember now. But I was only doing what she told me to, Wally.' He took a deep breath, purposely putting a pained expression on his face. 'Look, I didn't want to tell you this but for a while Frankie's been acting strangely.'

'She has? I hadn't noticed.'

'No, maybe not, but I'm her husband and with her all the time. She's been telling me she's done something, then I find out she hasn't. Stupid things like forgetting to take her garage keys home or going into the shops for something for dinner and coming out without anything. But this is more serious. I'd no idea her forgetfulness had gone this far or I'd have said something to you. I did have a word with the doctor about her memory lapses when she landed up in hospital and he said it was all to do with her pregnancy. Sometimes it affects women's brains, he said.'

He was privately thinking thank goodness he hadn't done anything by way of extracting illicit money from the garage since Frankie's accident, if only because the opportunity of doing so hadn't presented itself.

'Oh!' exclaimed Wally, most upset. 'Oh, I see. That's what must have happened with Mr Robinson's car then. Frankie thought she had replaced the gasket when she hadn't. Poor girl.'

'You won't say anything to her about this, will you, Wally?' Eddie urged. 'Only it might set her recovery back. I'll pay for the gasket myself . . .'

'No, no, I wouldn't dream of it,' he insisted as Eddie knew he would. 'And 'course I won't mention anything to Frankie, that poor child has suffered enough. I've already told Mr Robinson I'd replace the gasket free of charge. Well, there wasn't much else I could do except call him a liar which I wasn't prepared to do, and I'm bloody glad I didn't after what you've just told me. I just hope Frankie hasn't done this to any other of our customers.'

Bernard returned with the milk which Eddie took from him and poured a large measure into his mug. 'Do you want a cuppa?' he asked Wally, satisfied his employer was convinced by his version of events and wanting to change the subject.

'I don't mind if I do. And while you're playing tea lady, Eddie, I'm sure Bernard could do with one, couldn't you, lad? And one for our new mechanic. Matty!' he called. 'Tea's up.'

So distracted by what Eddie had told him was Wally that he missed the look of utter contempt on Eddie's face and the scowl he gave Bernard and Matty as he thrust their mugs of tea at them. Both men rapidly went off to resume their work.

Wally took a sip and studied his mug, grimacing in distaste. Like all the others used in the garage it was badly chipped and ingrained with tea stains as well as greasy around the handle. 'Frankie would never have let the mugs get into this state, nor let the milk go off, and our mashings never taste quite like hers. I miss her around here, I really do, can't manage without her really. Matty's proving a God-send, but he's not Frankie. Oh, that reminds me, Eddie. Me and Hilary were thinking of going to the hospital tonight. That won't hinder your plans, will it? Only I know what the ward sister's reaction is if there are more than two visitors at a time.'

'You go,' Eddie urged. 'I know Frankie would love to see you, and if I'm honest I've a few things to do in the house.'

Wally looked at him, confused. 'I thought Nancy was helping you keep the house straight and looking after you?'

'Oh, she is, can't fault her, but I can't expect her to do everything, can I?' he said, his eyes falling on the Bull-nose Morris just being finished off ready for its owner to collect the next day. Usually Eddie preferred a more upmarket model but nothing exciting had been brought into the garage for repair recently and he hadn't taken a car out for over a week and was desperate to do so. Now he had ready access to Frankie's set of keys, something Wally hadn't questioned, coming and going whenever he liked at the garage posed no problems.

Tonight with no need to visit the hospital he could go out earlier and take the car for a decent spin. He'd go by himself, not fancying Stella's company. Also he was becoming increasingly concerned that Frankie's recovery, although slower than the doctors would have liked to have seen, meant she would be allowed home soon and that state of affairs was bound to restrict his freedom.

Downing the last of his tea, Wally put his mug in the sink. 'Right, I'd better go and finish off what I was doing, then I must sort out the weekly takings for banking and get the paperwork together or Hilary will be after me. I must admit, though, her helping me keep the books up to date is a load off me mind, so I'm not grumbling.'

Eddie hid a smug smile. Over the past few months he had secretly noted Wally's method of handling the garage takings. What accumulated over the week was left in the safe – an old contraption hidden out of sight under the counter in the office, the key to it kept on a hook along with the set to the garage Wally placed there when he came in each morning and collected on his way out, it never crossing his mind that anyone would consider taking them, especially not a member of his own family. Wally was so stupidly trusting.

He banked on a Friday afternoon just before three after taking out the wages and dues to be paid. Eddie had decided that the best time to snatch the takings and make his departure would be on a Thursday afternoon, which would be easily done when everyone else was occupied. He'd arrange to slip them to Neil and now the theft wouldn't be discovered until he himself was long gone. It would be so easy! All Eddie hoped was that the week he did it would be one when the takings were good. He wanted to make away with as much as he could.

Running through his plans made him think of his brother. He really must make the effort to go and see him, find out when he was getting out, explain their plans had changed and his new scheme for the future.

He realised Wally was addressing him. 'Er . . . sorry, what did you say?'

'I was just saying there's no rest for the wicked. We'd better get back to it if we ever want to go home tonight.'

Chapter Twenty-Eight

Later that night Eddie was fighting hard to control his impatience. 'You don't have to do that,' he said to Nancy, her fussing around agitating him intensely. It was already past eight and he had planned to collect the car and be out for a drive by now. If she didn't leave soon it wouldn't be worth his while. The thrill of a drive alone, pushing the car to its limits on a deserted road, was just what he needed.

'I don't mind really,' she said, stretching up to press the iron's two-pin plug into the overhead light socket. 'It's the least I can do. You men are hopeless when it comes to looking after yerselves. I'll just press these shirts then I'll leave yer in peace. Besides, the last thing I want our Frankie to think when she comes home is that 'er mam ain't done her bit.' She shook out a shirt and examined it. 'Oh, I'm glad to see the lipstick stain that was on this collar has come out. Funny that,' she said, placing it on the thick piece of cloth on the table, substituting for an ironing board.

'What is?' he asked, lowering the newspaper, pretending to be relaxed and settled for the night when in truth as soon as she left he'd be out the door minutes after her.

'That you should have Frankie's lipstick on yer collar when she's been in 'ospital well over a month and I thought I'd washed all yer shirts,' his mother-in-law replied, spitting on the hot iron and beginning to smooth it over the shirt.

Bloody Stella, he thought, he'd told her to be careful. Or could it have been the shirt he had worn when he had taken out that pretty nurse last week? And the rumours *were* true, nurses were free with their favours. Well, that particular nurse was. Despite knowing he was married, she was really smitten with Eddie and had made it very plain she would be happy to see him again. But he had other ideas. He'd got what he'd wanted and nothing more about her was of interest to him. The only trouble was, he really shouldn't have done what he had, considering she looked after Frankie. It was a hell of a job avoiding that particular nurse when he visited his wife now.

'Oh, that shirt. That was one I found . . . er . . . hanging up in the wardrobe. Frankie must have hung it back up after I'd worn it, not realising it wanted washing. I didn't notice it was dirty 'til I came to wear it again.'

Nancy pulled a wry face. 'It's not like my Frankie to do summat careless like that. Still, it's clean now, and pressed,' she said, draping it around the back of a dining chair along with the rest.

Eddie was hardly able to contain his anger by the time Nancy had donned her coat and prepared to go home. 'Now are you sure, Eddie lovey, there's n'ote else I can do for yer? 'Cos I don't mind, it's no trouble. Yer dinner for tomorrow night is in the pantry ready for yer to heat up when yer get home from work, the ironing's all done and put away, and don't forget ter drop what other washing yer've got off ter me so I can get it done along with the rest at the end of the week.' She gave a chuckle. 'I shan't have Edgar's to do for much longer. The silly old devil must think I'm daft not to know Nelly Dawson's moved in with him. I shan't say n'ote though 'til he comes to tell me official. Good luck to them both, that's what I say. They should grab what happiness they can before it's too late.' She picked up her handbag, hooking it over her arm. 'Right, I'm off then.'

He glanced up at her. 'Yeah, cheerio. Oh, and thanks,' he hurriedly added.

Less than five minutes after Nancy had left, Eddie followed, first checking the coast was clear. It was a dark chilly night, no moon, hardly anyone about, perfect cover for him to steal into the garage and take the car out without being seen. Arriving at Champion's he undid the huge padlock, then pulled back the thick metal strip securing the doors and opened one just wide enough for him to slip through, pulling it to behind him.

The building was in pitch darkness and he groped around, seeking the torch he had hidden earlier behind a motor oil drum just beside the door. He switched it on and shone it around. The interior of the garage looked alien and ghostly, the floor space unusually empty, all the cars having been fixed and collected by their grateful owners except for the one Eddie had come for. It was parked near the doors, keys in the ignition. Opening the driver's door, he slid into the passenger seat and turned the key. At the first attempt the engine purred into life and Eddie smiled smugly. Leaving the engine warming up, he slid out of the seat again, meaning to open the large outer doors and make a quick getaway, when something in his pocket stabbed his leg.

He winced, thrusting his hand into his pocket and pulling out the set of garage keys which he'd put there for safety only moments before. He automatically looked at the keys, wondering which one was the culprit. As he studied them his eyes widened in surprise when he noticed the long key to the safe along with the others. He frowned, confused, then it hit him. This bunch wasn't Frankie's, it was Wally's. The bunches were exactly alike except that Wally's held the safe key, too. Eddie must have taken the wrong set off the hook when he had left that night. He wondered if Wally had noticed the mix-up when he had locked up to go home. Oh, well, he thought, it was a simple mistake and easily explained.

Then another thought struck him. It was a shame to waste such an opportunity, considering his future plan. While he was in possession of the safe key he might as well check how easily it opened. After all he would have to do it when the time came unobserved and as quickly as possible as others would be dangerously nearby.

Grabbing the torch which he had left on the passenger seat, he quickly made his way to the office, let himself in and, squatting down on his haunches, inserted the safe key in the lock. It took several attempts to jiggle the old key into position but finally it slotted into place and Eddie heard the click of the bolts releasing. Pressing down the cumbersome, stiff handle, he pulled open the door, which creaked and groaned so loudly he was afraid someone outside would hear it.

He frowned in concern. He'd have to do something about that before the time came, and opening the door had taken longer than he'd cared for. He would need to practise. He was about to shut the door and try again when curiosity made him shine the torch inside. What he saw there made his eyes light up excitedly, the adrenaline flowing. Inside was a pile of bank notes, far more than he had expected, and a lumpy canvas bag he knew contained coins, a lot by the look of it. Instinctively he grabbed the money and ran his fingers through it. It felt good in his hands, as if it belonged there. Eddie was extremely reluctant to let go of it.

As he looked at it and thought of all the things he could do with it a wicked plan began to form. There was no need for him to let go of this. Why not take it now, while he had the chance, instead of running such a risk later? All he had to do was relock the safe, throw the safe key away on his journey home and that way convince Wally he had lost it himself. Wally would never realise it was Frankie's set he had. Eddie could hide the money securely, somewhere where no one would think of looking, then sit tight for a few weeks. When the heat had died down, he would just tell Frankie their marriage wasn't working and that he was leaving. Afterwards collecting the hidden loot, of course.

Without the key it would take at least a couple of days to find a person qualified to get the safe undone as this surely wasn't a normal locksmith's job, and when the theft was discovered nothing could be connected to him. Not one thing. He had an alibi: Nancy. Hadn't she only minutes ago left him settled in front of the fire for the night? It was all so simple. The only sacrifice Eddie would have to make was not taking the car out tonight, or indeed any car in the future just in case what he had been up to after hours was discovered and then two and two put together.

An urgent need to leave the garage, hide the money and get home filled him. Stuffing the bank notes into the canvas bag, which he then put beside him, he shut the safe door and stuck in the key to relock it.

Half an hour earlier, arm in arm, Wally and Hilary had left the hospital.

'She looks better, don't yer think, Hilary?' asked Wally.

'On the outside, Wally, but inside is another matter.'

'Yes, well . . .' he said gravely. 'Her leg'll be in plaster for another couple of weeks at least and it'll be a while before she recovers completely from her surgery. Poor Frankie. Why her, Hilary?'

'Things like this always happen to the good ones, Wally. People say it's God's way, but I'm not so sure. More like the devil's work, something horrible like that. Anyway, I wasn't talking about her injuries, Wally, I was referring to her mental state. She might have a smile on her face, but Frankie is far from smiling inside. That girl, believe me, is grieving something terrible. She's just putting a brave face on it, covering it up.'

He sighed. 'Mmm. But what do we do, Hilary?'

'Just what we are doing, Wally, my love. Support her. Time is what she needs, and peace and quiet. No upsets for a while.'

'Not if I can help it. I was wondering about sending her and Eddie off on holiday somewhere as soon as she's able. By the sea, maybe. A nice boarding house in Mablethorpe or Skeggie. What do you think?'

Hilary smiled at him tenderly. 'I think, Walter Champion, that you're a lovely man. That's a grand idea.'

'I'm glad yer think so.' He looked at her earnestly. 'Problem is, it'll mean a big dent in the money I was going to spend on our honeymoon.'

'And I'd gladly go without one, for Frankie's sake.'

'Now who's a lovely person?' he said, smiling lovingly at her. 'Brrr, it's cold ternight. Let's get back and snuggle up in front of the fire with a nice cuppa cocoa.'

Hilary pulled him to a halt. 'We can snuggle up in front of the fire after we've made up the books.'

He pulled a face. 'It's not book night, is it?' he grumbled, that being the last thing he wanted to do.

'You know damned well it is, Wally, and we're not going to leave them and risk getting those books back into the state they were in when I started helping you. They were a nightmare to sort out.'

'Yeah, but now they're straight, leaving 'em for one week won't make that much difference.' The look on her face made him sigh. 'Slave driver.' Then his face lit up. 'We can't do them tonight. I've just remembered, I forgot to bring them home from the garage.'

'Oh, Wally,' she scolded. Then a thought struck her. 'Have you still got the garage keys on you or did you leave them at home?'

He patted his pocket. 'I've still got them, must have forgotten to put them on the hook in the kitchen in the rush to get to the hospital to see our Frankie. Why?'

She smiled at him. 'Most fortunate you forgot then because it means you'll be able to go and get those books.'

His face looked crestfallen. 'Surely you don't mean that, Hilary? We'll do 'em termorrow, eh? I won't forget to bring them home, I promise.'

'And you promised to take me to the pictures tomorrow night, remember?'

'Oh, so I did. I've a memory like a sieve at the moment.' Then a horrifying fact hit him. 'Oh, my God,' he exclaimed, slapping his hand to his forehead.

She frowned, worried. 'What? Wally, what is it?'

'I never did the banking last week. I completely forgot with all this worry over our Frankie. There's nearly two weeks' takings piling up in the safe.'

'Oh, Wally, I'm not surprised. But stop worrying. As you said, the money's in the safe.' She patted his arm reassuringly. 'It's all safe in the safe,' she said, chuckling. 'And you've said yourself, many a time, that safe has a mind of its own. It would take an expert safe cracker to get it open without a key, so stop worrying. Just make sure you do the banking tomorrow. Now go and fetch the books. I'll hurry ahead and get the kettle on.'

He pulled her to him and kissed her tenderly. 'You're a wonderful woman, I love you,' he said emotionally. 'I never thought I could meet someone who'd mean more to me than me garage, Hilary. But you do.'

'Oh, Wally,' she uttered, tears of happiness glinting her eyes. 'I love you too.'

His eyes suddenly shone with excitement. 'Let's not wait any longer to get married, Hilary. Wadda you say?'

A bright happy smile split her face. 'Is tomorrow soon enough?'

'Not for me it ain't, me darlin'. I'd do it right now if we could. But for Nancy it would be. Could you imagine her face if we announced in the morning we were getting wed in the afternoon? She'd go stark staring mad.'

'And she'd have a point,' Hilary said, laughing. 'We women need time to prepare. I want to look my best the day I say "*I do*" to you.'

'I'd marry you if you wore a sack.'

'I know you would, but a sack isn't quite what I had in mind,' she giggled. 'Shall we say next month? Is that soon enough for you?'

'It'll have to do, I suppose,' said Wally huskily, bending his head to kiss her again. 'You go and get that kettle on, I won't be long behind you,' he promised, playfully patting her backside.

'I'll be watching the clock,' she replied tenderly, and he turned from her to hurry off.

It wasn't until Wally was right up to the garage doors, about to dig his bunch of keys out of his pocket, that he noticed something odd. The doors were closed but the padlock was undone, the door's metal strip pulled back. But that wasn't possible, surely. The last thing he had done was secure the premises before going home, he knew he had, could remember distinctly. It was then the sound of a car engine running registered and a surge of panic filled him. He had no doubt in his mind what was happening. His garage was being robbed.

Wally hesitated momentarily, torn between the sensible course of alerting the police, with the risk that meantime the burglars could make their getaway, or the prospect of going in and tackling them himself.

There was no contest when it came to it. This was his garage and no one was going to steal from him what he had sweated blood to achieve. Without another thought he inched open one of the doors and slipped inside, flattening himself against the wall. The place was in pitch darkness and it took several long moments before he could see properly. He couldn't make out anyone, or sense another presence. Crouching, he inched his way over to the car then lifted his head, looking over the top to see if he could spot anything. Still nothing. Creeping around the car, the stench of its exhaust fumes nearly choking him, he tried to see if the intruder was over by the back, stealing whatever they were after besides this car obviously or why else was the engine running?

Still he couldn't see anyone or for that matter hear anything. Maybe the robbers had already left. But then why leave the engine running? No, they must still be here. But where?

He stood for a moment, deliberating, then it struck him. The robber or robbers must be in the office. Oh, hell, his mind screamed. The safe, inside which was nearly two weeks' worth of takings. It was heavy, cumbersome, it would be a struggle, but two strong men could lift it, carry it out, break into it at their leisure later. His face set grimly. Well, not if he could help it.

Frantically he searched around for something heavy. Wally was not at all a violent man, appalled at the thought in fact, but fearing for his own safety he felt he needed something to use in self-defence. Usually there were all manner of tools lying around. Why was it nothing was handy when you desperately needed it? Then thankfully he spotted his monkey wrench where he had left it earlier, lying on the edge of the wide counter running the length of the far wall. He grabbed it, then taking several breaths, crept over to the office. Raising the wrench menacingly, he stepped inside.

The sight that met him froze him rigid.

Eddie, so intent on trying to relock the safe and make a hurried departure, hadn't heard him enter.

In total shock and utter disbelief at what he was witnessing, Wally lowered the wrench. 'What are you doing, Eddie? I hope ter God it's not what it looks like?'

At the sound of his voice Eddie jumped up, face paling. 'Er . . . Wally, no . . . er . . .' Sheer terror filled his being. Never for a minute had he expected company, and not Wally of all people. His mind whirled, desperate for a plausible excuse to get him out of this mess. 'Oh, am I glad to see you! You've had burglars,' he blurted. 'Luckily, I was just passing on my way to the pub when I happened to spot the door to the garage open,' he continued, making the lies up as he went along. 'Well, at first I thought you'd forgotten to lock them. Then

I . . . er . . . heard the car engine running, and the place being in darkness, well, I realised what was happening. Obviously the garage was being robbed. I couldn't let that happen, could I? So I just charged in here and put the fear of God up them. There was two of them but I scared them off. I've never seen blokes run so quick.'

Wally sighed with relief. 'Oh, I see.' He slapped Eddie's arm in a thankful gesture. 'That was very brave of you. I much appreciate it, really I do. With all this happening to Frankie, I forgot to bank last week and there's far more than usual in the safe. I bet they're kicking themselves for leaving that bag behind,' he said, inclining his head towards the bulky bag to the side of Eddie.

His eyes flashed to it, then back to Wally. 'Oh, yeah, I bet they are. Only they never intentionally left it, I managed to grab it before they scarpered.'

Wally gave a sigh of relief. 'Thank God for that!' Then a thought struck him and he raked his hand through his hair, bothered. 'It doesn't look like to me they broke in, there's no sign of damage to the front doors.' His eyes fell on the safe. 'And . . .'

'They had the keys,' Eddie cut in hurriedly, waving them. 'They dropped them when I surprised them. It's my guess the cheeky beggars, whoever they are, swiped them off the hook sometime today when we were all busy.' He elaborated without thinking, 'We left together tonight so you must have picked up Frankie's set, not realising the safe key wasn't on it. And as there wasn't another bunch on the hook when I went to get ours, I must have thought I already had them in my pocket. I was just putting the money back in the safe, then coming round to tell you about it.'

To Eddie's relief, Wally seemed to accept that explanation. 'Yes, I suppose that's what happened then,' he said. 'I'll have to find a proper hiding place for the keys in future. Can't risk this sort of thing again. It's a good job you were around to put a stop to their game, Eddie, or I dread to think . . . Still, you were, and thanks. Thanks so much.' He took a deep breath. 'Well, I suppose you'd better fetch the police while I put the money back in the safe and have a look around to see if anything has been taken, though that's going to be difficult 'cos the trouble is in a place like this, you don't know something's gone 'til you come to use it.

'And I'll tell you something for nothing, Eddie, lad,' he continued. 'After this, I'm getting a phone put in. I've always shied away from them contraptions before, managed well enough without one really, but it's emergencies like this when a telephone is a Godsend.' He managed a smile. 'I forgot to tek the books home, I only popped back to fetch 'em. Well, we won't get them done tonight. The police are ages taking statements, so I believe. Oh, on yer way back from the telephone box, can you pop to my house and tell Hilary what's happened else she'll be worried I've been kidnapped or something?'

Eddie was terrified by this mention of the police. Their involvement was the last thing he wanted. They'd automatically want his name, then would obviously check their records, and if what the security guard at Rootes had said was true then Eddie's name could be on some sort of list. If it was, his true background would all come out and he could kiss goodbye to what he had hoped to achieve here.

Once again he could feel his whole future crumble. Why did Wally have to pick tonight of all nights to forget to take the books home?

Eddie clenched his fists, fighting an urge to grab the bag and make a run for it, but he doubted he'd get far. Somehow he had to persuade Wally not to fetch the police.

'Oh, surely we don't want to bother the bobbies, Wally? It's not like anything's been taken. They left here with nothing, I can assure you of that.'

Wally eyed him, shocked. 'Oh, but I must report this,' he said, aghast. 'Those robbers nearly got away with two weeks' takings and the rest they probably would've took if you hadn't happened to be passing. I can't just do nothing. What if they try this caper on someone else and those poor sods ain't so lucky as me? It's my moral duty to report this.'

Eddie swallowed hard, just managing by sheer will-power not to lose his temper. 'Well, if you do, Wally, please leave me out of it. It's . . . er . . . Frankie I'm worried about. I can't cause her any upset at the moment and this might set her recovery back.'

Wally gravely shook his head. 'Well, yer don't know Frankie very well if you think that, Eddie. Despite what she's going through, she'll be upset when she finds out all this but damned proud of you. And if I know her, she'll demand the police give you a bravery award.'

Before he could stop himself Eddie spat aggressively, 'Can't you just leave it, Wally? God, what is it with you people? Why can't you leave well alone?' Then, horrified, realising what he had said, he blurted, 'I'm sorry, I'm just tired and this had shaken me up.'

Wally stared at him, taken aback. Eddie was more than shaken up, he was very agitated. It was slowly dawning on Wally that there was more to this than Eddie was telling. But what? Thoughtfully he bent over and picked up the canvas bag containing the money, took the keys off Eddie, put the bag in the safe, relocked it and put the keys in his own pocket. Still thoughtful he walked back into the main garage and switched on one of the lights, affording a feeble light in an otherwise almost pitch-dark room. He made his way over to the car, leaned inside and switched off its engine. Then he leaned his back against it and looked across at Eddie, who by now had followed him through and was standing a few feet away.

'Why are you really so against me getting the police involved, Eddie?' asked Wally evenly, although his heart was thumping, not liking the way his mind was working.

Eddie fought with all his strength to remain calm. He had a dreadful feeling that if Wally had not already sussed the truth, he was getting close to it. 'I'm not,' he denied vehemently. 'I just think it's a complete waste of time, that's all.'

'Well, that's your opinion, not mine. I'm sorry, Eddie, but I'm fetching them. I can't just do nothing and let the buggers get away with it.'

He made to walk off, but Eddie, the fear of God on him, leapt over, blocking his way. 'I wish you wouldn't, Wally,' he said warningly, pushing his face close to his.

Wally grimaced, eyes narrowing as the awful truth hit him. He pulled the two bunches of keys out of his pocket and held them towards Eddie. 'You took my bunch of keys this evening, didn't you? There was no burglars, Eddie. You weren't putting the money *back* in the safe, *you* were taking it out.'

Eddie stared at him. He had been caught fair and square and all the lies in the world weren't going to get him out of this mess. He gave a menacing chuckle and pushed Wally backwards with the flat of his hands. 'Pity you had to come back and catch me at it.'

'Well, I did, unluckily for you. And push me again, Eddie, and you'll wish you hadn't,' he warned. 'This is going to break Frankie's heart.'

'And do you think I give a fuck?' he hissed. 'This is all her fault. She tricked me into marrying her. Told me she was an heiress. Promised me a business.'

Wally was staring. 'Our Frankie tricked you into marrying her? That I'll never believe. You're a liar, Eddie Taylor.' Suddenly he saw Eddie for what he really was. 'You have no wealthy family, have you? This has all been an act. It's *you* who tricked our Frankie.' He slapped his hand to his forehead, his expression horrified. 'Bloody hell, it all makes sense now. I wondered why you looked so shocked when you realised I owned the garage, not Sam. That was your game, wasn't it? You thought by getting Frankie to marry you, you'd get your hands on it when Sam died.' He gave a sarcastic laugh. 'When you realised you weren't going to get the garage you just bided your time 'til you saw an opportunity to steal the takings.'

Wally's temper rose now as the truth about several more things slotted into place. 'You bastard!' he spat. 'You've been blaming Frankie for things you've done yerself. Like charging my customers for work we haven't done, and the extra mileage on the cars. You've been taking them out. Been robbing other places and using them as getaway cars, is that it?' He poked Eddie hard in the shoulder. 'Come on, tell me I've got this all wrong. You can't, can you, because what I'm saying is the truth.'

Eddie smirked at him.

Wally scowled darkly and shook his head. 'You despicable bastard. How could you do this to us? We took you in, treated you more than fairly. We don't deserve this, least of all Frankie. Still, I'd sooner her be devastated when she hears all this than stay married to a lying thief like you. I'm fetching the bobbies whether you like it or not. Let's see what they have to make of it.'

Black fury filled Eddie. 'You get the filth involved,' he cried, 'and I'll kill you!'

Before he could stop himself he'd leapt at Wally, pushing him so hard he shot backwards. Wally let out a cry of surprise, the keys in his hand flying through the air. There was a dull thud then silence.

Eddie stared around him in the dim light. Where was Wally? What had happened to him? He was nowhere in sight. There wasn't a sound. Inching stealthily forward, Eddie peered all around him. Still nothing. He inched forward again, eyes searching frantically. His foot hung over the gaping hole of the pit; he just managed to steady himself before he stepped into it. Heart racing, he looked down but it was far too dark to see the bottom, the dim light that Wally had flicked on moments before not reaching that far. He lifted his head and glanced around, then his eyes rested back on the pit. Had Wally fallen down there and knocked himself out?

Rushing back to the office, he grabbed the torch and ran back, shining it down into the pit. What he saw made his blood run cold.

Wally lay sprawled face up, blank eyes staring. From the back of his head blood was flowing and forming a pool. He was dead, there was no doubt in Eddie's mind.

His thoughts whirled frantically. He was a murderer. He could spend the rest of his life in jail for this. What on earth was he going to do? Then it struck him. He'd got to make this look like an accident.

Quick as a flash, he searched around for the two bunches of keys. Much to Eddie's relief he quickly found them. Thrusting Frankie's bunch in his own pocket, he threw Wally's set down the pit. Then he ran over to the wall by the office door, flicked off the overhead light and slipped out of the garage, pushing the door to behind him, making it appear to any passers-by that it was shut securely. Collar up, shoulders hunched and keeping well to the shadows, he walked hurriedly home.

Chapter Twenty-Nine

Moving the net aside, Frankie stared out of the back-room window. Through the glass the brick-walled yard beyond looked bleak and uninviting. A grey sky hung low, thick frost causing next door's washing to hang stiffly on the line. Frankie shuddered. The weather mirrored her feelings, as if it was in sympathy with her. She gave a sad sigh. It would be Christmas very soon but neither she nor the rest of the family would feel like celebrating.

Wally's accidental death two months previously had hit them all badly. They were all trying to come to terms with his sad loss, but it would take a long time.

She heard the back gate creak open and her eyes went to it. She watched her mother struggle through, weighed down with shopping. As fast as her own injuries would allow Frankie made her way to the kitchen door and pulled it open.

'Hello, Mam,' she called in greeting.

Breathlessly, Nancy came up to her.

'Let me help you?' Frankie offered.

'No,' Nancy responded sharply. 'Now yer know what the doctor ordered. No lifting. In fact, no doing nothing. Move out the way and let me in, it's bloody freezing out 'ere.'

'Oh, sorry, Mam,' Frankie said, standing aside to allow her mother access and quickly shutting the door behind her.

'Now that's all yer groceries got,' Nancy said, piling the bags on the kitchen table. 'And there's a little treat from me for yer in one of the bags.'

'Oh, Mam, you shouldn't have.'

'Anything to brighten yer, Frankie, lovey. It's only a quarter of Mint Imperials. Me and yer dad are worried about yer, we are really.'

'I'm fine, Mam,' she fibbed, forcing a smile to her drawn face. 'How's Dad?'

'Oh, bearing up, lovey,' replied Nancy, stripping off her coat and hanging it on the hook on the back door. 'Best as can be expected. He's working hard and it helps keep his mind off things. Maybe Eddie would come and fetch him on Sat'day afternoon and wheel him down, 'cos he'd love ter see yer.'

'I'll ask him, Mam, but you know at the moment he's working all hours too.'

'Yes, I know he is. He's a grand lad, Frankie. Eddie's rallied round when we most needed him. The way he's keeping the garage going is teking the burden off you 'til yer well enough to go back.'

Frankie looked nervous. 'I don't know whether I will ever go back, Mam.'

Nancy eyed her sharply. 'We'll have less of that talk. Anyway, now's not the time for you to be meking big decisions.'

'Mam, like you said, Eddie seems to be managing fine and I might just leave him to it. Do something else.'

'Such as?'

She shrugged her shoulders. 'I don't know. Become a housewife.'

'You, a housewife? Huh! Well, we'll see. According to the doctor you've at least another couple of months' recuperation before you can even think about returning to work. Lots of things can happen between now and then. Did yer granddad and Nelly pop in today? They said they were going to when I saw them this morning.'

'Yes, about eleven. Oh, Mam, they're so happy together and I'm so glad Nelly's been able to help Granddad through this awful time.'

'Yes, me duck, so am I. She's a dear old lady and having her to fuss over Edgar has been one less problem for me to worry about. Now let's get that kettle on,' she said, bustling around. 'You park yer body while I get this shopping put away and then I'll make us a nice mash.'

'I'll mash the tea, Mam.'

'You will not,' she said, wagging one finger. 'How many times do I have to tell yer, Frankie? You should be resting. The sooner you do as you're told, the sooner you'll be better.'

'I am resting, Mam. I'm sick of resting. It's driving me mad doing nothing all day. And it's not fair to you, having to do all this. It's not as if you haven't enough to do of your own.'

'Of course it's fair, yer me daughter. Now sit down, you're in me way.' Nancy suddenly stopped what she was doing and eyed Frankie tenderly, holding wide her arms. 'Come and give yer old mam a hug. Just a gentle one. A proper squeeze'll have ter wait 'til yer better.'

Frankie didn't need to be asked twice.

'There, that's better,' said Nancy, smoothing a protective hand over her daughter's head. 'N'ote like a good hug from yer mam.' She pulled away, holding Frankie at arm's length and eyeing her hard. 'Now listen here, my girl. You've to stop blaming yerself for what happened to Wally. Don't look at me like that. Me and yer dad know fine well yer do. It was an accident, lovey, pure and simple.'

Frankie sighed despondently. 'I know, Mam, I know. But I can't help thinking that if I hadn't been so stupid as to fall down the stairs, Uncle Wally wouldn't have had so much on his mind and fallen into the pit like that. And it doesn't really make sense to me, Mam. Uncle Wally knew that garage like the back of his hand. For Christ's sake, he dug that pit out himself. How did he come to fall into it?'

Nancy shrugged her shoulders. 'Yer dad and me have gone over and over just that fact, Frankie. The Lord only knows. Wally just did, and that's that.' She eyed Frankie sternly. 'He'd be turning in his grave if he knew you were blaming yerself. Yer've got ter stop it, Frankie.'

She took a deep breath. 'I'll try, Mam.'

'You'll do more than try. You will,' Nancy ordered. 'And another thing, my girl. Wally left his garage and house to you. That's what he wanted and you've to accept them both as the gift he meant them to be.'

Frankie's face set tightly. 'I can't, Mam,' she said resolutely. 'We've had this all out before and I won't change my mind. It should all rightly go to Dad and you.'

Nancy frowned. 'Why?' she demanded. 'Look, I don't think for a minute Wally expected to go so young. I expect he thought when he made his will that he'd see me and yer dad out, which is only natural as he's younger. But Wally loved you, Frankie, as much as if you were his own, and he left you his worldly goods because he knew of no one better. You must honour his wishes, my darlin'.'

Tears of distress filled her eyes. 'Oh, Mam, I can't go back to the garage. That place was his life, he built it up from scratch, loved it so much.'

'And you don't? Come on, Frankie, in your way you've put as much blood, sweat and tears into it as Wally did. You gave it yer all, you know you did. And yer don't think Wally remembered that when he made his will? He left it to someone who loved the place as much as he did. And that's you, Frankie.'

'I know you're right. I just wish . . . Oh, Mam,' she cried, falling back into her mother's arms, burying her head in Nancy's shoulder. 'I just miss him so much,' she sobbed.

Nancy swallowed hard. 'We all do, me darlin',' she whispered emotionally. 'Yer granddad lost a beloved son, yer dad his best friend, me a very dear brother-in-law. As for Hilary . . . well, that poor woman lost her future happiness the day Wally died. And you, my darlin', as if you weren't suffering enough, lost the best uncle a niece could ever have. It's hard for all of us, Frankie, but we have to accept he's gone and get on with things.'

'I know, Mam,' she whispered. 'I know and I'm trying, really I am.' Frankie sniffed hard, pulled a handkerchief from inside her sleeve, wiped her eyes and blew her nose. 'About, Hilary, Mam. Not that I think for a minute she'd expect anything, but Uncle Wally loved her so much. Don't you think he would have wanted her to have something?'

Nancy smiled at her tenderly. 'I'm sure he would, Frankie, and if you want to give her whatever you feel fitting then that's your decision, not for me and yer dad to question.'

Frankie took a deep breath. 'I was thinking of the house. I begged you and Dad to move into it, I'd like nothing better, you know that, but you won't, will you?'

Nancy smiled affectionately. 'We're happy as we are, Frankie. We manage fine there and yer dad's customers know just where to find him. But we did appreciate the offer very much.' She eyed her in concern. 'Are you sure about giving it to Hilary?'

'It seems the fitting thing to do, Mam, all considering.'

'I agree with yer then, it is, and if it makes you happy you do it, lovey,' Nancy said sincerely. 'Now let's make that tea afore I pass out wi' thirst.'

Chapter Thirty

'Oh, Ed, I really thought yer'd abandoned me.'

Eddie leaned across the table and eyed Neil earnestly, his voice low, conscious of listening ears all around him. 'Don't be stupid, man. You're my brother. I just couldn't get to see you, I've explained why. Anyway, that's not a problem any more. I can come and go as I please now,' he said, smiling smugly.

Neil sat back in his uncomfortable chair and nodded. 'I can't believe it. You, a garage owner. Well, yer wife owns it, but that's the same thing, ain't it? And a house. Fancy owning a house.'

'Well, believe it, brother. You and me are made for life. As for the house, I nearly had a fit when Frankie told me she was offering it to her parents. How I stopped myself from going for her, I'll never know. Anyway, thank God, they don't want it. I can't get Frankie to move into it at the moment but she will eventually if I have to drag her.'

'You ain't gonna leave her then?'

'What? Why should I?'

'Well, you don't exactly love her, do you? And what about this Stella woman yer knocking off?'

'What about her? She's just my bit on the side. Not that she realises that, of course,' Eddie added, grinning maliciously. 'Don't worry about her, she's easy to keep sweet. I tell you, Neil, it's so much fun having a mistress. I couldn't settle for Stella anyway, she'd drive me mad, and she's a selfish cow, always on the want. If I left Frankie for her, which I've no intention of doing, she'd bleed me dry within a matter of months. Anyway, I'd be stupid to leave. Not only would I kiss goodbye to the garage, which is going to be the backbone of our empire, but I kinda like having someone to look after me. The occasional token marital poke and night out at the pub is a small price to pay to keep Frankie thinking everything's hunky-dory between us.'

Neil grinned. 'You're a nasty bugger, ain't you?'

Eddie smiled winningly. 'Yeah, I am. Mam taught us well, didn't she? I told you after the Amanda business that no woman was *ever* going to control my life again, and I meant what I said. And talking of that woman, I'm going on a visit after I leave here. I'm going to pay that little madam and her dad back for how she treated me and they're both going to be sorry, believe me.'

'Oh, I don't doubt that for one minute. Anyway, look, visiting time is nearly up,' said Neil, leaning forward. 'Just go over again what I've to do when I get out in case you don't manage to visit again?'

Eddie nodded. 'Good idea. And make sure all this is tattooed on your brain because I want no mishaps.'

Later that evening Frankie looked at the clock and sighed. It was coming up to eight. Eddie was getting later and later these days. But she knew it was unavoidable and wasn't cross. Her husband had assured her he was doing his best to keep the business going and she couldn't be annoyed with him for that. Like her mother had said, he had rallied around when the family had most needed it and she was very grateful to him.

Very carefully, mindful of the doctor's and her mother's warnings to take things easy, she turned the heat down under the pan of boiling water which was keeping his dinner hot and was just about to return to the living room to settle back in her chair when there was a knock on the back door.

'Come in,' she automatically called.

Hilary entered, the smile on her lips not disguising the deep sadness in her pretty blue eyes.

'Hello, Hilary, how lovely to see you. You're just in time for a cuppa.'

'That would be nice, Frankie. Thank you. But I'll make it.'

'Hilary, please,' she begged. 'Everyone's treating me like I'm about to break in two. I appreciate your gesture but surely I can be allowed to mash a cuppa? It's not like it's heavy lifting or anything, and if I hold myself around the middle like this,' she said, placing one arm around herself, 'it protects my ribs and they don't hurt so much.'

Hilary looked at her. 'Just take it slowly then, and be careful. I'll stay here in case you need me.'

A while later, Frankie placed the teapot on the table and slid a cup towards Hilary. 'See, I know it took much longer than usual but I managed and didn't come a cropper. But don't tell my mam, she'll have my guts for garters.'

'I won't,' Hilary replied. She put a spoon of sugar in her tea and stirred it. 'How are you, Frankie?'

'Oh, so, so. You know. Getting there. It'll just take time.'

'You still don't remember what happened?'

She shook her head. 'No, and to be honest I don't want to know. I'm fed up with trying to remember and want to forget that night altogether. It was just a stupid accident. Anyway, enough about me, how are you, Hilary?'

She shook her head but declined to comment.

Frankie looked at her, worried. Hilary was so bereft it was hard to know what to do to try and ease her suffering. Frankie hoped the gift of Wally's house might do something to bring even a brief smile to her lovely face.

'Hilary, I'm glad you've come. There's something I want to discuss with you.'

'Funny, I have with you too, but you go first.'

'All right. Uncle Wally's house . . .'

'Oh, you're going to move in? Good, Frankie. Wally would be very happy, knowing you're living there.'

'Oh, no, Hilary, not me. You.'

'Pardon?'

'My uncle would have wanted you to have his house, Hilary, I know he would. He loved you so much.'

'No.'

Such a final response shocked Frankie. 'Oh, Hilary, I'm sorry if I've offended or hurt you. Please, please, forgive me?'

'Nothing could be further from the truth. I'm . . .' She took a deep breath. 'I'm very touched by your thoughtfulness, but I can't take the house. Wally willed it to you, wanted you to have it, and you must honour his wises. And, you see, I've come to say goodbye. I'm going away.'

Frankie's mouth dropped open. 'No, Hilary, you can't! You're part of our family.'

She swallowed hard. 'Thank you, but I can't stay around here, Frankie.' She clasped her hands tightly and lowered her head to hide the tears in her eyes. 'Wally is everywhere I go. He's all around me here. Frankie, I miss him so much, I can't bear it. I have to go away, start afresh. I hope you understand?'

'I do,' she replied, feeling tears prick her own eyes. 'When . . . when are you going?'

Hilary lifted her head and looked at her. 'First thing tomorrow morning.'

Frankie gasped. 'So soon?'

'There's no point in my staying now I've made up my mind. I would only be prolonging the agony.'

'Where will you go?'

'I thought Devon. It's nice and peaceful there, and very pretty judging by pictures I've seen. I have some money put by to tide me over until I get a job. I have good references so that shouldn't pose a problem.'

'Oh, Hilary, I'll miss you,' Frankie said emotionally.

'Me too,' she said, sniffing back tears. 'I can't tell you how much.'

'Have you told my mam and dad?'

She nodded. 'This afternoon. They were both very sad but understood, bless them.' She took a deep breath and forced a smile to her face. 'When I get settled you must all come and visit,' she said. 'Before I go, will you make me a promise?'

'What is it?'

'That you'll move into Wally's house and be happy there. It's a lovely house, just right for a fa— Oh, Frankie, I'm so sorry!' she cried in distress, clamping her hand to her mouth.

'It's all right,' Frankie soothed her. 'I have to get used to the fact that I can't have children. I don't expect other people to feel they have to watch everything they say for fear of upsetting me. You're right, Hilary, the house would make a lovely family home. It's just a sad fact that my own children will never run happily around in it.'

'You will move into it, though? You gave me that house as a gift, now I'm giving it back to you.'

'Oh, Hilary.' Frankie took a deep breath, sighing heavily. 'I won't make you a promise I can't keep.'

'Maybe in time you'll feel differently.'

Hilary scraped back her chair and rose. She walked around the table and gave Frankie a gentle hug. 'I'd love to squeeze you tightly, but I daren't for fear of hurting you. I must go now, I've so much to do.' She released Frankie and looked at her tenderly. 'You'll take care, won't you?'

She nodded. 'And you.'

Chapter Thirty-One

'How was your day?' Frankie asked Eddie when he eventually came home much later that evening. 'I'll get your dinner,' she said, making to rise. 'You must be famished.'

'Don't bother. I grabbed a sandwich earlier,' he said, stripping off his working coat and throwing it on the back of a chair.

She settled back down. 'So how was your day?' she asked again.

Eddie had had a wonderful day, very productive. Not only had he managed to see Neil, putting his brother's mind at rest on what the future held for them, he'd also seen Amanda and started things moving towards getting his revenge on her and her father.

What a picture her face had been when she had spotted him waiting for her outside her workplace. Her greedy eyes had travelled over the car he was leaning against – and it was his own car, bought with cash Eddie had siphoned off from the garage and which he kept under lock and key in the building at the back. A 1955 Triumph TR2. A very sporty two-seater model, black, low and sleek with a soft top. Admittedly it was two years old but a new model was beyond him at the moment. It suited him, though, told people he was somebody important. And that, to Eddie, was everything. Dressed in an immaculate outfit he kept especially at the garage which Frankie had no idea about, he had looked Amanda over in a superior fashion as she had stopped short, shocked to see him, then made her way across.

'Just thought I'd let you see what you're missing,' he had said, smiling at her charmingly. 'You said I'd never amount to anything, Amanda, and I'm here to show you you were wrong.'

Her eyes travelled over the car, then him. 'I was wrong, wasn't I?' she said remorsefully.

He made to turn from her and get into the car. 'Going so soon?' she said, just like he had known she would.

He turned back to face her. 'Well, there's nothing for me around here, is there?'

'Isn't there?'

'You're not married then?'

She shook her head. 'Not yet.'

His heart leapt and he hid a smug smile. If his plan worked she'd never be married. Well, not to the kind of man she'd had in mind anyway. 'Hop in,' he said.

As they had driven along he had spun her an elaborate tale about owning several garages now in Birmingham and told her how well he was doing, even producing a wad of bank notes from his pocket to prove his story. He did not even attempt to make any advances towards her but drew to a halt at the end of a street near her house. She got out of the car and looked at him expectantly.

'It's been nice seeing you again, Amanda,' he said. 'Goodbye.'

Her face dropped in disappointment. 'Oh, aren't you going to ask to see me again?'

'I don't think so. You might not be married but you're still engaged and I had enough of playing second fiddle the last time we went out together. I'm serious about you, Amanda. Why else would I travel all this way?' He flashed her one of his winning smiles. 'Come on, Mandy. You'd seriously consider staying with a dull bod like Peter when you could have me? I bet he hasn't a car like this or a wad of notes in his pocket as fat as mine. And you haven't seen my house yet. Does six bedrooms whet your appetite?'

'Oh!' she exclaimed. '*Six* bedrooms, you said?'

He nodded. 'And a tennis court at the back.'

'You have done well, haven't you, Eddie?' And she added without further hesitation, 'Okay, I'll give Peter up for you.'

He smiled winningly at her. 'Good girl. Make sure you do it by Friday and that you tell him it's because you've found someone better than him. If I find out you haven't, I'll drop you like a ton of bricks. I want you all to myself, Amanda. I'll meet you here at eight o'clock next Friday. Don't be late because I won't wait.'

Before she could respond he had pressed the throttle down hard and roared off, leaving her staring after him.

Amanda had taken the bait. The trap was set.

Plonking himself down in the armchair opposite Frankie, Eddie pulled off his shoes and stretched his long legs out, feet resting on the hearth. He relaxed and gave a loud yawn. 'My day's been so busy, I've not stopped. I'm bushed.'

'Is it too much for you?' Frankie asked.

'Too much? What do you mean?'

'Running the garage. Is it too much for you, Eddie?'

'Of course it's not,' he snapped. He saw her flinch at his abruptness and quickly said, 'Look, I'm sorry, I'm just tired, okay? I'm managing fine, Frankie. I've run things before for my father, so this is nothing new for me.'

'Yes, of course, I was forgetting that. The men? Are they all right with you being in charge?'

They had had two choices. Eddie had gathered Bernard and Matty together on the morning after Wally's funeral and told them what was what. Either they accepted the need to do things his way or they could leave. They had both stayed, knowing good jobs were hard to come by, and had learned quickly that so long as they did their work and never questioned his orders, Eddie left them alone. And so did the new man he had brought in to oversee the work when Eddie wasn't there, which was quite often. He himself dealt with the money side of the business. He supposed he ought to mention the new chap's presence to Frankie in case she found out. 'The men are fine, Frankie. Did I tell you I'd taken another chap on?'

'No.'

'Oh, must have slipped my mind with all I have to do. I suppose I should have spoken to you first but with you being so grieved and still recuperating after your accident, I didn't want to bother you. I had no choice, Frankie. Well, let's be honest, I'm not a fully qualified mechanic, and neither is Bernard, and Matty couldn't cope with all the fully skilled work all by himself so I had no choice if the business is to carry on like Wally wanted. He's a good bloke, Saul his name is. Been in the trade for years.'

'Oh, I've no doubt he's good if you set him on. You did right, Eddie.'

'Thanks. If you want the truth, Frankie, working with my hands isn't really me, I'm better at running things. I let the men do most of the heavy work but lend a hand when necessary. Mostly I concentrate on the customers and keeping the paperwork side straight. It's paying off. The customers seem to like the attention I pay them. I don't want to speak ill of the dead, but Wally really fell down on the office side, as you know.' He planted a sorrowful expression on his face. 'What happened to him was very sad, Frankie, but life goes on. For me, running this garage is making up for what I lost with my own family. And I'm doing it for *you*,' he emphasised.

'Oh, I know, Eddie. I just feel sorry I can't help you, that's all.'

'I'm managing. All you have to do is concentrate on getting better.

We'll talk about you helping out when the right time comes.'

'I wish I could help you do the books,' she mused. 'That would take some of the burden off you. But I haven't got a clue how to do them. I could learn though, couldn't I? It's something I could do sitting at this table. And it would help keep me occupied.'

'I've already told you, Frankie, all that side of things is up to date. In fact, that's why I'm late tonight,' he lied. 'I was sorting out the banking and making up the wages. You just concentrate on getting better and let me manage the garage as you authorised me to.'

She smiled gratefully at him. 'Thanks, Eddie.'

'No need for thanks, Frankie, I'm your husband and I promise you I'm going to make this business a success. Of course it's gone down a bit after what happened to Wally but I'm doing my best to convince the customers we still work to the same high standards. I'm confident we'll get back on track in time.' In truth the business hadn't suffered at all, despite loyal customers being devastated by Wally's accidental death. Everyone wanted to show the same loyalty towards Frankie, knowing she had inherited the business and trusting her workmanship. But Eddie wasn't going to tell her that. He wanted her to think the business was thriving entirely because of his own hard work.

'Oh, I know it's in safe hands,' she agreed. 'And we owe it to Uncle Wally to keep his business going as best we can.'

Sod Wally, Eddie thought. It's *my* future I'm thinking of. 'Yes, we do.' One good thing – Frankie hadn't mentioned resuming her work as a mechanic when she was well enough, and she never would if he had his way. He didn't want to risk her finding out what he was up to.

She looked at him. Feeling so wretched still, she was gratified that he was taking this burden off her. It couldn't be easy for him, stepping into Wally's shoes, but he seemed to be thriving on it. Maybe this was what Eddie needed, something to give him an aim in life, a purpose, restore the self-respect that had been stripped from him when his family had ostracised him. Running the garage certainly seemed to suit him.

'Er . . . Frankie?'

'Mmm?'

'What about moving into Wally's house? Have you given it any more thought?'

He knew her parents had declined her offer of the house but she hadn't told him about wanting to give it to Hilary. Since making her decision she hadn't seen him long enough to have any kind of proper talk, with him working so hard and most nights coming home so late.

Anyway, now Hilary was moving to Devon there seemed no point. 'Not yet, Eddie. I couldn't.'

He looked annoyed. 'Whyever not? It seems silly us living in this poky place when a good house is sitting empty. The longer it stays like that, especially in this weather, the more damp and mildewed it'll get.'

'Oh, I hadn't thought of that,' she said, frowning.

'Wally's gone, Frankie. The sooner you take that on board, the better. It's just a house. And it's a house more fitting for a business-man to live in than this place,' he added.

'Surely that doesn't matter?'

It does to me, he thought. 'Maybe I said that wrong. I meant, it would be much more fitting and comfortable for *you*. There's a nice garden for you to sit in in the summer, and a bigger kitchen. Much more room all round.'

She said dully, 'I see your point. Once the doctor gives me the all clear, we'll talk more about moving in.'

'Good. I . . . er . . . might know someone who'll have this place.'

'Oh? Who?'

This house was ideal for Neil, he thought, casting his eyes around. Perfect for him to move straight into. Well, certainly a damned sight better than the cell he'd described to Eddie. 'Just an acquaintance of a customer I got chatting to today. He's a relative who's moving to the area and will be looking for somewhere to live. This would be ideal for him, and as Wally's house is furnished and it's good stuff too, we could leave this lot behind, couldn't we? Be a nice gesture. We were grateful for it when we moved in. Apparently the man's wife has left him and taken every stick of furniture and all his money so this chap's got to start again from scratch.'

'Oh, poor man,' exclaimed Frankie, thinking of Taffy. 'Yes, we would be helping him, wouldn't we?' A thought struck her. Maybe this was what she needed to help her mental recovery, something to concentrate on. Moving house would certainly give her that. 'All right, Eddie, we'll move in. And I'd be glad to leave the furniture if it'll help this man out.'

He fought hard not to look too pleased. 'Right, that's settled then. I'll mention it to the customer when he comes to collect his car.' He paused for a moment, eyeing her covertly from under his lashes, his mind briskly concocting the next lie to cover up his planned visits to Coventry. 'Frankie, I've decided to try and make it up with my family. What do you think?'

'You have? Oh, Eddie, that's wonderful news,' she said, her delight obvious.

'I thought you'd be pleased. I don't know whether I'll succeed but I've got to try. It'll mean me going over to Coventry once or twice a week and I'll be late back. It'll take me a couple of hours each way on the train.'

'Mmm. Pity we can't afford a car. Be much better for you than taking the train. That's something else we could think about when the business gets back to normal. A little Ford Anglia would be ideal for us, wouldn't it?'

'Yes, great,' Eddie said with false enthusiasm. A Ford Anglia might suit the likes of Frankie but he wouldn't be seen dead in one.

'Do your family know you're going to see them? Have you made any arrangements?' she asked gently.

'My brother does. I'm meeting him on Friday night to talk about tackling my mother and the best way to do it. Hopefully he'll persuade her to meet me. It might take me some time to win her over, but I think I will then she can persuade my father.'

'Oh, Eddie, it's a start. If your brother can talk her into meeting you, I could come . . .'

'No,' he cut in harshly, her travelling with him to Coventry the last thing he wanted. He couldn't seduce Amanda with his wife tagging along, could he? 'Sorry, Frankie, I didn't mean to shout. It's just that my family see you as the enemy in all this and it will take me time to convince them they're wrong.'

'Oh.' A thought struck her. 'Eddie, is that why you want to move to Uncle Wally's house? So we have somewhere nicer for them to come to when you do make amends? As I'm sure you will,' she added.

'Eh? Oh, yes, that's exactly my thinking. You can make it really nice, Frankie. It'll show them how well we're doing and how happy we are. It'll impress them, and I don't like to admit this but that's the kind of people they are. Us having a nice house will go a long way to convincing my family that they should change their minds.'

'I'll do my best,' she promised. 'My mother will help me. I'll keep my fingers crossed all goes well for you. I can't wait to meet them.'

Eddie sat back again. 'And they'll love you when they do, I just know they will,' he said, hiding a smug smile.

Chapter Thirty-Two

Frankie patted the cushions and glanced around. 'What do you think, Mam?'

Nancy nodded, impressed. 'I think you've done yerself proud, gel. Looks beautiful. Like a picture from one of them women's magazines. I have ter say, it seems strange walking past yer old house. I have ter stop meself from automatically turning down the entry.' She gave a laugh. 'I don't think the young man who's moved in would be pleased, me charging through the back door demanding a cuppa. From what I can gather from the neighbours he's settled in well enough but keeps himself to himself. I wonder what he does for a living? Still, none of my business.' She gave Frankie a satisfied nod. 'If Eddie's family ain't impressed with you and this house then they ain't worth knowing. I don't know what all the effort is for meself. What difference does it make whether you've a posh home or not? Eddie's family should count themselves lucky he's landed a lovely wife like you.'

Frankie sighed. 'Eddie said that's what they're like. Judge people by what they've got. He's told you and Dad how his father dragged himself up from humble beginnings, and after their reaction when he married me, Eddie just wants to prove what he's made of. He wants to make them proud of him, that's all.'

Sighing heavily, Nancy shook her head. 'I can't understand some people. Proud ain't a strong enough word for what me and yer dad feel for yer both. So when are you getting to meet this family of his? I can't wait meself, and I ain't putting on no airs and graces. They either accept us as your family or they can swing, for all I care. Don't look at me like that, 'cause I'll mek an effort but only 'cos I know it means so much to you and Eddie. I'll never understand why they cut him off like that just 'cos he fell in love. Still, I can't fault the effort he's bin to trying to make amends. Teking long enough, though, isn't it? Just before Christmas he started secretly meeting his mother, hoping she'd bring his dad round, and now it's nearly Easter.' Nancy pursed her lips. 'Seems peculiar to me.'

'Yes, I have to admit it's a strange state of affairs. Still, Eddie tells me he's winning her over, slowly but surely. He's going over again tonight and will ask her if she's willing to meet me. I must say, I'm nervous at the thought but for Eddie's sake I do hope she agrees. He misses his family so much.'

'Well, he must do to make all this effort. I feel sorry for the lad, I really do. Still, that's families for yer.' Nancy looked at her hard. 'Now, my girl. What about you?'

'What do you mean, Mam?'

'You know exactly what I mean. The doc's given you the all clear, you've got this house spick and span and yer time's yer own. So when are you going back to the garage? You miss it, I know you do.'

Frankie nodded. 'Yes, I do. Having this house to arrange has done a lot for me and given me time to think properly and sort things out in my mind. Eddie seems to be doing a grand job of running things and it's been the making of him, Mam. He seems so happy with himself, I feel it best to let him carry on. He might see it as an intrusion if I go back.'

'An intrusion? God forbid. As if you'd ever be an intruder there. Anyway, it's your business, I suppose, Frankie. But if you want to work there, you've every right.'

'Yes, I know that, Mam. But Eddie's my husband and I have to consider him. He gave up everything to marry me, and, well . . . I feel so guilty that I can't give him children.'

'Oi, that state of affairs ain't your fault. It's not like you did it on purpose.'

'I know, Mam, but all the same I feel that leaving him free to run the garage somehow makes up for it, if that makes sense?'

'No, it doesn't.'

'Well, it does to me.'

Frankie's eyes grew distant and she gave a sad sigh.

Nancy eyed her. ''Ote wrong?'

Frankie looked at her mother hesitantly. She longed to open up and tell Nancy how things really were between herself and Eddie, ask her advice as to what she could do to forge the closeness between them she longed for. Despite the passing of time it never seemed to happen, regardless of all her efforts. But then, how could it? Eddie worked such long hours and was so tired when he came home at night, they hardly spent any proper time together. Even their Friday nights down at the pub had never resumed, despite the fact that for weeks now the doctor had said Frankie could slowly return to her normal life. But, of course, since Eddie had been making such an effort to make it up with his family, Wednesdays and Fridays were the nights he travelled over to Coventry to have his secret meetings with his mother. It would be unforgivable of Frankie to insist he give them up to take her out.

Maybe once everything was back on an even keel with them, matters between Eddie and her would get better. Frankie certainly hoped so.

'No, nothing's wrong, Mam,' she said brightly. 'What made you ask that?'

'Oh, er . . . you looked so sad then. You and Eddie are happy together, ain't yer? Me and yer dad would be so upset if we know 'ote was wrong between yer. And yer would tell me if summat was, wouldn't yer, lovey?'

'Of course I would. I'm very happy, Mam,' she vehemently insisted. 'Things couldn't be better. Eddie's happy, Mam, and if he's happy so am I. Now how about I mash you a cuppa?' she asked to change the subject.

'That'd be grand, gel. Only when you meet Eddie's parents you'd better not say mash. A *pot of tea*, is what people like *that* say.'

They both giggled.

Later that afternoon, pursing his lips, Eddie scanned his eyes across a car and shook his head. 'You're asking too much. I'll offer you forty and that's being generous.'

The seller eyed him in astonishment. 'Forty? That car's worth at least eighty pounds. It's six year old and hardly any mileage. I'm only selling it because I'm strapped for cash.' He patted the bonnet lovingly. 'I'll miss this little car. The wife loved her Sunday afternoon rides out into the country in this.'

And that's your mistake, telling me that, Eddie thought smugly. 'It might only be six years old but your big end's going and it's costly to replace.' He put both hands on the car and pushed against it hard. 'Did you hear that noise?'

The man frowned. 'No. I didn't hear anything.'

'Ah, well, that's because you don't know about cars, you see. I've always tinkered with them. Know every creak and groan and what it means. That groan you said you never heard tells me your big end's going.'

The seller glanced him over. Dressed in a pair of shabby working trousers and donkey jacket Eddie certainly looked the sort to mess around with motors and came across as the honest type. Strange, though, the man around the corner in the little workshop who had kept the car maintained for the owner since he had bought it from new with an inheritance had not mentioned the big end going the last time it had had an overhaul. Funnily enough the other young chap who had been interested in buying it earlier had said just the same thing when he'd come to inspect it. He'd left without even offering for it.

Eddie decided it was time to go in for the kill. He smoothed his hand over the roof, sighing. 'I've always wanted a Morris Minor. Lovely cars they are. I've been saving like mad. Couldn't believe me luck when I saw your ad in the paper.' He fixed his eyes directly on the man. 'Look, sir, I'm not going to push you. I'll take it off your hands for forty and I'm willing to do the work on her. But she's your car and maybe you should stick it out to see if anyone else will take her. It's been nice meeting you,' he said, turning away. 'Good day.'

The man gulped. 'Er . . . just a minute, young man. The big end? It's definitely on its way out, you say?'

Eddie nodded. 'I'd stake me life on it.'

The other man sighed, 'Okay. Look, er . . . what if we said fifty?'

Eddie grimaced. 'Forty-five? I can't go any higher, not considering how much it's going to cost to put her right, I can't.'

'Done,' said the seller, holding out his hand to shake it. 'Deal.'

Eddie drove around the corner and pulled the car to a halt. The passenger door opened and Neil got in.

'Another bargain,' he said, patting the dashboard. 'Great team we make, you and me, brother.' Eddie was grinning. 'Right, you can slap a ninety-quid price tag on this little beauty and put it out for sale tomorrow. Some mug will snap her up.'

Neil grinned back. 'Sure thing, Eddie. This selling lark's a doddle. The coffers are building up nicely, I'm happy to say.'

'I told you we'd be rich and I meant it. And what Frankie doesn't know, doesn't hurt her. She knows nothing about the car lot and never will.' He rubbed his hands together gleefully. 'I've got the life of Riley and so have you. I'm loving every minute of it. We'll have to see about getting you a better house, then you can get your own housekeeper and mistress,' he said with a wicked laugh.

'How's your mistress?' Neil asked.

'A pain in the neck. She ain't happy with that little flat I rent for her. All she goes on about is me leaving Frankie. But I quickly shut her up and she believes what I tell her, silly cow.'

'Get rid of her, Eddie. You could get someone else.'

'I've thought of it, but someone else might not be so gullible as Stella, nor so good in the sack, and she looks great on my arm when we do go out. She bloody should do, it's cost me a fortune buying her all those clothes.'

'You ain't half taking risks, Eddie. What if Frankie should find out?'

'There's no chance of that. I'm too clever. Besides, taking risks is part of the fun. The way things are suits me just fine, Neil, and I can't see that changing. Can't compare it to the life we did have, can we? No comparison. I wonder what Mam'd say if she could see us now? Not that I give a damn. Right, we'll take this back to the car lot, then I must go and get changed ready to go over to Coventry. And, boy, am I looking forward to tonight. Crunch time, brother. That cow Amanda isn't going to know what's hit her. All this time and money I've spent has been well worth it, believe me.'

A couple of hours or so later, Eddie drew up alongside Amanda where he had arranged to meet her.

'You're late,' she complained slipping into the seat beside him and shutting the door. 'I was worried you weren't coming.'

'I got held up. Business.' He glanced over at her. 'You look . . . blooming.'

She smiled, smoothing her hands over her swelling stomach. 'It's been a job to hide it, Eddie. But I don't have to any longer, do I?'

'You told your father then, like I asked?'

She nodded. 'Last night. It was awful, Eddie. He was so furious I thought he'd burst a blood vessel. He called me a slut! My father's never spoken to me like that before. You should have seen his reaction when I told him *you* were the father. He slapped me, Eddie, so hard he bruised my cheek,' she said, turning her face to show him the angry bluish wheal. 'Anyway, he's demanding we get married as soon as possible. He's waiting for you now at home. I hope you're prepared? This isn't going to be nice.'

Eddie hid a smile. Sutton would have to wait a hell of a long time to meet him. He turned fully to face her. 'I've something to tell you, Amanda.'

'Oh?' she exclaimed eagerly, the look on her face telling him she was expecting him to produce an engagement ring at the very least.

'Come on then, tell me,' she cried impatiently.

Eddie took a deep breath, purposely stalling for time, wanting what he said to have the maximum effect. 'I can't marry you.'

She froze. 'What?'

'I said, I can't marry you.'

She playfully slapped his arm. 'Eddie, stop it, this is no time for jokes.'

'Oh, I'm not joking, Amanda. I'm deadly serious.'

She looked incredulous. 'But you *have* to marry me. I'm having your baby.'

He grinned. 'I don't have to do anything, Amanda. I can't anyway.'

'Can't? What do you mean, you can't. Why?'

'Because I'm already married. Didn't I mention my wife to you?'

'Wife! WIFE?' she screamed, and stared at him blindly as the implications of what he had just so cruelly told her sank in. Then she raised her hand and with all the force she could muster slapped his face. 'You bastard! You've ruined me,' she wailed.

His cheek smarted but he wouldn't give her the satisfaction of rubbing it. He just nodded, a wicked glint in his eye. 'Yes, I have, haven't I?'

'You seduced me on purpose. You had it all planned, didn't you?' she screamed.

He nonchalantly added, 'Afraid so. To pay you back for how you treated me. And to even things up with your father. I know he was responsible for putting my brother in jail and possibly having the police watch me. We're quits now.'

Panic-stricken, she grabbed his lapels and shook them. 'But you can't leave me like this, Eddie. You can't, you can't! My father will kill me. I'll be an unmarried mother, never able to hold my head up again for shame. Surely you don't want our baby to be illegitimate? Look, I'm sorry for the way I treated you before. It was only a bit of fun. You know that, Eddie. You could divorce your wife,' she begged. 'Please, Eddie, please say you will?'

Grabbing her hands, he forcibly wrenched them off him. 'I don't think she would like that. Anyway, I've no intention of divorcing her. Why would I want to, just to give a slut like you a name for her bastard?' he hissed. Before she could put up any resistance, he leaned over her, flicked the catch and pushed open the passenger door. 'Now get out,' he ordered her.

'What?'

'You heard.' He put both hands on her shoulders and with one mighty push shoved her off the seat. She tumbled out to sprawl face down in the gutter. Then he leaned over and peered down at her. 'That's where you belong,' he said, sniggering maliciously. 'So long, Amanda.' He slammed the car door shut and pressed down on the accelerator.

Whistling happily, he sped down the country road back towards Leicester. His vengeance on the Suttons was achieved. Now all that remained was to deal with Kelvin Mason, but there was plenty of time for that.

Eddie arrived home just after eleven after first garaging the Triumph and changing his clothes to more downmarket ones for Frankie's benefit. Stripping off his coat, he flopped down in an armchair, by the fire exhaling loudly. 'What a day it's been.'

From her chair opposite Frankie eyed him worriedly. She hadn't been able to relax all night knowing what Eddie was facing and the look on his face wasn't encouraging.

'Does that mean things didn't go so well as you hoped, Eddie?' she asked tentatively.

He issued a heavy sigh. 'You could say that.'

'Oh! Can I get you a drink?'

He shook his head.

She clasped her hands tightly. 'So I take it your mother wouldn't agree to meet me after all?'

He shook his head. 'No. I don't want to go into details, Frankie, but I've got to accept I'm wasting my time.'

Her face fell in dismay. 'Oh, surely not, Eddie? Please don't give up yet. What about approaching your father direct? I'll come with you . . .'

'For God's sake, Frankie, will you give over?' he erupted. 'Don't you think I've been through enough? This has been very painful for me. Unless I give you up and go back home and work for my father, he flatly refuses to have anything to do with me.' He sighed forlornly. 'I'm sorry for shouting but I thought I was getting somewhere, Frankie. My mother and I seemed to be making progress. I actually think she's willing to let bygones be bygones. I did do my best to tell her what a wonderful daughter-in-law she's missing out on. But she won't go against my father.

'Anyway, I'm not putting myself through this any more. I told her straight that you are my wife and if Father can't accept that, then that's his loss. Anyway, I don't want to talk about them again. My life is in Leicester now and that's the end of the matter. As I won't be going to Coventry any more maybe you'd like to go out next Friday night?' he suggested to change the subject, also feeling it was about time he made a token gesture towards keeping his marriage on an even keel.

'I'm sorry about your family, Eddie.' She planted a bright smile on her face. 'But I'd love to go out on Friday. I'll look forward to it, in fact.'

He rose. 'If you don't mind, I'm off to bed now. Good night.'

'Oh,' she exclaimed. She had wanted to discuss with him her return to work, make him understand she didn't want to interfere with what he was achieving, that her coming in for a few hours each day was purely to make her feel useful again, give her something to do. Rattling around this house all day was driving her mad. Housework took up part of her time, but not all of it. It wouldn't be so bad for her if Eddie came home at a reasonable time, and she felt strongly that her input into the business would help to ease his burden. Not that he didn't seem to be thriving on all this hard work which obviously suited him, but it was doing nothing for their marriage. Still, he had offered to take her out on Friday night. Maybe that was the beginning of better things to come. She did hope so. She smiled at him warmly. 'Good night, Eddie.'

Long after he had gone upstairs, Frankie sat on deep in thought. It was such a shame his family were being so stubborn. Being alienated from them was tearing Eddie apart. Surely, if they'd just meet her . . . Why, that was it. As a last resort, to try and reconcile son and parents, she would go and see them herself. She was very aware of Eddie's warning to keep away from his family but, as he seemed to be getting nowhere, what choice did she have but to disobey him? It was worth a try rather than do nothing and have Eddie live the rest of his life with their loss.

Chapter Thirty-Three

With a loud hiss, a jolt as the brakes were applied and a belch of thick white smoke, the train slowed down to a juddering halt. Having dressed carefully, wanting to look her best to meet Eddie's parents, in a pretty blue full skirt and crisp white Peter Pan-collared blouse, her hair piled becomingly into a fashionable French pleat, Frankie alighted at Coventry station mid-morning on Saturday. With the throng of other passengers she made her way outside.

Never having been out of the city of her birth before she was surprised to find the buildings of Coventry very similar in design to those of Leicester. She was very aware, though, that Coventry had suffered terrible bombing in the war and wasn't surprised to see gaping holes where once fine buildings had stood, and signs of rebuilding in progress.

Since making her decision to approach Eddie's family herself she had had plenty of time to formulate a plan of action and had deduced that the sensible approach would be to ask the police who were bound to know where such important people lived. She just prayed they would give her the address.

It had been very hard keeping her plans secret from Eddie, especially this morning when she had blatantly lied to him, saying that she was going shopping. She had also had to put her mother off from their usual fortnightly visit for tea. She hadn't liked telling a fib to either of them but felt sure she would be forgiven when she returned home with good news for Eddie, which she desperately hoped would be the outcome. Should she fail, there was no need for anyone to know what she had done.

Frankie hailed a taxi and climbed inside. 'The main police station, please.'

The driver looked at her curiously. 'Did you say the cop shop, missus?'

'That's right.'

The seasoned Desk Sergeant shook his head on hearing her request for information. 'Never heard of such a family. The Taylors, you said? Prominent people? Lots of businesses in the city?'

'Yes.'

'You sure you've got the right town? I've been a copper here for twenty-five years and I know all those worth knowing and those who ain't, if you get my meaning.'

'Yes, I'm positive.'

'I'm sorry but the name Taylor doesn't ring a bell, not in connection with the sort of family you've described. What sorta business is this Mr Taylor in then?'

'Well . . . I'm not sure. All sorts. Oh, he was doing something connected with selling car spares but I'm afraid I don't know whether he actually opened a business or not?'

'Oh, well, that's a lead then, missus. Try the car plant. If this Mr Taylor you're after is anything to do with cars, someone at Rootes should have heard of him.'

She smiled gratefully. 'Thank you, Sergeant.'

'My pleasure, missus. I hope you get lucky. There's a bus on the corner goes right past the plant. If you hurry you should just about manage to hop on the next one.'

Twenty minutes later Frankie got off the bus and gazed in awe at the vast assembly of brick buildings that made up the huge factory. She could just see the tops of them over the high brick wall that surrounded Rootes' premises, which seemed to stretch endlessly in all directions. So this was where some of the cars that came in to Champion's for repair had been made. She wondered what it was like to work inside on the assembly line. The thought didn't appeal in the least to Frankie, although she admired the men and women who did. But that sort of job was not for her. Putting cars together she preferred to leave to others. Fixing them when they broke down was what she enjoyed.

Through the large iron gates she spotted a building with a sign over the door reading ENQUIRIES. That was the place she needed. Straightening her coat, she raised her chin and prepared to march inside.

'Oi, missus.'

Frankie stopped short and turned around. 'Me?' she said, putting a finger to her chest.

'Yeah, you,' said a security guard, running towards her. 'Where do you think yer going?'

'To the enquiry office. I have an enquiry.'

'Well, you can't just enquire willy nilly, yer know. You have ter report to the gate house first to be signed in.'

'Oh, I'm sorry, I didn't know that.'

'Well, the sign is printed big enough. Still, never mind. Follow me and I'll sign you in. What . . . er . . . kinda enquiry you making anyway?' he asked noisily as he made to march her across.

'I'm trying to find out the address of some well-known people. I believe someone at Rootes might know them as I understand they had dealings in the motor industry. Car spares to be more precise.'

Sid Armstrong stopped and looked at her keenly. 'I've worked here over twenty-odd years and I know most people who pass through these gates. I should, I have ter sign everyone in and out. What's their name?'

'Taylor.'

'Taylor?' He gave a grimace. 'Common name but the only Taylors I know are Eddie and . . .'

She beamed in delight. 'Yes,' she cut in. 'That's my husband. You know those Taylors?'

'Well, yes, but . . .'

'Oh, you couldn't tell me their address, could you? I'd be ever so grateful.'

'Yeah, sure. Eddie did live in the Dales but . . .'

'The Dales?' she repeated. That must be it, she thought. It sounded grand. The sort of place Eddie's family would live. 'Thank you. You've been very helpful. Could you tell me how to get there, please?'

Sid gave her directions and watched thoughtfully as Frankie headed off.

'What did that woman want?' his boss asked when he returned to the gate house.

'She wa' looking fer the Taylors.'

'Taylors?'

'Yeah, you remember Eddie Taylor?'

'I sure do, that thieving git the company was glad to see the back of a couple of years ago. We put his brother in jail, didn't we? Got a big pat on the back for that,' said the man proudly, puffing out his chest.

'She was Eddie's wife. Well, said she was.'

'Wife? She looked too good for the likes of him. You sure that's who she wa'?'

'That's what she said. She was looking for the mother, so I told her where Ma Taylor lives. I don't know what she's expecting but I reckon by the look of her she's in for a bit of a shock.'

Frankie stared around her. The street she was in was grim, the houses badly neglected, reminiscent of the vast slum areas that were being systematically cleared in Leicester. Only these were worse, if that were possible. She must have mistaken the security guard's directions, taken a wrong turning somewhere. But they had been very precise directions, and she had taken careful note.

A slovenly, pinch-faced woman was shuffling towards her, straggly greying hair covered by a dirty scarf tied turban-style. She was wearing a shabby skirt and clutching around her a huge threadbare man's cardigan, full of holes and snags. On her feet she wore a dingy pair of grey socks bunching at her ankles and an over-large pair of holey slippers which slapped the cobbles as she approached.

'Excuse me,' Frankie said, addressing her, 'I'm lost. Took a wrong turning somewhere. I'm looking for the Dales.'

'Yer in 'em.'

'Pardon?'

The woman took her cigarette from her mouth and flicked off the ash. 'The Dales. Yer in 'em, missus.'

'This is the Dales?' Frankie exclaimed.

'Yeah, what us locals call "this Godforsaken 'ole".'

'Oh, well there must be another Dales. A house. A big house, I think.'

The woman shook her head. 'This is the only Dales I know of, missus. No big houses round 'ere. Who yer after anyway?'

Frankie didn't want to hurt the woman's feelings by saying, 'No one who would live here,' so she answered politely, 'the Taylors.'

'There's a Taylor that lives there,' she said, pointing to a house across the street. 'Mother Taylor. Old bag she is. Fleece yer dry sooner than look at yer. If yer buying 'ote from her, watch yerself, gel. Oh, talk of the devil, 'ere she is.'

Frankie turned around. Coming towards her was what appeared to be an elderly woman equally as shabby as the one Frankie was talking to. She was laden down with brown carrier bags. With her was a younger woman who appeared to be in the early stages of pregnancy if Frankie wasn't mistaken. It was the look on her otherwise very attractive face that commanded attention. She seemed the very picture of misery. But then Frankie supposed she would look miserable if she had to live in such a dire place as this. These were very obviously not the Taylors she was looking for. She opened her mouth to make her escape but the woman beat her to it.

'Oi, Mother Taylor,' she shouted. 'This young woman's looking fer you. Had a good day I see, Evelyn,' she said, grinning as they came up and eyeing the bags Evelyn Taylor was lugging.

'You shut yer mouth, Betty,' Evelyn hissed at her. She eyed Frankie up and down. 'What you after then, gel? Ain't you gorra 'ome ter go to, Betty?' she snapped aggressively at the other woman. They sneered at one other then Betty tightened her cardigan around her, stuck her nose in the air and hurried off. Evelyn turned her attention back to Frankie. 'If it's a bit of business yer after we'd best get inside.'

'No,' said Frankie hurriedly. 'I was looking for someone with the same name as yours. I must have got the address wrong.'

'I'm tired, Mrs Taylor. I need to get inside and put my feet up,' the young woman at Evelyn's side whined.

'Oh, stop moaning, Mandy. All you do all day is moan, moan, moan. Yer like a stuck gramophone record. No wonder yer dad kicked yer out. You want ter thank yer lucky stars I took pity on yer, else where would yer be? Now let me deal with this woman.' She turned back to Frankie. 'I'm the only Taylor in these parts, ducky.'

All Frankie wanted to do was get away from this awful creature. 'I'm sorry to have bothered you.'

'Sure yer don't wanna buy n'ote? I'm bound to have summat that'll interest yer. Come inside and have a look.'

'No. Thank you, but no,' Frankie declined hurriedly.

'Let's get inside, please, Mrs Taylor. My feet are killing me.'

Evelyn turned on the young woman, face thunderous. 'The trouble wi' you, gel, is that yer dad pampered yer something rotten. Well, don't expect the same treatment from me. If yer think yer suffering now, gel, wait 'til yer further on. When I was expecting our Eddie, my feet swelled up like elephants and I couldn't walk for a month. If your baby has much of Eddie in 'im, you could do the same. *Then* you'll have a right to complain, girl. 'Til then, shut yer gob or I'll be doing the same as yer dad did and turfing you out on the street.' She turned back to Frankie and when she saw the horrified look on the young woman's face, demanded, 'What you gawping like that for?'

Frankie's mind was whirling. 'Eddie?' she uttered. 'Did you say your son's name was Eddie?'

'Yeah, 'course that's 'is name. Edwin Taylor. The worst son any mother could ever give birth to. Why?'

Frankie was too shocked to speak.

Evelyn frowned at her. 'You know 'im, don't yer?' she accused. 'You're looking for him. What that's fucker done now?'

'Do you know where that bastard is?' shrieked Amanda. 'I want money for our baby from him. You tell me if you know where he is,' she shrieked louder, grabbing Frankie's arms and shaking them hysterically.

Ashen-faced, she was shaking her head. No, no! her mind was screaming at her. This couldn't be true. 'We're not talking about the same person. We can't be,' she said vehemently.

'Is he tall with dark hair, handsome, looks like Rock Hudson?' Amanda demanded. 'Got a black car. Sporty type with a soft top. Got car sales showrooms in Birmingham. Well, if you find him, you tell him from me I want money for our baby. And you can tell his poor wife what a bastard she's married to as well. If you find him, you will tell him, won't you? You will?' she screeched frenziedly.

The breath having left her body, Frankie gulped for air. Amanda had described her husband exactly, except that he hadn't a car and neither had he car showrooms in Birmingham. Tremendous relief flooded through her. Despite the coincidence of their likeness, and regardless of feeling dreadfully sorry for both women's plight, she felt gratified that her Eddie definitely wasn't the Edwin Taylor to whom they were referring.

She wrenched herself free from Amanda's grasp. 'I'm sorry, we're not talking about the same man. The Edwin Taylor I'm talking about hasn't got a car and neither does he live in Birmingham or own several showrooms.'

With that she spun on her heel and hurried away, desperate to get home and put behind her her wasted trip to Coventry.

Chapter Thirty-Four

With the rigours of the day still telling on her heavily, and disappointed at coming back to Leicester unsuccessful, Frankie was cold, exhausted and ravenously hungry by the time she eventually arrived home just after four. To her relief the house was empty, Eddie obviously still at work.

Hurriedly letting herself in, she put a match under the fire she had laid that morning before setting out and lit the gas under the kettle. Having refreshed herself with a mug of hot sweet tea, she busied herself preparing Eddie's meal, making an extra effort to cook something tasty and setting the table with special care.

By six he still wasn't home. Leaving the oven on low so the dinner dind't ruin, she decided to walk to the garage and insist he finish for the night, thinking it would do him good. She would suggest they popped in for a drink at the local on their way back, feeling that a couple of pints was the least Eddie deserved after his arduous day. Having first checked her appearance, wanting to meet her husband looking her best, Frankie happily set off.

She was just about to cross the road opposite Champion's when a taxi drew up a little further down which blocked her view of the oncoming traffic. Rather than risk being run over, she waited for the passenger to pay his fare and the taxi to move off. A car coming out of Champion's caught her attention, her immediate thought being that it was very late for a customer to be collecting a car. She glanced it over admiringly. It was a two-seater, sporty and black, and despite the bitter weather its soft top was rolled back. It was a handsome-looking car, the sort a moneyed young man would own. Then she frowned at a memory. Funny, this was just like the car the pregnant woman in Coventry had described. Then Frankie got a good view of the driver and her heart pumped erratically. It was Eddie.

She froze, face white with shock. So it *was* her Eddie those women had meant! Her heart thumped, the pain of betrayal gripping her whole body vice-like. Oh, no, God, please, please don't let it be true! But she knew it was. The damning evidence had just driven past her. Her mind whirled, thoughts chasing each other wildly as she realised with horror that their whole marriage had been built on lies. But through that terrible sickening realisation rose a great need to know where her husband was going. Stumbling across to the taxi, she almost knocked the departing passenger out of the way as she clambered inside. 'Follow that car,' she ordered the driver.

'Eh? Now look 'ere, missus, this ain't . . .'

'I'll pay you double,' she cried. 'Please, please, hurry before you lose him.'

'Double! Say no more, missus,' the driver replied eagerly, roaring off.

They followed the little black two-seater as it sped right across town to the Clarendon Park area. It finally pulled to a halt in front of a large imposing three-storey house that had been converted into flats. Frankie asked the driver to stop well before it, so as not to be noticed. Low in her seat, she watched Eddie jump out of the car and swagger up the steps at the front of the house and let himself in. She leaned forward and thrust a ten-shilling note at the driver. 'Thank you.'

'My pleasure, missus. Wish all me customers were as generous. D'yer want me to wait?' he asked, hoping for the same payment on the journey back.

Regardless of what was going on here she'd need to get back. 'Yes, please.'

Keeping in the shadows she slowly made her way to the house Eddie had entered. It had a four-foot-high privet hedge planted outside. Crouching behind this, she slowly rose just high enough to peer over the top. At every window in the house hung good-quality drapes and more expensive nets than were to be found at windows in the street where she and Eddie lived. Obviously these flats weren't cheap to rent. Eddie must be paying a visit to a customer, she thought, because who else would he know who could afford to live in a place like this?

She jumped as the front door opened, two people emerging, and automatically shot down out of sight. Hushed voices reached her ears. She held her breath. One of them was Eddie's and she strained to hear what he was saying.

'I told you I couldn't see you tonight, and what have I told you about ringing the garage? For Christ's sake, I've hardly had the telephone connected two minutes and you've been on it constantly. I wish I'd never told you I'd had it installed now.'

Frankie's mind raced. Telephone? Eddie had had a telephone installed in the garage and hadn't told her. And the way he was talking to this woman, this was no customer he was visiting. Before she could think any further the woman spoke and wasn't very happy judging from her tone.

'But I had to telephone, Eddie. I haven't seen you for days. What was I supposed to do? You could have been dead for all I knew. Look, don't be mad with me. Please don't go. Stay for a while.' Her voice lowered huskily and Frankie could just hear, 'We could go to bed.'

She clasped her hands to her face, closing her eyes, not believing what she was hearing. Eddie was having an affair? Wasn't it enough that he'd already got that young woman in Coventry pregnant? Did he really have another woman in Leicester too? Was that it, or was there anything more? Dear God, she had married a monster. Something else occurred to her then. The woman's voice seemed familiar.

She felt an overwhelming need to run, get far away, but before she could move Eddie was speaking again and Frankie strained to overhear.

'I've got to go. She'll be wondering where I am. I warned you about this when we started seeing each other. Now, I've told you I'll leave her and I will but you've got to be patient. If you don't stop going on about it, I'll stop seeing you,' he threatened. 'Look, we'll go out . . . Monday, somewhere nice. Book that restaurant you like. Come on, Stella, be a good girl. Calm down and give us a kiss.'

Frankie gasped. Stella! She felt the blood drain from her body and her legs buckle. Slowly a memory came back to her. She was at the top of the stairs. Arguing . . . She was arguing with someone. Roger. Why him? She saw a clenched fist coming towards her, aiming for her chest. She saw herself step back to avoid it. She was falling, down, down. Then like a bolt from the blue she saw it all. The nightmare, the terrible event she had blocked from her mind, flashed before her again and she gasped in horror. It was Eddie she had been arguing with, it was Eddie's fist she was trying to avoid when she had fallen down the stairs because she had found out through Roger that he was seeing Stella again. And he was still seeing her now.

Her vision swam and her head felt light. Her legs buckled. A hand grabbed her arm.

'You all right, missus?' a worried voice asked.

Through a haze she looked into the kindly face of the taxi driver.

'I'm sorry, but yer looked ter me like you was going to faint.'

She grabbed his other arm to support herself. 'Please take me home,' she begged.

Hands clasped so tight her knuckles pained her, a stone-faced Frankie was sitting rigidly in her armchair when Eddie sauntered through the door forty minutes after her.

'Oh, there you are,' he said matter-of-factly, flopping down in the chair opposite. 'Get your shopping done?' he asked, pulling off his shoes and putting them to the side of his chair, expecting her to put them away later. 'I've had a hell of a day. I was so busy I didn't realise how late it was.' He eyed her expectantly. 'Something smells good. What is it, I'm starving?'

'It's liver and onions, and if you want it it's in the dustbin,' she replied tersely.

He frowned his annoyance. 'I said I was tired, Frankie, I'm not in the mood for jokes. Now be a good girl and get my dinner.'

'I wasn't joking. If you want your dinner you can fish it out of the bin, and it's the last meal I'll ever cook for you.' She took a deep breath. 'I know, Eddie. I know it all. Every last sordid detail.'

He frowned at her quizzically. 'Know? Know what?' he asked.

'Don't act so innocent. You know perfectly well what I'm talking about. All the lies you've told me. How could you, Eddie? How could you do this to me?' Her voice rose hysterically. 'How could you make me believe that I caused myself to fall down the stairs and lose my baby, *our baby*, and damage myself that badly I can't have any more? Do you know how much guilt I suffered because of that, Eddie? Have you any idea? When all the time it was *you* who caused my accident. We were arguing over the fact that you had been seeing Stella behind my back, and *you* pushed me, Eddie. I fell down the stairs because I was trying to avoid your fist. I remember it all, so don't give me any more of your lies to cover up what you did.'

She took a hurried breath, face filled with contempt. 'I went to Coventry today, Eddie, and do you want to know why? Because I wanted to help you be reconciled with your parents. Thankfully I never had the pleasure of meeting your father but I certainly met your mother. She had a young woman with her – Amanda. Ring any bells? It should do, she's carrying your child. And as if that's not enough, I find out you're still seeing Stella. How long has that been going on, Eddie, and is there anything else I should know about? Well, is there?'

He took a deep breath and said matter-of-factly, 'No, I think that just about covers it. You've been busy today, haven't you, Frankie?'

She gazed at him, astounded. 'What! Is that all you've got to say to me?'

He nonchalantly shrugged his shoulders. 'What do you want me to say? So you found out about me? So what? It makes it easier for me. I won't have to cover my tracks in future, will I?'

'FUTURE! Eddie, we have no future. I want you to leave. Now. Please get your things and go. And I want a divorce. I don't ever want to see you again.'

Without warning, he jumped from his chair and leaned over her, pushing his face into hers. 'You can want all you like but you'll get nothing. I'm not leaving and I'll not divorce you. We married for better or for worse. Unfortunately for you, Frankie, you've got the worse. It's your own fault. You shouldn't have stuck your nose in.'

She saw the venom in his eyes, felt his hatred of her oozing from every pore. Her whole body shook. 'Why did you marry me, Eddie. Why? Despite all you said to get me to marry you, you've never loved me. So why did you do it?'

He stabbed his finger hard in her chest. 'You stupid woman, haven't you guessed why? You had something I wanted, or rather your uncle did, but when I married you I thought it was your father.'

She gasped as a terrible realisation struck her. 'The garage?'

'What else would I marry *you* for when a man like me could have anyone I wanted?' He grabbed her shoulders, pulled her to her feet and slapped her hard on the face. He pulled her back like a rag doll and thrust his face right up to hers, eyes blazing. 'Now you listen to me and listen good,' he snarled. 'I enjoy my life, I've worked hard for what I've got and I'm not giving it up for you or anyone.'

'It was my uncle who worked hard for that garage, not you.'

He slapped her again, harder this time. 'I told you to listen and that means keeping your mouth shut. Your uncle opened his mouth and he's regretting it now.'

Her eyes widened in horror. 'You . . . you had something to do with Uncle Wally's death?' she cried. Then she blurted out, 'Did you push him down the pit like you practically pushed me down the stairs? Is that what happened, Eddie? You're a murderer if you did.'

Uncontrollable rage and hatred for this terrible man filled her. She clenched her fist and swung it at him. Before it reached its target, he caught her wrist, gripping it, sharp nails digging into her skin and drawing blood.

He sneered at her maliciously, 'I'd be very careful just what you're accusing me of, Frankie. Even if I did have something to do with Wally's death, nothing could ever be proved.'

'I don't care,' she shouted, shaking violently at the shock of these terrible revelations. 'I'm going to the police. I'll tell them . . .'

'Tell them what?' he erupted savagely. 'That I was with your mother all night? Because I was, Frankie. You can ask her. Your mother will say I never left the house. She was doing the ironing, fussing around, *getting on me nerves*,' he emphasised harshly. He pushed Frankie from him and she stumbled back to land heavily in the armchair. He wagged a finger at her menacingly. 'Now I told you to listen and you'd better. You knowing all this changes nothing. You're my wife and you'll stay my wife. Breathe one word of this to anyone . . .'

'And you'll what?' she hissed. 'I'm not scared of you, Eddie Taylor. You're a monster. You'll have to kill me to stop me from going to the police. And I'll tell you something for nothing – Champion's is mine. My uncle left it to me and I'd sooner give it away than let you have another penny from it. You've plundered it already, probably bled it dry. I saw the fancy clothes you were wearing tonight and the car you were driving.'

He smirked wickedly at her. 'Yeah, nice, isn't it? Great thrill that gave me, walking into a car showroom and paying cash. Three hundred smackers.' He leaned over her again, face hard. 'The garage might have your name on it but it's under my control and it's staying that way. And you might not value your own safety, Frankie, but what about your parents' and Stella's? How much do you value *their* welfare?'

'What? You . . . you . . . wouldn't . . .'

He grinned wickedly. 'Oh, wouldn't I?' he cut in. 'We carry on as before or else you'll find out, won't you? The choice is yours, Frankie. Can't say fairer than that, can I?'

Her hand went to her mouth, horrified eyes staring wildly at him. She knew now without a doubt that Eddie was capable of carrying out his threats and she dare not go to the police. She cared far too much for her parents' and Stella's safety, and Eddie knew it.

As he watched her whole body sag, her head droop despairingly, a malicious smile spread slowly across his face. 'Right, now we understand each other. I'm glad we've got that sorted out. It's a weight off my mind.'

Face like death, she raised her head and looked at him. 'Your child? What are you going to do about it?'

He gave a nonchalant grunt. 'Its mother's a slag. It's probably not even mine anyway. I hate kids. Never wanted them. Even if it is mine, I want nothing to do with it. And you, Frankie, keep yer nose out. Amanda got what she deserves and that's the end of the matter as far as I'm concerned.'

He sat down in his chair, leaned back and rested his feet comfortably on the fender. 'Well, liver and onions is obviously off the menu so what else have you got?' He rubbed his hands together. 'I fancy a bit of steak. Nice and bloody. And chips. Yes, that'd do. You have got some in, haven't you, Frankie? You know I like a decent dinner after a hard day's graft. Come on, chop, chop. You must be starving yourself after the day you've had.'

Chapter Thirty-Five

The following Monday morning Eddie pushed his plate away and scowled at his wife. 'Those sausages were undercooked. I like them well done, Frankie, and you know it. Get it right tomorrow or else.' He leaned back in his chair, glancing at her scathingly. 'How long are you proposing to keep this silence up? It's makes no odds to me, I couldn't give a damn whether you talk to me or not, but what I can't put up with is having to face you looking like that. Pull yourself together, woman. You look worse than those old bags I grew up surrounded by in the Dales, but even they washed their face every day. And get this house cleaned! It's a pig sty.'

He scraped back his chair and rose. 'Right, I'm off, got a heavy day in front of me. I'll be wanting my dinner at six sharp because I'm off out tonight.'

With that he grabbed his coat and left.

When he'd gone Frankie sobbed in despair. She couldn't live like this, she couldn't. Just having him near her repelled her. But if she did anything to antagonise Eddie he might just do as he had threatened and harm her parents and Stella. She dare not risk that. She was going to have to suffer to protect her family and her once best friend. She had no choice because she loved them too much.

The knocker sounded on the front door and she jumped. She couldn't answer it, not feeling and looking like this. At this moment she felt she'd never find the energy to leave the house again. The knocker resounded again, then again. Whoever it was they weren't going away. Then she heard her name being called. Someone was shouting through the letterbox. It was a man's voice. It couldn't be the milk or coalman as she knew they'd never do something like that.

She got up and made her way to the hall. 'Who is it?' she called.

'Oh, thank God, it's me – Roger. Frankie, I need to speak to you. Please open the door.'

Oh, God, no, not Roger. She knew what he had come for. 'I'm . . . I'm not well, Roger.'

'Please, Frankie,' he pleaded. 'Just give me a minute. I've got to talk to you, I've got to.'

She saw his eyes peering at her through the letterbox.

'Two minutes, Frankie. That's all I ask.'

Sighing heavily, she made her way to the door, twisted the knob and inched it open just wide enough to see him through.

He gasped in shock when he saw the state she was in. 'My God, Frankie, you look dreadful,' he exclaimed. 'I thought you'd be a lot better by now. Can I come in, please?'

'What do you want, Roger?' she asked tonelessly.

'You know, don't yer, Frankie? I need to ask if you've spoken to your husband. He's still seeing Stella. She's living in a flat now and he pays the rent. Well, he must do, it's not the sort of place she could afford. Did yer know that, Frankie? Stella won't talk to me. I've tried and I'm desperate. I know she loves me deep down, it's just that she's been fooled by him. He's using her, Frankie, meking an idiot of her. And you,' he added. 'You've got to do something to stop him,' he begged. 'You can't let this go on. I stopped meself from coming before 'cos you was so poorly.'

She took a deep breath. 'I can't help you, Roger.'

He eyed her, astounded. 'What?'

'I'm sorry, there's nothing I can do.'

'Eh? But, Frankie, you can't mean that. He's your husband. You of all people could do something to put a stop to this.'

Her heart went out to him. How he loved Stella! But how could she tell him that to intervene in this lamentable situation would be to put Stella at risk and possibly her own parents too?

'I'm sorry,' she said resolutely. 'Now, if you'll excuse me, I've things to do.'

'You can't mean this, Frankie? This isn't like you. What's happened to yer?'

'I'm sorry,' she said, shutting the door.

She was sitting slumped at the table, her head in her hands, when her mother bustled in through the front door over an hour later.

Frankie inwardly groaned. She had completely forgotten they had arranged to go into town this morning. She hurriedly wiped her face over with her cardigan sleeve and forced a smile to her face.

'Hello, Mam, I'm in here.'

'I've loads of shopping ter do, so get a move on we'll miss the next bus. Oh,' Nancy exclaimed, stopping abruptly on spotting her daughter. 'Ain't yer ready yet?' Then Frankie's state registered. 'What on earth has happened, gel?' she asked.

'Nothing,' said Frankie with forced lightness. 'I've just got a terrible headache. The doctor did say I might suffer from those for quite a while yet. Would you mind if I gave it a miss today?'

Lowering herself on to the chair next to Frankie's, Nancy stared at her, frowning. 'That's more than a headache you're suffering from, lovey, so don't try and tell me otherwise. I asked what was wrong and I want to know.'

'Nothing, Mam,' she insisted. 'Will you please stop fussing?'

'Stop fussing! You're my daughter and the day I stop fussing is the day I die. Don't try and tell me there's n'ote wrong with yer, I've only got to look at yer to tell yer lying. You look like doom itself, gel. When was the last time yer washed yer face or changed yer clothes? Or slept for that matter? Right, get up them stairs, swill yer face and put summat clean on. You're coming with me.'

'Mam . . .'

'Now, Frankie. Don't give me no nonsense. Do as I say and mek it quick.'

'Where are we going?'

'To see yer dad. See if he can talk some sense into yer.'

A while later, Sam shook his head. 'Well, I'm sorry, me old duck, that daughter of ours isn't telling me anything she ain't told you. She reckons she's fine, just got a bad headache.'

Nancy stared at Frankie through the backroom window. Out in the yard she'd crouched down to examine a motorbike her father had had brought in for repair. 'And she's a liar,' said Nancy. 'She might fool most but she don't fool me.'

'Well, I agree she's covering up summat, but getting it out of her is another matter. Why don't we leave her, eh? Let her tell us when she feels she's able.'

Without taking her eyes off Frankie, Nancy patted his hand affectionately. 'I know yer right, Sam, but all the same . . . It's got to be what happened over the baby, 'cos she can't have any more. It can't be anything ter do with her and Eddie, I know she'd tell me if there was anything wrong between 'em, and surely she can't still be grieving so badly for our Wally? I know she misses Hilary, but not enough to cause this. So it's got to be the baby.'

'Mmm, you must be right. All we can do is be there for her, Nancy, like we've always been. Our gel needs time, that's all.'

She sighed. 'I hope so. Look at her, Sam, she's so beautiful and such a lovely girl, it pains me so much to see her like this.'

'Me too.' He squeezed her hand. 'It's just a thought . . .'

She turned and looked at him. 'Oh? What is?'

'Well, yer know how Frankie's having a struggle to get herself back to the garage? I was thinking, would it help if I asked her to come and give me a hand here? Mek out I'm so busy I can't manage. D'yer think that'd maybe pull her round?'

She looked at him tenderly. 'Oh, Sam, that's a great idea, and while she's 'ere I can keep more of an eye on her. Go and ask her. Put it in such a way that she can't refuse.'

'Well, give me a push out then and I will. I'd love having her work alongside me again. Be like old times.'

Chapter Thirty-Six

'My God,' Roger exclaimed in surprised delight. He clasped his arms briefly around the man before him then released him, standing back to look him up and down admiringly. 'I can't believe you're here. After all this time I was beginning to give up hope of ever clapping eyes on you again. Goodness me, it must be . . . well, five years since I last saw you. You look well, I must say. Filled out a bit but it suits you. Don't stand there, man, come in, come in!

Ian smiled broadly at his longlost friend. 'It's good to see you too, Roger. I thought we could go for a pint and catch up. Unless you've other plans for this evening?'

Roger slapped him on the arm. 'If I had other plans, Ian, I'd drop them. I've missed you, mate. You don't know how much. Just let me get my jacket and I'll be with you.'

A while later, both armed with a pint of foaming bitter, the men found a secluded corner in the busy public house and settled down. Elvis Presley's 'Hound Dog' was booming out from the jukebox, several flare-skirted girls grouped around it eyeing up the boys in Teddy-boy gear nearby. Two attractive older women sitting at a table close by Ian and Roger looked across at them, one giving Ian a come-on look. He appeared not to notice.

'It's not too noisy for you, is it, Ian?' Roger asked.

He laughed. 'Eh, I'm only twenty-seven, not too old yet to enjoy a good bit of music. Must say, I'm a Sinatra fan myself. But then, I still enjoy a bit of skiffle, too. Do you remember when we all used to go down the folk club . . .' His voice trailed off as memories of happier times he'd fought hard to bury flooded back. The pain was still as acute as ever. He forced them away and changed the subject. 'Well, life's obviously not been bad to you,' he said, taking a sup of his pint.

'Can't complain, I suppose. Starting to go a bit thin on top, but can't do much about that,' said Roger, grinning. 'I'm in charge at Barsby's now. It's a good position. As you saw, a nice house and a car. Only a little Austin Seven but it gets me about.'

'A car, eh? You must be doing all right. And Stella? How's she? You must have a couple of kiddies by now, I expect.'

A brief look of sadness crossed his friend's face. 'Oh, no, it didn't work out between me and Stella, Ian. I'm not married. Well . . . when you can't have the best, settling for less doesn't seem right, does it? Not fair on the other person. I suppose it's all or nothing for me. Anyway, that's all in the past. Life's obviously treated you well, too,' said Roger, taking a sip of his beer. 'Are you married?'

'Oh, no, me neither. Met a few nice women over the years, but as you say, when you can't have the best . . .'

Both men sat for a moment in silence, remembering.

It was Roger who spoke first. 'Your job seems to suit you. You look well on it, Ian.'

'Best thing I've ever done. You certainly see life,' he said, smiling knowingly.

'I bet you do. I must admit, I got quite a shock when your mother told me what you were doing.'

'My parents were both livid when I told them I was changing my job, and especially when I told them what I was going to be doing. My mother hated me going away for a while . . . she was very upset, but I talked them round and they were fine about it in the end.'

'I don't expect she realised you'd be away all this time, though?'

'Nor did I then, but when I got the opportunity to work in Northampton after I'd finished my training it seemed the best idea at the time. In another town you've no chance of bumping into people you're trying to forget.'

'So why are you back here now, if you don't mind me asking?'

'A job offer came up I'd have been stupid to refuse, one with good promotion, and to be honest I wanted to come home, Roger. When you've lived in some of the towns I have, you realise Leicester isn't so bad. Besides, I've found it doesn't matter where you are, you still have to face facts and deal with them mentally, if you understand my meaning.'

Roger nodded. 'I do, Ian.'

'I'm sorry I left without saying my goodbyes, Roger, but I hope you understand I wasn't myself at the time. And apologies, too, for not keeping in touch.'

'That's all right, mate. I understand. It was a hard time for both of us.'

Ian took a long gulp of his beer, eyed Roger hesitantly, needing to ask a question he'd been desperate to broach since first arriving on his doorstep an hour or so ago. 'How . . . how is Frankie? Do you know?'

'I never see her, Ian. Living on opposite sides of town, our paths never cross but as far as I know she's all right.'

'She still married to that Eddie fella?'

'As far as I know.'

Ian gave a sad sigh. 'Well, as long as she's happy.' The grunt Roger issued made him sit up straight and eye his friend sharply. 'Something I should know?'

Roger laughed wryly. 'They have you well trained, haven't they?' He shrugged his shoulders. 'I should leave well alone after all these years, but I can never get my head around it, no matter how hard I try. I thought I knew Frankie. Well, we practically lived in each other's pockets when we were all going out together.' He raked his fingers through his hair. 'Oh, I dunno, Ian, it just didn't make any sense her being like that over something so . . . I just know if it was my better half that was messing about, I would have to do something about it.'

Ian frowned darkly. 'Are you saying Frankie's husband has been messing around behind her back? I think you'd better tell me everything, Roger, don't you?'

Chapter Thirty-Seven

Frankie sat back on her haunches and ran her eyes over the bike admiringly. 'Well, what do you think, Dad? Should fetch a good bit, don't you reckon?'

'More than a good bit, Frankie, lovey. It's not often a Silver Hawk comes up for sale. You've done a grand job on the restoration. Couldn't have done better meself.'

She gave a laugh. 'I never thought I'd find all the bits. Digging around a scrapyard under piles of junk in search of one specific part can be a little bit soul-destroying.'

'Yeah, but you did find all the bits, Frankie, and yer should congratulate yerself. You've enjoyed doing this, ain't yer?'

She smiled at him. She'd enjoyed it more than she would ever let on. Sam had left her no option but to come and lend him a hand three years ago after . . . well, she had much for which to thank her father. This was her one place of sanctuary. Enclosed in the bosom of her family was the one place she could forget she was saddled for life with a monster for a husband. For a few hours each day she could lose herself doing something she loved and was cut out for.

Back at her own house – she never called it home, as to Frankie a home was filled with love and laughter and the place she lived in wasn't – she kept things clean and tidy, cooked Eddie his meals, washed and ironed his clothes. Conversation was kept to polite enquiries about simple daily matters that affected them both, nothing more. Frankie had moved into the back bedroom straight after that awful day when Eddie had confessed the truth and had not left it since, a fact her mother had never uncovered thankfully. Frankie did not relish having to concoct further lies in order to cover up her real reason for sleeping alone.

As for the garage and how it was doing, she had no idea and never asked. Eddie had made it quite clear she was not to interfere or she'd suffer the consequences. He gave her a fairly generous amount each week in housekeeping and out of that she managed to clothe herself smartly, outwardly at least the picture of a prosperous businessman's wife, which helped complete the illusion that Eddie and she were a happily married couple.

The only social occasions they spent together, apart from Christmas Day which was automatically spent with her parents, were rare trips to her mother's for tea on a Saturday afternoon when Frankie couldn't use the excuse that Eddie was busy. He seemed to enjoy these events, amused to see how uncomfortable she was through what were for her terrible ordeals. It was almost unbearable for the hours they were together in her parents' company to have to play the role of the loving, dutiful wife, but Frankie suffered in silence. It was a small price to pay for Nancy, Sam and Stella's continued welfare.

There was one matter that preyed heavily on Frankie's mind, and that was the plight of Eddie's illegitimate child. Unbeknown to Eddie, and she prayed that it stayed that way, she had been sending money anonymously on a regular basis, hoping it would help the child in a small way. Nothing, of course, could ever make up to it for the awful way it had arrived in the world, or for the fact it had such a despicable father who had abandoned it in a terrible place, but Frankie felt that what she was doing might in some way help to make amends. At least he or she would know that someone cared.

'What are yer gonna being doing with your share?' Sam was asking her.

'Pardon, Dad? Oh, now, we've had this all out before. What I do is for the love of it and to help you out. I don't need any money, Dad. We're doing well enough, thank you. What money we make is for you and Mam.'

'Come on, lovely. Through your 'elp me and yer mam for the first time in our lives have a decent bit put by. We're happy with that, Frankie. You've got to start teking some fer yerself. Yer mam feels the same. We were only saying as much last night.'

'Dad, I won't discuss this again.' She scrambled over to him, knelt before him and took his hands. 'I love working with you, and now we've partly covered the yard over I'm so happy you're protected from the elements.'

He smiled tenderly at her. 'That were a grand idea of yours, Frankie, having this covered-up bit. Not that I ever let on to yer mother but I used ter feel the cold summat rotten. And it were so good of yer, paying for it out of the profits from those bikes you fixed.'

'It was my pleasure and I'm glad you're pleased with it. It makes me feel happy, Dad, that I've done something for you. And Mam still has room to hang her washing out in good weather.'

'Trust our Nancy to be worried about that,' he said, grinning. 'And not giving a thought to the fact that having this shelter means she doesn't have to get wet in the rain when she needs the privy or a bucket of coal.'

'Well, you'd soon complain if you never had a dry shirt to put on, and that's all Mam was thinking of.'

'Eh, yer know I've never complained about anything yer mam's not managed to do. I might have passed a comment but never complained.'

'Oh, the Silver Hawk is finally finished then? Took yer long enough, our Frankie.'

'Hello, Granddad, Nelly.' Frankie smiled happily as she saw two faces peeping at her and Sam through a gap in the yard gate.

'Come away in, Dad,' said Sam. 'Nancy's in the kitchen, Nelly,' he said, smiling at the old lady as she and Edgar came through, shutting the gate behind them. 'Yes, it's a beauty all right. Our Frankie's done herself proud, ain't she, Dad?'

'Well, I ain't surprised merself,' Edgar said gruffly, lips pursed as he gave the bike a close inspection. 'I've always said it's in her blood.' He looked across at Frankie, a mischievous look in his eyes. 'Sure you got the right mudguards for this model, Frankie?'

'Oh, Granddad,' she scolded. 'You know fine well I have.'

Just then Nancy came bustling out. 'I thought I 'eard voices. Hello, you two. Good timing, I'm just about ter put the dinner on so yer can both stay for a bite to eat. That all right wi' you, Nelly? I don't want to interfere with any of your plans.'

The old lady gave her a happy smile. 'That's fine wi' me, me duck, as long as we're not putting you out?'

'Never,' said Nancy. 'You're me family. Welcome anytime.' She walked towards Frankie and put a motherly arm around her. 'Can't you pop over to the garage and let Eddie know we're all having dinner here tonight, then we could mek a family do of it? Be nice that.'

Frankie looked at her tenderly. 'Yes, it would, Mam. But Eddie told me this morning he'd a big rush job on and had no idea when he'd be finished.'

How she hated telling lies, but what else could she do?

'Oh, pity that. Still, another time, eh?'

★ ★ ★

Across town in the small prefab building which was the office of Ace Autos, Eddie leaned back in his leather chair, stretched out his long legs and put his expensively clad feet on the desk. 'I'm bored,' he complained, folding his arms at the back of his head.

In a seat opposite, Neil took a bite of ham sandwich and eyed his brother. 'Bored?' he said through a mouthful of food. 'In God's name, how can yer be bored, our Eddie? Bloody hell, there's men I know who'd give their right arm to have what we've got. You've a garage that practically runs itself and this car lot that's doing better than we ever expected. And we've got money saved. I've nearly five grand meself stashed in the back of the wardrobe, so I can't think what you've got.'

'And that's my business.' Eddie sighed heavily. 'The thrill's gone out of it, though. I used to love nothing more than knowing I'd got a car for half its value but now we've got Bill and Jimmy doing that for us, it seems to have taken the fun out of it all.'

'Well, we could always expand,' Neil suggested.

'Yeah, I suppose we could. We could get a fancy showroom, brother, couldn't we?' Eddie answered, his voice full of sarcasm. 'And what would that achieve? The bloody tax inspector pouncing on us, that's all. This little car lot hides a multitude of sins, Neil, and you know it. No one would ever guess how many cars come and go through here. We can put most of the cash straight in our pockets and no comeback. What does go through the books is enough to keep the officials happy. We could never get away with that in bigger, posher premises. Not so much as we do here anyway.'

'Yeah, I suppose. Well, what about opening another garage? You've kept Champion's legit, you say, so why not have another legit one. Give yer summat to occupy yer, wouldn't it, setting it all up? And think of the profits.'

'Mmm,' Eddie mused. 'It's crossed my mind before. Pays to have a kosher concern, keeps official eyes from looking too closely at the not-so kosher ones,' he said, grinning. 'But before I do that I'd sooner start another car lot, same working practices as this one. I've got to start thinking about my retirement. I want to retire by the time I'm fifty and have enough money to go anywhere I want and live like a lord for the rest of my life. The lot brings in far better profits than the garage. Yes, that's what I'll probably do. I'll put some thought into another car lot. But right this minute, I'm still bored.'

'Well, I tell yer what, how about spending a few quid of your profits? You might be saving for your retirement, Eddie, but meantime you've got to have a little fun. I'm teking that new bird I landed last week down the casino tonight. What about you and Stella coming?'

'Gambling's a mug's game, Neil. It's a wonder you've anything put by, knowing how much you lose.'

'I might lose a bit, Eddie, but I know when to stop. And I know for a fact Stella's not averse to a bit of a tickle. She won twenty quid the last time you took her greyhound racing. Anyway, are you coming or not? We could tek the women for supper first.'

'No, not tonight. Another night I might but I don't think I'll bring Stella. Time for a change, I reckon.'

'What, you'd give her up after all this time?'

Eddie nodded. 'I'm fed up with her now. She's getting a bit long in the tooth for my tastes.'

'And you think she's going to take it lightly?'

'She won't have any choice. Rest assured, Neil, I'll leave her in no doubt that should she dare cause any trouble, she'll bloody wish to Christ she hadn't. This new bird of yours, has she got any good-looking friends?'

'Yeah, she has. Want me to fix you up?'

'Yes,' he said, grinning wickedly. 'Do that. Tomorrow night.'

Neil smiled. 'Done.'

Eddie lapsed into a thoughtful silence. Several minutes passed before a slow smile spread across his handsome face. 'I've got it,' he cried jubilantly.

'Got what?'

'The way to ease my boredom.'

'Oh, yeah?' Neil said eyeing him keenly. 'Come on then, brother, spill the beans?'

'It's time to make a visit to Coventry.'

'Coventry? What on earth do you want to go back to that hell-hole for?'

'It's payback time, Neil.'

'What?'

'Time to settle the score with Kelvin Mason.'

Neil looked worried. 'Oh, Eddie, I thought you'd forgotten all about that.'

'Never. Just put it on hold while I waited until the right idea came along. Now it has.'

'Well, are yer gonna tell me what this brilliant idea is then?'

'I will when you've dealt with that punter out there,' he said, pointing out of the grubby window to a man browsing through the cars on the front lot. 'Try and palm him off with that old Vauxhall we did the quick respray on. The rust is beginning to bubble through and I want rid of it before we have to touch it up again.'

'Leave it to me,' said Neil, hurrying off. 'Can I help you, sir?' he asked the man strolling purposefully up to him.

'I hope so,' said Ian.

Chapter Thirty-Eight

Kelvin Mason eyed Eddie warily. 'You sit there seriously thinking I'd believe you wanna do business wi' me after what I did to you? Sorry, mate, but leave me out of this. I wouldn't trust you, Eddie Taylor, no matter how well you tell me you're doing now.'

'You can't hold grudges where business is concerned, Kelvin. So you did the dirty on me – I'm not so sure I wouldn't have done the same, given the chance. I couldn't produce the cash you wanted so you sold to someone else who could. I can't say I was exactly overjoyed at the time but, well, when all's said and done, you probably did me a favour.'

'I did? How the 'ell do you make that out?'

Eddie smiled secretively at him. 'Let's just say that if you hadn't double crossed me there's a good chance I might not be such a successful businessman now. Another pint?'

'Don't mind if I do.'

A few minutes later Eddie returned with the drinks and sat down. 'This place doesn't change any, does it? Still the same old faces.'

'Yeah, and still the same stinking lavvies,' Kelvin said, his voice rising. 'They stank to high heaven the last time we was here and that ain't changed.'

'Keep your voice down,' Eddie said, annoyed, noticing the attention Kelvin was attracting which was the very last thing he wanted. 'So, do we talk business or what?' he asked, taking a large gulp of his pint and glancing at Kelvin. 'Looks to me like you could do with a bit of cash coming your way. You could buy yourself a decent coat for a start. You were wearing that old thing the last time we met.'

'Ah, cash I ain't short of but Sandra spends it as soon as I make it. You were right, Eddie, I should 'ave listened ter yer. I left one scheming cow for another, only Sandra bleeds me drier than me first wife ever did.'

'Should have kept her as a mistress, mate, works far better.'

'I will the next time round, believe me. Okay, Eddie, tell me what's on yer mind and I'll let you know if I'm interested or not.'

A while later Kelvin eyed him sceptically. 'You expect me to secure at least six top-notch cars through my contacts, all with new identification docs?'

'That's the size of it. And that's just for starters.'

'And fer starters, mate, as you well know, I don't do anything without seeing any cash up front. This ain't gonna come cheap.'

'Money is no problem. Can you do it or not?'

''Course I can do it,' Kelvin scoffed. 'Might tek a couple of weeks, the kinda cars you're after.'

'That's fine. Now I'm also in the market for car spares . . .'

'Oh, that's more tricky, Eddie mate. Rootes ain't half tightened up security over the past few years. Hardly get much coming my way in that line any more.'

'I'm sure you'll sort something. I'm prepared to pay fifty percent to the men this time, and say thirty to you.'

'What? Only leave yerself twenty? 'Tain't like you, Eddie, ter be so generous.'

'Times have changed, Kelvin. I've got more money than I know what to do with, but I can always do with more. Let's say I don't need to be quite so greedy. You saying yes?'

Kelvin grimaced thoughtfully. 'All right. I'm sure the lads in the factory will think of some new schemes to get stuff out if they know they're getting that much return.'

'Good. I want a seven-tonner van's worth.'

'Eh? That's a shit load of parts, Eddie.'

'I might be well off, Kelvin, but I haven't lost my marbles. I know how much goes into the back of a van that size.' He put his hand into his inside pocket and pulled out a wad of notes, Kelvin's bulging eyes not lost on him. He peeled off several and handed them over. 'Five hundred to start, the rest on delivery. Then we'll discuss further business when I know you can produce the goods.'

Kelvin thrust the notes into his pocket and eyed Eddie, impressed. 'I won't let you down, trust me. You'll want the delivery made to one of yer garages in Birmingham, I take it? I need a telephone number where I can contact you when we're ready to go.'

That was the last thing Eddie wanted. 'No. These are going straight to the customers. I'll arrange my own drivers. No disrespect, Kelvin, but cars like these need a certain type of delivery driver behind the wheel when we make the drop off and I doubt you can come up with them. I'll bring my own seven-tonner along to transfer the spares into. I'm out and about all the time so giving you a telephone number is a waste of time. Best thing is to handle contact between us like we did last time. It worked very well. You just leave word with Grim Jack when you've got your end all sorted and a time you'll be here so I can speak to you direct on the Grapes telephone and arrange a meet. Somewhere between the two towns would be best.' He gulped down the last of his pint and rose. 'Right, I'm off. Other business to see to. Two weeks, yeah?'

'Give or take a day or so.'

Eddie nodded.

Seconds after he'd left the pub, a grim-faced man rose from the table in the alcove behind and followed him out.

Chapter Thirty-Nine

'But, Mr Cohen, I know Eddie will have paid the rent. There must be some mistake.'

'There's no mistake, Miss Simpson. Three weeks are owing and I want the money.'

Stella froze. She hadn't got anywhere near that kind of money herself. Where was Eddie? She hadn't seen him for three weeks now. She knew he hadn't had an accident or anything or the men at the garage would have said something when she had telephoned, and they had assured her they had passed all her messages on. Why hadn't he contacted her? Oh, this was so worrying. What on earth was she going to do?

She had no alternative but to go to the garage. It was Friday today. She knew Eddie always paid a visit in the afternoon to do the banking, dish out the wages and such like. It was just coming up to six and the other mechanics would have left for the night. She desperately hoped he hadn't gone home himself yet or she wouldn't know what to do.

Eddie's absence more than likely had something to do with Frankie, she thought. She'd resurrected her old suicide trick, no doubt, to keep tabs on him like she'd done in the past. Those times had been hell for Stella. For days at a time Eddie couldn't visit her, just like now, only this time for whatever reason he hadn't been able to let her know and put her mind at rest. But that still didn't explain why he hadn't paid the rent on the flat.

Oh, Eddie, she thought worriedly. This lack of contact was tearing her apart. How much she loved him. She must do to put up with this awful situation for as long as she had. She had only managed it thanks to Eddie's promises that he'd leave his wife one day. Surely he must do something about that soon. Three years this had been going on, and Stella was twenty-seven years old. She wanted a proper house of her own and a family. Time was passing so rapidly. Why was Frankie being so selfish in keeping Eddie tied to her all this time when she knew he didn't love her or want to be with her? Surely it couldn't give her any satisfaction, knowing he was only staying put because of her threats to harm herself?

Stella realised Mr Cohen was speaking to her. 'Sorry?'

'I want my rent, Miss Simpson.'

'And you'll get it. But not right this minute. Look, my . . .' Her voice trailed off. How she hated calling Eddie her boyfriend and not her husband, knowing people like Mr Cohen and others who lived in the flats must realise he paid the rent. Something that hadn't bothered her too much at first now made her feel uncomfortable. She was a kept woman, there was no other way to describe herself. 'You'll have your money tomorrow, Mr Cohen. All of it, I promise.'

He sighed. 'No later or I'm sorry, Miss Simpson, I'll have to arrange for the bailiffs to call.'

The shame of that didn't bear thinking about. Stella shut the door and rested her back against it. 'Oh, Eddie,' she cried, 'where are you? Why are you doing this to me?'

She grabbed her coat and bag and hurriedly departed.

A short while earlier Frankie glanced up worriedly at the clock tower in the centre of Leicester. She had so enjoyed herself browsing around the shops, she had lost track of the time. She should be home by now preparing Eddie's dinner. Not that she ever knew whether he would be home to eat it or not, but she had to get it ready just in case to avoid any conflict. Many times in the past she had wanted to express her anger at cooking so many wasted meals but she knew it was better not to cause any trouble. Eddie wasn't very nice when his temper was roused as she knew to her cost, and there was always the possibility he would do something to her parents or Stella and she dare not take the risk.

The town was busy, the traffic very heavy and pavements crowded with throngs of people making their way home after their long day at work, and shoppers late back just like herself. She stood anxiously at the kerb waiting for the policeman in the centre of the road to halt the flow of traffic to allow pedestrians to cross. Someone bumped into her and she automatically turned to see who it was.

It was a middle-aged man and he was muttering an apology.

'Oh, that's all right, no harm done,' she answered with a smile. Then she looked at him in surprised recognition. It was Mr Green, an old customer from the garage. He seemed upset.

'Mr Green, it's me, Frankie. Frankie Champion. I used to fix your car. Are you all right?'

He turned his head and stared at her from swollen red eyes. When he recognised her, he looked at her in disgust. 'I don't know how you've the nerve to talk to me.'

She gasped at his tone. 'I'm sorry,' she uttered, deeply shocked at such an unexpected reply.

'You're sorry?' he spat, turning fully to face. 'It's me that's sorry I ever had dealings with Champion's.'

Face filled with horror, she said, 'I don't understand . . .'

'Don't give me that! It's your business. Are you going to stand there and deny you don't know what's going on?'

Frankie was very conscious of other bystanders waiting to cross the road and looking at them interestedly. She shook her head. 'I don't know what you're talking about, Mr Green.'

'Don't lie to me, Frankie. I've had enough lies from your family. I trusted you. For Christ's sake, I'd been dealing with your uncle for years and was so sorry when he died. Lovely man he was. Straight as a die. I continued to have my car looked after at the garage out of loyalty to him and to you, Frankie, being's I heard you'd inherited the place. So I thought buying a car for my son from a place connected to Champion's Garage was going to be a good bet.'

'But Champion's doesn't sell cars, Mr Green,' she said, confused, absently putting down her shopping bags on the pavement.

'Ace Autos belongs to Champion's and don't try and tell me it doesn't. I know it does. When I was looking over the cars on the lot there I recognised your husband in the caravan they use as an office and asked the chap looking after me what he was doing there. He told me Eddie was the owner.'

Frankie gasped. 'What?'

'That's what decided me to buy the car for my son's twenty-first birthday as a surprise for him. The young man who sold it to me seemed so genuine. He assured me the car was as sound as a bell and I had no reason to believe otherwise. That car should never have been on the road!' he spat. 'Its underside was near rotten and it had hardly any brakes. I know because my son's now lying in hospital fighting for his life, having crashed into another car after his brakes failed. We don't know whether he's going to pull through or not. His mother is beside herself. And I've no comeback.'

'No comeback?' Frankie didn't understand.

'No. I can't prove I bought the car from Ace Autos. No receipt, you see. I was told they'd run out and one would be sent on. I should've realised then something dodgy was going on but I was so pleased with the car, couldn't wait to see my son's face when I gave him the keys.' He poked her forcefully in the shoulder. 'You ain't getting away with this, let me tell you. You're killing people, that's what you're doing, selling unroadworthy cars like that. I just hope for your sake my son pulls through and you haven't a murder charge on your hands. I'll prove somehow I got that car from Ace, you see if I don't. Anyway the police are involved now.'

With that he hurried off, leaving Frankie staring blindly after him. She heard a man at the side of her say, 'People like you want stringing up. All yer interested in is innocent people's money. Should be a law passed against villains like you.'

Heedless now of anyone around her, filled with horror at what she'd just been told, Frankie's mind raced frantically. If Eddie was selling lethal cars to innocent buyers then Mr Green was right. People were in terrible danger. All she could picture was that man's son, lying in hospital fighting for his life. Eddie had to be stopped. She didn't know how but she couldn't stand back and let anyone else suffer terrible injuries.

Forgetting her shopping bags, she kicked up her heels and ran as fast as her legs would carry her towards Champion's Garage.

Eddie meanwhile was speaking into the telephone, his voice huskily seductive. 'No I can't tomorrow night, pussy cat, but I can tonight. How about me and you having a nice meal together? I'd take you to my flat only I've let a friend stay for a bit, but sh . . . he'll be leaving next week. We'll have it all to ourselves then and we can be on our own. No, I'm not married, don't ask such stupid questions. I'm just a busy man. Businesses don't run themselves, you know. Tonight about eight, okay? I'll pick you up in my new MG and we'll go somewhere nice. Wear that red dress. That's right, the low-cut one. Yes, I do fancy you in that outfit.' What red-blooded man wouldn't? he thought. 'Look, I've got to go. See you tonight.'

He put down the telephone and grinned at the thought of the night to come. Rosalind was a stunner all right. Face of an angel, legs up to her armpits and breasts on her no woman would be ashamed to own. And she was very broad-minded, teaching Eddie tricks in bed even he never knew existed.

He smiled smugly to himself as he thought of Stella. It had been okay with her while it had lasted. He wondered if she'd taken the hint yet and realised her days with him were over. The landlord must have paid her a visit by now and Eddie knew only too well Stella hadn't the money to clear the rent. She'd never be able to stay on there with just her wages from a poxy office job, leaving him free to entertain Rosalind there whenever he wanted. He might even install her in it if she was agreeable. Hopefully Mr Cohen would do his dirty work for him very shortly and have Stella turfed out.

The door leading to the office opened and the sound it made caused Eddie to swing around in his seat.

'Coast clear, Eddie?'

'Bugger it, Neil, you made me jump. Yeah, come in, they've all gone home.'

Neil put a leather Gladstone bag down in front of him. 'The takings from the lot. Good day today. I finally got rid of that Vauxhall.'

Eddie smiled at him, impressed, leaning back in his chair and placing his feet on the desk. 'Good man. I was beginning to think we never would. You'll make a car salesman yet.'

'Cheeky sod.' Neil grabbed a chair from nearby and sat down. 'You look happy with yerself,' he commented.

'And so I should do, Neil. So I should. Life's brilliant. Couldn't wish for better. The garage is doing well, the car lot too it goes without saying. And . . .' He paused, rubbing his hands together gleefully. 'Tomorrow night Kelvin Mason gets what's coming to him. I've arranged a meet. All I've got to do is put a call through to the rozzers and Mason will be lucky not to get a ten or twelve-year stretch with what they're going to catch him with. And what it cost me to set it all up was worth every penny. Just a pity I can't be there to see his face.'

Neil laughed. 'You're a devious bastard.'

'Ain't I just? It's only what he deserves. I'm seeing Rosalind again tonight. Some woman she is, Neil. Best thing you ever did was getting me introduced to her. She's classy, I like that. More fitting type of woman for a bloke like me. You know, this might even be the one I leave Frankie for. Time will tell. Right, I'd better get myself ready. Want to look my best. Picked up my new suit today from the tailor. Italian style. Very nice. Cost enough so it should be. That tailor sure knows his business. I've ordered another two dozen shirts as well.'

'And Frankie never says anything about all the money you splash out on yerself?'

'She knows better, Neil, believe me.' His head suddenly jerked up. 'What was that?'

'What?'

'I thought I heard a noise.' Eddie listened for a minute. 'Probably something outside. Right, I'll see you tomorrow then. Oh, how's that new house you bought? Settling in all right?'

'Yeah, it's great, Eddie. Never thought I'd live in a place like that. It's really posh in Stoneygate. You should see the cars parked in the neighbours' driveways. Mind you, I wouldn't swap my Austin Healey for a Rolls if you paid me. The women love it. I'm not sure if it's the car that draws them or me,' he added, laughing. 'You'll come around soon to the new house, won't you, Eddie? And bring Rosalind with you. We'll crack open a few bottles of Champers to christen it.'

'As soon as I can find time, Neil. I expect you're keeping pretty busy yourself though with Nadine?'

Neil smiled. 'And the rest, brother. You ain't the only one who likes a couple on the go, yer know.'

They both leapt out of their seats when the office door suddenly burst open and several men walked in. The tall, lanky one in the lead stood before Eddie grinning. Then, hands thrust deep into his pockets, he looked around him. 'Bit of a dive for a posh car showroom like you described to me, Eddie, mate. And in Birmingham I could have sworn you said. Funny, I seem to recall when we drove here the sign saying Leicester. Not like you to get summat like that arse over tit, is it? Good job I decided to follow you that night you put the deal to me. Had a niggle, you see, that not everything you was telling me was kosher. Still, we'll just put that down to a lapse of memory on your part, shall we, Eddie?

'Anyway, being's I had everything sorted out my end, I thought it'd be decent of me to save you the bother of meeting me tomorrow and get the business done and dusted tonight. It's all outside. Six cars like you asked and a seven-tonner full of spares. So it's just a matter of sorting the spondulicks and we'll all be happy.'

Eddie flashed a glance at the menacing thugs behind Kelvin, then brought his eyes back to rest on his old enemy.

Panting hard, gasping for air, Frankie arrived at Champion's and stopped momentarily to catch her breath. Immediately the sight of six very upmarket cars – one a Daimler, another an Austin Atlantic – commanded her attention as did the large van blocking the forecourt at the front. Parked in the road was a red MG. Her face set stonily.

Eddie was into far more than she'd realised, but at the moment the expensive cars were not her main worry. It was the cheap and faulty ones she had to stop him selling.

Without another thought she raced into the garage.

'You've got to stop it now, Eddie. I demand . . . Oh!' The sight of six burly men and one tall, thin, very dubious-looking character made her pause. Then she saw Eddie and another man who looked very much like him. They were all staring at her.

'What the fuck are you doing here?' Eddie demanded. 'Get out. Go home. I'll deal with you later.'

Heedless of the others Frankie cried, 'I will not! I don't know what's going on here but I'll not go until you promise you'll stop selling those lethal cars?'

'Who's this then, the little woman?' Kelvin sneered. 'Got yerself a looker there, Eddie, mate. Done yerself proud. Anyway, lady, whoever you are, you can wait yer turn. When I've finished I'll happily leave him to you. So, Eddie, mate, you were telling me you're not in a position to take delivery tonight. Now it's funny that 'cos I had a suspicion you might not be. Couldn't be because you never planned to be meeting me at all, could it? That maybe you were sending the rozzers instead?'

Forgetting Frankie's presence Eddie went on the defensive. 'Of course not, what do you take me for?' he vehemently denied. 'How dare you think I'd stoop so low as to welch on a deal. You tell him, Neil.'

'I wouldn't believe a word you say any more than I do your brother, so you can shut yer trap,' Kelvin spat at Neil. He returned his full attention to Eddie. 'Took me for a mug, didn't you? I knew straight away what you had in mind, but I thought I'd play yer game and turn the tables on yer simply because the money I'm making out of all this is my ticket out of here. Got a plane to catch, see.'

Eddie's face darkened. 'Just what have you done, Kelvin?'

He grinned maliciously. 'Oh, put the word out about you, that's all. There's a dozen or so not very happy Rootes workers out for your blood, Eddie, 'cos I ain't paid 'em a penny yet, and I think the police will know by now who's got these cars. You shouldn't have tried to get even with me, Eddie. Not that I blame yer, but you should have just left it 'cos you made a big mistake underestimating me.'

Frankie was listening to all of this, stunned. Before she could stop herself she cried, 'You're using my uncle's garage to sell stolen cars and spares? I won't allow this, I won't!'

'Shut the hell up, Frankie, before I shut you up,' Eddie bellowed, grabbing her arm and yanking her out of the way. She stumbled backwards to land heavily on the floor. He spun back to face Kelvin. 'You bastard!' he shouted, temper erupting violently, grabbing the nearest thing handy which happened to be a lump hammer. Quickly sussing what was happening Neil likewise snatched a monkey wrench, waving it menacingly at the henchmen as he advanced on them. He grinned as the burly-looking men began to back off fearfully.

'You told us there's be no trouble, Kelvin,' one of them shouted.

Eddie raised his arm and waved the wrench warningly at Kelvin. 'Some protection that lot are. Fucking clever you are, Kelvin, to pick a load of nancies to protect you.' His face contorted threateningly. 'Now if you value your life I'd get those cars and van out of here quick sharp or I won't hesitate to use this.'

Kelvin leapt over to Frankie. He grabbed her arm and forced her in front of him, his arm tight around her throat, forcing the breath from her. 'Lay one finger on me and she gets it!'

Eddie's laughter rang out loud and clear. 'Do what you like to her, I don't give a fuck. Sorry, Frankie, but I did warn you to go home.'

Unable to move an inch from Kelvin's tight lock on her, shutting her eyes, heart pounding painfully, Frankie prepared to face the worst.

'Right, men, we've heard enough,' a loud voice boomed as the garage doors burst open and several uniformed policemen armed with dangerous-looking truncheons spilled inside.

'What the hell . . .' Eddie cried, panic-stricken. 'Neil, quick, scarper!' he shouted frenziedly, knocking the policemen out of his way as he bolted for the door.

Next thing Frankie was aware of she was being thrust aside. She stared in disbelief at the mayhem around her. Policemen seemed to be everywhere, shouts of protest filled the air. In the distance she heard the screech of wheels as a car sped off, then another roaring after it.

A hand caught her arm and she spun around then gasped in shock on seeing the uniformed man before her. 'Ian,' she uttered, astounded.

'Hello, Frankie. You're safe now.' He took her hand. 'Come on, let's get you home.'

Moments earlier, all thoughts centred on his getaway, a desperate

Eddie rammed the car key into the ignition, smashing his foot down hard on the accelerator. As his car roared into life a brief smirk kinked his lip. It had certainly paid to buy a decent car from a reliable dealer. Conscious that the police were close behind, Eddie sped off, wheels squealing, forcing an approaching car to skid to a halt, making the driver inside shake an angry fist. Eddie's mind was too full of his own problems to even notice.

As he steered the car expertly through the congested streets that headed out of the city, followed by the ringing of police bells close behind, a sudden furious annoyance that he was in this position reared up inside him. But the bulging roll of bank notes in his pocket and the Gladstone bag of takings he had grabbed as he escaped the garage were more than enough to give him a start somewhere new. When he had settled down he would make plans to retrieve the rest of the money he felt he'd laboured so hard for during his time in Leicester. And he would get it back, every last penny of it, and he didn't care one iota how he did, or how much suffering he would cause.

As he cornered a tight bend he thought fleetingly of Neil. Not that it was of any importance to him at the moment, but he did wonder how long his brother's prison sentence would be this time.

The police car chasing him was only yards behind now and Eddie could see the late evening traffic becoming thicker ahead. He issued a loud profanity in protest; the heavy traffic was hampering his escape route. Without another thought he swerved into a side road, knowing that the warren of streets that led off it would take him out to the edge of the city. Once he was there he'd be safe, he could lose himself easily down country lanes. Not far now, he thought smugly, praying the police would have difficulty following him.

Suddenly, out of nowhere a loaded coal lorry loomed. Eddie slammed on his brakes. But it was too late. As the back end of the lorry flew up to him, his eyes bulged with terror, and all Eddie had time to do was mouth, 'Oh, hell.'

'Frankie . . . oh, Frankie, lovey,' was all a devastated Nancy could say later that night after hearing the dreadful tale her daughter had to tell her. Hugging her tightly she looked across at Ian. 'How can we thank yer?'

Sam placed his hand on Ian's arm. 'Thanks ain't enough for what you've done, lad. If you hadn't taken an interest in Eddie, I dread to think of the outcome.'

Ian smiled awkwardly at him. 'Well, I didn't like what Roger told me. It didn't make sense that Frankie should turn a blind eye to her husband openly having an affair. I knew her better than that. There had to be a good reason why she was allowing it to happen. So I decided to watch him. The more I did, the less I liked what I was seeing so I took my concerns to my superior officer. He didn't like the sound of what I was telling him either and felt we should have Taylor checked out properly. We've had a tail on him for three weeks. We were just waiting for something like tonight to happen so we could catch him good and proper.'

'Well, thank God yer did, Ian, that's all I can say.' Sam took a deep breath. 'And Stella? Will she be all right?'

'Concussion, thankfully, not serious. A couple of days in hospital should see her as right as rain. Knowing what was going on inside, and us just waiting for the right moment to go in, I nearly had a heart attack when I saw Frankie go charging into the garage. I couldn't stop her. Then just after her, along came Stella. Well . . . I was a bit over-enthusiastic in stopping her. Leapt on her just as she went to open the office door and she fell and hit her head on the ground. Anyway, Frankie's in safe hands now. I'd best get back to the station.'

'The brother's going to be locked up for a long time, I trust?' asked Sam.

'You can count on it, Mr Champion.' Ian's voice lowered to a whisper. 'I'll let you know when Edwin Taylor's body is being released from the morgue so you can arrange the funeral.'

Still stunned by the terrible story he'd just been told, Sam shook his head sadly. 'We had no idea, Ian, no idea at all that our Frankie was having to put up with all this because that . . . that . . . terrible man threatened our lives and Stella's.'

'She did it because she loves you. That's why, Mr Champion.'

'Yes, I know. Well, she's released from that purgatory now. And as long as I live and breathe I'll make sure nothing like this ever happens to her again.' He gave Ian a knowing look. 'Mind you, I have a feeling I won't need to watch over her now you're back.'

Chapter Forty

Nancy heaved a heavy bag on top of two others already piled in the alcove by the front door. 'Well, that's the last of 'em.' Tight-lipped, she appraised the pile. 'Eddie sure liked his clothes, me duck, and that's a fact. There's enough 'ere to open yer own second-hand shop and keep it stocked for weeks. And those clothes never came from Burton's. I ain't never seen a Savile Row suit but I suspect some of Eddie's are, as near as dammit.' Nancy turned and looked at the pain etched on the face of her daughter and deep concern wreathed her own. 'You sure yer fit ter go to the 'ospital on yer own, Frankie? I don't mind coming with yer, honest I don't. Nelly and yer granddad are seeing to yer dad's dinner tonight so it's no problem me coming.'

A totally exhausted and wretched Frankie smiled at her mother tenderly. 'I appreciate your offer, Mam, but you're done in. You've been constantly at my side for the last two days. Now enough's enough. You need to get off home and put your feet up, not that I expect you will do.'

'But . . .'

Frankie placed her arm around her mother's shoulder, pulling her close. 'No buts, Mam. Please don't take offence, but going to the hospital is something I have to do by myself.'

Nancy swept a tired hand across her forehead, folded her arms under her ample bosom and pursed her lips disapprovingly. 'Well, I don't know why yer have ter go and visit Stella at all. I mean, your so call friend was aiding and abetting your 'usband in adultery. One of the worse, if not *the* worst cardinal sins anyone could commit.'

Frankie sighed wearily. 'I know, Mam. But Stella had been blinded by Eddie's lies the same as me, so it's not what it looks like if you take it on face value, is it? I need to clear things up with her. I couldn't live with myself knowing she was mourning Eddie for the rest of her life and her not knowing what he was really like. I have to take the risk she'll hate me for what I'm going to tell her but I must do it, Mam, for my own peace of mind and for hers. Mostly for hers. You understand, don't you?'

Nancy let out a long loud resigned sigh. 'I might not quite agree with your way of thinking, but I do understand yer reasoning, me darlin'. I still wish you'd let me go with yer, though. Just for support. I could wait outside.'

'Mam,' Frankie gently scolded. 'You've worked like a navvy for the past two days and as I said you need a rest.' She glanced over at the pile of bags holding Eddie's belongings which were waiting to be taken to the local WVS. 'I would never have managed all this without your help but I want everything connected with Eddie gone from my life as quick as possible.'

'I agree with you on that. And that's what mothers are for, Frankie, to help their children through the good and the bad.' She grimaced hard and added, 'Well, what this one's for at any rate. I really don't like the sound of Eddie's mother at all. I doubt I'll ever have the pleasure, thank God. I don't suppose that she'll bother to travel to the funeral. She doesn't sound the type to do such things as paying last respects.'

At the mention of Eddie's funeral, Frankie's drawn face paled. It was something she wasn't looking forward to. Hearing the vicar proclaim Eddie an upright citizen whose life had been cut so horribly short, and how much his wife would grieve for him would be impossible when the opposite was true. She felt such a hypocrite having to play along with such a farce, but what else could she do? 'Ian did tell me that Mrs Taylor had been informed but I don't know yet what his family's intentions are. I'll have to cross that bridge when I come to it. Mind you, if they do come to the funeral it will save me a journey.'

Nancy frowned bewildered. 'A journey? To where?'

'Over to Coventry. The money that Eddie was carrying. I'm giving it to them. I want nothing to do with it. Most, if not all of it was made by dubious means, but I hope it's used wisely in respect of Eddie's son's future welfare.'

'Huh! Well, I think that's debatable from what I've learned about them. Still, it's your decision. What about the proceeds from the car lot? Have you decided what to do about them yet?'

'Oh, yes. I'm going to do my best to make sure every last penny of it is returned to the unsuspecting people Eddie and his brother sold the cars to. It's going to be difficult, as Eddie kept no records but once people have read the *Mercury* and word gets around about his